BOOK ONE OF THE
WORLDWALKER TRILOGY

TRIAL
BY
FIRE

JOSEPHINE ANGELINI

SQUARE FISH

FEIWEL AND FRIENDS
NEW YORK

**SQUARE
FISH**

An Imprint of Macmillan
175 Fifth Avenue
New York, NY 10010
macteenbooks.com

Square Fish books may be purchased for business or promotional use.
For information on bulk purchases, please contact the Macmillan Corporate
and Premium Sales Department at (800) 221-7945 x5442 or by e-mail at
specialmarkets@macmillan.com.

Library of Congress Cataloging-in-Publication Data Available
ISBN 978-1-250-06819-4 (paperback) 978-1-250-06425-7 (ebook)

Originally published in the United States by Feiwel and Friends
First Square Fish Edition: 2015
Square Fish logo designed by Filomena Tuosto

10 9 8 7 6 5 4 3 2 1

AR: 5.6 / LEXILE: 800L

For my family

CHAPTER
1

LILY PROCTOR DUCKED INTO THE GIRLS' ROOM, ALREADY yanking back her rebellious hair. Aiming for the toilet through a blur of tears, she vomited until her knees shook.

Lily had been symptomatic all day, but she knew she'd rather eat her own foot than get sent home. Tristan would never take her to the party that night if he knew she was having another one of her epic reactions, and Lily couldn't afford to miss this party. Not now. Not when things between her and Tristan had so recently—and so wonderfully—changed.

Tristan Corey had been Lily's best friend all her life. They'd grown up together, building tent cities out of his mother's clean sheets and space stations out of sofa cushions. Most kids drift apart when they start to grow up—Lily knew that. Some figure out the trick of being cool, and others stay runny-nosed geeks for the rest of high school. But to Tristan's credit, no matter how popular he got over the years, or how isolated Lily became as her allergies intensi-fied and embarrassing rumors about her mother spread, he never once backed away from their pinky-swear promise to be best friends forever. He never tried to hide how close they were or pretended not to care about her because other kids thought she was strange. The only reason he rarely let her go to parties with him was because lots of kids smoked at them, and Lily's lungs couldn't handle smoke.

Or at least, that's what Tristan said. Since Lily had never been to one of these parties herself she couldn't know for sure, but she had a sneaking suspicion that Tristan didn't bring her with him because he was usually going to hook up with a girl. Or several girls.

Everyone in their graduating class knew that Tristan was the biggest player in Salem, Massachusetts. Sophomore year, he'd come back from summer baseball camp a foot taller and achieved legendary status by dating a senior. Ever since then the girls—and women—of Salem had passed him around like a pair of traveling pants. Unfortunately for Lily, she'd had a crush on Tristan since she first realized that there was a difference between boys and girls—way before he rode the testosterone rocket to studliness. And she'd suffered for it.

For years, she'd had to pretend that she was okay with being his girl Friday. They'd run everyday errands together—driver's ed, shopping for cleats, studying—and then, inevitably, some girl would call and he'd leave. Lily never told him how much it killed her to see the excited flush grazing his cheekbones or the hungry shine in his blue eyes when he'd give her a distracted hug good-bye and dart off to meet his latest conquest. Tristan had never looked at Lily like that. And as she heaved monstrously into the toilet, Lily had to admit she couldn't blame him for taking so long to finally kiss her.

The kiss had come out of the blue. They'd been hanging out, watching TV, and Lily had fallen asleep on his leg like she'd done a thousand times before. When she opened her eyes, he was staring down at her with a stunned look on his face. Then he'd kissed her.

That was three days ago. Even thinking about it still made Lily shake. One second she'd been asleep, and the next Tristan was on top of her—kissing her, touching her, and slowly moving against her. Then he'd suddenly pulled away and tried to apologize. But Lily wasn't sorry at all, and she didn't want him to be, either.

They hadn't talked about it, but the next morning he'd held her hand at school. He'd even given her a sweet little kiss in front of his jock friends right before practice. Lily had never dated anyone and didn't really know how these things worked, but she was pretty sure that by taking her to the party tonight he would be announcing to everyone that they were officially together. So Lily didn't care if she coughed up her spleen or sneezed out an artery. She was going to that party if it killed her.

When she was finally done vomiting up the leaves, twigs, and roots that made up her vegan lunch, Lily staggered over to the sinks to mop her face.

She moaned when she looked in the mirror. It was worse than she'd expected. Her alabaster-white skin was flushed such a bright red it looked like someone had slapped her across the face. Crimson hives were rising like whip marks across her wing-like collarbones and her green eyes were glassy with fever. Quickly recounting everything she'd eaten that day, she couldn't think of what could have caused such a runaway reaction. Her allergy must have been caused by something she couldn't see, like the chemicals they used to clean the school, but she couldn't really be sure of that.

Lily twisted her slippery strawberry-colored curls up close to her scalp and stabbed the thick mass into a messy French twist with a pencil. She took off her SAVE THE WHALES T-shirt and bent over a sink in her bra, trying to coax colder water out of the lukewarm tap by batting it with her fingertips. She splashed the not-quite-cool-enough water over the angry rash that was rising like a hot tide up her hyperreactive body.

The bell rang, signaling the end of her lunch period, and Lily had no choice but to reach into her bag for one of her many emergency kits. She dug past a bottle of quick-dissolve steroid pills and her inhaler, and went straight for the Epipen. She took the green cap off the tube of sterile plastic and jabbed the tip through the jeans covering her thigh, gritting her teeth against the painful stab.

Technically, she wasn't supposed to use her Epipen except in a life-threatening situation, but since she had no idea what was causing such a violent reaction, she figured it was better to be safe than sorry. As the medicine cocktail from the Epipen flooded her system, Lily's symptoms began to diminish. Her eyes stopped watering and her vision cleared. She shivered violently as the adrenaline from the shot rushed through her system, then realized that her entire upper body was wet. Hands shaking with the jitters, she dabbed at herself with some paper towels and put on her T-shirt as the bell rang a second time, signaling the start of the next class.

Lily ran out of the girls' room, up the stairs, and thundered down the nearly empty hallway to Mr. Carnello's classroom just before he closed the door.

"Sorry, Mr. Carn." She panted as she ducked past him.

"Are you alright?" Mr. Carnello asked her, glancing down at Lily's top and then quickly away.

"Sure. I just had a . . . thing," she mumbled distractedly, and darted into the room.

Tristan looked up from his spot at their lab table and narrowed his eyes at her as she made her way over to him. She noticed a couple of people looking at her strangely as she sat down. She tried to smile back at them in friendly way, but they all looked away from her without making eye contact.

"Lily," Tristan hissed at her.

"What?" she hissed back.

"Why are your boobs wet?"

"My what?" Lily looked down at her T-shirt and saw that the white material was completely transparent where her soggy bra had soaked through. Mortified, she crossed her arms over her chest. She could hear a few guys snickering in the corner and saw Tristan's head spin around, silencing them with a look.

"Do you need a moment to collect yourself, Miss Proctor?" Mr. Carnello asked kindly.

"No. We're good," Tristan answered for Lily as he quickly pulled his sweater over his head.

The shirt he was wearing underneath hiked up accidentally as he did so, and a few girls whispered excitedly at the glimpse of rippling muscles and velvety skin. Tristan helped Lily into his sweater as if he didn't even hear them. Considering the fact that he just had to walk past most girls to make them groan out loud, he probably didn't. But Lily heard them, and felt herself flush with even more heat as she resisted the urge to strangle them.

"Do you have a fever?" he asked.

"I always have a fever," Lily replied grumpily, which they both knew was true.

Lily's body ran hot—about 102 degrees on a normal day. On a bad day, her fever could shoot up as high as 111 degrees. The doctors had no idea how she'd survived some of her worst attacks, but then again, they had no idea about a lot of things where Lily was concerned.

"I'm serious," replied Tristan, pointing accusingly at the spot of blood on her jeans where she'd impaled herself with the Epipen. "Do you need me to take you home? Or the hospital?"

"I'm *fine*," she replied emphatically. "Really. I feel great." She paused and smiled ruefully. "Well, apart from the whole wet-boobs-in-class thing."

Lily gave him a saucy look and nudged his arm, brushing the whole thing off. After everything that people had said about her and her family, a wet T-shirt was the least of Lily's problems. Tristan's big blue eyes sparkled and his light-brown hair fell across his forehead as he ducked his head with quiet laughter. He had a million little gestures like this that left her star struck. He was almost too pretty to look at sometimes, and Lily couldn't believe how lucky she was that he was finally hers.

"Pay attention to Mr. Carn," she chastised, like Tristan had been the one to disrupt class. He nudged her back and they focused on the lecture.

"If any symbol fits the universe better than this one"—Mr. Carnello spun to his projector and drew the sideways figure eight that represented infinity—"it would be this one." He drew an equal sign. "Newton proved that if you hit a ball with a known amount of force, that force doesn't disappear. It's turned into kinetic energy, and the ball flies a distance that you can measure with accuracy. Why? Because energy in"—he tapped one side of the equal sign—"is equal to the energy out." He finished by tapping the other side of the equal sign. "So. Energy changes. Matter can even change into energy—we'll get to Einstein's E equals mc squared later—but you can't make something out of nothing. This is the first law of thermodynamics. Now! *Thermo*, which is Greek for 'heat,' and *dynamics*, from the Greek *dynamikos,* which means 'power.' Heat and power are two halves of the same whole."

Mr. Carnello began to scribble furiously as he mumbled to himself. Lily and Tristan looked at each other and grinned. They both loved science. In fact, Tristan had scored higher on his Biology Achievement Test than anyone else in the state that year, and he was seriously thinking about enrolling as a premed student in one of the Ivy League schools that he would apply to this winter. It was only early November, and seniors still had another month or two to pick colleges, declare their majors, and basically figure out the rest of their lives before they all turned eighteen. Lily was sure Tristan had already decided to be a doctor someday. After spending so much time visiting her at Mass General when she was having one of her more severe attacks, he certainly knew his way around a hospital.

Lily wasn't particularly interested in being a doctor herself, but she studied all the sciences with a passion. She had always been able to understand physics intuitively, and on the days she was feeling particularly put upon, Lily believed this was because her body was a wacky science experiment gone wrong. Every year, Lily's ailments grew worse, and not even the cadre of specialists in Boston she went to see every month knew how to treat her. She'd always dreamed of chaining herself to an endangered redwood tree or participating in a long sit-in to stop animal testing, but the truth was, her body would never let her do those things. She probably wouldn't even be able to live on campus when she went to college next year—if she was healthy enough to attend college at all.

A wave of anxiety overtook her at the thought of Tristan going far away to college. Harvard and Brown were close enough for him to commute easily, but what if he decided to go to Columbia—or worse, Cornell? Ithaca was a six-hour drive from Salem.

As Mr. Carnello delved into the finer points of thermodynamics, the adrenaline from the Epipen shot abandoned Lily all at once, leaving her with a killer headache and a raging case of paranoia about her changing status in Tristan's life. She resisted the urge to rub her temples and beg Tristan to stay in Boston. Every time Tristan looked over at her to see if she was okay, Lily smiled brightly to prove how great she felt. What she really needed was about a gallon of water to wash away the bitter film that was coating the inside of her mouth, but she'd have to wait until after class to go to the bubbler or Tristan would know she felt sick. Lily nearly sighed with relief when the bell rang.

"Thanks for the loaner." She pulled Tristan's sweater off and handed it to him. "I think my boobs are sufficiently dry now." She fanned her flushed face. "Actually, I think they're cooked. I was roasting all period."

"And I was freezing." Tristan gratefully put his sweater back on with a shiver. "Mr. Carn always keeps his room so damn cold."

"The half-dissected cats like it better that way."

"You're just lucky I love you."

"Yeah, right. You just didn't want me flashing the whole room!" Lily exclaimed a bit too loudly.

She watched Tristan grab his stuff and hurry out of the room, not even thinking twice about his choice of words. He said he loved her every now and again. It didn't mean the same thing to him as it did to her, and Lily knew it. But she also knew that he did care deeply about her, which made the situation all the more confusing. Since their steamy episode on the couch, Tristan hadn't tried anything sexier than a few chaste kisses and a lot of hand-holding. He loved her—Lily had known that for years—but he just didn't seem to be all the crazy about her body.

Not that she had a bad body, Lily thought as she grabbed a sip from the bubbler and then followed Tristan to their side-by-side lockers. Sure, she had skin that was much too fair for the current style and she was painfully skinny, but even she was aware of the fact that she had a great face. Well, Lily conceded, she had a great face when it wasn't leaking snot or covered in hives, which wasn't very often. And the hair was a problem. Bright red, thicker than polar bear fur and curly as scissor-skinned ribbons on a birthday present, Lily's hair was a force to be reckoned with. She wouldn't be surprised if it could be seen from space, and she spent most of her time pinning it back, pulling it up, and generally trying to convince it not to eat her face.

Lily hated her hair, probably because it reminded her so much of her mother's. Her big sister, Juliet, had pin-straight locks in a perfectly respectable shade of brown, but not Lily. Oh, no. On top of having to wear a battalion of medic-alert bracelets that proclaimed her freakiness to the world, Lily had also been saddled with her mom's crazy hair.

Lily fervently hoped she hadn't gotten her mom's crazy mind to go with it.

"Are you sure you want to go to your last class?" Tristan asked skeptically as he watched Lily pull her Spanish textbook out of her locker. "I could get a pass and drive you home right now," he offered.

"What for?" Lily said brightly.

Tristan straightened to his full height of six foot two and turned toward her. He reached out with one of his long, supple arms and boxed her in against the wall of lockers. She went still and looked up at him. Tristan was one of those rare guys whose skin always managed to look dewy and fresh, like every inch of him was utterly kissable.

"No jokes. No acting tough," he said, easing closer to her until his thighs rested on hers. Tristan brushed her cheek with the backs of his fingers. "You don't have to come with me to the party tonight."

Lily frowned. If he thought she was so sick, why would he go to the party without her? She was about to ask him when a shrill voice interrupted them.

"Are you *serious*?"

Lily and Tristan broke apart and turned to see Miranda Clark staring at them, her hands planted on her shapely hips and an exaggerated look of disgust on her spray-tanned face. Half the hallway full of students slowed to gawk.

"What, Miranda? You got something to say?" Tristan said rudely.

"Yeah, I got something to say," Miranda retorted, her lower lip trembling.

Lily felt bad for her. Under all that lip gloss and chemically treated blonde hair, it was easy to see that she was hurt. Tristan didn't talk about his love life with Lily, but she was pretty sure that Miranda and he had been involved a few weeks back. Lily wasn't sure exactly when they'd stopped seeing each other, but from the stunned look on Miranda's face, Lily guessed that it had been recently. Maybe too recently.

"This should be great," Tristan said, crossing his arms and smirking. "Remember to use your big-girl words, Miranda."

Lily gaped at Tristan, surprised at how cruel he was being. True, Miranda Clark wasn't the smartest girl in school, but she was two years younger than they were. Of course her vocabulary wouldn't be on the same level as theirs. What was he doing hooking up with a fifteen-year-old to begin with? The whole episode was leaving a bad taste in Lily's mouth.

"Miranda. I'm sorry you're upset, but maybe we should talk about this later?" Lily said. Miranda didn't appreciate Lily's peace offering. In fact, she looked like she was just about to pounce on Lily and beat the crap out of her.

"This isn't your mess, Lily," Tristan said tiredly. "Go to Spanish. I'll handle her."

"Mess?" Miranda said, focusing her rage on him. "You think I'm a *mess*?" she repeated, her tone sliding up an octave.

The bell rang, breaking up the knot of bystanders, but Miranda didn't move. She waited, eyes bright with furious tears, for Tristan to deal with her.

"Go," Tristan repeated to Lily. "I got this."

Lily turned and went to her class. Behind her, she could hear the two of them arguing. The volume rose steadily until Lily could catch the last retort from all the way down the hall.

"Whatever, Miranda," Tristan said. "I honestly don't care about what you think." Then Lily—and half the student body—heard Miranda slap Tristan across the face.

Lily ducked into her classroom rather than go back and defend Tristan as she might have a few days ago. This wasn't the first time a girl had slapped her best friend, but it was the first time Lily believed he'd really deserved it.

After school, Lily felt a bit strange getting a ride home from Tristan as she usually did. Having no other option, she waited in the parking lot by his car and grimaced when she saw the hassled look on his face as he came toward to her.

"I could have my mom . . ." Lily began halfheartedly.

"Your mom? Driving? Like I want innocent blood on my hands," he said, raising an eyebrow.

"She'd never make it out of the driveway, anyways," Lily said dryly. "The garage confuses her."

Tristan unlocked the doors on the Chevy Volt that he kept immaculate for Lily, and they both got in.

"Sorry about today," he said sincerely. "I didn't mean to drag you into it."

"That was some slap. How's your face?"

He sighed dramatically. "Unfortunately, the nurse said that slap was loaded with cooties."

Lily sucked in a pained breath. "Cooties. You know what that means?"

"They'll have to amputate."

"Girls across the tri-state area will be inconsolable. A national day of mourning is sure to follow."

He smiled at her lazily, his mouth inches away, eyes locked with hers. Lily desperately wanted to forget the whole thing and kiss his cootie-infested face, but something held her back.

"How's Miranda?" Lily asked, looking down at her hands.

"How should I know?" Tristan turned back to the steering wheel and started the car. His coldness toward Miranda disturbed her. Was this how Tristan treated every girl he was finished with?

"Do you want me to talk to her?" Lily offered. "I can tell her it was unexpected. That she's got the wrong idea about us and what happened."

"Miranda has so many wrong ideas in her head I don't see how setting her straight about one of them will make any difference. She's not the sharpest tool in the shed, Lily." Tristan glanced at the look on Lily's face while he drove out of the parking lot and knew what she was thinking. "I know, I know," he said with exasperation. "If I think she's an idiot, I probably shouldn't have fooled around with her in the first place, right?"

"She's a lot younger than us, Tristan. Two years is a big deal," Lily objected gently.

"I guess." He sighed. "But trust me, Lily. Miranda's not some innocent little girl. I didn't, you know, ruin her or anything."

"Ruin her? What century is this?" Lily chuckled. Tristan's lips turned up in a tiny smile. Lily took a second to steel herself for the next question. "Were you still involved with Miranda the other night?"

He rolled his eyes. "She wasn't my girlfriend. I never made any promises to her, and it was idiotic of her to think we were going to be a couple."

They drove in silence for a bit.

"Just out of curiosity, how would a girl know if you *were* going to be a couple?" Lily was reaching—fishing for a commitment from him like she was one of his desperate admirers. She disliked herself for it, and as the silence stretched out, her question hanging like a bad smell in the air, she started to dislike him for not answering her. They pulled into Lily's driveway, Tristan's face never even twitching to show that he'd registered what she'd said.

"I'll pick you up at seven for the party," he said, then drove off.

Lily stood outside in the cold sea air after Tristan left. She liked the cold. She especially liked the clean, salty air that blew in off the Atlantic Ocean, which was pounding away at the rocky shore just a few blocks from her house. Cold, damp air cleared her head and soothed her skin. Luckily for Lily, growing up in Salem meant that there had always been plenty of blustery winds off the water.

When she was comfortable and cool, Lily turned and went inside the ancient Colonial house that had been in her family since the Pilgrims had landed. Literally. Lily's parents, Samantha and James Proctor, could trace their families back to the *Mayflower*, and both of them had family members who had either lived in Salem or the surrounding Essex County since there was such a thing as an Essex County on this continent. Sometimes Lily wondered if her raging allergies were from inbreeding, but her sister told her that was ridiculous. Tristan's family, the Coreys, had been in Salem just as long as the Proctors had, and there was certainly nothing inbred about Tristan.

Lily put her stuff down on the kitchen table and listened to the house for a moment. "Mom?" she called, when she decided it sounded empty.

"Is that you, Lillian?" Only Samantha, Lily's mom, called her by her full name.

"Yeah, it's me. Where are you?" Lily wandered toward her mother's voice, confused. It sounded like she was out in the garage.

"Ah, Mom. Look at this mess," Lily exclaimed when she saw what her mother was up to out there.

Samantha sat at her old potter's wheel, her curly red hair sticking out wildly, throwing clay in her pajamas and robe. She was in the spot where Lily's dad parked his car, but she hadn't put a tarp down underneath her. The floor was covered in drippings that were already beginning to harden. They'd have to be chipped off, but that was only half the problem. In the parking spot next to that, her mom's old Jeep Grand Cherokee was splattered with clay. Lily dug her hands into her hair, surveying the disaster.

"There she is—no bumps or bruises! I almost came to get you at school," Samantha said in chipper way. She only garbled her words a little, and that concerned Lily. The meds made her slur, and the slightly clearer speech could mean that she hadn't taken all of them today. "But when I didn't get the phone call from your principal, I knew that my Lillian wasn't the one that trashy girl had attacked in the hallway. See? That's how I knew the difference between what happened *here* and what happened *elsewhere*."

Lily tried and failed to work out her mom's logic.

"And then I saw my wheel!" Samantha continued happily. "And I wondered, why did I ever stop throwing pots?"

Lily looked at the watered-down lump of poorly mixed clay in her mother's shaky hands and couldn't think of a way to say the phrase *you lost your mind and the meds destroyed your talent* so it didn't sound cruel.

It hadn't escaped Lily's notice that before she'd gone to Spanish, Miranda had looked like she'd wanted to attack her but had settled for Tristan instead. Yet, according to her mother, the fight *had* happened. Elsewhere. The new medication obviously wasn't strong enough. If her mother was underdosed, things could get ugly. She'd need help.

"Hey, Mom? Aren't you cold?" she asked brightly. Samantha nodded, like it had just occurred to her that she was. "Why don't you go inside, and I'll finish up out here for you."

"Thank you, dear," Samantha said placidly. She slid out of her dirty Crocs and took off her ruined robe, handing it to Lily.

"I'm going to take you upstairs, tuck you in, and then make a few phone calls, okay?" Lily said carefully. When her mom got confused like this Lily knew the best way to keep her calm was to be as clear as possible.

"Yes, call your sister and tell her exactly what happened," Samantha said. Her face suddenly got serious and she grasped Lily's hands with her clay-covered ones. "There isn't a Juliet who doesn't love you," she said desperately. "Remember that."

"Sure, Mom," Lily said, smiling brightly as she pried her fingers free. "Let's get cleaned up, okay?"

Samantha nodded and shuffled inside. Lily pulled out her cell phone and called her dad, just in case he decided to answer. When she was shunted to voicemail after two rings, Lily didn't even bother to leave a message. He was obviously avoiding the call and probably wouldn't check his inbox for hours. She speed-dialed her big sister, Juliet, instead.

"What's wrong?" came Juliet's immediate response.

"Mom's having a bad day," Lily said, not at all surprised that her sister already knew something was out of place. The two sisters often joked that their phones were so used to making emergency calls that they had somehow learned how to ring more urgently when there was trouble. Lily walked over to the refrigerator and checked her mom's meds.

"Did she get loose again?" Juliet asked.

"No," Lily replied thankfully as she counted her mom's pills. "She just decided to make a few pots. But she neglected to take the car out of the garage first."

"Fantastic." Juliet paused. She and Lily started laughing at the same time. "How bad is it?"

"Oh, it's pretty impressive, Jules." Lily finished counting the pills. "I just checked, and she took all her meds today, so we'll have to talk to the doctors about her dosage again. I can clean up the mess myself, but I'm worried about leaving her alone tonight. And I have this thing."

"A date?" Juliet practically screamed with excitement.

"Sort of." Lily felt her cheeks heat with a blush. "Tristan's taking me to a party."

"A party." Juliet sighed heavily. "Lily, are you sure about that? With all the hair products and perfume that the girls will be wearing, and the alcohol and smoke?"

"Can you come or not?" Lily asked quietly. "It would mean a lot to me."

Juliet paused. "We'll talk about the party when I get there," she said, and ended the call.

Lily decided to start on the Jeep first. Her dad's spot could wait. It wasn't like he'd be coming home that night anyway.

Technically, Lily's parents weren't divorced, but her father had pretty much abandoned the family about the time her mother started wandering around sleepy Salem, screaming at everyone to shut up. James had hung in there for a few years. Lily was in eighth grade when her allergy symptoms started escalating exponentially and, as luck would have it, at around the same time Samantha began accosting people at the grocery store. She'd started walking right up to people, telling them she knew about the affair they were having, the bankruptcy they were hiding, or the Adderall they were stealing from their kids to lose weight.

Sometimes she was right, and sometimes she wasn't. When she was wrong, she simply said that another "version" of the person she'd accused had done what she'd said. Samantha caused a lot of trouble for some good people, but she'd downright humiliated anyone with the last name Proctor. In a small community like Salem, having a crazy mother was not something that was easily overlooked. By the time Juliet went to college two years ago, it seemed like all of Salem had turned on the Proctor family and wanted to run them out of town.

That's when James stopped coming home most nights. He couldn't take the embarrassment of being married to the town kook, but he knew that if he filed for divorce he'd end up getting burdened with Lily. No court would grant Samantha custody of a minor with as many medical problems as Lily had, and James didn't like sickness, either mental or physical. He didn't file for divorce or involve the legal system in any way because he knew he would end up with more responsibility. Instead, he just stopped showing up.

Lily filled a bucket with soap and water and opened the garage door so she could let out the fumes of the cleaning goop while she scrubbed. Even the non-toxic stuff her mom bought at Whole Foods still irritated Lily if she was around it in its undiluted form for too long. Ten minutes later, her eyes were watering from the chemicals so badly she could barely see. She ignored them. She had a party to go to, damn it, and after everything that had already happened that day, a couple of leaky eyes weren't about to stop her. Another twenty minutes later, she was mostly done with the Jeep, when she heard Juliet's car pull into the driveway and park.

"You know what? The way the clay's all flung out like that, it almost looks festive," her sister said from the garage door.

"I'll be your best friend if you check on Mom," Lily said, wiping her hair off her damp forehead.

"Fever?" Juliet crossed the garage to Lily. Her giant brown eyes were rounded with concern. Lily edged away from her sister's smooth, cool hands before Juliet could touch her face.

"Just warm from all this exercise," Lily said.

Juliet cocked her chin as she judged Lily's health. The gesture accentuated the heart shape of her face, and as she pursed her naturally red lips with worry, Lily thought, as she always did, that Juliet's mouth looked like a heart inside a heart—a small red one inside a larger, pale one. Lily knew most people considered her sister a bit plain. Juliet dressed conservatively and never wore makeup or styled her straight, mousy-brown hair. But to Lily that stuff was irrelevant. She thought her sister was the prettiest girl she'd ever seen.

"Check on Mom. I'm awesome." Lily turned Juliet by the shoulders and gave her a playful kick on the rump to get her to go inside.

When Lily finished, she found her sister sitting in bed with their mom, taking her pulse. At twenty, Juliet was already a registered EMT and moonlighted at a hospital to pay her way through Boston University. Sometimes it seemed like everyone closest to Lily had decided at an early age that it would be a good idea to go into medicine—probably because at some point they'd seen paramedics fighting to keep Lily breathing. That kind of experience tends to leave a lasting impression on a kid.

"How is she?" Lily whispered when her sister looked up. Juliet tilted her head to the side in a noncommittal gesture before easing herself off the bed and taking Lily out to the hall.

"Her pulse is racing. Which is kind of hard to do when you have two hundred milligrams of Thorazine and an Ambien in you."

"Is she alright alone?"

"She's fine for now," Juliet whispered, her big eyes downcast.

"Did she say what's bothering her?" Lily asked. She took Juliet's arm and led her down the hall to her room.

"She's paranoid." Juliet sighed as she sat on Lily's bed. "She said another Lillian was planning on taking *her* Lillian."

"That's—" Lily stopped, overwhelmed.

"—the way she explains her hallucinations to herself," Juliet finished for her. "The hallucinations aren't wrong if they really happen *somewhere*. She isn't crazy if there are multiple versions of people and multiple worlds that only she knows about."

"Yeah." Lily agreed reluctantly. Something about this explanation bothered her. She knew her mom made stuff up, but how had she known about Miranda nearly starting a fight with her in the hallway? It hadn't happened, but it almost had. It certainly could have happened if one or two things had worked out differently. "But it's spooky how close to true her lies sound sometimes."

"Yeah. I know."

"And it keeps getting weirder."

"Schizophrenia is a degenerative disease."

Juliet said things like that sometimes. It wasn't to edify Lily, who already knew the ins and outs of their mom's condition. It was to remind herself that no matter how much of a nightmare all of this seemed, it was still considered normal in some textbook somewhere. Feigning normalcy didn't help Lily much. Cracking a joke usually did, though.

"Ah, schizophrenia. The gift that keeps on giving."

Neither of them laughed, but they both smiled sadly and nodded in unison. It helped to have someone to nod with. That's how Lily and Juliet survived. A textbook answer, a bad joke, and a sister to lean on, and so far they'd managed to keep their dysfunctional little family from going completely down the drain.

"So what's all this about a party?" Juliet asked.

Lily sat down next to her sister. "It's the only one I've been invited to since junior prom. Which I missed because I got sick," Lily said quietly. Juliet wanted to interrupt. Lily took her hand and kept going before her sister could argue. "Look, I know what's happening to me. I know that soon I won't be able to go to school anymore. I'm out of time, Jules. And it's okay. Well, no, it isn't okay, but I've accepted it at least. I just want to go to one high school party before I'm stuck inside a plastic bubble for the rest of my life."

"So. Tristan's taking you," Juliet began cautiously.

"Yeah." Lily looked down, smiling softly. "And I'm pretty sure we're going as a couple."

"But he doesn't care if you don't go to parties. You know that."

"I also know how long I waited for this. How long I waited for him. I can't miss this party, Jules."

Juliet tilted her head to the side and rested it on Lily's shoulder. They sat together for a while, comforted just to be close to each other.

"Want me to blow out your hair?" Juliet asked after a long silence. She sat up and looked Lily in the eye, smiling.

"Would you?" Lily jumped off the bed and pulled her sister up with her, as if the melancholy exchange they'd just had was miles away already. "I can never get the back."

CHAPTER
2

THREE AND A HALF HOURS LATER, LILY HAD LUXURIOUS, bouncy, Hollywood-starlet hair. She even managed to get some all-natural, nonirritating makeup on her face and a slinky dress on her bean-pole body without getting too overheated. The dress wasn't fancy, but it did compliment her slender build and tricky coloring. Lily didn't want to look like she was trying too hard, but she still wanted to look good.

"You and Tristan are easing into the whole relationship thing, right? Taking it slow?" Juliet asked a little too casually.

"We have sex six times a day, and we're thinking of making a porno together," Lily said, poker-faced, while she rubbed almond oil on her bare legs. She glanced up to see Juliet glaring at her. "Yes! We're taking it slow. Maybe a little too slow."

"Good!" Juliet shoved Lily playfully. "I love Tristan, but he has a really bad track record with girls. He's hurt a lot of people."

Lily's smile faded. Tristan was the best friend she could ever imagine. He'd been there for her through things that would have sent most people running for the hills. But he didn't treat his girlfriends nearly as well. Lily had seen it firsthand with Miranda, and she wished she hadn't.

"He's different with me," Lily said. She stood up and wiped the rest of the oil from her hands. "It'll different with me," she repeated emphatically.

Juliet's big eyes grew even bigger with concern. "Okay," she said. "But maybe it'd be a good idea to change out of that dress. Make him wait for it."

"Wait?" Lily said, grinning at her sister. "I'm the one who's been waiting. Not him."

"Exactly. And after this long, what's your rush?" Juliet joked. They both heard Tristan pull into the driveway. "Last chance to run upstairs and change into jeans and a T-shirt?"

"Not going to happen, Jules," Lily replied cheerfully as she went to let Tristan inside. She pulled the door open and smiled at him, her stomach filling with butterflies even though she saw him every day.

"What did you do to your hair?" Tristan immediately asked, a scowl forming on his face.

Lily's hand darted up automatically to smooth her already smooth hair, her excitement disappearing. "Juliet did it for me."

"Hey, Tristan," Juliet called out.

"What's up, Jules?" he called back in greeting.

"You don't like it?" Lily asked him, feeling defensive. This wasn't how she'd imagined this moment at all. After she'd spent hours sweating it out under a hair dryer, he was supposed to be staring at her slack-jawed.

"It's okay." Tristan shrugged in a noncommittal way, his eyes scanning her. "What are you wearing?"

"A dress."

"Kinda little, isn't it?" He grimaced. "I can see, like, all of you."

"Oh, the horror," Lily deadpanned. She pushed him outside and called back to her sister. " 'Night, Jules."

"Have fun," Juliet said, her face apologetic. Lily gave her sister a pained look before she closed the door and followed Tristan to his car. He didn't start the engine immediately. He turned to Lily, starting to say something, but Lily cut him off.

"The next thing you say had better be a compliment," she said incredulously. "Tristan. I'm wearing *makeup*. This may never happen again."

Tristan shut his mouth and started the car. He pulled out of the driveway and was halfway down the street before he spoke. "Cute shoes."

"That wasn't so hard, now was it?"

They drove the rest of the way to Scot's in comfortable silence. Scot's street was already lined with cars. He had the kind of parents who went out of town a lot and didn't seem to mind that their son threw huge parties in their absence. They had to know about it— everyone in town knew about Scot's parties—but since being the "party guy" made Scot incredibly popular, his parents turned a blind eye to the whole thing. All they asked for was plausible deniability in front of the other kids' parents, and Scot was good about that. He always hid the valuables, covered the furniture, and cleaned up thoroughly before his parents got home.

"Vomit," Tristan warned, yanking Lily out of way before she could step in a chunky, orange puddle in the grass.

"Good eye."

"Lots of practice. Scot's front yard is always touch and go."

Lily slowed down and tried to take shallow breaths. A bunch of kids were smoking out front on the wraparound deck, and she could smell it halfway across the yard. Several of the smokers spotted Tristan and started calling out to him, peering through the gloom at the girl on his arm.

"Hey, man! You made it. Who's that with you?" a kid everyone called Breakfast asked. Lily realized no one recognized her without the usual meringue of curly hair on top of her head.

"Hey, Breakfast. It's me. Lily."

"Lily?" Breakfast immediately put his cigarette behind his back— thoughtful, but like that would help. "Are you okay? I mean does this bother you?"

Her eyes were watering, but she smiled and waved at him. "Don't worry about it."

She didn't want to make him feel bad. She liked Breakfast. He'd always been a bit on the goofy side, but he had a way of winning people over—even the bullies who wanted to harass him.

"Lily?" Tristan's brow creased with worry, and he tugged on her arm, angling her away from the smoke.

"I'm fine. Come on."

They left Breakfast and his smoking buddies on the porch with a parting wave and went inside. More people called Tristan's name as soon as they spotted him, like he was a celebrity.

It's not that everyone loved Tristan. In fact, most of the guys glared at him as he passed, their jealousy palpable. Everyone either wished they were Tristan or that they were with him, and he knew it, but the attention didn't make him stuck-up. It made him cautious. As Lily fielded some withering glances of her own, she finally understood why Tristan had always worked so hard to maintain their friendship. He didn't have that many real friends. But then again, neither did Lily.

Lily smiled and waved at a girl from her poetry class whose writing had always impressed her. The smart girl, Una, waved back politely, but then returned to her conversation without inviting Lily to join her. It wasn't meant as an insult—they just didn't know each other outside of school. To be honest, Lily hadn't really hung out with anyone besides Tristan since her mother started screaming destructive nonsense in public. After that, most girls were only nice to Lily so they could get closer to Tristan.

It had hurt a lot more than she would ever admit. Once she'd realized she was being used, Lily had become guarded around anyone who tried to be friendly toward her—even people who didn't deserve it. Her chilliness had been a twisted form of self-preservation. But now that they were so near the end of high school, Lily regretted how she had behaved toward some of the girls in her class. Like Una.

"Hey, man," Scot said smoothly as he greeted Tristan. "Wow. Lily. I think this is a first."

Scot faced Lily, taking in her altered appearance. He was a big guy, as tall as Tristan, if not quite as developed, and Lily had to tilt her head back to look him in the eye. He stood close to Lily, smiling down at her in a friendly way. Scot had always seemed a bit too sly to Lily, like he was trying to find an angle on any situation, and she'd avoided him because of it. Now she wondered if she had judged him too harshly. He had a nice smile, she decided. Lily didn't want to be the snide, cold loner anymore. She wanted to be a part of her class—if only for a few months.

"You don't mind, do you?" Lily asked, smiling back at him.

"Are you kidding? I'm going to have to throw another party to celebrate you actually showing up to one of my parties." Scot flashed his smile even wider, making Lily feel truly welcome. "Drink?"

"I'll have a beer. Water for Lily," Tristan answered. Scot raised an eyebrow. "Lily doesn't drink," Tristan stressed, a hint of a warning in his voice.

"That's cool. I'm not drinking tonight, either," Scot said as he waded through the crowd to the kitchen. He pulled a beer and a bottle of water out of a giant tub of ice on the counter and brought it over to them. "Just a heads-up. Miranda's here," Scot said as he politely opened the water bottle for Lily and handed it to her.

"Christ," Tristan said under his breath, scanning the growing crowd.

"She's downstairs in the family room. Dancing. Or stripping. I can't figure out which at this point," Scot said with a wry grimace. "Why don't you go and talk to her before she comes up here and starts throwing things at you?"

Tristan glanced at Lily, silently asking permission.

"Go. Seriously. You need to take care of that," Lily replied immediately, sounding much more encouraging than she felt.

"I'll keep Lily company," Scot offered. "Make sure she doesn't get trampled by the hockey team." He gestured into the kitchen with his head, where four beefy dudes were downing shots and doing a lot of unnecessary shoving and bellowing.

"Okay. I'll be back in a bit," Tristan finally decided. "Or I'll be back *in* bits, depending on what kind of mood Miranda's in." He drank most of his beer in one gulp.

"Courage, man," Scot said bracingly, fixing Tristan's shirt.

"Thanks, dear," Tristan replied, like they were husband and wife. Lily watched their joking around, feeling the warm glow of inclusion.

When Tristan had gone, Scot took Lily's elbow and steered her in the opposite direction. "I think it would be a good idea to keep you as far away from Miranda as possible."

"There's no reason for her to be upset with me," Lily said.

"Maybe, maybe not." Scot stopped to admire her. "You really look great tonight."

Lily dropped her eyes, feeling her cheeks heat up. "Thanks."

"Look out." Scot grabbed Lily's arm and pulled her toward him suddenly, making her drop her bottle of water. Behind Lily, two drunk girls stumbled past, debating which path to the bathroom would lead them by the cutest boys.

"Sorry about that," Scot said after the girls had left. "I'll get you another."

"It's okay, really," Lily began, but Scot had already picked up the bottle and was making his way to the kitchen. Lily took some napkins off a nearby coffee table and mopped up the spilled water as best as she could while she waited for Scot. He came back moments later with a glass of bubbly red juice.

"No more water. Sorry. The only thing in the fridge was cranberry juice and seltzer. I mixed them. Is that okay?"

"It's fine," Lily said, taking a sip of her fizzy cranberry juice. It tasted a little sour, like it had gone bad, but she swallowed it and smiled anyway. "You don't have to stay with me if you don't want to, you know."

"I know." It was Scot's turn to blush. "I want to, though. I've always wanted to hang out with you. Did you know that?"

"No. I didn't."

Another wave of partygoers passing through the busy living room made Lily and Scot reposition themselves.

"Do you want to go somewhere cooler?" he asked. "I know you get hot easily. Tristan told me once."

Lily was so surprised she just nodded. She had no idea that Scot knew anything more about her than her name.

"How's your drink?" he asked as he led her upstairs.

"Great." Lily took another big gulp to be polite, even though the mix of seltzer and cranberry burned her tongue a bit. "It's really stuffy in here."

"There's a balcony off my room." Scot swung the door to his

bedroom open and went inside. Lily stopped on the threshold. Something didn't feel right.

"You don't have to worry," he said, holding his hands up in a surrender gesture. He rushed over to the balcony doors on the other side of the room and opened them for Lily. She felt a gust of cool, clear air rush toward her and nearly sighed with pleasure. "It's just, everyone's smoking on the patio out front, and my room faces the back. You can leave the door open if that makes you more comfortable."

She felt stupid for doubting him.

"It's okay. And you're right. I'd rather be on the non-smoking side of the house." Lily resisted the urge to giggle. Her body felt warm and gooey. She crossed the bedroom and joined Scot on the balcony, breathing in the crisp air, trying to clear her head. "Can't catch my breath."

"The heat got to you. Sit," Scot urged, and Lily sank down next to him on the outdoor love seat.

"This is really nice. I've never seen a teenager with his own balcony. But then again, I haven't been in many guys' rooms." She had no idea why she'd just said that. For some reason, she felt like telling her life story, and she shut her mouth to stop herself from spilling her guts.

"You've been in Tristan's room," Scot countered quietly.

"Sure. Thousands of times." Lily saw a question steal across Scot's face, and then disappointment. "Oh—but not like *that*."

"Really?" Scot narrowed his eyes, disbelieving. "Never? Isn't he your boyfriend?"

"We only just started seeing each other like that." Lily started laughing. She had no idea what was so funny, she just couldn't seem to stop herself. Lily took another sip of her drink, trying to calm down, but instead of cooling her off, the drink only made her feel hotter and more flushed. She put the sweating side of the glass against her cheek.

Scot stared at her for a long moment, an unreadable expression on his face. "I knew you were it."

"What?"

"The only girl in town he hasn't been with yet." Scot took the drink out of Lily's hands and slid closer to her. She moved away and her back hit the arm of the love seat. Lily tried to stand up, but Scot leaned over her, putting his hand on the armrest and caging her against the cushions. Lily's vision swam unsettlingly, and she froze, trying to keep the horizon from tilting back and forth.

Lily was still trying to make the floor stop spinning underneath her when she felt Scot's tongue in her mouth. She tried to squirm away but she felt dizzy, like any sudden movement would make her slip off the edge of the world. Heat prickled under her skin. She twisted her head and closed her mouth, evicting Scot's slug-like tongue. Her skin burning with fever, Lily pushed against his chest.

"Stop. Scot, stop now," she managed to say as white and blue blobs of light flashed in front of her eyes.

"Why?" he said, annoyed. "You think Tristan isn't doing exactly the same thing right now?"

"What do you mean?" Lily asked.

"You really have no clue, do you?" Scot stood and pulled Lily up after him. "Okay. Let's go find your brand-new boyfriend," he said with a sneer. "Let's see what he's up to."

Scot nearly dragged Lily after him. Her legs were heavy and clumsy. As she stumbled down the steps, Lily heard a few bystanders on the landing say the word "drunk" and something clicked in her fuzzy head. Lily stopped dead and yanked on Scot's arm, turning him around to face her.

"Did you put alcohol in my drink?" she asked. She must have

said it louder than she'd intended because the room got quiet all of a sudden. "Did you?" she repeated, intentionally raising her voice this time.

"A little vodka," Scot admitted with a casual shrug.

"How could you do that?" she asked. The only other time Lily had tried alcohol, she'd spent the night in the ICU with a fever of 115 degrees. She ran her hand across her forehead, and it came back dripping sweat. "Oh, no."

Scot's eyes widened with fear when he registered just how pale and sweaty Lily was. "It was half a shot. I swear," Scot said, pleading his case to the gathering crowd.

"Are you okay?" Breakfast asked in her ear.

Bleary as her vision was, Lily felt Breakfast take her arm before she actually saw him do it. She leaned against him, her head spinning and her vision bending sickeningly around the edges.

"Tristan. I need Tristan," Lily whispered desperately. She felt a building sensation in her body, as if she were a roller coaster reaching the top of its climb. She knew that in a moment she would be powerless to stop the descent.

"I don't know if that's such a good idea," Breakfast said gently.

"I need Tristan now!" Lily insisted, shouting over him.

"He's in there," Breakfast said, pointing to a door a few steps away from where Lily was standing. It was the bathroom door.

Breakfast kept a steadying hand on Lily's arm while she knocked. Tristan didn't answer her, but she could hear him talking to someone else in there. His voice sounded low and urgent. Something was terribly wrong. Lily pulled open the door.

At first it didn't make sense. Why would Tristan be half naked in Scot's bathroom? Then Lily saw Miranda behind him. She had her bare back turned away from the door, but Lily didn't need to see her face to recognize her long, bleached-blonde hair.

"What?" Lily started to ask, and stopped herself. She knew what was going on—she just couldn't believe it.

Tristan finally managed to pull his shirt over his head and noticed Lily's condition. "Lily," he said, taking a step toward her.

Revolted, Lily backed away from him, plowing into Breakfast. She latched on to Breakfast when her legs gave out. It felt as if her own clothes were smothering her. Her muscles began to twitch as the electrical storm in her overheated brain took over. Her arms and legs went rigid, and her entire body convulsed with the superhuman strength of a seizure.

Frightened voices rose up from the crowd that had gathered around the humiliating scene. "What the hell is wrong with her? Is she's having a fit?" the voices murmured.

Breakfast guided Lily gently down to the floor as the seizure descended on her in earnest. Blobs of light in her eyes and a clanging in her ears crowded out all of Lily's other senses. She couldn't feel anything. She was on the floor, her fever eating her up inside, and then it all shifted.

She saw herself lying there, teeth clacking together, spine bowing and arching as her muscles pulled her bones and joints to their limits. She hovered there, above herself, watching her body tear itself apart. Then—she didn't *hear* a girl's voice, not exactly. It was fainter than that, like it was coming from far away, and the words were being placed inside her head.

You are sick in this world.

Lily wondered if she was talking to herself.

Come to me and be the most powerful person in the world.

But . . . I don't want to go, Lily thought. The faint voice went away, and Lily fell back into her body.

She saw Tristan's face, desperate and yelling over hers, but all she heard was the *whoosh* of the blood in her veins. She tasted leather and blood. Hands held her down. She felt herself being lifted and carried. Pale faces, frightened faces, flashed past her.

"Tristan?" she lisped. Something was in her mouth. She got her fingers to obey her enough to pull it out, and stared at a leather strap. A belt.

"It's okay, Lily," Tristan said, his voice high and fearful. "I'll take you to the hospital."

"Won't make it," she whispered. Her tongue was so swollen it filled up her mouth. "Too hot."

"Okay," he said, immediately understanding. "I'll take you to Juliet."

Lily saw Breakfast running in front of them. He opened the car doors and helped Tristan put Lily in the front seat and buckle her up.

"Oh my God. She's burning," Breakfast said in a quavering voice.

"Just leave it. There's no time," Tristan growled. "Shut the door."

Breakfast obeyed and got in the back. Tristan sped to Lily's house, and he and Breakfast carried her inside.

"Tristan? What's going on? What happened?" Juliet cried as soon as she saw Lily.

"Some bastard slipped vodka into Lily's drink. Get ice."

Juliet ran to the fridge as Tristan and Breakfast carried Lily upstairs to the bathroom. Tristan put her in the tub and cranked on the cold tap, tilting her head under it. Lily sighed when the water spilled across her roasting forehead. Juliet joined them and dumped ice into the tub. Tristan's face floated over hers. She wanted to cry and scream and push him away from her, but she couldn't move.

"Please tell me she's not going to die," Breakfast said in a slightly hysterical tone. "I don't think I could handle watching someone die."

"How did this happen, Tristan?" Juliet asked, ignoring Breakfast. "Did you leave her alone?"

Tristan didn't answer for a while. He scooped water over Lily, his hands stiff and white with cold. "Yeah. I left her."

Water filled the tub. Lily's slack limbs floated up around her. She looked at them, breaking the surface of the water. She watched how the surface of the water clung to her and formed liquid webs between her fingers. Finally, she felt the fire go out. Exhaustion followed, nearly paralyzing her with its quick onset.

"Her fever's dropping," Tristan said from far, far away.

Lily's eyes shut and she slipped into sleep.

Lily felt Tristan's arm, heavy and smooth, draped over her shoulder. He was tucked against her back, all the covers piled on top of him to keep him warm while Lily stayed cool. The window was open. Lily watched her white curtains swell and sink on the cold November breeze. A day ago, she would have been over the moon to lie like this with him, but now she felt nothing for him. In fact, she wanted him to leave so she could figure out why she felt so empty. Lily was looking for a way to wiggle out from underneath his heavy arm when Tristan's breathing hitched and he woke up.

"Lily?" he said anxiously, rising up on his elbow behind her.

"I'm awake," she answered.

"Are you okay? How do you feel? Do you need something?"

"No, Tristan. I don't need anything."

She felt him looking down at her, studying her, but she couldn't bear to meet his eyes. Again, she wished he'd go away so she could think.

"I'm so sorry—I can't believe Scot did that to you," he said quietly. She could feel angry heat radiating off of Tristan and saw his fist clench. "I'm going to beat the shit out of him."

"Why?" Lily asked. "He's not the one who abandoned me for another girl."

A long, awkward silence stretched out between them. Lily felt Tristan grow tenser with every passing second. He flopped onto his back with a frustrated sigh.

"I'm sorry you saw that, okay?" More silence. She didn't know what to say. He took her shoulder and rolled her onto her back. "Will you at least look at me?"

Lily did as he asked. She half expected to burst into tears or start screaming at him as soon as she saw his face. But she didn't feel anything for Tristan except a growing sense of disgust.

"Say something," he urged. He was afraid.

Lily had never been the cold anger kind of girl. She was a yeller, a foot stomper, and a pillow thrower. This blankness she felt toward him was completely unlike her, but she couldn't help it. All she could see when she looked at Tristan was a guy who'd taken a sophomore girl into the *bathroom* for a quickie at a party. It was nasty— borderline nauseating—and she wished she'd never seen it. It had stolen something from her, but she didn't know what it was just yet.

"What?" she replied when his expectant look intensified. "What do you want me to say, Tristan?"

His eyes narrowed. "You're punishing me. Fine," he said tersely. "Just remember I never made any promises. And I never lied to you, Lily."

"Let me get this straight," she said, sitting up and turning to him. "As long as you don't verbally promise anything to anyone, you can treat girls like dirt, and you aren't technically doing anything wrong. Aren't you going to accept any responsibility for this?"

He looked away. He couldn't meet her eyes. "I'm just pointing out that I never said we were exclusive."

"And that's your justification? The same justification you gave me about Miranda yesterday?" Lily felt like she'd been tricked. Like some huckster had sold her snake oil and blamed her for not reading the fine print when it made her sick. "I used to think I meant more to you than they did, but I don't, do I?"

"You know I care more about you than I ever have about anyone else." Tristan was yelling now, and in a way he seemed relieved—like having a big fight would clear the air. "You have no idea the things I've gone through for you. I've been there for you, defended you, protected you. I could have slept with you the other night on the couch, but I didn't. I stopped before we went too far because I knew I wasn't ready to be faithful to you, and I didn't want to hurt you."

"I bet you think that makes you a good person." Lily wasn't angry anymore. She just wanted the whole thing to be over. "It doesn't, Tristan."

Lily had never shown this side of herself to Tristan—the harder side that had protected her when girls started whispering about her family behind her back—and he didn't seem to know what to do with it. The look on his face, after the shock had passed, was pure hurt. Then the anger set in. Proud anger.

She saw the shape of him put on his shirt and storm out, but the image was blurry because she didn't have the strength to focus her eyes. She just couldn't find a reason to try and stop him. What was the point, really? He wouldn't be coming back. And if he did, nothing would ever be the same anyway. Their friendship was over.

She repeated the phrase *Tristan isn't my friend anymore* in her head, trying to convince herself that it was real.

Lily sat in her bed, legs pulled up, chin resting on her knees, not seeing anything but blurry shapes and colors. Things would never be the same again. Especially not after half the school had witnessed one of her seizures. Lily had been embarrassed many times in her life, but no one outside of Tristan and her family had ever seen her foam at the mouth before. As messed up as her life had been, it was about to get exponentially worse. And this time she would have to face all the jeers and taunts in school alone. Tristan wasn't her friend anymore and he wouldn't be there to help get her through it. He wouldn't stand up for her, or protect her, or drive her home and make her talk about it. Lily didn't know what to look forward to after a day of horror at school if she couldn't look forward to seeing him.

Lily stood up and got dressed. Her legs and arms still felt rubbery and weak from the seizure, but they still worked, and that was good enough. Jeans. T-shirt. Chucks. She went outside and down to the shore. She sat on a rock and stared at the water. Gray. Cold. Wild. She let her mind drift out there somewhere with the waves, farther and freer than ever before. There wasn't one thought in her head. Usually when Lily tried to empty her mind, it became ironically crowded, but not this time. For once, there was silence inside of her, an empty space that seemed to be expanding. Tears slid down her face. She wished she could just disappear.

She heard a faint voice again from far away, a voice that sounded just like hers.

Are you ready to go now?

"Yes," Lily answered, only feeling half crazy. Maybe this is what her mother felt, she thought. Maybe being crazy didn't feel crazy at all—it just felt like you were having a conversation with yourself. "I'm done here."

I watch the flames rise around me and hear the wood of the pyre pop and groan. Even though I'm prepared for this, the fear I feel is unavoidable. No matter how strong you think you are, fire has a way of bypassing rational thought. It talks directly to your skin. Your brain never enters into the conversation.

Heat builds around me, and the fire begins to eat into my flesh. Yes, fire has teeth, and it chews at you like a living, breathing animal. It even roars like an animal. When you're in its mouth, you have to fight for air. Fire, like a lion, likes to suffocate its prey.

The flames rise, and I twist and scream, trying to get away, but the iron shackles on my wrists keep me bound to this stake.

I'm a witch. And witches burn.

There are other ways for a witch to gather power, of course, but the pyre is the best. When I'm burning, I'm completely focused. Every micro-joule of energy is converted into power. It's almost like I can't waste any part of my pain. Like agony itself is another source of power. When I come to the pyre, I remember that I am alive.

I also remember what I owe for my life—what I did to keep it. I remember what I must do, even if it makes me the villain of my own story. Most importantly, I remember that the good of the many really does outweigh the good of the few. Even if one of those few is me.

It took me eight months to find the right candidate, to watch and wait, and now she's finally ready to come. She's strong. She's independent. She's a survivor. She has all of my power, but in her world she is powerless—sickly, even. I need to be certain that I'm not stealing the savior of another world in order to save mine. But most importantly, there is no Rowan in her world. If there were, I'd never be able to convince her to leave. I wouldn't bother trying. I know what it is to love Rowan and what it feels like to lose him. I'd never ask that of another.

I feel like I've been roasting on this pyre for days, but I know that in reality only a few seconds have passed. I haven't even begun to transmute the energy of the flame and use it to bring her body from her world into mine. Funny how quickly the mind moves, but how slowly time does when you're in pain. I always think of Rowan when I'm in pain, probably because the comparison comforts me. If I survived the pain of losing him, I guess I can handle anything.

This logic has served me well over the past year. Whenever I've felt weak *and doubted my path, all I've needed to do is think of Rowan and what I did to him. If I didn't have mercy on him, why should I be merciful with others? There's a clarity that comes with cruelty. When you've alienated everyone who means something to you and you've sacrificed every last sense of self, then there really is nothing left to lose.*

This girl I'm about to steal has no concept of loss. She doesn't understand the difference between infatuation and love. That's a good thing. I don't want her broken like me. I want her wounded, yes, but stronger for it. There comes a day when every girl loses the stars in her eyes. And then she can see clearly.

This is Lily's day.

The voice went away for a few moments, and Lily thought that was that. She didn't really think anything would happen. Then all sensation left her body and the voice came back.

It will be terrifying. It was for me.

There was no more warning than that. At first, she was too stunned to be frightened, but then the fear came, just as the voice had promised.

It was like being numb, but not the warm, tingly numbness of Novocaine. This was absolute sensory deprivation. Lily couldn't feel the clothes on her body, the hard rock under her legs, or the weight of her skin on her bones. She couldn't even feel the panic that she knew she was experiencing; she could only think it. She was disembodied and she wondered if that meant she was dead.

Then the vibration began. Lily didn't know if it was a sound, a sensation, or something in between, but a steady thrumming became her only focus in the void. It was a distinct pattern, a unique combination of rhythm, intensity, pitch, and duration that was as recognizable as a friend's voice. It was a song without notes, as complex as a symphony, and startlingly beautiful. It ended and another began. The second vibration was as unique and as infinitely complicated as the first, and it ended just as abruptly.

As fast as a light being switched on, Lily could feel her body again. She could feel, see, taste, and smell the world again. She was still sitting on the same rock, still staring out at the same Atlantic Ocean, but several things were off. The air smelled clearer and fresher. The sky lacked the vaguely brownish smudge of smog ringing the horizon. There were more barnacles on the rocks and more starfish in the tide pools.

Her skin prickling with a preternatural sense of wrongness, Lily turned and looked behind her.

She was still in *a* Salem. The shape of the shoreline, as familiar to her as the whorls of her own thumbprint, told her that.

She just wasn't in *her* Salem anymore.

CHAPTER

3

Lily sat and stared at the impossible sight before her.

A massive castle-like structure loomed where her house was supposed to stand, and beyond that, Lily could make out the outline of a city. She stared at the skyline, trying to make it register. A city larger than Boston stood where little Salem used to be. A city made up of weird buildings that were shaped unlike any she'd seen before. Twisting high above even the tallest skyscrapers were spiraling towers that seemed to be crawling with vegetation. Lily jumped down off her rock and ran up the steep path from the beach, hoping that as she got closer the whole thing would dissolve like a mirage in the desert.

"I'm dreaming. I fell asleep on the rock and now I'm dreaming," she muttered under her breath, but she knew it wasn't true. Her skin tingled with awareness of the world around her. She felt completely awake. Whatever was happening to her was real.

Lily crested the rise and met the implacable wall of the castle. Running along its side, she reached a turret that blocked any further progress along the edge and quickly realized that there was no way around the fortification. This structure was built to keep invaders out, whether they approached by land or sea.

She put her hands on the stones, feeling the lichen covering them and inhaling their flinty smell, but still not fully believing they were there. Pacing back and forth along the precarious edge, Lily kept looking over her shoulder at the unchanged shoreline. *This* view, the one facing out to the ocean, was exactly the view she remembered. She'd seen the same rocks and the same unmistakable shape of the shore nearly every day of her life. Then she turned back to the wall that looked like it had stood there for hundreds of years. It had no business being there.

"What the hell!" Lily shouted, hysteria threatening to take over.

She heard footsteps along the top of the wall, and clapped a hand over her mouth to stop her screams. Men's voices drifted down to her from the thirty-foot-high barricade—hostile voices barking orders. There was nowhere to hide. Lily looked around frantically, but she knew that if she ran or stayed it would make no difference. She was trapped between a rock wall and the ocean.

A man dressed in dark clothes and holding some kind of foreign firearm aimed his weapon at Lily from over the wall. She stuck her hands in the air in surrender.

"Lady! How'd you get out there? When did you . . ." The young soldier bit off his questions, as if realizing that he shouldn't be asking them, and lowered his weapon.

An older soldier joined the young man. He stared down at Lily for a moment, his mouth agape, before finding his voice and addressing her cheerfully.

"Forgive us, Lady. Would you like to take a walk on the beach? We'll send a detail down to you," the older soldier said evenly.

"A walk? No, I . . . Who are you?" Lily asked. Her voice broke, and she found herself shifting from foot to foot, trying her hardest not to cry. "I just want to go home."

Half a dozen more men joined the two soldiers. They all stared at Lily in disbelief. The older soldier called the others to attention.

"Go down and escort the Lady of Salem back inside her Citadel," he said crisply. The two soldiers stiffened and saluted.

"Yes, Captain Leto," they chorused, then rushed off to obey.

Lily stared up at the men on the wall, holding her tongue. Silently, she took in their clothes, which seemed to be made of a new kind of fabric that looked a bit like leather but moved and bent with more ease. The weapons were strange to her as well. From what she could see, most of the soldiers were carrying crossbows, but not old-fashioned crossbows. These were high-tech and looked lethal. In fact, very little about this place struck Lily as medieval—somehow it seemed both modern and old at the same time.

And, judging from everyone's deferential tone, apparently she looked like their ruler. Before she could crack that mystery, two soldiers who were hardly older than she was called to her from the beach.

"Would you like us to come up the rise and carry you down, Lady?" one of them asked, still out of breath from running to get her.

"Of course not," Lily replied warily. "I can make it down to you just fine."

She had no idea what was expected of her at this point, or more accurately, what was expected of this Lady of Salem they seemed to be confusing her with. Regardless, Lily didn't want two armed soldiers carrying her anywhere. She half walked, half slid her way down to them. The two soldiers flanked her, waiting for her to take the lead.

"Which way?" she asked in as neutral a voice as she could manage.

The two soldiers shared a confused look, but quickly collected themselves and led Lily around the side of the Citadel to a path that didn't exist on her version of this beach. She tried to act as naturally as she could, even though she had no idea what passed for natural here. Her eyes darted down to the odd, vicious-looking sidearms strapped to the soldiers' belts. She guessed that her best bet at making it through this episode was to play along.

It was a long walk around. The Citadel was a castle on top of the highest hill, surrounded by a circular wall that was backed up against the ocean. Ballooning out from the seawall that Lily had walked alongside stretched a much larger wall that seemed to go on forever. Lily tried to see around it and decided that this larger wall must encircle the whole city. She scoured the landscape for something familiar but saw no landmarks she knew. The tallest buildings of a strange city poked up above the massive wall. Looking at the soaring spires, Lily had to forcibly calm her breathing so she didn't start to hyperventilate. A busy metropolis had somehow sprung up to replace her little town.

From her vantage point on the Citadel hill, Lily could see a section of the city. It was dense and imposing, but the buildings were not the modern glass-and-steel skyscrapers she was used to seeing in her world. There were no rigid pillars of concrete, rising like arrogant middle fingers into the sky. Instead, a congregation of airy hives and nests spiraled and arched into the air in twisting ringlets, dripping green plants off their tiered sides. This city bloomed with vegetation on every available surface. It looked like a latticed bouquet, reaching high into the sky.

"Lady? Would you care to open the gate?" asked the soldier on her left. They had come to a stop while Lily had been gawking and now waited expectantly. She looked up at the massive portcullis in front of her, feeling exposed and vulnerable. Did they expect her to lift it up with her bare hands?

"I c-can't," she stammered. Her escort gaped at her, perplexed. The soldier on her right glanced down at her neck and drew in a sharp breath.

"Your willstone. Lady, was it stolen? Were you attacked?" he asked urgently.

Lily touched her bare throat. She noticed that both of the soldiers wore similar silver stones around their necks, and they were staring at her so intensely that it was clear that *not* wearing one of those willstones was a big deal. Lily had to think fast. The soldiers' distress was quickly turning to fear, and she knew from experience that people do strange, even irrational things when they are afraid.

"I can't discuss it with you," she said, pulling rank for the first time in her life. The only thing Lily had in her favor was their deference to the Lady that they had mistaken her for. "I need to go home. Now."

The soldiers responded to her imperious tone immediately and yelled for the gates to be opened. The portcullis slid to the side like it was weightless. There was no groaning metal or clanking chains, just a faint whisper of wind as the thirty-foot-high and three-foot-thick wall of latticed metal swept to the side to let them inside. Ignoring that this effortless entry flew in the face of physics, Lily strode forward fearlessly, playing the part of a lady for dear life.

Holding herself to the calmest pace she could manage while her heart hammered away, Lily passed more staring soldiers and entered a large courtyard. Beyond the courtyard stood the keep of a giant castle. Lily recalled the old soldier calling it *her* Citadel. Forcing her shaking legs to carry her, she clenched her jaw and strode toward the entrance as if she owned it.

The keep looked like an ancient structure with a futuristic makeover. It had enlarged windows and outbuildings that were designed in an open style, as if some brilliant minimalist architect had gotten his hands on an old castle and had refitted it from top to bottom.

The inside was the same blend of old and new. Lily entered and found impossibly large flagstones beneath her and airy skylights above her. There were large, open areas all around, but despite the fact that she found the place beautiful, her throat closed off with disappointed tears. A part of her had been expecting to step inside the keep, fall back through the rabbit hole, and find herself home again. When it occurred to Lily that her *Alice in Wonderland* moment hadn't happened and that she had no idea how to get home, she turned to her escort and shrugged.

"I don't know what to do," she said hopelessly.

"Lillian?" Juliet's voice called down from the great staircase. Lily turned to the voice at the top of the stair, sighing with relief.

"Juliet! You're here, too?" Lily rushed up the stairs, suddenly feeling like it was all going to be okay. Her sister was with her, and together they would sort this mess out as they had a hundred others. But as Lily neared the top of the stairs, her relief faded and she slowed to a stop.

The woman waiting with a frightened expression looked exactly like her sister—from her large, dark eyes to her red heart-shaped lips and pale heart-shaped face. But the ornate gown she wore and the yards of hair that snaked over her shoulder and down to her waist in one long braid were not Juliet's. Lily's sister never wore fancy dresses and not once in her entire life had she ever grown her hair past her shoulders. Lily stared at this other woman, this other Juliet, and heard her mom's voice inside her head.

There isn't a Juliet who doesn't love you.

Lily was so desperate for something to believe in that she wrapped her arms around the startled woman's shoulders.

"I'm lost," Lily whispered in her ear.

"It's okay," the woman whispered back. She wrapped her arms around Lily and held her close. Lily tucked her face into her neck and relaxed. Whoever this other Juliet was, she smelled just right and her hug was full of the same familiar mix of worry and tenderness that Lily recognized as her sister's. "Let's get you back to your rooms."

Juliet led Lily down the hallway to a spiral stone staircase that seemed to lead up to the top of the keep. Lily clenched Juliet's hand in hers, urging her along. She wanted to wait for the two of them to be alone before she started to speak about what had happened—if she ever found the words to describe it at all.

They got halfway down the hallway of the topmost floor before Juliet stopped. She placed her hand lightly on the surface of a huge door. The small, pinkish stone on her neck flashed, its surface coruscating with lights, and the door, which was twelve feet tall and at least a foot thick, swung open effortlessly. Just like the portcullis had. *Like magic*, Lily thought.

"How did you do that?" The words flew out of Lily before she could snatch them back. Juliet's brow furrowed, and she grabbed Lily's arm with a rough shake.

"Who are you?" she asked, her voice low.

"She is *me*," croaked a worn-out but still hauntingly familiar voice.

"W-what?" Juliet stammered. She didn't understand what was going on any better than Lily did.

46

"It's alright. I brought her here, with her consent, of course. Couldn't do it without her consent. . . ." The voice trailed off with exhaustion, and Lily saw a slender figure stand up from the edge of a giant gaping fireplace, which was easily larger than Lily's garage back home. The fire had long since gone out, and the room was cold. Lily froze in the doorway, unwilling to enter.

"What have you done?" Juliet breathed. She looked at Lily, her jaw slack with fear as her eyes skipped over every aspect of Lily's face and body.

"You're not going to believe it, Juliet," answered the girl. She picked up a silken robe and pulled it around her naked body. There was a sickly smell in the air, like flowers that had been left in old water for too long, their stems starting to rot. "I brought another version of me into this world," she said, and then suddenly swooned.

"Lillian," Juliet gasped. She crossed the room quickly to catch the girl and half carried her to the wide bed in the giant suite. Lily noticed that under the robe, the girl was covered in soot, as if she had been lying in the dirty fireplace. "This is insane. You are far too weak to go to the pyre. It could kill you."

"As if I have a choice about that now. Which is why I brought her here."

"Have you lost your mind?" Juliet asked in a strangled voice.

A tense moment passed between the sisters. The girl in the bed looked at Lily and waved for her to approach.

"Come in, Lily. That's what you prefer to be called, isn't it? I pre-fer Lillian."

Lily entered the room as if drawn there by invisible hands. A creeping chill raised all the hairs on the back of her neck. Lillian had Lily's voice, her hair, her body, even her way of moving. The clothes were different, and Lily desperately hoped that the cynical gleam she saw in Lillian's eye was different as well, but apart from those small variations, there was no mistaking it. Lily was looking at herself. Not her mirror opposite, but her absolute double—right down to the swirl in her left eyebrow that made all the little hairs spike wildly in the wrong direction.

Lillian's eyes darted down to Lily's No Nukes T-shirt, and she gave a wan smile. "I've watched you long enough to know that the important things inside of us are exactly the same."

"You can't be me," Lily said, shaking her head as if that would change what her eyes were telling her. "I'm me."

"You are me and I am you—we are versions of each other," Lillian said. She raised a hand and held her thumb and forefinger apart by the most miniscule of distances. "In worlds that lie this close together, and yet never touch."

It was the word "versions" that rang inside Lily's head. She thought of her mother. "No. I'm crazy. That last seizure did it. I've finally gone crazy like my mother."

"Your Samantha isn't crazy," Lillian said sadly. "She's cursed. She sees and hears an infinite number of universes that she can't block out. It's a terrible thing. Our version of mother couldn't take it. Not even with guidance from what you would call an expert."

"So it's true?" Juliet interrupted hoarsely "The shaman wasn't talking nonsense?"

Lillian looked at her sister, and for a moment, a tender emotion crossed her forbidding face. "Mom wasn't crazy. Other universes exist, Juliet." She gestured to Lily. "There's the proof."

"Then why did she . . . ?"

"It was too late for Mom," Lillian said abruptly. "Even with the shaman's help."

There weren't many things that Lily was sure of at the moment, but even in a different universe, she could read her sister's face. This version of Samantha was dead, and Lily was pretty sure that she had killed herself. Fear shot through Lily as she considered whether or not her version of Samantha would do the same someday. If she were distressed enough, she might. Say, if one of her daughters disappeared into thin air, for instance.

"I have to go back," Lily whispered. "Please. I don't belong here."

"But you do, Lily. You do. And you will stay," Lillian answered calmly.

"We can't keep her here," Juliet hissed at her sister disbelievingly. "Enough, Lillian. I don't know what the shaman taught you in those secret meetings—yes, I know about them," she said when Lillian shot her a surprised look. "Don't worry, I'm the only one who does. I assumed you were sneaking around for a reason, so I never mentioned it to anyone. Not even Rowan. But we brought the shaman here to help Mom, not so you could do *whatever* it is you're doing." Juliet threw her hands up, staring at Lily. "This is wrong. You have to send her back to her world." A half-hysterical laugh escaped Juliet's lips. "I can't even believe I just said that."

"Juliet. I know this is a shock for you," Lillian said slowly. "But I brought her here for a reason. And when she gets past her fear, she'll realize that she wants to stay." Lillian's tone was icy and final.

"But I don't!" Lily exclaimed. She felt like she was choking. "I want to go home!"

"To what?" Lillian asked derisively, her sweaty cheeks flushing red with anger. "A world that makes you sick? Armies of reckless doctors and scientists who don't have a clue what to do with you because they only know how to cut and destroy?" Lillian said the words "doctors" and "scientists" with sneering hatred, but her brief, passionate tirade was curtailed by bone-rattling coughs.

Juliet tried to soothe her sister, but Lillian pushed her hands away. Lily watched, silent and still, as Lillian fought the paroxysm, and after several painful moments of gasping, she could speak again.

"Or maybe you want to go back to your Tristan? That fickle prettyboy who doesn't want you? Or back to the family that would be better off without you?"

"My mother," Lily said, her voice catching. "She'll—"

"She'll suffer more with a sickly daughter like you in her life than out of it. Believe me." Lillian's eyes drilled into Lily's, cold and unrelenting. "You're useless in your world. Worse. You're a burden. But here, where you belong, you could be the most powerful woman in the world."

Lily didn't have much experience with hate. She didn't even hate her dad for abandoning her, even though no one would have blamed her if she did. But as she watched Lillian finish her bitter speech and fall back against the pillows, she realized that she hated her. Lillian looked so pathetic, but Lily couldn't help hating her. In fact, she'd never hated anyone or anything as much as she hated this evil other self in the big white bed.

"And what are you going to do to keep me here? Tie me up? Put me in a dungeon?" Lily asked, trying her hardest not to think how similar her vicious tone, even the cadence of her sentences, was to Lillian's. A thought dawned on her. "You said you brought me here for a reason. You need me, don't you? You need me so much, you can't even stop me from leaving."

"By all means, go," Lillian said with a calculating smile. "Run along."

Lily turned and walked away from the bed, marveling at her own audacity. She had no idea where to go. She felt light and strange, like her blood had filled with cold bubbles and her belly with slippery rope. Her vision shrank in from the sides, collapsing until all she could see was the door. Lily lunged for it, praying that she didn't faint first.

"Lillian!" Juliet cried.

"Let her go," Lillian said. "She *needs* to go."

"She could get hurt out there. It's too dangerous," Juliet said, incredulous.

"She'll be back."

"How do you know?"

"Because you can't run from yourself forever."

Half blind and numb with shock, Lily stumbled past the guards, through the gate, and down the steep hill of the Citadel toward the strange city. She heard people calling out to her, telling her to stop, pleading with her to come back to the safety of the keep, but she was too overwhelmed to respond. All she wanted to do was get away—to get as far away from this waking nightmare as possible.

As she walked, she told herself that what she was experiencing had to be some kind of hallucination. Something happened to her when she'd had that seizure, she decided. Maybe she'd never even woken up this morning.

The more Lily thought about it, the more convinced she was that none of this was really happening. Tristan hadn't cheated on her. They'd never had a fight or ended their friendship. She'd never gone down to the water or agreed to come to this strange place. None of this was real.

Lily paced down a cobbled street and headed into the heart of the strange city. She wasn't really paying attention to which way she went; she was just following a vague sense inside her that told her when to turn or continue straight ahead. She talked to herself sternly the whole way, convinced that this was all some fever dream she couldn't wake up from, probably because the doctors had drugged her.

"That's it," Lily said loudly, making several pedestrians stop and stare. She lowered her voice but continued to mumble to herself, trying to keep panic at bay. "When I heard that voice inside my head, the one that said it would be frightening, it was just the doctor warning me before she gave me a shot. She was telling me that the drugs were going to do this to me. That's all."

No matter how real it felt, she knew that she would wake up eventually and the meandering streets that she now wandered through, with their tall, latticed towers of vegetation, and their tinkling sounds of running water, would all disappear.

Lily's wild eyes bounced from one strange sight to another. Colonial-style carriage houses and brick townhouses, right out of her version of Salem, were interspersed with modern wood-beam and glass buildings that had a tent-like feel. A few steps down, she saw spiral-shaped domes that had gardens growing on side tiers, interspersed with glass windows. They looked like hives that housed plants instead of honey in their combs. Lily glanced into the glass windows of these hive houses and saw only more greenery inside. They were multifaceted greenhouses that were growing things both inside and out.

Rotating around, she realized that there was one on every block, and where there wasn't, there was one of the tall, latticed green towers that went up to find the sun rather than wait for it to hit the ground. Lily wandered closer to one of the towers, trying to look inside the soaring double helix of greenery.

Something growled. Lily looked down slowly. At her feet, chained to the base of the tower, were three monstrous dogs. Or were they bears? One of them hissed, showing fangs like a tiger's.

Lily screamed and threw her body back, away from the unnatural creatures, and didn't stop until she slammed into something hard. She spun around frantically and saw that she had backed up against a large glass window. It was the front of a café.

Peering inside at the startled patrons, Lily's eyes locked with a young man's. They were dark eyes, such a deep brown they were nearly black. His eyes widened, momentarily, stunning Lily both with their intensity and with the recognition she saw inside of them. She'd never seen him before, but he knew her. The young man stood up from his table abruptly, tipping his heavy chair to the ground behind him. His lean body was tense and his angular face was immobile with fury. She saw his fists clench and his lips mouth a single, unmistakable word. *"Lillian."*

The malice she saw in him was breathtaking. He hated her—really hated her—and he looked like he wanted to hurt her. The dark-eyed boy took one stiff step toward her. Lily turned and ran.

The monsters chained to the bottom of the green tower roared at Lily as she streaked past. She shied away from them with horror even though they were chained and couldn't get at her as long as she stayed on the sidewalk.

Lily could hear the footsteps of the boy with the dark eyes behind her. He was gaining on her easily. Any vestiges of the adrenaline rush she'd experienced when she had found herself surrounded by men with crossbows was long gone. She was still dangerously drained from the seizure and from the fact that she hadn't eaten since lunch the day before. After running only a few blocks, Lily's legs were turning to jelly, her inner ears were burning, and all she could hear was the ragged wheeze of her own breathing. A cold sweat broke out across her upper lip and down her back, but her head still felt unbearably hot. Lily knew this feeling. It meant she was going to faint.

In a desperate effort to shake off her enraged pursuer before she passed out, Lily darted down a narrow alley, hoping to hide until the dark-eyed boy ran past. She took several sharp turns, ducked into a low niche in the solid wall of stone and crouched down, trying to hide herself in the shadows before he rounded the last corner.

Her legs shook and she half sat, half fell into what she belatedly realized was a garbage-filled drainage grate. She heard his footsteps pounding past her, then held her breath when she heard the footsteps stop and turn. A pair of black boots pointed into her disgusting niche, blocking most of the light. She heard him sigh.

"You know you can't hide from me, Lillian," said a deep, rich voice. The ringing in Lily's head turned to clanging, and her ears popped. Two hands reached in and scooped up her spent body. The young man placed her on her feet and examined her sweaty face carefully. Lily's vision was wobbling in and out of focus, but she could have sworn the dark-eyed boy actually looked worried for a moment.

"Who are you?" she asked.

"You know damn well it's me," he said angrily. He searched her eyes, and realized that she truly didn't recognize him. "Rowan," he said slowly. Lily shook her head, the action making her wobble unsteadily. His expression changed. "What did you take, Lillian? Belladonna?"

Rowan ran a hand over her face in a clinical way, checking her for fever like he had been her doctor for years. His hands were warm, but they still made Lily shiver. He trailed sensitive fingertips down the sides of her throat, feeling lightly over her glands. Confusion darkened his face.

"Where's your willstone?" The anger and impatience she'd sensed in him earlier were completely gone. He looked afraid now, as afraid and lost as Lily felt.

"Help me, Rowan? Please," Lily begged, figuring she had nothing left to lose.

She saw his dark eyes narrow with suspicion. He hooked a finger into the divot at the bottom of her throat, pressing hard on a sensitive point buried deep inside that U-shaped hollow. A chill swept up Lily's already exhausted body, and she blacked out.

Gideon pushed his way into Lillian's chamber. It should have been sealed, impossible for him to enter, but the heavy door swung open with the slightest nudge from his willstone. Lillian must be very ill, he thought. Or dead.

"What are you doing here?" Juliet asked.

She stepped in between him and the bed. Her eyes darted behind Gideon to the door as he closed it, her nervousness apparent. The willstone on her neck pulsed, but no power followed it. Juliet was a latent crucible. She carried the gene but not much talent, as if being the sister of Lillian had sapped most of her potential gifts. Gideon brushed past Juliet's weak intervention and went straight to the bed.

Fiery red curls snaked up from under the covers and coiled over the white pillow, but the rest of Lillian's fragile frame was buried in blankets. She was so thin now that her body looked to be no more than a wrinkle in the plush duvet.

"So she is here," Gideon said. "The guards said she'd run away. They also said that before she left, they saw her on the beach, wandering around aimlessly. Like she didn't know where she was."

Gideon watched Juliet's face. It was a pretty face, although she frowned too much. He'd break her of that when they were married. His father had arranged the match, and the Witch didn't oppose it. It made sense for them to wed, even if Juliet wasn't to Gideon's taste.

"The Witch is sleeping," Juliet replied in a lowered voice. "Please get to your point *quietly*."

"Fine. Is she going crazy like your mother did?" he asked bluntly.

"No," Juliet replied, offended even though she shouldn't be. It happened every now and again in families that had true power. The dark side of great talent was often madness. It went hand in hand with genius, and it was nothing to be ashamed of. It meant the Proctor family had true power in its bloodline. Power that Gideon wanted for his own offspring, even if it meant he had to get them from Juliet.

"Then why was she wandering around on the beach—dressed very strangely, the guards said—and without her willstone? How'd she even tolerate being separated from it?" Gideon leaned close to Juliet. He saw her lips pinch together with distaste and considered slapping her, but the Witch would punish him for that. *Soon*, Gideon promised himself. She'd learn her lesson soon. "We all know the Witch has been struggling with a sickness of some kind for the past few months," he continued. "If she would let me—or any another competent mechanic of her choice—look her over, we might be able to help."

"I know her behavior must have seemed strange to the guards," Juliet said, ignoring his request to lay hands on Lillian for what seemed to Gideon the thousandth time. "But Lillian has her reasons."

She was hiding something for her sister, something other than the cause of Lillian's mysterious illness. Gideon was sure of it now. "Well, when she wakes, let her know that both me and my father would love to know what those reasons are."

Juliet's colorless face blanched an even paler shade at the mention of Thomas, and Gideon repressed a pleased smile as he turned and left. The Witch might rule, but she still had to deal with the Council and its leader. His momentary triumph was marred by the nagging feeling that something important had just happened. Something *huge*. And it was being kept from him.

Gideon was tired of being pushed aside. He was the Witch's head mechanic in name only, and that fact was not lost on the rest of the Coven. If Lillian wouldn't give him responsibility, then he'd just have to take it.

Lily woke, but not to the sterile bleakness of a hospital or to the familiar four walls of her bedroom. It was dark out—dark and cold. She could smell loamy earth under her and wood smoke on the air. Flickering firelight revealed crisscrossed wooden bars all around her. She tried to move her arms, only to discover that they were tied in front of her. She was a prisoner. Leather creaked as she tried to twist her wrists out of their bonds. There was writing on the leather straps. Lily squinted in the low light and tried to make out the unfamiliar shapes. They looked like something carved on the side of a standing stone, or engraved on the cover of a leather book. *Runes*, Lily thought, recalling the description from an old movie she'd seen once.

Lily heard the snap and crackle of a campfire and wind buffeting the tall trees above her. She caught a glimpse of a thick tree trunk a few yards away from her cage and realized that she must be in a deep, dark forest. Some place old and full of wildlife. She could hear all kinds of rustles and scratches from what she hoped were just small, furry animals in the forest—preferably animals that didn't have too many teeth.

Long shadows, cast by legs standing around the campfire, reached into her primitive cage and darkened her view. Lily swallowed hard to moisten her throat and stifle the hacking cough that threatened to burst out of her. She could smell all kinds of fecund things in the ground beneath her—mushrooms, pulpy woodbark, and leaf mold. Mold spores could kill her. She had to get out of this world, but she needed more information. Her heart pounding and her eyes and nose watering, Lily stayed very still and listened to the conversation by the fire.

"I don't trust her," Rowan said, his voice heavy with hatred.

"That's nothing new," replied an unfamiliar man sardonically.

"No, something's wrong with her, Caleb. Off." Rowan's deep voice was nearly a growl of frustration. "And it's not just because her willstone's gone. Her body felt different. Clogged and neglected. Like it had never performed magic."

"An imposter?" Caleb asked in a lowered voice.

"No. It's her," Rowan replied passionately. "Down to the deepest parts of her cells—that's Lillian."

"Well, no one knows her body better than you." Caleb sighed. "A genetic copy then?"

Lily swallowed again, trying to suppress another cough. Wherever she was, they talked about human clones as if they were easy to make. What kind of a world was this? The hybrid monsters tied at the base of the greenhouse flashed across her mind's eye, and Lily wondered if they'd been grown rather than born. Rowan's urgent tone interrupted her frightening thoughts.

"How, Caleb? They're the same age. I can read it in her body. Someone would have had to copy Lillian on the day of her conception. I knew Samantha well, and she would have rather died than let anyone copy her daughter. That's Lillian. It has to be." Rowan's shadow paced restlessly.

"We're not arguing with you," Caleb said, trying to placate him. "There have been rumors that the Witch is ill. Maybe that's why her body felt 'clogged' or whatever it is you mechanics call it when a crucible gets sick."

"It's not just her body," Rowan continued.

"What, then?" Caleb said patiently. Rowan exhaled a shaky breath and paused.

Lily's throat clenched. She stopped breathing in order to suppress a coughing fit. She needed to hear the rest of what Rowan would say. She needed to find out how he knew that she was different. It might give her some clue as to how to get out of here.

"I know this sounds like such a little thing, but . . . she said *please*." There was another long pause. Lily's eyes streamed irritated tears. She wished Rowan would hurry up and get to the point. "Until last year, I'd spent nearly every day with Lillian since she was six and I was seven. Not once in that entire time had she ever said please for anything."

"She's the Witch," said a third and intimately familiar voice. "She wasn't supposed to be polite to us, Ro."

It was Tristan. He sounded exactly the same. Any thought of being angry with him fell away. Just knowing he—or some version of him—was there made Lily feel safer. It didn't matter what universe this was, or what had happened between them, Tristan would never let anyone hurt her.

"Tristan, help!" Lily yelled. "There's mold everywhere!"

Coughs racked her body. She scrambled up onto her knees and leaned against the latticed wood and leather cage as the three men rushed to her. Lily coughed so hard she gagged.

Rowan knelt down, slinging a pack off his back as he did so, and pulled out a few leaves. While Lily continued to cough, she heard Rowan light a match. "Mold hasn't bothered her since she was eight," he growled.

"Well, obviously it's bothering her now," Tristan growled back. "She's really weak, Ro. You laid hands on her. You should have known that."

"She's not *weak*," Rowan began to argue back.

"Enough bickering you two," Caleb said impatiently, and Tristan and Rowan fell silent.

Lily smelled fire, burning, and then smoke. She scrambled away from the fragrant smoke, hacking and gasping, convinced that Rowan was trying to kill her.

"Tristan," she gasped. "Please. Don't let him."

"Breathe in the smoke, Lillian," Tristan said, cutting off her plea.

"Are you *crazy*?" she managed to reply through her rib-rattling coughs.

Rowan's dark eyes narrowed. Just as she sucked in a pained breath, he waved the smoke in her direction, making sure there was no way she could avoid it. Lily prepared herself for a terrible fit, but instead she felt the burning in her throat ease and the itching in her lungs begin to subside. She breathed again, and the urge to cough went away. After a few moments, she felt her chest open up completely as she inhaled the tangy, scented air.

"How did you do that?" Lily asked.

"Sage," Rowan replied, holding up the smoking bundle. "It purifies the air. You know that."

"Lillian knows it." Lily slid off her knees and sat cross-legged in the dirt while the three men exchanged baffled looks. She felt better, but she was still so spent that she could barely hold herself up. She slouched over her lap tiredly. "May I have some water?"

"Water!" Caleb called over his shoulder. A canteen was brought immediately, and Tristan passed it to Lily through a little slot at the bottom of the cage. "Start explaining, Lillian. And don't get any funny ideas. You don't have your willstone. Try to cast one spell against me or my men and women, and I'll let Rowan kill you."

Lily swallowed and regarded Caleb's earnest face. He was older—maybe in his mid-twenties—and dark-skinned. His face was painted with streaks of red and white. Lily couldn't put a finger on his heritage, but he was definitely a mix of several races. He was also enormous, and Lily could tell from the level way he looked at her that he didn't make idle threats.

She didn't have many options. She could pretend to be Lillian and try to escape later, or tell the truth and hope they would let her go. If they knew she wasn't the girl they all seemed to hate, then maybe they would realize that they had no reason to keep her locked up in the first place.

"I'm not Lillian. Please, you have to believe me," Lily begged. She heard Rowan make a scoffing noise and desperately raised her voice to be heard over him. "I'm a *version* of Lillian."

They all stared at her blankly.

"Lily. That's what I like to be called," she continued, trying to sound as calm and as rational as she could even though she still couldn't believe what she was saying. "I know this sounds crazy, but I'm from another world—another Salem, Massachusetts."

"Another world? Really?" Rowan said mockingly. "And how did you get here?"

"Lillian brought me," Lily said. Rowan started shaking his head before Lily had even finished that short sentence. He didn't believe a word of it.

"What are you doing?" Rowan asked. "How can you sit there and expect me to believe this?"

"I don't know," Lily replied quietly. The way he was looking at her was so raw it shook something inside her. "Juliet was with the two of us, me and Lillian. We were all standing together in the same room, and she didn't believe it right away, either. How am I supposed to make you believe it?" She frantically tried to recall the conversation that had convinced Juliet. "There was something about a shaman."

"Hold on," Caleb said. "What about the shaman?"

"Juliet said something about Lillian studying with a shaman in secret. She said it like it was something really important. And that's what made her finally believe that I was from another world, like Lillian was saying."

"Is this true?" Caleb looked at Rowan, like he couldn't believe it. "Did a *shaman* go to the Citadel?"

"He was there to help Samantha," Rowan said impatiently. Tristan looked at Rowan sharply, and Rowan continued. "Lillian didn't want anyone to know about it. Not even you, Tristan. The shaman said that Samantha wasn't crazy. He said that she was like him—a spirit walker—and that she just needed to learn how to control it. But who believes that nonsense anyway? Caleb, you and I both know only old-timers and children believe in other worlds. It's a tall tale shamans use to comfort the weak."

"If Lillian brought a shaman to the Citadel, then *she* believed it. And Lillian is anything but weak." Caleb's brow creased with conflicting thoughts. "Did she study with the shaman, too?"

"No," Rowan said vehemently. Then his face changed. "I don't know," he admitted. "But even if there is such a thing as spirit walking and multiple universes—which we all know is pretty farfetched—that doesn't explain this." Rowan gestured to Lily. "It's impossible. Universes are closed systems. You can't get matter or energy in or out."

"Conservation of energy," Lily muttered, nodding her head. She desperately wished she were back in Mr. Carnello's class talking about this, rather than living it.

"What did you say?" Rowan asked sharply.

"It's the first law of thermodynamics," Lily replied miserably. "Energy can be transformed, but it cannot be created or destroyed." She slumped against the bars of her cage, accepting that they were never going to believe she was from another world. "So, basically, my being here makes this universe *not* an equal sign. It goes against a fundamental law of physics—the most fundamental law, actually."

Tristan looked at Rowan, and then back at Lily. "Thermo-what now?"

"Thermodynamics." Lily looked at their puzzled faces. "You guys *do* study physics in this world, right? You know—science class?"

Tristan and Rowan shared another look. "Not exactly," Tristan said. He looked her up and down. "Where did you say you were from?"

"Are you falling for this, Tristan? She's playing us," Rowan said bitterly.

"Ro. She doesn't have her willstone. How can she be parted from it and just sit there?" Tristan asked plaintively. "If that were Lillian, she'd be screaming in pain."

"I don't know how she's doing it." Rowan's dark eyes burned with hatred. "But I know her. I know every cell in her body. That's Lillian."

"I'm not Lillian. I'm Lily! She tricked me and kidnapped me!" Lily choked out, her frustration and desperation nearly bringing her to tears. "I wasn't thinking straight. I thought any place would be better than—" Lily broke off before she said more than she wanted to. She took a shaky breath and swallowed down a sob. "All I want is to go back to my own world and forget this ever happened to me."

"Fine. You're not Lillian? Then prove it."

"Just look at me," she pleaded, her eyes skipping from Rowan to Tristan to Caleb. "Look at how I'm dressed. Obviously, I'm not from around here."

"She has a point," Caleb said.

"If other worlds exist, like the shamans say, and if Lillian studied with a shaman, then she would know how they dress in parallel universes because she can spirit walk into them," Rowan replied stubbornly.

"Will you just *stop* it?" Lily asked, her voice breaking with frustration. "I can't argue with you, because I don't even know what's going on. How am I supposed to prove to you I'm not the evil witch I look exactly like?"

"You know how, Lillian." One corner of Rowan's mouth twitched up in a bitter smile. "Let me in your head."

"Ro. Be serious," Tristan said with an uneasy chortle, like he was hoping that Rowan was kidding.

"I am serious," Rowan replied, his eyes never leaving Lily. Tristan took Rowan's arm and pulled him around to face him.

"If that is Lillian, and you let her into your head, she could kill you with a thought. Or worse," Tristan said in a low, warning tone. "Even without her willstone, she's powerful enough to work you like a puppet."

"I'm aware of that."

"Really? Are you also aware of the fact that getting control over your new willstone might have been her plan all along?"

"Then you monitor our mindspeak," Rowan said evenly. "If she tries to key into my willstone, smash it."

A stunned silence stretched out between the two young men.

"Hold on," Caleb said, stepping between Rowan and Tristan. "The shock will incapacitate you for weeks." He fingered the golden stone around his neck nervously, like the thought of smashing anyone's willstone made him cringe. "I'm not sure it's worth it."

Rowan looked over his shoulder at Lily, who glared back at him. His lip curled. "It's worth it to me."

"I can't authorize this," Caleb said with a shake of his head. "You'll have to talk to the sachem."

"Then bring me to him," Rowan demanded. "The sooner we find out what she's really doing here, the safer we'll all be."

A tense silence passed as the three of them searched each other's eyes. "Tristan, stay here and watch her," Caleb ordered softly. "And be careful."

"I will."

Tristan walked over to the edge of the fire with Rowan and Caleb. They exchanged a few words that Lily couldn't hear before Rowan and Caleb left, sinking silently into the shadows outside the dim glow of the campfire. Tristan stayed where he was, his back turned to Lily, pointedly ignoring her.

For the first time since she'd regained consciousness, Lily looked out beyond the small bubble of light that immediately surrounded her. She saw halos cast by other fires. They seemed to be clustered together, hundreds of yards away from her handmade cage. Lily realized there must be a large group out here in the woods, holding her captive, but apart. Like she was a threat.

Muted voices softened the silence of the thick forest around her—a forest so dark it seemed to eat the light out of the air. Lily looked up. Stars, more stars than she had ever seen, left a milky streak across the deep black of the night sky above her, like a pearlescent river of light.

"So that's why they call it the Milky Way," Lily sighed to herself, awed by the sight.

"Quiet," Tristan commanded nervously, his head snapping around. He stood up from the edge of the fire and came toward her quickly, watching her lips the whole way. "Don't even try to cast a spell on me."

He was genuinely afraid of her. Lily thought she knew every expression on Tristan's face, but she had never seen him like this before. For the first time in their relationship, Lily sensed that she was the one in charge. It made her brave.

"Tristan," she said, smiling ruefully. "If I ever knew how to cast a spell on you, I wouldn't be here right now."

He paused with a bemused half smile on his lips, like he was trying to decide if she was flirting with him. This Tristan was much more humble than hers. "Rowan said you didn't recognize him at first. But you recognize me?" he asked, intrigued.

"Oh yeah," Lily replied. "You're my best friend. Or you were my best friend before last night."

Tristan came toward her. He thought about it for a moment before deciding to sit down next to her.

"What happened?" he asked, resting his elbows on his knees.

Lily knew that he wasn't her Tristan, but she needed a friend right now, and the way this Tristan sat, the sound of his voice, even the way he rubbed the pad of his thumb across the tips of his fingers when he was anxious were all the same.

"We had a fight."

"What did I do?" Tristan winced, automatically assuming that their fight was his fault.

"You cheated on me. Well, sort of." Lily rubbed her forehead tiredly. "It's complicated."

Tristan looked like he didn't believe it. "Are you sure?"

"I saw you with another girl."

"Oh."

"Yeah. It was really horrible actually." Lily looked at him, momentarily taken aback by the weirdness of the situation. "I'm sorry, but this is freaking me out a little. I'm explaining to you how you cheated on me."

"This is pretty weird for me, too." He flashed her one of his brilliant smiles. "So we're lovers?" he asked. He tilted his head toward her slightly, a smile melting on his pretty lips. It was an inadvertently seductive gesture—yet another thing he had in common with her Tristan even if the phrase he'd used was not something a seventeen-year-old guy from Lily's world would ever say. Lily regarded his smile carefully. She didn't trust it anymore and that made her sad.

"No. We're not *lovers*," she said, and then breathed a silent laugh. "I think we were on our way to that eventually, but—"

"I ruined it." He grimaced. "With who? Someone special?"

"No." Lily felt sad all of a sudden. Now that she wasn't angry, she felt the hurt much more deeply. She cleared the thickness from her throat and continued. "You don't even like her."

Tristan nodded, like that made sense to him somehow. "Sounds like I ruined things between us on purpose."

"Yeah," Lily mused, surprised that he was so perceptive. This Tristan seemed older than hers, somehow. Wiser. "You didn't *decide* to hurt me, but I do think you did it on purpose to get away from me."

"And what about the Rowan in your Salem?" he asked in a subdued tone. "What does he think about you and me?"

Lily shrugged. "There is no Rowan in my Salem."

"Oh," Tristan said, almost as if he were disappointed. "That explains it then." Before Lily could ask him what he meant by that, he continued. "So. In your world, I'm an idiot."

Lily laughed and nodded. "Yes, you are," she said, not unkindly.

The firelight, and the harsh shadows it cast, seemed to cut Tristan's face into confusing halves. But even in the unforgiving light, Lily saw a drowned spark rising up out of the well of shyness in him.

"You really aren't her," Tristan said, his voice full of awe. "You're not Lillian."

"No. I'm not her."

He stared at her, the silence stretching out between them.

Tristan's head suddenly pricked up in alarm. Lily heard whipping sounds surrounding them. It took her a moment to identify the noise as bodies running through the brush. Eerie howls filled the air. Lily tried to jump up to her feet but hit the roof of her low, dome-like prison. Wrenching at the rune-engraved bonds holding her wrists together, Lily looked around for Tristan.

He was already up by the fire and digging into the dirt with a spade. He threw the earth onto the flames, smothering the smoke in a few quick shovelfuls. Instantly, their little camp, a distant satellite of the main group, was plunged into darkness. Peering through the bushy conifers, Lily could see motion and hear shouts from the main settlement. A desperate fight was taking place. Flashes of light and shadow blinked in the distance as fast-moving shapes struggled around the campfires. She could hear strange yips and growls blending with the screams of men and women.

"What's out there?" Lily whispered into the dark, thinking of the monsters at the bottom of the green tower.

"The Woven," Tristan whispered back, his face pale with fear. He shucked off his jacket and pulled something out from behind his back. "Hold up your hands." Tristan cut the leather bindings with one flick of his blade. He pulled off his dark shirt and threw it at her.

"Your hair is too bright, and they're attracted to bright colors. Cover it completely. If something happens to me, stay down and hide your face as best as you can. Play dead, and they might not try to get at you through the cage."

Lily nodded numbly, too frightened by the look on Tristan's face to ask questions, and started wrapping up her hair with his shirt. Tristan circled around to the other side of her cage, facing out toward the dark forest, and stood firm. He was guarding her, Lily realized.

The distant shrieks and howls piercing through the darkness

pinned Lily down with fear. Tristan paced around her cage, obviously anxious to join the battle, but his orders to guard Lily kept him at his post. They both watched, helpless, as the screams turned to groans and the frenetic flashes of light from the fires died down. It was impossible to guess which side had won.

A long silence followed the burst of noise and motion of the raid. Lily strained her senses into the darkness. Something moved out there.

Tristan changed position, facing the sound of approaching footsteps, and crouched down into a braced stance. The underbrush shook. Lily saw Tristan's bare back striate with tensed muscles, his knife ready in his hand.

CHAPTER
4

"LADY JULIET."

Juliet looked up from her writing desk. "Yes?"

"The Witch is awake."

"Thank you." Juliet nodded at the footman, dismissing him, then stood, taking the hastily scrawled note she'd been reading. The other Lillian—Lily—had been spotted by one of Juliet's informants outside a nearby café. Rowan had been inside the café, and he'd seen Lily, too. Apparently, he'd chased after her. Juliet's man had lost them both in the winding streets, but he had written in the note that he believed Rowan had caught her. Juliet threw the paper in the fire on her way to the door. She'd learned the hard way that Gideon wasn't above riffling through her private documents.

It was late. Long past sunset. The thought of Lillian—Lily, Juliet reminded herself again—out there in the dark was enough to make her ill. It comforted her some to know that Rowan had most likely taken her off the streets, although it probably shouldn't. Rowan had more reason to want Lillian dead than just about anyone.

And how were they going to keep this quiet? The Outlander shamans—whom even most Outlanders thought were insane—were right. There really were an infinite number of worlds on the other side of every shadow, and Lillian had found a way to access them. They had to keep this a secret, above everything else, but Lillian had allowed Lily to go running off into the city. Alone.

Juliet noticed she was wringing her hands. The thought of how Lily must be feeling—kidnapped and surrounded by strangers in a strange land. Juliet stopped herself and opened the door to her *real* sister's bedroom, trying with little success to convince herself not to worry.

Lillian was sitting at the tea table in front of the fireplace. She was looking out the window, her gaunt face frozen. Sometimes, like now, when Juliet looked at her sister, she could see flashes of terror in her eyes, as if she were screaming on the inside.

Juliet had tried to get her sister to talk, to tell her anything about what had happened to her during those three weeks when she'd disappeared a year ago, but Lillian had never said a word. For days, she didn't speak at all or let anyone touch her. When she finally did start talking again, the only thing Lillian had said was that she had a plan and she needed Juliet to trust her. And Juliet had trusted her, supported her, and defended her when nearly everyone in her inner circle began to speak out against her ever-crueler laws. Juliet had even stayed loyal to her sister when she had started hanging people. To her growing shame.

"Are you going to explain why you let her go, Lillian?" Juliet asked, without much hope for a response.

Lillian shook her head in answer, her blank face hardly registering that she'd heard Juliet at all.

"She's lost," Juliet persisted, taking a seat on the opposite side of the table. "People saw her, and if anyone figures out what you've done, it will change everything. Nothing about our world will stay the same. The possibilities are just . . ." Juliet broke off and shook her head, overwhelmed. "Gideon's already poking around, you know."

"Oh, Juliet," Lillian said tiredly. "Let him. It's not like anyone would see her and think the truth. It's too fantastic for anyone to just assume."

"And what if they *ask* her where she came from?"

Lillian laughed. "They'd think they were talking to me and that I'd lost my mind. Like Mom."

"Even Rowan? He found Lily, you know." Lillian gave her sister a flat-eyed smile, and Juliet sat back in surprise. "You led her to him, didn't you?"

"Of course I did," Lillian said, her voice cracking with fatigue. "She's from a world that's so mind-blind that she still thinks my nudging her this way or that is intuition. She has more to learn than I thought." Lillian frowned and reached for the glass of water in front of her, barely wetting her lips with the smallest of sips. Juliet had noticed months ago that too much of anything seemed to make her vomit these days. Even water.

"Why, Lillian?" Juliet pleaded.

"To train her." Lillian looked out the window again. "Without Rowan, she'd never be strong enough in time. We need him as much as we need her, or this won't work."

Juliet leaned forward, reaching across the table for her sister's hand. "*What* won't work? Please tell me."

Lillian took Juliet's hand but didn't turn her head to look at her.

Lily nearly screamed bloody murder when something burst through the underbrush, but she found herself strangely comforted when she realized that it was Rowan. She saw Tristan's tense back relax a bit as he recognized his friend.

"Caleb?" Tristan asked, searching behind Rowan.

"Tracking the Woven's trail, looking for their nest," Rowan replied tersely, making his way to Lily's cage. "We have to move her."

As Rowan got close enough for her to see him clearly, Lily recoiled. He was covered in blood. Sweat-slicked skin peeked out from under his shredded shirt, and his face was stamped with the grim hollows of violence. His breath gusted out of him as steamy clouds in the frigid night air.

"Where are you taking me?" Lily asked, backing against the far side of her cage. Rowan ignored her and touched the lock on the door. His large silver willstone glowed, and the lock sprang open. He reached in for Lily, grabbing her arm and pulling her out forcibly.

"Easy, Ro," Tristan protested. "You're hurting her."

"Then you take her." Rowan shoved Lily in Tristan's direction. "But if she bolts for the woods, her death is on you."

"Fine. It's on me," Tristan replied. He took his shirt from Lily and pulled it back on angrily.

"No, it's not, Tristan. I'm responsible for me." Something snapped in Lily. She whirled on Rowan, her anger finally overpowering her fear. "Why the hell would I run into the woods when it's crawling with monsters? I'm not a frigging moron. And I don't appreciate being ignored, Rowan whatever-your-last-name-is. Where are you taking me?"

"Like I'd tell you that," Rowan said, offended, as if she'd asked him for his bank-account number. He turned to Tristan with a sardonic smile. "She's all yours."

Lily sputtered impotently at Rowan as he busied himself, collecting useful tools and supplies from the camp. She wanted to scream that she wasn't his to give away, but she couldn't ignore the fact that she was a prisoner—Rowan's prisoner, apparently—and therefore without much say in the matter. And if she were to be completely honest with herself she wasn't even sure she wanted to be freed—at least not yet. She had no idea how to get back home and even less of an idea how to protect herself in this strange and dangerous world.

They marched through the near pitch dark of the forest for what seemed like hours. The only light Rowan permitted were the stars whirring overhead, and that feeble illumination seemed to be all he and Tristan needed to move silently through the forest.

Not so for Lily. She could barely see her own hand in front of her face and crashed blindly through the dark. Every time she stumbled over the uneven ground, she could hear Rowan chuff with displeasure. As the night wore on Lily could sense Rowan growing more and more impatient with her, like he thought she was intentionally trying to break every twig and fall down every gopher hole in the damn state. More than once Lily laid herself out flat, landing hard on the heels of her hands in the brittle, frost-covered leaves on the forest floor. After a few hours of this, she was cut and bruised in a dozen places, and by the time she twisted her right ankle so badly it made her cry out loudly, she was already on the verge of tears.

"Quiet, or you'll get us all killed. You're not fooling anyone," Rowan growled as he tugged her roughly up off the ground. "And I won't tend to that ankle for you so you'd better drop the act."

Lily wrenched her arm out of his hand, desperately trying not to cry. She put her right foot down to move away from him, and the pain that shot up her leg like lightning was the final straw. Tears that had been gathering in her eyes tipped over and spilled down her cheeks.

Rowan turned away from her with a sound of disgust,

whispering the words "so manipulative" under his breath. Lily rubbed the tears off her cheeks and felt their salt sting the scratches on her hands. She took a few deep breaths to quiet her crying. There were still those things—the Woven—out there in the dark, and even though she was lost, confused, and hurt, she knew Rowan wasn't joking. Any sound she made could alert those things and get them all killed. Still dwelling on the Woven, she startled and nearly screamed when she felt Tristan's hands cup her ankle.

"This is bad," he whispered. Lily felt his cold fingers gently prod a spot that was so sore she jerked away spasmodically. "I think it's broken."

Lily looked around at the looming forest, growing desperate. She was quite sure that they weren't anywhere near a hospital. "Isn't there anything you can do?"

"I can get you to camp." Tristan stood up suddenly. Before Lily could figure out what he was thinking, he'd already lifted her and started carrying her silently through the trees.

"Wait," Lily pleaded. She pushed against his chest, trying to get him to put her down. He even smelled the same as her Tristan. "You can't—"

"Yes, I can. Don't worry. We're nearly at the rendezvous point," he said, hefting her easily in his arms. "You weigh next to nothing anyway."

Rowan had gone ahead. When they caught up to him, he saw Tristan carrying Lily, and even in the dark Lily could read frustration oozing out of him; frustration and some other emotion she couldn't quite place. Despite his displeasure, he didn't object to Tristan carrying her, even though he clearly wanted to tell his friend to drop her on her behind.

The rendezvous point was close, as Tristan had promised. In less than ten minutes, Rowan stopped and called out softly, holding his hand to the side to indicate that Tristan should keep still. A moment later, Caleb came through the underbrush.

"You made it," Caleb said, his wide grin showing brightly against his dark skin in the starlight. He and Rowan clasped hands briefly. "What happened to her?"

Rowan made an irritated sound and brushed past his friend, leaving Tristan to explain.

"She fell in the dark," Tristan said hurriedly.

"She fell?" Caleb repeated, grimacing like he'd never heard anything so silly.

"Her ankle's broken." Tristan shook off Caleb's next question and continued. "She's not Lillian—I'm dead sure of it, Caleb. We need to get this straightened out right now. She's in a lot of pain."

"Come on. I'll take you to the sachem," Caleb replied reluctantly. He led the way through the small camp, occasionally glancing back at Lily warily. He still didn't trust her.

"Isn't a sachem, like, an Indian chief?" Lily whispered to Tristan, and quickly corrected herself. "Sorry—Native American chief?"

The only reason Lily knew this was because, being from Salem, she'd had to learn about the Pilgrim settlement in Massachusetts. A lot of land had been purchased from the sachem of the Algonquin tribe, including entire islands, like Nantucket. Lily was pretty sure there were no more Algonquin left in her world, although she knew that there was a high school in Northborough named after them. Not really a fair trade, in Lily's estimation—a high school for your whole tribe.

Tristan gave her a puzzled look. "The sachem is the leader of the Outland people in this particular area. Well, what's left of the Outland people, anyway," he replied darkly. They passed a few guards, who inspected them carefully. Every time one of the guards recognized who it was that Tristan was carrying, Caleb had to stop to calm him down.

"What's an Outland person?" Lily asked while Caleb argued with a few heavily armed men and women.

"An Outlander is someone who lives outside the walls of the Thirteen Cities," Tristan replied.

"You only have thirteen cities in this world?"

"Why? How many do you have?"

Lily recalled the vibrant city encircled by those towering walls—vibrant, but not bigger than New York. In contrast, she looked at the old and thick forest that she had battled through for hours, and a strange feeling settled over her. Tristan carried her past an expansive oak that must have been growing for hundreds of years. If there were only thirteen cities in this America, just how *large* was this forest? This world suddenly felt much wilder then her own.

"So there are thirteen cities and this big, spooky forest, but what about the suburbs?" she asked in a hushed voice as more and more eyes peered at her as they neared the camp. "Where are they?"

"What's a *sub-urb*?" Tristan replied, his mouth tentatively pronouncing the foreign word.

Stunned silent, Lily was still trying to figure out how to shape her next question when they entered a large glade. At first, she could only make out vague shapes looming here and there around the clearing. As Tristan carried her closer, she realized that the shapes were perfectly camouflaged tents, made of some kind of unfamiliar material.

They zigzagged their way in between the tents, which grew denser toward the middle, until Lily finally saw a light. A campfire burned, its light blocked from the rest of the forest by the clever positioning of the tents. The fire struck Lily as an oddly rustic centerpiece to what was otherwise a futuristic-looking camp. It was too small to keep them all warm, and she wondered why they bothered lighting it at all.

Tristan set her down next to the fire and shook out his exhausted arms. Caleb disappeared into one of the tents, indicating that they should wait there. Lily tried to keep her throbbing ankle elevated as best she could while she waited for him to return with the sachem. Even in the low light, she could see that her ankle was swelling alarmingly fast and already starting to bruise.

Lily looked up to see a man, about thirty years old, coming toward her with a forceful yet halting stride. He had prematurely graying hair and a pronounced limp, but other than that he looked incredibly fit. The man was flanked by Rowan on one side and Caleb on the other. He wasn't particularly large—Caleb stood a full head taller—but Lily didn't doubt his authority. This man was a leader. The sachem stood above her, taking in every aspect of her appearance. His dark eyes drilled into hers for an uncomfortably long time, and Lily found she couldn't hold his gaze.

"Look at me, girl," he snapped when she tried to drop her eyes. Lily obeyed even though his searching look unnerved her. "Who are you?" he asked.

"Lily Proctor," she replied.

"Where are you from?"

"Salem, Massachusetts."

The sachem raised an eyebrow at Lily in surprise. "Massachusetts? We haven't used that name for this territory in hundreds of years. Not since the Great Witch Trials."

Rowan made an impatient sound, and the sachem raised his hand for quiet. "This isn't Lillian, Rowan," he said.

"But it *is* her," he argued. "Every cell in her body . . ."

"Is exactly the same," the sachem finished for him. He put a hand on Rowan's shoulder and squeezed reassuringly. "I believe you and I trust your skill as a mechanic completely. But impossible or not, this girl isn't the Lillian we know."

"How can you be so sure?" Rowan asked pleadingly.

"Because *this* girl has never killed anyone," he said with certainty. "Look in her eyes, Rowan. There's no death there."

Rowan looked away, chewing on his lower lip. "You willing to bet your life on that?" he asked.

The sachem smiled indulgently. Lily could tell that if anyone else had questioned him this way, the sachem would have lit into him, but for some reason he had more patience with Rowan. She wondered if they were related. They both had the same sweeping brow and strong features, and they projected a similar strength.

"We both heard the stories of spirit walking when we were kids, Rowan," he said gently. "All Outlanders do."

"We hear them, and then we grow up," Rowan replied. "Do you honestly believe that she isn't Lillian?"

"Do you honestly believe she is?"

"I don't know." Rowan looked at Lily, and his dark eyes softened with uncertainty.

"Is this one still powerful?" the sachem asked.

"There's none stronger," Rowan responded immediately.

"Can she do everything that Lillian can?"

Rowan shrugged. "Maybe. With training."

The sachem crouched down stiffly in front of Lily. An old brace that spanned from the thigh to the calf kept his right leg straight. Something awful must have happened to his knee to require that much hardware, and Lily wondered what it was. "I'm Alaric," he said, introducing himself.

Lily nodded once, but was too intimidated to say anything back. Alaric touched her broken ankle with his fingertips, and Lily gasped, tears springing to her eyes.

"That's definitely broken," he said. Alaric removed his hand and stood. "Get to work on that ankle, you two," he ordered in Rowan and Tristan's general direction. "And Lily?" he added over his shoulder. "In the morning, I have some questions for you." Alaric paused to look at Lily, shaking his head. "The shamans were right. Who'd have thought that?"

The sachem chuckled to himself as he and Caleb disappeared into the dark outskirts of the camp, leaving Lily with Rowan and Tristan. She exhaled slowly and realized that she'd been half holding her breath under Alaric's intense scrutiny.

Rowan knelt down at Lily's feet, avoiding her eyes. He stripped off his jacket and began rolling up his sleeves. His face grew pensive as he considered her ankle.

"I'll get the phosphorous and chalk," Tristan said, and turned to go.

"And bring iron," Rowan called after him. "The marrow's smashed."

As Lily watched Tristan hurry off, she barely bit back the urge to call after him and beg him not to leave her alone with Rowan. But as she watched Rowan staring at her ankle, her fears about whether or not he would take this opportunity to slit her throat drained away. He was completely focused on her injury.

Rowan placed his fingers on her ankle and pressed gently, but unlike everyone else who had prodded her sore spots, he didn't hurt her. In fact, she felt some of the pain diminish. Rowan's willstone flared with a strange, oily light, and the campfire behind him pulsed brighter and then dropped to an almost imperceptibly duller intensity. Lily felt heat under her skin—heat and a slackening of the swollen pressure in her ankle. She felt something like hot fingers prodding the muscle and sinew around her bones. Then the hot fingers dropped deeper and started rearranging the bones themselves like they were nothing more than another kind of stiff tissue.

It didn't hurt, but the sensation was so foreign and off-putting that she tried to pull away from Rowan's touch.

"Easy," Rowan said, his deep voice rumbling.

"It's too weird," she said, still trying to shy away.

His eyes darted up and met hers. Lily saw fire in them—actual *flames* licking around his irises.

"Holymarymotherofgod, your eyes are on fire!" Lily blathered.

Since she'd been brought to this alternate Salem, she'd seen necklaces glow and huge doors swish open automatically, but this was the first time she'd seen anything that was flat-out impossible. Lily had never believed in magic, not even when she'd first found herself transported to this alternate universe, but she believed in it now. Like it or not, she'd just felt magic in her bones.

The fire in Rowan's eyes went out, and the gentle pressure of his fingers suddenly hurt. He released her immediately, almost as if he could sense that he was hurting her, and scooted away.

"You're not Lillian," Rowan said roughly.

"No, I'm really not," Lily replied, taking the opportunity to scoot away from him, too.

They stared at each other, both regarding the other fearfully.

"She did it," Rowan said, breathless. His eyes left Lily's and he stared blankly at the ground. "How?" His eyes darted back up to Lily's and rested there for a moment.

He fell silent until Tristan returned, he and Lily staring at each other skeptically.

"What's going on?" Tristan asked. He dropped a pack on the ground between them, ending the staring contest. "Lily? Are you okay?"

"It's not that," she replied. She motioned to Rowan with her chin. "He believes me now, and it's freaking him out."

Tristan turned to Rowan and shrugged. "I tried to tell you."

"Yeah, I know you did," Rowan replied, with a look that said Tristan didn't need to rub it in. "Let's get to work."

He started rummaging through the pack Tristan had brought and pulled out a few small lumps of brightly colored stone and a few handfuls of leaves, flowers, and something that looked like a gnarled bit of beef jerky. Lily had studied enough chemistry and botany to know that the yellow lump of rock had to be the phosphorus; the white one chalk; and the red iron. The flowers she wasn't too sure about, but she thought they might be arnica. She knew arnica was a homeopathic remedy for swelling and muscle cramps, and she recognized the simple white flower from the picture on a tube of gel she used in the hospital whenever she ached from lying in bed too long.

"I'm going to have her do it," Rowan said to Tristan as he unpacked a small pot and a mortar and pestle.

"She has no idea how," Tristan replied.

"I'll guide her." Tristan started to object, but Rowan cut him off. "She resisted me when I was prepping her, and she'll only fight me harder the deeper I go. If I try to do it, she might block me entirely, and it won't heal at all."

Tristan stared at Lily for a moment, his eyes narrowed with concern. "She doesn't even have a willstone."

"*She* doesn't need one," Rowan replied confidently. "All she needs is for me to point the way."

"It's never been done."

"But it's still going to work."

Rowan and Tristan stared at each other, long and hard. Lily got the strange sense that they were still speaking to each other, even if she couldn't hear what they were saying.

Without another word, Tristan turned and started scraping off tiny bits of the phosphorus, iron, and chalk. He began grinding them down to dust with the mortar and pestle while Rowan plucked bits of the herbs and put them in a small pot of water he'd set to boil on the edge of the fire. Their actions were quick and precise, as if they had been trained to do this. After a few moments of orchestrated movement, Rowan held out his hand to Tristan, who poured the ground minerals into his palm, like a nurse handing a surgeon a scalpel.

"Here. Inhale this," Rowan said, holding his hand under Lily's nose.

"What's it for?" she asked, already inhaling. Rowan gave her a quizzical look.

"You're just going to inhale it without waiting for an answer?" he asked, cocking an eyebrow at her. Lily squinted back at him. His face had started to blur.

"Please don't tell me I'm going to pass out again," she pleaded.

"Focus," Rowan said. He brushed his hands together in the direction of the fire, sending the leftover particles into the flames. The fire shot up, changing color as it burned the phosphorus, calcium, and iron. Lily's vision cleared.

She had no idea what Rowan wanted her to focus on, so she just stared at him and Tristan. The two of them sat cross-legged next to the fire, waiting. Rowan stared at the little pot of water, absent-mindedly touching his willstone with the tip of his middle finger. The pot boiled, and he wrapped his hand in the sleeve of his jacket to remove it from the flame. He turned to Lily.

"Drink," he said, offering the red-bottomed pot for her to take.

"But . . . it's burning hot," she said, not understanding what he wanted her to do.

"Heat is energy. You are a crucible. Take this cauldron, drink this brew, and use the energy to change the elements I've given you into blood, marrow, and bone."

Lily gaped at him.

"Do it now, Lily." He shoved the small cauldron into her hands, and tipped the rim toward her face. Left with no other option, she gulped the liquid down rather than let it splash over her face and hoped that if she got it over with quickly she'd suffer less.

Lily didn't feel a thing. The hot brew didn't scald her tongue or mouth. Her hands weren't singed. She turned the ashy cauldron around in her fingers, feeling pulsing warmth, but not pain. She saw Rowan's willstone flare as he moved closer to her.

"I'll help you guide it," he murmured, his eyes half closed.

Rowan reached out and took her shoulders, slowly drawing her closer to him until they were nearly pressed against each other. The slippery, silver light of his willstone pulsed in the scant inch that was left between them. Rowan pushed her back until she was lying down, and leaned over her. The light from his willstone began flashing over her body and arcing down in little tendrils, like lightning.

Lily felt a tingling storm in her body that drew the heat from the brew in her belly down to her ankle. When it reached her injury, the heat burst into life and crawled like fingers of fire under her skin.

Suddenly, Lily could *see* the damage. She saw the smashed bone, the torn ligaments, the shredded blood vessels, and she knew what she had to do. She told the fingers of fire to put the broken bits back together, to use the free elements that she'd inhaled to mix with the collagen, proteins, and minerals that came from the brew to knit her body back together. In seconds, Lily's ankle reassembled.

"Now. Call out the fluid—the swelling and the blood. Remetabolize it," Rowan whispered, his soft mouth brushing against her jawbone as he spoke. Lily saw what he meant and released the pressure, calling all the fluid back to her organs to be recycled.

The light from Rowan's willstone went out, and he sighed, drooping on his elbows for a moment before he pushed himself away from her. Lily sat up. She turned her ankle around effortlessly, drawing a circle with her big toe. It was as good as new.

Lily pressed her foot against the ground, testing whether or not it could handle weight. There was no pain. She stared at her perfect ankle, not really believing that five minutes ago it had been swollen and broken.

"Magic," she whispered, not convinced that she could handle this.

"Of course," Rowan said, looking at Tristan. Again, Lily got the feeling that they were communicating without words.

"What?" she asked defensively.

"We've decided that you don't need to be locked up. You can sleep in a tent tonight," Tristan said. He crossed to Lily and helped her up off the ground. "This one behind you should be fine. Rowan and I will be in that one," he continued, and gestured to the tent next to hers. "Are you tired?"

"Of course I'm tired," Lily said in a quavering voice. She was trying to stay calm, but too much had happened. She'd been teleported, kidnapped, tied up, raided by monsters, frog-marched through the woods in the dead of night, and now this. *Magic.* And she'd been the one to do it. Before she lost it completely, Lily whirled around and dove into her tent.

"There should be a canteen of water in there if you get thirsty," Tristan called after her. "Good night."

Lily didn't answer. She pulled the flap down over the entrance and stood in the dark tent, panting hysterically. When her eyes adjusted, Lily saw what looked liked a rolled-up sleeping bag in the corner. She went to it quickly and laid it out on the ground. Her breath was coming in and out of her in fretful little gulps, and her hands were shaking. Kneeling on her makeshift bed, Lily cupped her hands over her mouth and tried to slow her breathing down.

She wanted to go home. She wanted her sister to come into the tent and tell her everything was going to be okay. Lily crawled onto her bag, tears spilling down her face. All she could think about was that Juliet must be worried sick about her. Lily had disappeared into thin air, abandoning her without warning. Lily laid her head down and wished with her whole heart that Juliet could hear her.

Help me, Juliet!

Gideon heard a furtive knock on the door of his personal suite of rooms at the Citadel. It was late, so late it was almost early morning.

The girl across from him stiffened with fear at the sound. She was an Outlander who'd tapped on his window out of desperation. Or stupidity. Gideon didn't know which yet. He didn't think she had the right papers to allow her inside the city walls after dark, and she certainly didn't have permission to be inside the smaller circle of the Citadel walls. If she was caught by one of the guards, she would end up in prison for sure. She looked at him pleadingly and Gideon smiled. He liked her better when she was scared.

"Who's there?" he called out.

"Carrick," answered the man on the other side of the door.

"Give me a moment."

Gideon flicked his head toward the window. "Get out," he said to the girl.

"My brother?" she whispered, her eyes downcast.

"That depends on you," Gideon replied, "and on how nice you are to me."

She looked up at him, her mouth tight. She wasn't an idiot, or pretending to be so virtuous she didn't understand what Gideon meant, which was good for her. If she'd tried to play the shy violet after climbing in his bedroom window, he'd have hung her alongside her wretched brother just for wasting his time.

The girl swallowed. "Then you'll let him go? He's not a scientist or a rebel. Really."

Gideon was surprised she had the nerve to ask him for a promise. He wondered how old she was. Thirteen? Maybe fourteen. Some of those Outland girls had smart mouths and seemed older than they were. After a lifetime of being passed over by the high-and-mighty Salem Witch herself, Gideon did not find female spunk endearing.

"Ask me again and he'll hang for sure," Gideon said, watching a choking hatred rise up in her throat. Good. Now she knew where she stood. He smiled at her. "Get out, drub. For now."

She wasn't crying, which could be a problem. If he hadn't broken her spirits completely, she could come back demanding something. If she wanted her brother to live, she'd have to learn patience. And manners. Gideon decided it might be fun to teach her both.

While the girl scurried out the window, Gideon put on a robe and crossed through his suite to the main entrance. He opened the door and led Carrick, his Outlander spy, into the sitting area. He marveled, as he always did, at how drubs seemed to walk without stirring the air. A necessary ability, Gideon assumed, for those stuck down precarious mine shafts all day and surrounded by roving bands of Woven all night. It made them good fighters. That, coupled with the constant near starvation of their poverty-stricken lives, gave them a survivor's mastery of all the herbs and animals of the forest. Strength and knowledge of herb lore—those were two of the reasons Rowan had been chosen to be Lillian's head mechanic, rather than Gideon himself.

An Outlander, a drub no better than that piece of rubbish he'd just kicked out of his room, was head mechanic to the Salem Witch. Or he had been until she sent him away.

"Set the wards," Carrick whispered.

Gideon shook off the all-consuming swell of irritation that

always accompanied any thought of Rowan and concentrated so that he could cast a ward spell around the room to be neither heard nor felt by anyone else inside the Citadel. A pulse of silvery blue light throbbed around the room as Gideon's ward formed a bubble of protection around them.

"The room is sealed," Gideon said, moving his hand away from his willstone. "Speak freely."

"Minutes ago, I saw Lady Juliet leave the Citadel," Carrick responded, the words bursting out of him urgently. "She seemed distraught—frantic, even. I sent a team of guards to shadow her, of course."

"Why so many? Where was she going?" Gideon replied, already on his way to the clothespress to dress.

"The forest." Carrick sounded pleased. "She left the city and went into the Outland."

Gideon stopped momentarily. First Lillian was found wandering around the Citadel, half crazed, and now dependable Juliet was behaving like she'd abandoned all sense. What was going on? Gideon needed Juliet alive—at least, for a little while—to get children out of her. "Did she have her bodyguard with her? A weapon?"

"She stole out the southwest gate with nothing but a cape and a small handbag. I have horses ready," Carrick said, his wiry shoulders already tilted toward the door.

"Horses," Gideon said resignedly.

Gideon hated riding the damn things, and growing up in the city like a civilized person he'd rarely had reason to. He much preferred his luxury elepod, or even one of the trains that connected the Thirteen Cities underground, but unfortunately electric vehicles were nearly useless in the woods, and the whole idea of above-ground trains had been abandoned when the Woven were accidentally brought into being. Horses it was, then.

"I have a tracking ward set to the guard captain's willstone," Carrick said, his own willstone flaring slightly with the touch of its master's mind. He raised his eyes and met Gideon's. "We have to hurry. Juliet is going deep into the Woven Woods."

Gideon finished pulling on a pair of pretty but stiff riding boots and turned to Carrick. "Lead the way."

Lily felt a hand shaking her awake. She would have jumped at the touch, but she smelled a scent that was as familiar to her as her own.

"Juliet?" Lily called plaintively into the dark.

"Shh. Yes, it's me," Juliet replied. She was half in, half out of the tent. Lily sat up and saw that her sister—or, rather, her sister's long-haired other self—had lifted up the backside of the tent and scooted only part of the way inside. Her luminous eyes were wide and wild. "What happened? Are you injured?"

"No. Well, I was, but not anymore," Lily replied, still struggling to kick-start her exhausted mind.

"You're healed?" Juliet asked, her face frozen.

"Yeah." Lily tried to tug Juliet into the tent with her, but Juliet resisted.

"Come *on*," Juliet whispered angrily, tugging back at Lily to draw her out. "We need to go! Anyone could walk by."

Lily crawled out of the tent wondering if she could trust this woman. She looked like Juliet, but that didn't mean that she was Juliet. Every instinct in Lily screamed that Juliet would always be on her side, no matter what universe they were in, but Lily didn't know if she could trust herself anymore. After all, it had been another version of herself that had kidnapped her to begin with.

"I'm going to get you out of here," Juliet said, her voice quavering with fear, but her delicate jaw set with determination. "You have no idea how dangerous these woods are, even in the middle of an armed camp like this. You're not safe out here, Lily." She clasped Lily's hand in hers and crouched down, making a beeline for the trees.

"How did you know where to find me?" Lily asked, ducking down like her sister did.

"Seriously?" Juliet whispered, glancing back at Lily as though she didn't believe what she'd been asked. "You were *screaming* for me to come and get you!"

"In my head, yeah, but . . ." Lily stopped talking as soon as she saw that look in Juliet's eyes. It was the same *I can't believe you scared the crap out of me for no reason* look that her sister had given her about a million times before, and it confused Lily even more. "Wait. How did you hear that?"

"Close blood relations like sisters can mindspeak without will-stones," Juliet answered automatically.

"But I'm not Lillian," Lily replied. She didn't understand will-stones yet, but she did know one thing: Her whole life she'd felt as if she and her sister, and her mom sometimes, could read each other's minds—without glowing magic necklaces. And now she knew that it was true.

"I guess even if you're not exactly Lillian, you're still my little sister. Not that I ever asked for two of you, but there it is." Juliet nibbled on her lower lip and then nodded her head once, as if she was making a final decision. "I'm not leaving you out here in the Woven Woods. I can't. You don't know how important your being here is yet, but please believe me. You're in terrible danger."

"Where are we going?" Lily frowned suddenly. "You're not taking me back to Lillian, are you?"

"Not if you don't want me to." Juliet's brow furrowed. "But I have to hide you somehow. If people find out about you and what you could be capable of—Lily, I'm frightened for your life."

Lily squeezed Juliet's hand. "Okay. Let's get out of here. I'll follow you."

"Stop, Juliet."

Lily and Juliet spun around to face the deep voice that came out of the dark. Juliet thrust Lily behind her protectively, even though neither of them could see where the words had come from yet.

"Rowan," Juliet scolded, her familiar tone making it obvious that the two of them had known each other a long time. "How could you endanger her like this? She's not Lillian. She's lost and she's frightened."

Rowan sighed. Apparently, Juliet was just as good at scolding in this universe as she was in Lily's.

Lily tried to pinpoint where he was. She could see bushes and even a bit of the trail, but she couldn't see him. Rowan seemed to be able to blend into the shadow and starlight.

"I don't want to fight with you, Juliet," he said, disarming Lily with his honest tone. "But I can't let you take her."

"She's in shock and she's terrified. You allowed her to get *injured,*" Juliet continued, as if the Rowan she knew would never allow something like that to happen.

"And I'll kill her if I have to," Rowan answered, finally stepping into view. He had his knife out.

Lily heard Juliet gasp, like she was fighting back tears. Feeling rather ridiculous, Lily tried to mindspeak again.

Hey, Jules. Can you hear me? Hello? But she didn't see or hear any reaction from Juliet.

"What's happened to you, Rowan?" Juliet asked, dismayed. "Has Alaric turned you into another one of his painted savages?"

"Careful, Juliet." Rowan's expressive mouth was pinched into a thin line of warning. "You don't know what you're talking about. You don't know the man."

"I know he's little better than a wild animal." Juliet pressed on with increasing heat. "Alaric has killed hundreds of guards—in all the Thirteen Cities—and he won't even entertain the notion of peace. Rowan," she said pleadingly, "I can understand you wanting to help your people, but how can you align yourself with *him?*"

"Because Lillian and the Covens have made peace impossible," Rowan said. "Only when the Thirteen Cities grant Outlanders basic rights and stop killing the people who can give them a better future will peace ever be an option again."

"Lillian says there's a reason she's taken this path," Juliet said in a slightly more subdued tone. "That it's for all our sakes."

"What reason could she have for killing scientists, teachers, and doctors?" Rowan ran a hand through his thick hair. His face was sad and lost. "Come on, Juliet. How can you align yourself with *her?*"

Juliet looked down at her hands. She fidgeted with her fingers the same way Lily's Juliet did when she was anxious. "She's my sister."

The argument was over. Rowan approached Lily and took her hand out of Juliet's. Lily tried to fight him off, but Juliet stopped her.

"Don't struggle, Lily. He really will kill you if he has to." Juliet turned to Rowan. "And what about me?"

"You have to leave immediately. I can't hide you from Lillian's mind if she seeks you, and I can't have the camp discovered."

"She's asleep," Juliet said, shaking her head so that he needn't worry. "She's sick, actually, but I don't know what's wrong with her because we haven't shared mindspeak in almost a year now." Juliet seemed almost relieved to be able to tell this to someone, and despite the fact that Rowan was the enemy, Lily got the distinct sense that Juliet still trusted him. "No one knows I've left the Citadel, Rowan. I don't want to get you all killed."

"I know you don't, Juliet." Rowan's face pinched with a painful thought and his voice softened. "You never want anyone to get hurt, but people do. Every day. Go back to Lillian and keep arguing with her. Try to save as many people as you can." He turned to the bushes and whistled softly. A painted warrior appeared out of the darkness. "Take two men. Escort Lady Juliet through the woods. Protect her with your lives."

The guard took Juliet's arm, pulling her away. She smiled bravely at Lily, which only made Lily more afraid for her.

"Are you going to be okay?" Lily asked.

"Don't worry about me," Juliet replied.

Lily watched, her heart climbing up her throat, as her sister's narrow shoulders disappeared into the clutching branches of the autumn-bare trees.

"She'll be okay, right?" Lily asked.

Rowan didn't answer. Instead, he took Lily's wrist firmly in hand. She wondered if he could feel her loathing for him through her skin. He stopped briefly to give instructions to another warrior, ordering her to inform Caleb and to send out scouts to make sure that Juliet had come alone, and then pulled Lily back to the camp. He led Lily back to her tent, opened the flap, and hauled her inside.

"How did you reach Juliet? You aren't really her sister," he said harshly. "Did you touch her willstone?"

Lily glared at him, refusing to answer.

"Juliet isn't a witch, and she has no fighting skills," he persisted, his tone accusing. "She isn't fit for the woods. You could have gotten her killed, coming here. She's still in danger, even with the guards I sent with her. You understand that, don't you?"

"I didn't mean to," Lily said, frowning with worry.

"Explain."

Rowan's dark eyes glittered, and Lily was suddenly aware of how much bigger he was than her. She saw the knife in his belt and took a step back, glancing around the tent for anything she could use to defend herself. Rowan's expression shifted. He backed off and put his hands on his hips.

"I'm not going to hurt you, okay?" he said, as though regretting scaring her. "But I need to know how many people you contacted, or we're all in danger, including Tristan. I know you don't care about the rest of us, but you care about him, don't you?"

"I don't want anyone to die—not even you, if you can believe it. I just want to go home," Lily said, exhausted. "Juliet said that even if I'm from another universe, I'm still her little sister, and sisters don't need to touch stones, or whatever."

"Can you mindspeak with Lillian?" Rowan asked calmly.

"I think so. I think I heard her in my head before she kidnapped me." Lily dragged a hand over her face. "But I thought it was my own voice, like I was talking to myself."

Rowan nodded, visualizing what it would be like to hear your own voice in your head. "Have you reached out to Lillian in any way since you've been at camp?"

"She brought me here. She *tricked* me," Lily said, her anger rising swiftly. "I wouldn't reach out to her if she was the last person on Earth. Any Earth."

Rowan gave her a puzzled look, his eyes searching hers. Lily looked back at him, feeling the odd sensation again that there was a complicated language the two of them could speak if only she could recall the first few words. He looked away and swallowed hard.

"Stay here," he said over his shoulder, and left the tent.

She heard him speaking quietly outside by the fire with Tristan and Caleb, telling them everything that had happened and deciding what to do next. They started arguing again. Yawning, Lily sat down on her sleeping bag and struggled to keep her eyes open while she waited to hear what they were going to do about her little jailbreak.

Her body ached from the unaccustomed exercise and from the dozens of little bumps and scrapes she'd incurred. Her nose was stuffed up, probably from the leaf mold, and her head was throbbing. She rubbed her puffy eyes, wishing she could fall asleep and wake up from this nightmare. Finally, Rowan returned with another sleeping bag.

"You're tired," he said, like he was reminding her she needed to buy milk at the store. She regarded his sleeping bag meaningfully, arms crossed.

"I thought this was my tent."

"Your single-tent privileges have been revoked," he said, looking down at his own hands as he unrolled his bag. For a second, it looked like he was smiling to himself, but when he looked up at her, his face was stern. "Lie down."

Rowan set his sleeping bag down against the foot of hers, in a T formation. She was just about to argue with him when a giant, jaw-cracking yawn overtook her. The truth was, Lily felt so exhausted that she didn't really care where he slept. She stretched out on top of her bag as he climbed into the bag at her feet. He reached out for her, pushing his hand under the hem of her jeans and clasping on to her newly healed ankle. She tried to jerk her foot away, but he only held on tighter.

"In case you try to wander off again," he told her. His expression made it clear that there was no point protesting—he wasn't going to let go. Lily settled back hesitantly while Rowan lowered the lamplight and settled down.

His hand was refreshingly cool on her hot skin—almost as if he were pulling some of the heat and congestion out of her through the palm of his hand. Lily felt her nose unstuff, the ache behind her eyes lessen, and her fever begin to drop.

She knew she should probably be terrified of someone who'd

threatened to kill her only moments ago, but she wasn't. The gentle pressure of Rowan's fingers on her calf soothed her. But as her muscles started to slacken, his seemed to get tighter and tighter. Even though Lily was exhausted, his tension was keeping her awake.

"What is it?" she finally asked.

"You're really dehydrated," he replied, throwing off his blankets and crossing the dark tent. "Didn't Tristan tell you about the canteen?"

He brought it over to her without waiting for a response.

"I'm fine," she said stubbornly.

"You're not fine. Drink," Rowan urged, his voice softer than she'd ever heard it. She took a few swallows, realized how thirsty she was, and drained the whole canteen in one long draw that left her gasping for breath at the end.

"Thanks," she said, handing the canteen back to him. "How did you know I was so thirsty?"

Rowan didn't answer her right away—he just shook his head and smiled to himself. After a long pause he finally said, "I've been taking care of you for so many years now, I know your body better than you do."

Rowan stowed the canteen and climbed back into his bag. He reached out and grabbed on to her ankle again, but this time she didn't try to pull it away.

CHAPTER
5

LILY OPENED HER EYES AND SAW AN ARM. A BIG, THICK male arm. The skin was smooth and a few shades darker than her nearly translucent shoulder, which was pinned beneath it.

She knew it was Rowan's arm—the same guy who had said he would happily kill her—but she couldn't seem to get herself to pull away from him in disgust. Every part of her felt like it was in exactly the right place.

Lying on her side as she was, she normally had to put a pillow between her skinny thighs to keep her knees from pressing too hard against each other, but Rowan had placed his bent leg in between hers. She had no pillow for her head either, but it didn't matter. Rowan had put his lower arm under her head to cushion it. Lily always needed something clasped to her chest when she slept or she would feel untethered, only to dream of falling and shake herself awake. This morning she found that she was clutching Rowan's hand to her heart as if it were her anchor.

She felt Rowan pull in a shuddering breath as he awoke, his

diaphragm fluttering against her back. Lily eased away from him, embarrassed. No matter how good he felt, she didn't know this guy, and she had no business cuddling with him.

Lily was trying to figure out how to crawl away as inconspicuously as possible when Rowan untangled himself from her, stood, and left the tent in a few swift motions. She sat up and stared after him, confused.

The way he'd spoken to her when they were alone last night in the tent, the genuine concern he'd shown over her well-being, had made her think that they could eventually make it through a conversation without wanting to throw rocks at each other. But he stormed out as if she'd wronged him somehow.

Lily got up and puttered around the tent for a few minutes, rolling up the sleeping bags, trying to convince herself that there was no reason for her to feel ashamed. She was a prisoner. It's not like she'd asked to share a tent with Rowan, and she certainly hadn't asked for him to spoon with her.

"Lily? Are you awake?" Tristan asked from outside the front flap of her tent.

"Coming," she called, and lifted the flap. Tristan glanced behind her and into the tent.

"Where's Rowan?" he asked, his eyes cautious.

"He got up and left a few minutes ago," Lily replied, joining him outside.

"He just left you alone?"

"Not too good at guarding people, is he?"

Tristan and Lily shared a tentative smile before his eyes drifted up to look at the froth of hair on top of her head. Lily's hand automatically shot up to try to smooth it down. It felt even bushier than usual, and there seemed to be an impressive collection of sticks and leaves in it.

"I'm going to need a personal moment," she said wryly. "I don't suppose there's any way I could get a bath out here, is there?"

"I'll take you to the lake," Tristan replied with a laugh. "You're going to need some fresh clothes too."

Lily looked down at her stained No Nukes T-shirt and torn jeans. She was filthy. "Yeah, I guess so. Thank you, Tristan."

"What's a nuke?" Tristan asked, leading her through the maze of tents.

"A nuke is short for a nuclear weapon or a nuclear power plant," she answered, winding her tangled hair into a bun and knotting it on top of her head. "Do you have nuclear energy here?"

Tristan's brow furrowed. "Describe nuclear energy to me."

"Oh boy," Lily said. She took a deep breath and dove in. "Okay, well. There are these things called atoms, teeny tiny bits of matter that are the building blocks of the elements."

Tristan unhooked the front flap to a large tent, holding it open for Lily to enter, with a wry grimace on his face. "That sounds like what we call elementals. They're the smallest parts of the elements."

"Exactly!" Lily said excitedly. "Same thing, different name. Well, long story short, nuclear energy comes from fusing or splitting the insides, or nuclei, of the heaviest elements to turn matter directly into energy."

"The heaviest elements are really unstable," Tristan said, his eyes narrowing. "They throw off particles that corrupt cells and cause a wasting disease. If it isn't caught in time, the corrupted cells overtake the healthy ones. It's a very painful death."

"We call it cancer in my world," Lily said solemnly. "Which is why I, and a lot of people who think like I do, want to get rid of the nukes. Problem is, not only does nuclear energy power our cities inexpensively, but it's also the source of our most powerful weapons. My world runs on inexpensive energy and powerful weapons."

"That sounds very familiar," Tristan said with a dark look. "And your shirt helps to change people's minds about nuclear energy?" he asked.

"Probably not," Lily said with a self-deprecating shake of her head. "But a girl can dream."

Lily wandered into the center of the tent, taking a closer look. It was a storeroom for all kinds of supplies, including clothes. She turned to find Tristan, still standing by the entrance, thinking deeply.

"Tristan?"

"Sorry," he said, snapping himself out of it. He led her to a small pile of dresses. "Do you see anything you like?"

"I don't really do dresses," Lily said, balking. "Is that okay?"

"Sure," Tristan replied, gesturing to the jeans she was wearing. "Women wear breeches here, too, although not usually women of your station. But whatever you prefer."

"My station, huh?" Lily mumbled uneasily.

Tristan didn't comment, but he watched her carefully. She was an American. In her mind, everyone was supposed to be equal. To mask her disapproval, she turned more attention than necessary to the pile of "breeches," feeling the odd but supple material between her fingertips.

"What is this? Is it leather?" she asked, pulling her hand away. "I don't wear leather or fur."

"It's wearhyde. Very much like leather, except it's grown from a culture."

"So this was never part of a living animal?"

Tristan shook his head. "A few cells taken from a living animal, but that's all. Raising an animal takes a lot of green and a lot of space. It's much less expensive to just grow replicas of their skin in the stacks. I've noticed you wear a lot of cotton."

"Yeah," Lily said, looking down at her outfit. The way he'd said "cotton" made it sound like gold. "Is it expensive here?"

"Most natural textiles, like cotton, wool, and linen, take a lot of land to grow," Tristan said.

"It's a big country. Plenty of room," Lily replied. She thought of the towers of vegetables and the hydroponic greenhouses she'd seen in the cities, and of how they seemed now, in retrospect, to be a kind of vertical farming. She also recalled how heavily guarded they were. A strange notion occurred to her. "You do have farmland and ranches here, don't you?"

"Yes, but not many. The Woven started to overrun most of the continent almost two hundred years ago. All the large farms and home-steads in the west were lost," Tristan said.

"Tristan?" she asked carefully. "What are the Woven?"

"They are a mistake," he began quietly. "About two hundred years ago it was decided that in order to build our cities larger and more efficiently we needed stronger, bigger animals that didn't require as much food. Animals specifically designed for new types of labor."

"Two hundred years ago, huh?" Lily interjected. She wasn't a his-tory genius, but she'd just studied this period in depth last year for a civics project. "We had an industrial revolution about that time in my world. So, how did you make the Woven? Did you breed them?"

"No, that wouldn't have been possible, not on the scale that we needed. The witches wove the germinating cells of many different types of creatures together. Some generations of Woven were very successful. We still use them today."

"The things at the bottom of the vegetable towers," Lily guessed.

"Guardians, they're called," he replied, nodding. "Others, espe-cially those that were part insect—"

"Part *insect*?" Lily exclaimed. Tristan nodded and continued.

"They were harder to control. They got loose."

"*Insect?*" Lily repeated again, trying and failing to tamp down her culture shock.

"They're very strong," Tristan said with a shrug, like that would explain why they were made.

"So is iron. We made a bunch of machines to build our cities." She made a rueful face. "But I guess they sort of took our world over, too."

Tristan gave her a puzzled look.

"Forget it. I'm just trying to understand it all."

"It's a lot, isn't it?" he said, his brow furrowing compassionately.

"Yes." Lily shrugged, feeling overwhelmed. "Is there anyone who can help me get back to my world?"

"Honestly? We thought it was impossible to do what Lillian did." Tristan sighed helplessly. "None of us has a clue."

"I just want to go home, Tristan."

"I know you do." He moved closer to Lily, and put his hand on her upper arm to comfort her. "But I'd be sorry if you did. I much prefer you to the Lillian we have here."

"Yeah." She smiled up at Tristan. "But she's a hag."

They shared a much-needed laugh, and Tristan gestured to the piles of clothes. "Pick whatever you'd like. We should hurry."

Lily started shuffling through the clothes, looking for something that might fit her. There was only one pair of pants that looked about her size. While she tried on the buttery soft leather-like jackets, Tristan found her a shirt. Lily touched it, noticing that it was made of something like linen.

"Is it okay for me to take this?" she asked, aware that he was choosing something expensive for her.

"Of course," he replied, giving her a funny look. "You can have anything you want."

The whole way down to the lake, Lily worried that Tristan had given her the linen shirt because of some misguided belief that she, like Lillian, had the right to certain privileges that others didn't. Lily didn't believe in elitist nonsense like that. It bothered her so much that she stopped Tristan, turning him around to face her, as they reached the shoreline.

"I'm not a lady, you know," she blurted out. He narrowed his eyes at her, and she wondered if that statement implied the same thing here as it would in her world. "What I mean is, I'm not entitled to any kind of special treatment. In my world, I'm just an ordinary girl. Well, mostly ordinary."

Tristan looked surprised at first, and then pleased. He tilted his head down closer to hers, moving slowly. For a moment, Lily wondered if he was going to kiss her, but he stopped a teasing distance away from her mouth. "I don't think you could be considered ordinary in any world," he said.

He was flirting with her, she realized, and she immediately felt suspicious. Not because he was technically her guard and she was his prisoner, but because flirting came too easily to him. Just like it did to her Tristan. She took a step away from him.

"I thought you wanted to clean up?" he asked after an awkward pause.

"That's the plan."

"Well, go ahead."

"Aren't you going to give me some privacy?" she asked incredulously.

"Can't. Wouldn't want you to run away again, now would I?"

"I'm not going to undress in front of you," she said, offended.

He stepped back and turned around. "Is that better? I promise I won't peek."

Lily stared at Tristan's back while she peeled off her mangy

T-shirt and shredded jeans. Her white Chucks had been on their last leg before she'd come to this world, and after a night of marching through the forest primeval they were utterly destroyed. She quickly stripped off her underwear and bra, jumping when Tristan faked a turn around with his head.

She squealed and ran into the water, shouting, "Don't, Tristan! I'm totally naked!"

His shoulders shook, and he tilted forward with laughter, but he honored her wishes and didn't turn around. "It's really charming that you're so modest. Are people usually this shy in your world?"

"Yes!" Lily shouted through chattering teeth. "Sweet jeezus, this lake is cold!"

Lily took a few deep breaths and dunked her head underwater. She washed as quickly as she could, then ran out of the water. She took up a small square of material that Tristan had brought. It was some kind of synthetic fabric that turned out to be incredibly absorbent, and she dried herself with it in a few fast swabs. When she was fully dressed in her new outfit, she told Tristan he could turn back around.

"What?" she asked, when he gave her the once-over.

"You look like a rebel," he replied with a little shake of his head. The way he said the word "rebel" made it clear that he wasn't talking about disaffected youth. "I know you don't understand yet, but trust me, it's incredibly ironic."

Lily fell into step next to Tristan, scrunching her curls dry with the ever-thirsty bit of fabric as he led her back to the fire. Apart from the growling in her empty belly, she felt remarkably at ease.

The wearhyde pants and jacket moved like the softest of leather on her legs and across her back, the boots were well-balanced and light, and the smog-free air was like a blessing to her lungs. The hills rolled and stacked themselves into the distance, just as they did in

Lily's world. The leaf-covered ground shuffled and crunched under-foot in exactly the same combination of birch, oak, and beech leaves as she remembered from her woods. The landscape was bigger, the trees older, and wildlife wilder than anything she knew, but this was still a New England forest in late autumn.

Lily had read Emerson and Thoreau. She'd read *Walden* sitting on the shores of Walden Pond, but she hadn't felt like she was experiencing that same natural wonderland that they'd been moved to expound upon so long ago. It might have been because even at Walden Pond, she could hear the traffic on Route 126 droning away a few hundred yards behind her. But she finally understood all the poetry. Like a fish that had been pulled from its bowl only to be placed on the other side of the glass, she had a new perspective on a room she'd lived in her whole life. Except unlike the fish, she could breathe better outside the bowl.

Then there was Tristan. She glanced over at him as they neared the center of the camp. His shape, his scent, even the length of his stride were all the same, and all were second nature to Lily. He wasn't the version of Tristan who had hurt her, but he was still basically the same person, and that was the problem. He had the same easy way with women—the same flirtatiousness. Even though this Tristan had never done anything to hurt her, Lily found herself bristling at the same charming smile she used to love.

As they joined the main group congregated by the fire, she recalled Lillian's words. *You belong here,* and wondered if it was true. Then she thought about the Woven out there in the woods, and decided that she most definitely did not. This world was far too scary for Lily.

She looked up and saw Rowan staring at her over the fire, his eyes searching hers. Any thoughts of belonging were abruptly discarded. Rowan definitely didn't want her here, and his distrust colored everything else. Rowan glanced from Lily to Tristan, and then his eyes darted swiftly away, like he knew her well enough to make assumptions about her character. It annoyed her beyond reason.

Lily had just taken a seat by the fire with Tristan when the sachem came striding stiffly into view. Everyone jumped to their feet at his approach and Lily followed suit.

"Don't get up," Alaric said gruffly. He bent over the fire and ladled out a bowl of what looked to Lily like lentils and potatoes. "Did Lady Juliet's guard return yet?" he asked Rowan while he served himself.

"No. We should move camp as soon as possible," Rowan replied. The sachem shook his head gravely.

"The elders have been summoned," he said. "We can't leave until they've seen her."

"Wait," Lily interjected anxiously. "Juliet's guard is missing? Is she okay?"

The sachem looked up at her as he ate. "You would know that better than we would," he said. "Have you felt like she's in distress?"

Lily sat very still and searched around inside herself. She had no idea what she was looking for. "I don't know. I don't feel anything."

"That's good. It means she probably isn't dead," Alaric replied. Lily stared at him while he ate, trying to figure out if the sachem was being intentionally callous or if he was always so blunt. She stared a bit too long.

"You'd better feed this girl before she steals my bowl," Alaric said with a sideways grin. Embarrassed, Lily was about to protest that he'd misunderstood her stare when he continued. "What can she eat, Rowan?"

"She needs poultry and salt, Sachem," he answered immediately.

"No. I don't eat anything that came from an animal," Lily insisted, shaking her head. "I'll have what the sachem's having."

Rowan met her eyes, his face unmoving. He looked back at Alaric. "She'll have poultry and salt."

"No, I won't," Lily said simply. "I don't eat meat." She glared at Rowan, but he wouldn't look back at her. Alaric held up his hand in Rowan's direction, trying to stave off the impending argument. He turned to Lily.

"Why?" Alaric asked, a curious glint in his eyes. "It is perfectly natural for people to eat meat."

"Maybe it was once," Lily conceded. "But the world I come from is very crowded. The animals live in cages, stacked on top of each other in horrible places in order to feed people more meat than they need. I stopped eating it years ago."

"To make up for the sins of everyone else in your world?" Rowan snapped, an eyebrow raised in derision. "Or do you just do it to prove that you're superior?"

"I do it because I believe it's wrong," Lily said, standing up and facing Rowan over the fire. He jumped to his feet and met her eyes, his body straining toward her like he wanted to launch himself over the flame and shake her.

"And would you force that belief on everyone else?" he yelled back. "Even if not eating meat made them sick? Even if it made you sick?"

Lily didn't have a response to that. She repressed the image of her dresser drawer full of slogan-emblazoned T-shirts, especially the one that read I'M VEGAN. AND YES, THAT DOES MAKE ME BETTER THAN YOU.

"What a lively debate we're having," Alaric said wryly. He waved his hands at both of them, indicating that they should sit down. "Tristan, would you serve Lily some lentil stew?"

"She can't have it, Sachem, there are potatoes in it," Rowan said, taking his seat next to Caleb. "Potatoes are a nightshade. They are poison for her until she learns how to transmute their alkaloids into power. If she refuses to eat poultry—which is a neutral, nonreactive food for you, by the way," he added, shooting Lily a withering look before continuing, "she may have cooked oats for energy. For protein I'll figure something else out. Lentils without potatoes, maybe."

"Problem solved. Amazing what we can accomplish in a morning," Alaric said with the faintest of eye rolls.

Lily smiled hesitantly at Alaric. His dry sense of humor took some getting used to, but Lily could tell he was pleased that the conflict was solved. Alaric liked finding solutions to problems—even silly ones, like what Lily could and couldn't eat.

Tristan returned with a wooden bowl of oatmeal for Lily. She smiled up at him in thanks, but her thoughts were still fixated on what Rowan had said. She'd always thought potatoes were so bland that they couldn't possibly cause a reaction, only to find that an hour or so later, she was burning with fever. It bothered her that she had never noticed this connection before, but it bothered her even more that Rowan had.

"May I ask you something, Rowan?" she called over the fire when she couldn't stand it any longer. He nodded. "My doctors did test after test, but they could never figure out what triggers my fevers. How do you know what I'm allergic to?"

"You're not allergic to anything," Rowan replied with a shrug. "You're a crucible."

"Okay, you keep calling me that," Lily said, putting down her bowl, and addressing the group. "But what's a crucible? I know what a crucible is in my world—it's a container that's used to heat things up. Are you calling me a crucible because my body runs hot and I heat things up?"

"You don't just heat up substances," Tristan said. "You change them inside your body."

"And what do I change substance into?" Lily asked.

"All different kinds of energies and forces," Rowan replied. "You can also take outside heat, which is a form of energy, and turn it into force." He gestured to the fire.

"My ankle," Lily said. She remembered the fingers of fire and how she was able to manipulate the blood, tissue, and bone on the smallest level—right down to the cells. It was impossible. "I turned the heat from that brew you made me drink into a force that rebuilt my ankle?"

"Along with the calcium and other elements we gave you in the brew," Tristan amended. "You can change things—chemicals into energy, and energy into force—but you can't create matter or energy out of nothing, which is why we gave you the brew." He smiled at her. "Your thermodynamo law."

"Thermodynamics," Lily corrected absently.

"Your body is a place where matter and energy get transmuted. That's why you're called a crucible," Rowan said, his dark eyes flicking up to catch hers. "Get it?"

"Yeah, I get it," Lily whispered.

All those baffled doctors, all the allergy tests that came up inconclusive, all the fevers that didn't come from any kind of infection scrolled through Lily's mind. They'd never found anything wrong with her because what was wrong with her was so unbelievable, no rational person would ever think to look for it. Lily's hands were shaking. She clasped them together to steady them.

"I'm a witch."

"Not yet," Rowan said seriously. "That's a title you have to earn."

"God, you say that like it's a good thing," she said with a gasp. Her hands kept shaking, even though she was squeezing them together so hard she was practically wringing blood out of her fingertips. Lily felt a hand on her arm, and looked over at Alaric.

"I think that's enough for now," he said.

Lily stood up and nearly ran away from the campfire.

"Lily? The elders are here to see you," said Rowan.

Lily had been hiding in her tent for the last half hour, trying to calm down. She paused and took a few steadying breaths, preparing herself to go out there. The last thing she wanted to do was lose it as she had at breakfast and run off crying like a little girl again. She could hear Rowan on the other side of the thin material of the tent, shifting from foot to foot as he waited for her to collect herself.

"Are you okay?" he finally asked.

"Yes," she said, and pushed the flap of the tent open.

Rowan looked her over. "You're feverish."

Lily swiped the back of her hand across her forehead, and it came back glistening with sweat. "Great," she said. Half her mouth tilted up in a wry smile. "Maybe if I'm lucky, I'll have another seizure and wake up back home."

A frown creased Rowan's brow. "Come on," he said sharply.

As they walked back to the campfire, he reached out and took her by the wrist. She tried to edge away but he persisted, lightly pressing on her pulse point with soft, sure fingers. She glanced over at Rowan and saw the willstone at his throat glittering subtly. Her fever ebbed out of her, like hot water swirling down a drain. Before she could ask Rowan what had happened, they'd reached the fire.

Several conversations, spoken in a language Lily couldn't even begin to place, hushed at once. A dozen men and women sat in a circle, staring at Lily with wide eyes and blank faces. Some of them had graying hair and craggy faces, but they all seemed to be remarkably fit and strong. Lily wondered why they were called elders when none of them seemed all that old. There were certainly no frail or elderly people among the Outlander elders.

"Well—that's *Lillian*," said a wiry woman with a thick mane of salt-and-pepper hair. She had cinnamon-colored leather for skin, and a dried and spicy voice to match. "Kill her," she said with a shrug, like she couldn't believe no one had done it yet.

Half a dozen bows were drawn, creaking ominously to fulfill the woman's order. Lily stared over the fire at a semicircle of arrows pointed at her face. Her jaw fell open and a whimper squeaked out.

"Wait!" Alaric shouted, his hands up in appeasement. "Yes. She is a Lillian, but not the Lillian we know from this world. Rowan. Explain."

Lily realized that she had grabbed on to Rowan's arm. He had stepped in front of her so quickly she hadn't immediately noticed, and now he pulled her forward so she stood in front of him. Lily's knees shook, and she leaned her back against his chest. A dozen arrows were still aimed at her face. Rowan slowly took a hold of the collar of her shirt in both hands and opened it so everyone could see her bare throat and chest.

"No willstone," Rowan said. His voice rumbled against her back. The tips of half the arrows dropped to the ground hesitantly, then Rowan continued. "I brought the shaman to the Citadel almost two years ago. I didn't know that Lillian trained with him, and I still don't know how this is possible, but somehow Lillian has managed to spirit walk into another world, locate another version of herself, and bring her here."

The fire popped and Lily felt the weight of everyone's hate and fear pressing in on her. Her breath hitched in the back of her throat. Deep in the crowd, she saw Tristan's worried face staring back at her and Caleb's stern face right next to his. Rowan slowly shifted her behind him and out of the remaining line of fire.

"This version of Lillian is from a world so different from ours that she studies *science,* not witchcraft," he said with disbelief. A murmur swept through the mob. "And she likes to be called Lily," he finished, allowing a note of humor to enter his tone.

That strange language rose up again as the elders began to argue. Rowan's head snapped around in reaction to what some in the crowd were saying, and as he listened, he became increasingly tense. He reached back for Lily, keeping her close to his body. As the infighting between the Outlanders escalated and braves began to stand and face off with each other, Lily could see Tristan and Caleb weaving their way through the crowd toward her and Rowan. Rowan suddenly held up his hands again, waving for everyone's attention.

"Who here knows Lillian better than I do? And who here has more reason to want her dead?" Rowan announced loudly. The bickering ended abruptly. "I swear on my life this is not Lillian. If it was, I would have strangled her myself."

The wiry woman stepped forward again. "Alright, Rowan, we believe that you believe. And since we knew your father, that's good enough for most of us." The wiry woman paused in a moment of reverent silence, and the crowd followed suit, some of them even bowing their heads. "But if what you're saying is true," she continued after a suitable amount of time, "what does it mean?"

"I don't know yet," Rowan said quietly, his eyes reaching back to meet Lily's. "But the possibilities are literally infinite." Rowan kept his eyes on Lily. She didn't know what he was thinking, but whatever it was, it frightened him.

"She'd have to be trained first," Alaric said into the long silence. "Where's the shaman?"

"He hasn't been seen in months," answered a voice from the crowd.

"Is he dead?" another voice asked.

"Who would be daft enough kill a shaman and risk being haunted forever?" the wiry woman said derisively. "He's probably out on the Ocean of Grass, smoking funny herbs and doing one of those vision quests."

"Find him," Alaric ordered. Two of Alaric's specially painted braves nodded in obedience and left the group.

Distant yips and cries from the perimeter guards reached the group at the fire. Lily felt Rowan grab her by the arm as his eyes flew to the treetops, his knife glinting in his other hand. Her heart flew to her throat, and she scanned the trees, like Rowan, for Woven. The call "Citadel guards!" was heard and Rowan's eyes dropped back down to the ground.

"Take Lily," Alaric ordered. "Hide in the woods for five, six days if you can. We'll try to get word to you before a week is past." Alaric's painted warriors flocked to his side, forming a circle around him. Caleb was among them, but Lily didn't see Tristan anywhere. "If we don't make contact in a week, try to smuggle her back into the city when things have died down," he said hurriedly to Rowan. One of Alaric's guards handed Rowan a pack. He opened it quickly and scanned the contents. Lily heard the *whiz* of arrows. "Run, Rowan!" Alaric shouted. "And keep her alive."

Rowan nodded once and pulled Lily along beside him. His face was drawn and intense, his eyes skipping through the trees as he looked for the best route. Lily could hear the pounding of horses' hooves, shouts, and screams. Rowan dragged her into a run, leading her away from the sounds of chaos.

"What do they want?"

"To capture as many of us as they can," Rowan answered, his eyes still darting this way and that. "You can't be seen. Here," he rasped, and pulled Lily down behind the trunk of a large tree.

He pushed her between the thick roots and into a shadowy

hollow that was barely large enough to conceal her, and covered the opening with his body. She saw his willstone flare, and his face relax in meditation. The dark wearhyde jacket and backpack that he wore seemed to blend with the shadows cast by the tall tree. He didn't disappear, but he was so well camouflaged that he was nearly impossible to see.

Horses thundered past, carrying men heavily armed with crossbows, blades, and what she thought was a kind of gun. The men wore the same uniforms Lily had seen on the guards of the Citadel. She looked at Rowan's calm face. His eyes were closed, his breathing regular. At any moment, she expected to hear the *thwap* of an arrow as it sank into his back, but the horses rode right past. Rowan opened his eyes and met Lily's, the focus of his gaze swallowing all of her thoughts. She heard herself breathe, in and out, and didn't dare move any more than that.

Rowan's head flicked to the side, an ear cocked to listen behind him. Lily looked over his shoulder and saw a group of elderly men and women hurry past their hiding spot. They began to shout to each other. They tried to run, but they were too old to do more than shuffle through the leaf litter with frantic hopelessness. The mounted soldiers ran them down easily, trampling the unlucky ones. Lily heard the cries of pain and she tensed, her body straining to go to their aid. Rowan put his hands on her shoulders to stop her.

"No," he whispered, his eyes pleading with her. "You can't help them now."

A young man rode forward, taking command. He jumped off his mount and stood over an old man who had been knocked down and couldn't get back up to his feet. The young man was well-dressed and had pale skin and white-blond hair. He looked like an overgrown choirboy.

"But I'm not a scientist," the old man said in a wavering voice. "I'm a history teacher."

"You've been found guilty of teaching the history of science," the baby-faced commander said in a whiny, unpleasant voice. Rowan stiffened when he heard it, like he recognized it, and turned slightly to look.

"But it's not the same thing," the old man pleaded. He rose up on his forearms, trying to explain himself better. The commander began to hit the old man over the head with a baton. He was smiling, his baby face leering obscenely.

"Don't look." Rowan put his hand over Lily's mouth, his eyes locked with hers as they listened to the old man being beaten to death. It seemed to take hours. Lily found herself counting the blows, her lips silently tracing the words "six, seven, eight, nine" against the palm of Rowan's hand. When it was finally over, the rest of the elderly people were rounded up, tied together, and led away.

Rowan eased his hand away from Lily's mouth, his other arm still holding her close to him. Lily looked over Rowan's shoulder at the old man.

She'd never seen a dead body before. He was so still, and he looked smaller, barely the size of a child. Lily heard herself hiccup and realized that she was crying.

"Shh," Rowan breathed. He squeezed her shoulders and tilted his face toward hers. "Look at me."

Lily gulped a few times and tried to control herself. When she met Rowan's eyes, she was surprised to see that they were soft instead of angry.

"I'm not going to let anything happen to you. Okay?" He ran a hand across her face, brushing her wet cheeks dry.

"That man—" Lily broke off, her voice had come out louder and rougher than she'd intended. "Why did that guy just kill him like that?"

Rowan shook his head and looked away, his lips pursed as if he didn't want to discuss the matter any further.

"Why?" Lily demanded. "He was just a history teacher. What did he do wrong?"

"That's just it. He was a teacher. The truth is, he got off easy," Rowan said bitterly. "The rest of them are going to be tortured and then hanged."

"By whom?"

"Haven't you figured out who runs things in this world?" He didn't have to say it. She knew it was Lillian.

"You recognized him. The killer."

Rowan nodded and dropped his eyes. "Gideon," he whispered. Rowan clasped her hand in his and pulled her up. "We have to move. Now."

"Where's Tristan?" Lily asked, clutching Rowan's wrist.

Rowan paused, his gaze turning inward for moment. "He's okay. He got away."

"Are we going to him?"

"It's too dangerous," he replied, shaking his head and frowning. "There are guards everywhere. We stand a better chance if we split up for a while."

Lily nodded reluctantly and followed Rowan. He stopped momentarily to pick up a discarded gun. He flicked open the chamber, saw that it was empty, and cast it aside. He didn't waste any more time trying to scavenge a weapon and led Lily out of the glade. She ran alongside him, trying to move as quietly as she could. She could barely hear Rowan's footsteps hitting the ground while she seemed to make so much noise that she was convinced at any moment they were going to get caught. But try as she might, she couldn't figure out how to make her feet quieter.

Rowan led her deep into the woods, neither of them speaking. Years ago, Lily had come to terms with the fact that she wasn't in control of her own body, that at any moment a fever or seizure could overtake her and potentially kill her, but this was different. Now she was at the mercy of a whole world she didn't understand.

Rowan brought them to water, tasting it carefully before he slung the pack off his back and took out a water pouch. He filled it and passed it to Lily. Hands shaking, she drank from the pouch while he scooped water into his mouth with his cupped palm. When she'd drained the pouch, he refilled it and they moved on.

Every now and again, Rowan would stop, brush some fallen leaves aside, and pick acorns or mushrooms off the ground. The mushrooms he'd hand to Lily, indicating that she should eat them, and the acorns he stowed in his pack. Lily eyed the mushrooms warily, her stomach still churning from what she had witnessed, but after the first taste of them—woody, earthy, and surprisingly meaty—she didn't hesitate when he handed more to her the next time they stopped. After she ate, Rowan would reach out to touch Lily's wrist in that odd gesture again, like he was taking her pulse. She wondered vaguely what he was doing, but was still too shaken to question him.

They never stayed in one spot for more than a few seconds at a time before moving on. Rowan ate nothing at all and drank only a few sips of water. Everything he gathered, he gave to Lily to eat or saved for later, even though she urged him to take some for himself.

"I don't need it," he'd said simply when Lily offered him the water pouch. "I drank my fill at the stream."

He wasn't acting tough, or trying to be noble. He'd stored those acorns against some kind of emergency. Lily could tell from the detached way he pulled up a handful of wildflower bulbs, scraped them clean with his knife, then gave them to Lily to eat without sparing them even one hungry look, that he was someone who'd learned how to live with very little. He didn't get thirsty or tire as quickly as someone with Lily's upbringing. Rowan was a survivor.

Unlike Rowan, Lily felt her sore feet, thirst, and pounding head, but she was too sickened to put too much thought into them. All day long, she'd been able to think of little else besides the old history teacher.

Rowan pushed the pace, never letting them stop for more than a few minutes at a time, his eyes constantly darting through the trees, scanning for Woven. At dusk, Rowan built a fire and threw a handful of herbs on the flames. Their fragrant smoke smelled almost like a citronella candle, used to keep mosquitoes away in her world.

"Barely enough for one night," he whispered to himself, scowling. Rowan looked up at the looming canopy of branches, his face pinched with fear. "But it should keep the Woven away for a few hours."

Lily hardly registered what he'd said. She was so tired and numb she stretched out on the ground and fell instantly into a nightmare-filled sleep. She woke several times with a shake, seeing Gideon's twisted baby face above hers and only fell back to sleep because of the steady, soothing pressure of Rowan's fingers wrapped around her ankle.

It was late afternoon the next day before the shock had faded enough so that Lily could speak. "Did I bring the soldiers to the camp?" she finally asked, barely able to raise her voice above a whisper.

Rowan didn't look at her as they walked along. "You can talk normally. No one's following us."

"Is it my fault?" she asked again, needing to know.

"No. It's mine. I should have insisted we moved camp that night after Juliet showed up, even if the elders were on their way."

"Do you think she told Lillian?" Lily asked, unable to believe any version of Juliet would do something like that.

"No. But Juliet's not the stealthiest woman in the world. She could have been followed from Salem. Considering how fast the attack came, I'm pretty sure that's what had to have happened." Rowan angrily kicked a pinecone aside. "I should have fought the sachem harder about moving the camp."

"Are they okay? Can you tell if Tristan is still—"

"Tristan's fine," Rowan replied impatiently. "He, Caleb, and the sachem are all out of danger."

"Why you?"

"Why me what?" he asked, confused.

"Why did you agree to take me out here and not insist Tristan do it? You hate me."

"I don't hate you," he said gruffly. "And Tristan is city bred. He wouldn't last a day out here on his own, although I'm sure you'd have preferred his company to mine."

"I didn't say that," she replied quietly. She actually felt safe with Rowan. There was something about him that made Lily think he could protect her from whatever lurked out there in the shifting darkness between the enormous trees.

Lily stared at his profile for a few moments, trying to decide if she should keep questioning him when he looked so forbidding. He had a straight, aquiline nose, and full, well-defined lips. His skin was a light-caramel color, and his cheekbones were high and sharp. It was a strong face. He was very handsome, she decided, but his fierce expression made him almost impossible to approach.

"What?" he finally asked, his tone just short of snapping. Lily looked away, and silence drew out between them. "What?" he repeated, more gently this time.

"Are you, Caleb, and Tristan related?"

"Not by blood," he replied. "We're kin of a different kind."

"But you can all mindspeak with each other, right?"

"Yes. When we have to."

"Why wouldn't you do it all the time? It seems really handy."

He glanced over at her, his eyes measuring her. "You can't lie when you mindspeak, or hide how you feel. Sometimes people need to keep things to themselves."

"Were you mindspeaking with them just now?"

"No. Not at this distance," he said. The corners of his mouth tipped up with a little smile. "I'm not you."

Lily couldn't decide if he was giving her a compliment or making fun of her. She didn't understand Rowan, and she had no idea how to read him.

"Our willstones are tuned to each other. That's why we can mindspeak. We are what's called stone kin," he said, surprising Lily by offering the information. "But only a powerful witch can sync up her willstone to other people's and get into their heads from a large distance."

"Into their heads?" Lily repeated, not sure she liked what that implied.

"That's why they're called willstones. The crystals get keyed to a person's unique brain waves. Once a crystal is keyed, it answers to the will of its wearer, directing and amplifying a mental want or desire. Everyone here wears them."

"So everyone here can do magic?"

"An average person can do small things, like seal something shut until they will it to open, turn lights off and on, or find something they've lost. Some of the more gifted can even share a little mindspeak with blood relations or stone kin. Mechanics can heal, regulate bodies, and strengthen the potions they create—along with a few simple spells, like camouflage and glamour." He stopped and looked at her. "But only crucibles can do real magic because of their natural ability to transmute matter into energy and force inside their bodies. Their willstones help to direct and intensify that ability."

Rowan fished his willstone out from under his clothes and showed it to Lily. She leaned close to peer at it.

"But a witch can do even more than that," he continued. Lily looked back up at him. "She can unlock another's willstone so that the wearer enacts her will. And that's just the start."

"What's the difference between a crucible and a witch?" Lily asked.

"All witches start out as crucibles, but not all crucibles have the strength or the talent to become a witch. Most just stay crucibles. Very few are capable of graduating to full witch. There's a level of magic—it's called warrior magic—that crucibles don't have the power to do."

Lily wondered what else a witch could do that a crucible couldn't, but just as she was about to ask, her eyes drifted down to stare at Rowan's willstone again, her mind going blank. It resembled an opal, except that the dancing lights inside of the stone seemed to flicker and glimmer independent of the sun. Like it was alive inside with sparkling thoughts. It was so beautiful. She wanted to dive inside it.

"Don't," Rowan said, jerking away from her. She hadn't even realized that she was reaching out for it. Lily dropped her hand, embarrassed.

"I'm sorry," she said, aware that she had offended Rowan in some way.

"It's an important thing to touch someone else's willstone." He tucked the stone back under his shirt protectively with a tight expression on his face. He turned and started storming off, like she'd just kicked his grandma.

"I said I was sorry," Lily called after him. "What's the big deal?"

Rowan stopped and turned to face her, his hands planted on his narrow hips. "Touching a stone is how you tune to it. It's intimate, okay?" He looked away again. "And dangerous—for me. When mechanics touch each other's stones, they become stone kin—like Caleb, Tristan, and I. We can hear each other's thoughts and feel each other's feelings. But when a witch touches your stone, she can key her mind to it and *claim* you."

"Claim you?" Lily repeated. Rowan nodded and started walking away from her again. She raced to catch up to him, wondering exactly what he meant by "intimate."

"A witch can take your will away. She can get in your head and control your body. Like a hand in a glove."

"That's awful!" Lily exclaimed, visions of Body Snatchers dancing gruesomely in her head. "I wouldn't do that to you, Rowan. Even if I did touch your willstone."

"Well, you couldn't unless I let you in first," Rowan said, his mouth pulled up in a guarded half smile. "No one can steal a willstone. A witch or a crucible needs the key, the right vibration from the wearer's mind, in order to possess it. That must be given willingly or the willstone cracks."

Lily remembered Lillian saying that she couldn't have brought Lily to this world without her consent. At the time, Lily hadn't known that her little pity party would get her transported to another universe—she'd just been having a good cry on a rock. She didn't know that wishing she could disappear would actually make it happen. She'd been tricked. Bitterness swelled in Lily at the thought of how deeply Lillian had wronged her.

"I'm not upset with you anymore," Rowan said quietly, looking straight ahead as they walked along. "You didn't know."

"What? No, it's not that," she replied, realizing that she'd been silent for longer than she'd realized. "I'm just wondering why anyone would knowingly allow themselves to be claimed by anyone else."

"With a witch inside of you, you can do just about anything—jump higher, run faster, and more. A *lot* more if the witch is powerful." Rowan's voice was low and serious. "But once you let a witch in, your willstone is keyed to her. You have to smash your stone to get away. Start over with a new stone. And that's really—"

"I'm guessing it sucks," Lily said, remembering how Caleb had gone stiff at any mention of smashing a willstone. Rowan gave her a funny look, and she laughed, realizing he had no idea what she'd just said. "It's just an expression from my world. When something sucks that means it's bad."

"Huh," Rowan said, not seeing the logic between sucking and being bad. Now that Lily thought about it, neither did she.

"It's stupid, isn't it?"

"But fun to say," Rowan conceded. "That sucks. This sucks. *You* suck."

"Hey!" Lily elbowed him, feigning offense. "Be nice to me or I won't teach you the difference between sucking and blowing."

Rowan laughed, and the sound was so startling to Lily she stopped walking and stared at him.

"What?" he asked, puzzled.

"You've got a great laugh," she replied.

He looked away and tipped his head in silent thanks, then started walking again. Lily watched carefully as the cheerful look on his face darkened.

"Come on," he said sharply, abruptly severing the connection they were so tentatively building. "We still have to make camp before nightfall."

They pushed on in silence for another twenty minutes or so and as the shadows around them deepened Lily felt Rowan growing more irritable. His eyes kept scanning the ground anxiously. Some ancient part of Lily's mind sensed that they were in danger.

"What is it?" she whispered. Her breath came out of her mouth in little puffs of steam.

"Woven tracks," Rowan whispered back. His skin was bleached an ivory blue from the cold air and his black eyes gleamed in the moonlight. "Fresh ones."

Lily looked down at the forest floor underfoot, but to her it was just a mess of leaves and sticks. How anyone could discern tracks from the general disorder of nature was beyond her, but she was grateful that Rowan could.

"And we're out of wovensbane," he added darkly. Lily recalled the pungent herbs he'd thrown on the fire that had smelled to her like citronella, guessing correctly that that's what Rowan meant.

"What do we do?" she asked, her breath fluttering in her chest.

"We climb." Rowan took her hand and led her to the trunk of a large conifer. "And hope they don't have simians with them."

Rowan gave her a boost up to the lowest branch, and then had to shove her hard so she could haul herself up on top of it. She peered over the side of the thick branch, wondering how Rowan was going to get himself up, and saw his willstone throb with that strange, oily light that seemed to call to her. He jumped easily up beside her on the branch, landing in a crouch on the balls of his feet with his fingers resting lightly in front of him.

"Climb quickly," he urged, steadying Lily with his hands. "They're drawn to magelight like moths."

The gray-colored bark was rough but powdery under Lily's tender palms. Her boots scraped it and sent clouds of lichen-laden dust showering down on Rowan. He took no notice and, despite the debris, didn't let even a few inches of distance grow between them. More than once his quick hands shot out to help balance her as they rose over a hundred feet into the rapidly darkening sky.

"Keep close to the trunk!" he admonished when a branch bent dangerously underneath her.

"I'm trying," Lily hissed back. "My arms are tired."

"Then stop." Rowan hauled himself up onto the branch just below hers. "We've gone as far as we should go anyway."

Lily sat back against the trunk of the tree and rubbed the blackened tree sap off her scratched hands. Rowan's shoulders suddenly tensed, and his volume dropped to nearly nothing.

"Hold still."

Lily froze immediately. The thin sweat that had coated her as she climbed shrank back into her skin. Rowan tilted his head ever so slowly to peer around the branch under him. Lily copied his careful movements, barely moving, and looked down.

A man ran, staggering into view from the underbrush. He was reaching desperately for the tree. He didn't make it.

From above, the thing that attacked the man looked like a giant bug. In the bright moonlight Lily could see a sectioned carapace that was covered in spikes and hair growing in between the large armor-like plates. The creature had to be at least nine feet tall and twice as long, and it picked its way at lightning speed toward the man on four spindly legs that ended in pointy barbs.

The man turned, saw the Woven moving in on him, and screamed. Rowan stood up on his branch without a sound. He unsheathed his knife and made a move to climb down. The front section of the creature was drawn up and hunched over like a praying mantis, but when its two front limbs shot out impossibly far to grab the hysterical man, it did so with human hands.

The man howled in pain as the Woven curled over him, its mouth pincers clacking together. Lily felt Rowan grip her forearm tightly as he melted back into the trunk of the tree. She looked down at him, her breath whistling in and out of her with panic.

"Shhh," Rowan whispered almost silently. "It's too late to help. Calm down, Lily."

She swallowed and forced herself to slow her breathing. Squeezing her lips shut and pressing herself against the tree, Lily narrowed her world down to one thing—the sound of the Woven as it tore into the man again and again. She saw parts of the man flying up and falling back down to the forest floor, an arm, a leg, even his insides. Lily put a hand over her mouth.

The Woven ate the man down to nothing. Every bit of skin, muscle, bone, and all of the entrails were consumed. Nothing was left of the man except scraps of clothes. The Woven sifted carefully over every last bit of the killing ground and then moved on.

It was a long time before Lily found her voice.

"Are they all like that?" she whispered.

"No. There are many different breeds, each with many variations." Rowan's voice drifted up to Lily from the branch below hers. "The Woven come in all shapes and sizes."

"Are they all dangerous?"

"To humans. They are territorial, but they tend to leave other animals alone unless they're hunting them."

Lily looked up at the stars. This sky here held the same exact constellations, but they seemed closer, brighter, and more varied in color and tone than anything she was used to.

"Let me wrap this around you." Rowan reached up and looped a rope around her legs a few times, tying her to the branch so she didn't slip off in the middle of the night. "Try to rest," Rowan said when he'd finished, his voice edged with concern.

She gripped the rope tightly even though she knew there was no way she would nod off that night.

"Lily?" he called up to her. She could hear him repositioning himself on the branch beneath her, trying to get a glimpse of her face.

"Go to sleep, Rowan. I'm fine."

"You're not fine. You're in shock. I can feel—" He broke off suddenly, and made an impatient sound. "Good night."

CHAPTER
6

IT WAS HALFWAY THROUGH THIRD WATCH BY THE TIME Gideon made it back to the Citadel with his prisoners. He ached from riding for so many hours on no sleep and with so little to eat, but he wasn't about to show his discomfort and look weak. The sachem had gotten away, but apart from that, the raid had been a success. Softhearted Juliet had inadvertently led many rebels to their deaths. Gideon couldn't wait to tell her that.

Carrick was already separating the potential talkers from the hard cases. He moved among them, planting the seeds of hope for a release in those he found pliant. The stoic ones—the ones who neither railed about their loyalty to the cause nor moaned about the injustice of the Witch State—he sent immediately to the dungeons. It was the quiet ones who always ended up as the worst kind of martyrs and needed to be kept apart.

How Carrick, who had never been a mechanic, could sense these differences in individuals and know how to deal with them so adroitly was of interest to Gideon. Carrick was far too old to be trained as a mechanic now, but the talent was certainly there. It was a pity that it had been overlooked when he was young and he hadn't been brought to the Citadel to be trained; Gideon was almost certain that Carrick knew more craft than he let on, and he was willing to let that go as long as Carrick made himself useful. If he had been given some kind of training, it had been without the consent of the Coven and could get Carrick and his teacher hanged—that, too, could be useful to Gideon as a way to control the inscrutable Outlander.

"A word?" Carrick asked politely when Gideon finally dismounted.

"Found something already?" Gideon guessed, handing the reins to a lackey. Carrick waited until the lackey was out of earshot before answering.

"Possibly," he said with his customary caution. "Two of the prisoners mentioned something that caught my attention."

"Go on," Gideon prompted. Carrick glanced around, surreptitiously checking each willstone for the telltale flare of magelight. When he was satisfied that no one was using his stone to listen in, Carrick continued.

"One was taunting me," he started, and paused. Carrick was an Outlander by birth, but he had sided against the majority of his people in this small and useless rebellion. Gideon nodded his understanding and motioned for Carrick to continue. "She said that soon the Salem Witch would *truly* meet her match. Then she laughed like a crazy old woman. I would have thought nothing of it if another prisoner, far removed from the first, had not also said that every coin had two sides and that the front was about to face off with the back."

"I don't see the connection." Gideon led Carrick inside the Citadel. "Explain."

"I couldn't help but think about the sightings in town three days ago."

"Of the Witch running through the city and throwing herself against the window of a café?" Gideon smirked over his shoulder as he led Carrick up to his private rooms. "Lillian hasn't gone anywhere without an entourage since she was six."

Except once, Gideon added silently in his mind as he opened the door to his rooms. A year ago she'd disappeared for weeks and returned half dead without ever explaining where she'd gone. She refused to allow her mechanics to help heal her. In fact, she hadn't allowed anyone but Juliet to touch her since. That was when Lillian had changed completely and began her crusade against science. But Carrick didn't know about that—no one knew about the disappearance except Lillian's inner circle.

"Dozens of people said they saw her running through the streets while you yourself confirmed that she was in her bed," Carrick persisted. "So many people claimed to have seen the same thing, and there's no reason for any of the witnesses in the city to have lied."

Gideon sat down heavily behind his desk and began yanking off his pretty but far-too-stiff boots. "Alright," he said with a reluctant sigh. It had bothered him as well, although he'd tried to overlook it. "So what do you think is going on?"

Carrick's dark Outlander eyes—eyes that looked solid black from pupil to iris to city folk like Gideon—had a glassy sheen to them. Gideon assumed this was Carrick's cold approximation of passion.

"Either the Witch has learned how to physically be in two places at once—or the prisoners are right. There are two of them."

Gideon looked at Carrick with a raised brow. "And how would there be two?" Carrick was agitated, which was rare. Usually, the Outlander was cold. Unruffled. Gideon was almost more intrigued by that than by the mystery of the "two Lillians."

"The shamans of my people believe that there are millions of versions of every single one of us."

"Millions of versions of each of us," Gideon repeated disbelievingly. He'd never heard anything so ridiculous. He stood and poured himself a glass of wine, flexing his cramped toes into the carpet. To his surprise, Carrick didn't take Gideon's turned back as a cue to leave, but continued to stand stubbornly in front of his desk.

"When I was a child, a shaman told me that I had the talent to spirit walk and that I should train with him. But shamans aren't respected as they once were among my people, and my father wouldn't hear of it."

Gideon had heard of the Outlander shamans. They were laughed at by the Covens, but the Outlanders believed that shamans had some kind of telepathic ability that allowed them to do something that only the greatest witches could ever do—farsee. Gideon had read about farseeing in an obscure book, and he didn't entirely rule out the shamanistic ability to do it, like the haughty Covens did. He also didn't rule out the possibility that Carrick was actually a great magical talent who'd been overlooked. Call it farseeing or spirit walking, either way the possibilities were intriguing.

"Continue," Gideon said in a level tone. He poured a glass of wine for Carrick and motioned for him to sit down.

"My father died when I was a teenager, and I went back to the shaman. After a few weeks he . . . decided not to teach me how to spirit walk." Carrick's face fell. Gideon had never had much talent himself, but he knew that for those who did have it, not developing it was like being a musician whose instrument has been smashed. How horrible for the poor drub. Carrick took a deep drink of wine before continuing. "But before I was sent away, I learned enough to believe that there are other worlds, and that they are as real as this one."

Instead of sitting behind his desk, Gideon opted for the other armchair next to Carrick. He brought the decanter of wine with him, and refreshed both their glasses.

"Tell me about these other worlds, Carrick," Gideon said with genuine interest.

Lily watched the stars whirl all night. Meteors streaked across the sky—dozens of them. She wished on every single one that she would be magically transported back home, but they all burned to black and left her exactly where she was. It didn't take Lily long to realize that no amount of wishing was going to get her anywhere. She had to act.

The stars faded, the sun came up, and Lily made a decision. No matter what happened, no matter how hard it was, she was going to find a way to get home.

She heard Rowan awake with a start before he reconciled himself to his surroundings. His back scraped across the trunk of the tree as he slid sideways—trying to see around the branch she was sitting on to get a look at her.

"Are you awake?" he asked, his voice still rough from sleep.

"Yeah."

"Did you sleep at all?"

"No." She heard him mumble something to himself and decided to cut him off before he could scold her again. "My butt did, though. Slept like a log all night."

"Well, obviously, your butt has more sense than you do."

"You're a funny man, Rowan whatever-your-last-name-is."

"Fall."

"I'd rather not."

She managed to get a tiny chuckle out of him, which she considered a huge achievement. Rowan stood up on his branch, bringing his head level with Lily's, and started to untie her. His lips were still pursed in a near smile.

"My *name* is Rowan Fall," he said, tossing the rope over her lap as he unwrapped her. His eyes briefly flicked up to meet hers and then back down to his task. "I was born Outland. My community traveled from site to site, gathering minerals or mining them as we could. Depending on the Woven, of course. Outlanders aren't allowed to own land or stake out permanent settlements."

"Why not?" Lily asked.

"The Covens and the Council—"

"Are those like two different branches of government?" Lily interjected.

"It's more complicated but, yeah, that works for now," Rowan replied, a hint of admiration in his eyes. "Anyway, the Covens and Council decided that it was too dangerous to try to establish settlements outside the thirteen walled cities because they'd be impossible to defend. If the Outlanders were citizens, they'd be entitled to all the rights that citizens have—and one of those rights is to be defended by the Guard. So the Council denied them citizenship."

"How brave of them," Lily retorted.

"Right?" Rowan smiled at Lily briefly, his face lighting up, before he dropped his eyes and went back to coiling the rope around his forearm. "But no citizenship means Outlanders have no rights to own land. It all stems from the fact that Outlanders weren't supposed to have survived the Woven Outbreak in the first place. But now that many generations have persisted, the laws keep it so Outlanders have no rights. That way they're a source of cheap goods and labor for the Thirteen Cities."

"Convenient," Lily said.

"And easier for Lillian to control. Thirteen established cities— who all look to Salem—are much more manageable than scores of scattered Outlander outposts. Her word is law, and that law is easily enforced inside the walls."

Lily knew that Rowan was very passionate about this topic, and she respected that he was resisting the urge to rant. He was trying to give her space and not shove his opinions down her throat. Lily didn't know if she'd have the willpower to do the same.

"You keep calling the Outlanders 'they.' Aren't you an Outlander?" she asked.

A complicated expression crossed Rowan's face as he thought about Lily's question. She found herself staring at him. As hard as his face was when he was angry, when his guard was down, it was incredibly expressive. She didn't know what he was thinking, but she imagined that she could almost *feel* it.

"When I was seven, my father took me to the Citadel to be tested. When I was accepted, I was given citizenship. Then I was trained as a witch's mechanic. As long as I'm a citizen, I don't think I have the right to call myself an Outlander."

Rowan tied off the tightly wound rope and put the bundle in his pack. "Okay. Swing your legs to the side, but don't stand yet." Lily did as he instructed. Her legs hung off the branch, unresponsive. She wiggled her toes and cringed as the pins and needles started.

"I may have tied you down a bit too tightly," he said, a brow raised in apology. Rowan stood between her numb legs and started rubbing the blood back into them.

"Better than plummeting to my death," she said, trying to ignore how good his hands felt. He certainly seemed to know how to massage thighs. Not that Lily had any firsthand experience with that sort of thing, but Rowan was definitely doing something right. Except that all the blood that was supposed to be going into her legs seemed to be rushing to her face. She felt like she needed to fill the silence somehow before she did something unforgivable, like sigh or, worse, moan.

"Well, it's nice to officially meet you, Rowan Fall. I'm Lily Proctor. I was born in a hospital. When I was seven, I went to camp. Five minutes later, I went back home with a full body rash. It was fun."

Rowan stopped massaging and looked up at her. "Your parents sent you to a work camp when you were seven?" he asked angrily.

"No, day camp," Lily replied, smiling back. "It's supposed to be, well, sort of like *this*." She gestured to the woods around them. "Canoeing, hiking in the wilderness, climbing trees. Except we climbed down the trees and slept in beds at night. It's recreational."

"Ah. I see," he said, still confused.

"What's a work camp?" Lily asked, not sure she wanted to know the answer.

"It's where the Covens send anyone who can't find enough work on their own in one of the cities but don't want to go Outland. They aren't nice places."

"But still better than being Outland with the Woven?"

Rowan shrugged in a noncommittal way and went back to rubbing her legs, his face clouded with troubled thoughts. His hands ran all the way up the inside of her thighs, and she jumped.

"Okay, I'm good. I can feel them again. Thanks." She pushed his hands away and went to stand.

"Lily—" he began, moving to stop her. As soon as she tried to put her numb feet down on his branch her knees buckled.

Rowan grabbed a fist full of her jacket with one hand, and the branch next to them with the other as they both lost their balance and tipped back and forth, swaying dangerously. He regained his balance first and pulled her to him. When she finally got her feet under her, he caged her against the trunk.

"What's the matter with you? You could have fallen!"

"I thought I could stand," she countered. He looked down at her with narrowed eyes, their faces inches away from each other as he studied her.

"No, you didn't. You just wanted me to stop touching you," he said knowingly. Lily's eyes darted away. "All you have to do is say stop. And I will."

Rowan moved back, but he didn't take his hand off her jacket. Lily busied herself with wiggling the blood back into her toes. He watched her, even though she didn't look up at him.

"You're embarrassed," he said disbelievingly.

"Are we going to spend all day in the tree?" she returned, hoping to end the conversation.

"I'm not trying to seduce you," he said seriously. "Believe me. You'd know if I was."

"I know you weren't," she responded, ignoring the boastful half of his comment. And the small sting she felt. Did he have to make it so insultingly clear that he wasn't interested in her? "But where I'm from people don't put their hands all over each other, okay? We don't get naked in front of each other, we don't share boy-girl tents, and we don't go massaging each other's groins."

"Okay," he said, raising one shoulder in a half shrug.

"Okay," Lily said back, not sure if she'd made her point—or simply made a fool of herself. With Rowan it was difficult to tell whether you'd won an argument or not.

Rowan turned and started climbing down the tree. Lily thought for a moment that she heard him whisper the word "Puritan" as he picked his way down the branches. She was tempted to yell down at him, but she couldn't really be sure that was what he'd said, and she didn't want to seem touchy or defensive. The fact that she couldn't even argue with him properly annoyed her.

"Are you coming or not?" he called up.

Lily turned toward a branch and began to climb down, muttering to herself the whole way.

Gideon waited for Juliet outside Lillian's suite of rooms. Listening at the door was pointless. The Witch had set her wards. When Juliet did finally appear, her face had the pinched look of someone who'd just been in a huge fight.

"You're back," Gideon said smoothly.

Juliet shut the door behind her and started down the hallway. "As if you didn't know that. How long have you been watching me?" she growled at him as she passed. Gideon followed her.

"I'm your sister's head mechanic," he said without a trace of remorse. "Anything that happens to you affects the Witch. Especially when you go running off into the Woven Woods to visit a camp full of your sister's enemies."

Juliet spun around to face him, her eyes flashing. "Are you accusing me of disloyalty?" she challenged.

Gideon had to admit Juliet could be quite pretty when she was angry. "No," he said honestly. He knew that even though Juliet disagreed with every policy her sister had enacted over the past year, there was no one more loyal to Lillian than her sister. And if anyone knew whether or not Lillian had been able to do the impossible and make a bridge to a parallel universe, it would be Juliet. "But maybe you'd better tell me why you were out there before others—who don't know you as I do—start to talk."

"Let them talk," Juliet said. She turned and started down the hallway again. "Lillian knows the truth."

"She knows that there's another witch out there in the woods—a witch who looks exactly like her?"

Juliet stopped and paused momentarily before turning to look at him. When she did, her face was a blank slate. "I don't know what you're talking about," she said lightly.

What a *terrible* liar she was. "Sweet Juliet," Gideon said, with something approaching true affection, "you must have the purest heart in this universe."

Gideon pivoted away from her distressed face and went to go find his father. They had plans to make. An infinite number of worlds had just opened up before Gideon, and he'd barely had a chance to imagine what those other worlds could offer. Or what he could take from them by force if they didn't offer it.

But first, he had to find this other Lillian.

Lily finished washing up as best as she could by a small, muddy stream and joined Rowan back by the fire. Bubbling away in the flames was the small cauldron he'd used to make Lily her ankle-healing brew.

"What's for breakfast?" she asked dubiously.

"Acorns. I have to boil them first, though. Too many tannins for you."

"I didn't know you could eat acorns," Lily said, sitting cross-legged by his side.

"White oak acorns are the least bitter," he said, stirring the pot with a small stick.

"I'll keep that in mind," Lily said with a little smirk. She had no idea what a white oak tree looked like, let alone one of their acorns. Rowan caught the look on her face and interpreted it correctly.

"Not a lot of woods in your world, I take it?" he asked.

"We've cut most of them down so we could build houses and stuff," she said, wondering how Rowan could read her so easily. "I don't know exactly where we are right now, but I'm pretty sure in my world it would be someone's backyard. Some sleepy little neighborhood in Nowhere, Massachusetts."

"Without the Woven, I'm assuming people spread out wherever they wanted?" he asked. Lily nodded. "Are there still large cities?"

"Huge ones. There are people everywhere in my world. Overcrowding is a big problem."

"Amazing," Rowan whispered to himself. "I'd love to see that."

Lily stared at his profile. The gentle expression that crossed his face as he imagined her world—a world that was safe enough to fill up with people—softened his usually sharp eyes. "How old are you?" she asked, suddenly not sure.

"Nineteen. Why?"

"You seem so much, I don't know. Older, I guess. You're, like, an adult."

"Well, yes," he replied with a small laugh. "Legally, I've been an adult for three years now."

"So you come of age here when you're sixteen?" Lily asked.

"In the cities. When do you?"

"Well, technically, it's eighteen. But in my country, there are still some things you can't do until you're twenty-one."

Rowan made a face, as if he thought that was insane. "In the Outlands we come of age at fourteen. Most men have families by the time they're sixteen." He put down the stick he was using to stir the acorn and wrapped his hand in the sleeve of his jacket. "But Outlanders don't have any time to waste. Most don't live to see fifty."

Disturbed by this, Lily frowned pensively as she watched Rowan pull the pot off the fire and drain away the red-brown water. At least that explained why all the elders seemed on the young side. Outlanders didn't live long enough to get old. Rowan fished out all the acorns and gave them to Lily.

"Did you already eat?" she asked him.

"I'm fine."

"Rowan, seriously." Lily tried to put half of the acorns into his hand, but he wouldn't take them.

"I don't have to eat. I'm taking all the energy I need from you."

"What are you talking about?" she asked, completely lost.

He placed two fingers on her wrist as he'd done many times in the days before, as if he were taking her pulse. Lily saw his willstone glow subtly under his clothes.

"Your body is an energy factory, Lily. You can take a handful of food—in the right chemical combinations, of course—and turn it into enough raw energy to sustain twenty people. Eventually I'll have to eat for the protein and vitamins that my body needs to maintain itself, but I can live for days off of your excess energy."

"That is so unbelievably weird," she said, shaking her head. "So when you touch my wrist like that, you're taking, like, sips of energy?"

"And regulating your reactions," he said, laughing a little at Lily's choice of words. "You haven't learned how to safely process all the different agents in the air and in your food."

Lily had been so overwhelmed since the raid she hadn't noticed that she'd gone two days without getting a fever or a rash or even a stuffy nose. She hadn't had a full day completely free of a reaction in years, and certainly not on a day spent outside.

"Can you teach me?" she asked, leaning closer to him.

"Of course," he replied with a small smile.

He had such an expressive mouth. Now that she was looking at him up close, she could see that even when his eyes were guarded, his lips conveyed every new emotion that sped through him, as if they were more sensitive than most people's. Lily couldn't stop watching them.

"Eat," he reminded her.

She pulled her gaze away and started in on her acorns, pleasantly surprised to find them quite satisfying, if a bit bland.

"Got any salt?" she asked jokingly. His face pinched with worry.

"You need it. Badly." Rowan rubbed his hand across the stubble on his chin and his leg started bouncing up and down nervously.

"It's okay. They're really good just like this," Lily said.

"It's not about taste," he replied with frustration. "Salt is an important mineral for a crucible."

"Why?"

"It's a special substance. It carries a charge," he said slowly, like she was a child. "Do you know what electricity is?"

"Yes." Lily tried not to sound offended or sarcastic. She knew Rowan couldn't possibly understand that to her, parts of his world looked like they still had one foot in the Stone Age. "And I know that salt is an electrolyte. We understand biology very well in my world."

"Okay." He paused, giving Lily another strange look before continuing. "Well, our bodies are electric, and we all use salt for a number of things—nerve impulses, muscle contraction, extracting energy from food. But a crucible's body speeds through these processes differently, and at an accelerated rate. As a result, you generate huge amounts of energy. You also use up a lot more salt."

"Is that why I freaking love Fritos?" Lily asked. He didn't get it. "Forget it. Keep going."

"Witchcraft and salt go hand in hand. Your body practically runs on it," he said, summing it up. "And I'm out of salt."

"I'll be fine. It's just a craving."

"When you crave something, it means you need it." He breathed a laugh and his eyes momentarily turned inward. "A crucible's craving is her mechanic's mandate." The way he'd said that made Lily think it was something he'd learned by rote, and that it had a much deeper meaning than was immediately apparent. "Trust me, in another day or two, this is going to become a big problem for both of us," he continued. "And I can't bring you back into Salem just yet. Not for another three or four days, at least."

"Okay. Is there any way to get more salt?" Lily asked equitably.

"Yes. I could kill an animal, and you could drink its blood."

Lily gave Rowan a withering look.

"Look, you don't have to eat the meat," he began, his tone near to pleading.

"I'm not drinking blood, Rowan."

"There are no other sources of salt out here. Otherwise, we have to go back to Salem."

"Then we go back to Salem," Lily said simply.

"Right. Because that's the smartest choice," he said sarcastically.

"I refuse to consume any part of any animal. It's not an option."

Rowan paced around the fire, biting his lower lip to keep himself from speaking.

"Just say it," Lily said, jumping to her feet.

"Fine. I really want to know if there's a universe, any universe, where you're a reasonable person who knows how to compromise even a tiny bit?" he yelled back at her. "Does every version of you have to be so ridiculously stubborn that you won't even do the littlest thing I ask?"

"Drinking blood is not a little thing," she sputtered incredulously.

"You do realize *who* you look like?"

"Yes!"

"And you realize that you're a bit conspicuous?" He pointed to her bright red hair. "And that it would be nearly impossible to get you back into Salem right now without someone spotting you from, say, a mile away?"

"So cut off my hair. Dye it," Lily said, her voice wavering when she realized what she was saying. Rowan's angry expression switched to surprise, and Lily strengthened her resolve. "Do what you have to do. But I am not drinking blood."

Lily saw the first tress of her hair fall at her feet and nearly told Rowan to stop.

She heard his knife slice through another hank, and tears started welling up in her eyes. She tried to tell herself it was just hair, and that she'd never liked her hair to begin with, but that only made her cry harder. If she didn't like it long, how much worse would it look short? Lily's breathing skipped with tears and Rowan's hands stilled.

"Do you want me to stop?" he asked quietly.

"No." Lily's voice came out high and childish. She cleared her throat and continued. "It's too late anyway, isn't it?"

"Yeah. Sorry."

"Keep going."

He lifted another lock and cut through it. "I think short hair will be really flattering on you," he said optimistically. "You've got a beautiful face. It shouldn't be covered by hair."

Lily watched more strands fall to the ground. Her neck could feel everything, even the weight of Rowan's eyes as he looked at her. She felt exposed.

When he was finished cutting, Rowan took up a bundle of Lily's shorn hair, a twig, and some twine from his pack. He sat down next to her while he wrapped the hair onto the end of the twig, binding it tightly with the twine. He trimmed the ends of the hair bundle evenly, and in a few moments he'd fashioned a rudimentary paintbrush. Lily watched every neat motion of his hands. His dexterity fascinated her so much she momentarily forgot about herself.

"Nifty," Lily said, truly impressed.

"We're almost done," he said, smiling encouragingly at her. He stood behind her and began painting the dye he'd made in his small cauldron onto her hair. Rowan dyed her hair in layers, getting all the way down to the scalp. He piled the dyed hair on top of her head, being very careful not to stain her face or neck with it. As he worked, the stench of the dye kept intensifying.

"That smells awful. It's making my eyes sting," she said. "What's in it?"

"Black walnut husks."

"They smell like pee," she said, sniffling.

"No, they don't," Rowan responded cautiously. "Pee is why the dye smells like pee."

Lily stiffened and turned her head carefully to look at him. "Please tell me you didn't."

"You can't make dye without a stripping agent, Lily," he said pleadingly. "I don't have any way to make peroxide or ammonia out here, but I do have uric acid in my urine."

Lily faced front again.

"Do you want me to stop?" he asked.

"No," Lily said through gritted teeth, trying to ignore what was seeping into her scalp.

"You can rinse it off right now if it's too disgusting. I'll go catch a squirrel, and we don't have to go back to Salem."

"No thank you."

"Lily, you really don't have to—"

"Are you going to finish or not?" she said, cutting him off.

"So stubborn," he said, more to himself than to Lily.

"I'm not stubborn," Lily said. "I have conviction. And I'm not afraid to do something difficult in order to stay true to my beliefs."

"That sounds familiar," he said in a slightly sad way.

They lapsed into silence while Rowan finished painting her hair with the dye and they waited for it to set. When Lily was done rinsing the dried dye out of her hair in the stream, Rowan made another, more careful, pass at trimming her hair with his knife. He took his time, making sure it was even and that it fell properly around her face. Finally he stood back and gave her a satisfied nod.

Lily's hand shot up to feel her hair. Rowan had given her what felt like a bob. She scrunched her damp curls, happily noting that he'd had the sense to give her some layers so she didn't have pyramid-head.

"How does it look?" she asked anxiously.

"I think it looks great short," he replied, still studying her. "But I've always preferred you with your hair up, so I can see your long neck."

Lily was thrown for a moment. Of course, he was referring to Lillian, but it was still strange to hear Rowan speak to her in such a familiar way when she'd only met him three days ago.

"And the color?" she asked, unable to hold his appraising gaze.

"It's dark," he warned. "Outlander dark, which works in our favor. If you don't let anyone see your light eyes, we might be able to pull this off."

They broke camp quickly. While Lily washed out the cauldron, Rowan took care to make sure all of her hair was burned before he buried the black walnut husks and the embers of the fire under a few layers of dirt. In minutes, it was as if they'd never been there. Lily looked over her shoulder as they left the campsite and headed back to Salem, conscious of the fact that they'd left no soda cans or ugly plastic wrappers behind.

"What's wrong?" Rowan asked, touching her arm.

"Nothing. It's just that in my world we're so concerned with everything being clean. Everything has to come in its own package." She gave Rowan a rueful smile. "And it makes such a mess."

His nose scrunched up as he puzzled out the contradiction. "Being clean makes a mess?"

"Unfortunately," Lily said, nodding.

"I don't think you're doing it right then."

"No. We definitely aren't."

"I guess every version of the world is flawed somehow," he said equitably. "Nothing's perfect."

Lily walked beside Rowan for a while, wondering if she agreed with him. If there were an infinite number of universes, didn't that mean that one of them *had* to be perfect? And if one of them was a paradise, then did that mean that another one had to be hell? Lily wondered how many versions of the world were better than this. And how many were worse.

"Teach me something," Lily asked, breaking herself out of her circular thoughts.

One corner of his mouth tipped up in a quizzical smile. "Like what?" he replied.

"Teach me how to control my reactions," Lily asked excitedly.

"That's going to take more than one lesson. But we can start if you'd like."

Rowan spent the next few hours showing Lily how to discharge unnecessary energy before it became a runaway reaction. Lily saw little sparks of energy flying off her skin, like glitter. It was pretty, but it required so much focus. Rowan said that a willstone would change the energy effortlessly, and without making her look so sparkly. They worked their way up from bark dust, and after a few tries, she was able to manage her reaction to a nettle scratch without Rowan's fingers on her wrist.

"It's not puffing up too horribly," she said, peering at the angry red line that traced an inch across her forearm. Lily sniffed. Her head was starting to get congested.

"You mostly did it," he said encouragingly. He reached out and pressed his fingertips to her pulse point. The red line disappeared, and her stuffy nose cleared. He grinned at her.

"Why can't I do it like that?" Lily asked with a pout. "What I need is a willstone."

Rowan's smile faded. He looked at the ground as they walked, his lips pursed together.

"What? Don't you want me to have one?" she asked.

"It's got nothing to do with what I want," he said.

"What does that mean?"

"If you get a willstone, you'll have to be trained. You'd be a menace if you weren't." He pulled his lower lip through his teeth.

"So train me," Lily said. His head snapped around and he stopped walking.

"Why?" he asked, suddenly angry. "Why do you want to be trained?"

"So I can control my reactions."

"You're lying," he said dismissively.

"I'm not."

"You're not telling me the whole truth, Lily. I can hear it in your voice."

"I want to control my reactions, *and* I want to go home!" she shouted. "Do you have any idea how I can do that? Do you know how to send me back to my universe?"

His eyes narrowed, warning her against using too much sarcasm. "It's never been done by anyone but Lillian."

"That means I have two options. I can beg Lillian to send me back—which I know she won't—or I can learn how to do it myself. If she figured it out, why can't I?"

"It's not that simple, Lily. You seem to have all her potential, but crucibles start their training when they're six years old. You have no idea how much you'll need to learn to get to the point she's at right now."

"I don't care what I have to do. Please, Rowan, I need to go back. My mother—"

Lily broke off, a wave of fear making her voice weak. She'd been so concerned with keeping herself alive the past few days she hadn't had any worry left in her to spare for her mother. The worry came back as Rowan searched her eyes. Lily got that feeling again—the feeling that there was a secret language the two of them spoke that she'd forgotten.

"And if I train you," he said softly. "How do I know you won't end up exactly like *her*?"

"Because I'm nothing like her," Lily replied, throwing up her hands like it was self-evident.

"Really?"

"Yes, really," Lily said, offended. "How could you even think that about me?"

Rowan looked away, his hands planted on his hips. "This isn't my decision, anyway. The sachem wants you trained."

"And you don't think I should be?"

"I think there are going to be a lot of people who are going to try to use you, whether I train you or not."

He turned and started walking again, his brow furrowed in thought. Lily followed him cautiously. She knew not to push him to explain anymore.

"How is she? Your Samantha?" Rowan finally asked after a long silence.

"She's sick, but still alive. I think, anyway." Lily watched Rowan's face. "You knew Samantha here?"

"Of course." His voice sounded like it was coming from far away. "We were very close."

"What happened to her?"

Rowan didn't answer right away. "About a year ago, Lillian disappeared for three weeks." He stopped again and swallowed hard. "Samantha said that Lillian was in front of us, inches away but beyond our reach. She said that Lillian was being destroyed from the inside out. We didn't understand. Samantha decided that she had to go get Lillian on her own. She went to the pyre even though she knew she wasn't a firewalker. It killed her."

Lily moved closer to Rowan until their shoulders were nearly touching.

"What's a firewalker?" she asked cautiously.

"It's the final level of witchcraft. Very few attempt it. Most die."

They continued along at a stroll, both of them slowed by the thought of losing Samantha.

"I've disappeared from my world just like Lillian did," Lily whispered. "I have to go back, Rowan."

He sighed and nodded. "I know."

CHAPTER
7

THE TEMPERATURE STARTED DROPPING EVEN BEFORE the sun went down. Frost fell, lining the leaf litter underfoot with flaky, white ice. Even Lily felt chilled. Rowan stuffed his hands under his arms as they walked, trying to stay warm.

"Come here," Lily said, putting her arm around his waist. Rowan startled at her touch, but when she didn't let go, he wrapped an arm over her shoulder and hugged her to his chest. His whole body was trembling.

"We need shelter tonight," he said through chattering teeth.

"How far are we from Salem?"

"Hours. I won't make it," he replied honestly. Lily started rubbing his arms with her hands, trying to chafe some warmth into him. She was really cold, something she couldn't ever remember happening to her before, but Rowan was literally freezing to death.

"Can't we build a fire?" she asked.

"Not out in the open. There are Woven tracks everywhere." He paused before continuing. "But there is a cabin nearby."

"What are we waiting for?" Lily asked enthusiastically.

"It was abandoned years ago when a Woven built her nest not far from it." Rowan watched Lily's face carefully. "The nest may be empty by now. And then again, it may not be. Are you sure you're up to it?"

Lily felt him shaking in her arms and pushed down her own fear. "Let's hurry."

A grateful look crossed Rowan's face, and he squeezed her a little tighter before turning and leading her quickly through the trees. They speed-walked for about half an hour, racing the lowering sun and the lowering temperature. Lily clamped on to Rowan's hand, frightened that he was going to freeze to death before they got there.

"Can't you take some heat from me?" she asked. Rowan shook his head tightly. "Does that mean you can't or you won't?" she pressed.

"W-won't. You're c-cold, too," he said haltingly, his lips nearly numb. Lily started to protest, but Rowan cut her off. "The cabin is over the next rise," he said, pulling her down behind a bush and crouching down next to her. "Wait here. I'll go check it out. Don't make a sound until I come back."

"Rowan—" Lily began, but he'd already pulled out his knife and crept away on cat-quiet feet.

Lily peeked around the bush, trying to figure out where he'd gone. She couldn't see anything but forest. She strained her ears listening for him, but all she heard was the wind and the creaking of the frozen limbs of the trees as they swayed and rubbed together. Lily stayed still, her breath tight in her chest as the forest darkened. More sounds joined the ghostly chorus of the trees—skittering, rustling sounds.

Lily edged her way back into the bush, drawing her knees up to her chin protectively as time passed. Too much time. She didn't know anything about Woven behavior, but surely if Rowan were attacked, he'd fight back. She'd be able to hear that. Wouldn't she?

Lily felt pressure on her forearm and jumped, clapping a hand over her mouth to keep herself from screaming.

"It's me," said Rowan's disembodied voice. "The nest is empty."

He dissolved out of the background and became visible again—the same way he had that night when he'd caught her trying to run away with Juliet. Lily almost threw her arms around him she was so relieved but settled for smiling at him instead.

Rowan pulled her up to her feet and held her hand as he led her through the dark trees. They walked for about five or ten minutes before Lily saw a clearing with a small stone cabin in its center. The cabin had a thick oak door studded with iron bolts, and a wide chimney that tilted atop the slated roof. It looked like it came out of a storybook. Lily could easily imagine a jack-o'-lantern by the front door and a black cat hissing at them from the crooked roof.

They pushed the door open, and Lily smelled the murky scent of moldering leaves and wet ash. Rowan's willstone glowed, lighting up the pitch-black room. As he walked in front of her, Lily saw that Rowan's body was edged with a halo of opalescent magelight. He looked big and otherworldly.

"There's a candle around here somewhere," he said. It took him a few moments to find it, and when he did, he brought it over to Lily.

One of his ice-cold hands snaked up the sleeve of her jacket and wrapped around her forearm.

"May I?" he asked tentatively.

Lily nodded, not sure what she was agreeing to. She felt a chill creeping under her skin and realized that Rowan was draining some of her heat. His eyes closed, and he swayed toward her until his sinking forehead nearly touched hers.

"Thank you," he sighed. "I just need a little bit more to light this."

Lily inhaled sharply as the cold sank down deeper into her. Rowan's willstone sparked and the wick ignited. She shivered.

"Sorry," he whispered, his eyes still closed.

"It's okay."

Lily watched the planes of his face, turned golden by the light of the candle between them. She wanted to touch his mouth. Rowan's eyes flicked open, and he lifted his sagging head up and away from hers. He released her arm and pulled his hand out of her sleeve.

"There are preserves put up in the cabinet," he said, turning toward the hearth.

A little bewildered about what had just happened, Lily followed the direction of his pointing finger to a small pantry while Rowan used the candle to light a fire in the hearth. Lily searched the nearly bare pantry and found four dusty jars.

"Blueberry jam," Lily said, reading the first label. She turned the second jar around. "Dried crickets," she read, confused. "Why would someone put dead bugs in the cabinet?"

"Because they're nutritious," Rowan replied evenly.

"No way," Lily replied. "You don't actually eat crickets, do you?"

"I haven't had them in years," Rowan said, more to himself than her, like he was reminiscing.

"Seriously?" Lily grimaced at the thought, but tried not to look too disgusted. She didn't want to offend him.

"Only the richest of the Outlanders can afford to keep and protect livestock from the Woven. But nearly all of them have cricket farms in their living quarters." He looked up at Lily's wan expression, his eyes glinting with humor. "I'd prefer the blueberry jam, though."

Lily went back to inspecting labels. "Pickles!" she exclaimed happily, and more than a little relieved that he wasn't going to try to make her taste cricket. "I love pickles."

Rowan laughed under his breath and nodded while he fanned a

small flame. "That's because they're mostly salt and vinegar. Two things you need desperately. Eat all of them."

Lily took down the pickles and the jar of blueberry preserves and brought them over to Rowan.

"Does this mean no squirrel blood?" she asked, placing the jam on the hearth and handing him the pickles. He stopped what he was doing and, without needing to be told, started wrenching on the tightly sealed lid. A satisfying sucking sound followed.

"No squirrel blood," he said, handing her the opened jar with a smile. "That ought to be enough salt to hold you over for a while." He frowned suddenly. "We should still get you back to Salem soon though. We can't live on our own in the woods forever."

"And I didn't let you cut off all my hair for nothing." Lily started munching on the pickles, and her mouth watered with pleasure. "So good!" she mumbled around her food. "You explained the salt part, but why do I crave vinegar?"

"Vinegar is an antimicrobial, antiviral, and antibiotic. The less you have to fight internally, the stronger you are," he said, feeding kindling to the small fire. "So you can fight your enemies instead."

Lily crunched and nodded, too happy with her jar to ask any more questions. She sat down on the hearth, right up close to the tiny fire, and ate pickle after pickle. She'd never seen anyone build a fire in person before. The way Rowan watched it and fed it was fascinating to her. He took such care tending to its every whim that she'd finished all the pickles before he was done. Lily couldn't think of anyone in her world who had that kind of patience.

"Aren't you starving?" she asked.

"I am," he replied, still stoking the growing flames.

"Eat," she urged, nudging the jam in his direction.

"I will." He glanced over at Lily's pickle-less pickle jar. "Drink the brine," he ordered gently.

Even though drinking pickle juice was something she would have considered disgusting just three days ago, Lily didn't hesitate. When she'd finished the last drop, Rowan reached out and placed his fingertips on the inside of her wrist. His willstone glittered at the base of his throat as he gathered some of Lily's excess energy. After a few heartbeats, Rowan released her, stood, and carried the unopened jam back to the cabinet.

"Why won't you eat?" Lily asked incredulously.

"I don't need to. I have you," he said with a shrug.

"Don't you want to *eat* something? I can give you energy, but that's not the same as feeling food in your stomach, is it?"

Rowan joined Lily by the fire, sitting close to keep warm.

"This used to be an Outlander shelter for those who couldn't quite make it to Salem," he told her. "Traders, some of them coming from as far away as the mountains, would stop here as a last resort. Most people who come here are desperate, and some are near to dying. This little cabin and those preserves have saved a lot of lives."

His expressive lips pressed together, like there was so much more he wanted to say, but was holding back.

"When did it save yours?" Lily guessed.

Rowan met her eyes with a touch of surprise, and then looked away. "When I was seven my father brought me to the Citadel to be tested," he said. "We had to leave our people and make our way east alone to do it. Outlanders don't usually risk it. Being chosen is a long shot, so they only bring their children to be tested at the Citadel if they happen to be near Salem during the child's testing year."

"Why did your dad risk it?" Lily asked. She couldn't begin to imagine trying to get through these dangerous woods alone with a little boy.

"My dad was a doctor. Most Outlanders don't have any book learning, but he did. He said he knew the signs, and he told me I had what it takes to make a good mechanic. Maybe even a great one." Rowan breathed a mirthless laugh. "Mostly, I think he didn't want me to die in the mines or fighting the Woven out on the Ocean of Grass."

An image of the Great Plains popped into Lily's head, and she nodded her understanding, encouraging Rowan to continue.

"At first, it was like we were charmed. We traveled for weeks without a single problem. It wasn't until we were two days from here that we finally came across a Woven." Rowan stopped and looked down at his interlaced hands, rubbing one thumb over the other. "She was an old thing, half blind, half deaf. But she still had enough venom to bite my dad before she died. I had to carry him here."

Lily reached out and took one of Rowan's hands, angling her head under his so he would look at her.

"Did he die here?" she asked.

Rowan looked at Lily, and a quizzical smile lit up his face unexpectedly. "No. My dad told me what to do. Even though we were in the middle of the woods and I didn't have a willstone yet, my dad knew how to heal without magic." Rowan's voice dropped and his eyes looked inward. "He was really sick. And heavy. By the time we got to this cabin, it was like entering paradise. A roof. A fire. Jam."

"Jam," Lily repeated, swallowing the tight feeling in her chest.

"The best jam I've ever tasted." Rowan cradled her hand in between both of his, running his fingertips over the blue veins that traced under her translucent skin and circling the swirls of her fingerprints. "So I'll leave that jar of jam for someone else. Someone who really needs it."

The first time Lily had seen Rowan glaring at her through the glass window of the café, she had been so overwhelmed by his anger she hadn't noticed much else about him. Now she couldn't believe that she hadn't seen, right from the first, that he was absolutely beautiful. His thick hair, sensitive mouth, even his hands were shaped in a way that appealed to her.

Lily stared at him, amazed. "I can't believe it."

"What?" he asked, confused. "What can't you believe?"

"I can't believe you're the same guy who peed on my head a few hours ago."

"I didn't pee on your head! I did it in the cauldron," he said, laughing, which was exactly what Lily had intended. It hurt her to see Rowan that sad.

"Six of one, half a dozen of the other," she said wryly, waving off his protestations. "All I know is that you cut off all of my hair and dyed it who-knows-what-color, and you used *your pee* to do it."

"You're never going to forgive me for that, are you?" he asked sagely.

"Nope."

"Well, it was worth it." He reached out and pushed a few stray curls away from her forehead. "I can see your face better with short hair. I do miss the red, though."

Rowan's eyes ticked over her face, her throat, her shoulders, as if he couldn't stop following the flow of her shape. When his eyes finally circled back to hers, Lily could barely meet them. She didn't have a joke ready to deflect the tension. All she could do was stare up at him, her mouth parted as if it were waiting for the smart comment that her brain failed to supply.

"We should get some rest," he said, looking away.

Rowan left Lily by the fire for a few moments and returned with two curious-looking wooden frames. Leaving those by the fireplace with Lily, he went to a small chest in the corner, opened it with his willstone, and returned with two tarps and two blankets. He had Lily hold the blankets while he stretched the tarps across the frames, making two cots that resembled something that was halfway between hammock and lawn furniture.

"The blankets smell fresh," Lily said, sniffing them. "Do you think someone's been here recently to replace them?"

Rowan shook his head in answer while he worked. "Travelers use their willstones to seal up storage chests with a universally known charm. All the next traveler has to do is touch their will-stone, think *open*, and it does. But until then, no leaks and no bugs."

"No wonder you don't need plastic," Lily said, regretting that there wasn't something like this in her world.

"What's plastic?"

"Never mind," Lily replied, too tired to get into it. She couldn't remember the last time she'd slept. She took off her boots and lay down on the cot, her eyes already closing.

"Good night," Rowan said, covering her with a blanket.

Lily mumbled something back and fell immediately asleep.

"Lily," Rowan whispered, shaking her awake.

She opened her eyes and saw Rowan's face over hers, his index finger pressed to his lips to indicate she should be quiet. He looked pale and scared. Lily sat up, her ears already filling with the high-pitched hiss of fear.

"Woven?" she mouthed, not daring to make a sound. Rowan nodded slowly, his eyes never leaving hers.

"The nest," he mouthed back silently, shaking his head like he wanted to kick himself. "Not empty."

Outside and to the left of the cabin, Lily heard a faint chittering noise. Rowan's head cocked in that direction, and he held up one finger. A rustling to the right made him crane his head in the other direction, and Rowan held up a second finger. A soft keening signaled a third Woven. Right outside the cabin door, they both heard scratching. Something pattered across the roof.

Rowan stopped counting at six, and the look on his face changed from fear to regret.

"I'm sorry, Lily," he said out loud, as if being quiet was of no use anymore.

A chorus of screeching howls erupted outside at the sound of Rowan's voice. Lily heard the shuffling and crunching of thousands of frozen leaves being plowed aside as the many-legged creatures scurried into position around the cabin. Their armored appendages began scraping at the shuttered windows and scrabbling up the sides of the stone walls.

"We have to do something," Rowan shouted over the sudden cacophony. His face was pleading with hers. "Something that you're not ready for. Something that probably won't even work because you don't have a willstone, but if we don't try, we're both going to die."

"Okay," Lily shouted back, her voice breaking with panic. "Whatever it is, just do it."

One of the Woven outside began to throw itself against the entrance, trying to ram it down. The thuds of its body against the door and the sound of its frustrated wails boomed through the little cabin. Rowan picked his knife off the floor and stowed it in the sheath at his belt. He threw the rest of the spare wood onto the fire, sending sparks flying up the chimney in a plume of ash and smoke. The creatures on the roof squealed as if the sudden upwelling of heat had burned them.

"Sit here," he said, placing Lily on the hearthstones right in front of the roaring flames. He pulled off his linen shirt. His bare skin picked up the light of the fire and seemed to blaze like copper.

He looked down at Lily, the wails of the Woven bearing down on them from all sides. Lily saw him clench his hands into fists, squeezing his eyes shut tightly for a moment. Then he shook out his hands and puffed his breath like he was preparing to plunge into icy water. He knelt in front of Lily, leaning close to her. His eyes were wide and bright with terror.

"Touch my willstone," he said, taking her hand and raising it to his throat. His voice dropped to a whisper, almost like he was praying. "And please don't hurt me."

Lily looked at Rowan's willstone, dancing with inner light, and felt as if she were falling toward it. Her panic disappeared. The cacophony silenced. The whole world cupped itself around the one, gorgeous point hanging from Rowan's bared throat.

She'd meant to touch his stone gently, hardly brushing it with a feather-soft caress, but before she could control herself, her hand shot out greedily and grabbed it.

Mine.

Rowan gasped and shook as if she'd strummed an open nerve, his eyes rolling back in his head.

"Lily, please," he begged, his voice high and breathy.

She wanted to swallow his stone, or squeeze it so tightly it ground into her skin and buried itself in between her bones. She heard Rowan moan. She was hurting him. She forced herself to relax her grip until the stone rested lightly in her palm. It was warm and it pulsed, like a living, beating part of Rowan.

"So beautiful," Lily said, and sighed. Her breath blew over the stone and Rowan shivered.

"Look into it. Find my stone's rhythm." He stopped and panted. "Find my pat—"

Lily could feel his willstone pulsing in her palm. The lights rippled like waves and flashed like particles at the same time. Lily felt a vibration all through her—one particular frequency that felt like a single, rich note played on her body as if she were an instrument.

She memorized it and locked its copy away inside her. It was the rhythm of Rowan's mind inside this particular stone. She played that rhythm back to his stone and the room around her changed.

It was suddenly daytime. There were no Woven charging through the door. It was quiet. She heard Rowan's voice in her head but she knew instinctively he wasn't talking to her. He seemed to be simply thinking his own thoughts. He was so young—just a little boy—and so scared. Lily realized with a jolt that she was inside one of Rowan's memories, reliving it from his perspective. She saw . . .

. . . A man with dark eyes. Dad. His normally tanned skin is green with sickness. He's lying on one of the cots in the cabin. He smiles. He doesn't know his gums are bleeding. He is trying to encourage me, but I'm scared. I don't know what to do. The bite wound stinks of rot. We need time to let the pus drain, but the jars of preserves won't last forever. I know I'll have to go out, out into the Woven Woods to hunt, or we'll starve.

No more of that.

. . . A pillow. Silky, strawberry curls spilling toward my face. I run my hand up her naked back, feeling the knobs of her spine and her bird-like rib cage. My hand is dark and big against her skin. She inhales, waking, and reaches for me under the covers. My body responds. I roll on top of her, my face in her white neck, her hips arching up to meet mine.

Don't. That's private.

. . . The courtyard inside the Citadel is muddy and the sky is the dark silver color of unfallen snow. The smell of vomit and piss is everywhere. A gallows—one noose hanging, waiting.

Stop!

. . . Tristan, young, maybe eleven, and a blond-haired boy are laughing like crazy. The three of us have had such a long day that laughter is the only way to blow off the enormous pressure we're under. But even now, I feel a little removed from Tristan and Gideon. Lillian favors me. The poor Outlander. The drub. It galls the two city-bred boys, especially Gideon. I want to feel closer to these two who are tied to me like brothers, my stone kin, but I want Lillian's attention more. She's still too young—I'm still too young—but I already know that I'm in love with her.

Lily. Enough.

. . . Tristan. He is visiting me in the hospital, lounging at the end of my bed with his shoes kicked off. I swear that guy could find a way to lounge in a torture chamber. I'm inside a plastic tent, which is a sort of torture chamber, for me anyway. It's meant to keep me in a sterile environment, but I'm cheating. I'm sticking my hands out of the bottom so I can play cards with Tristan. Not that I ever win. Whenever we play cards, I spend most of the time staring at him instead of my hand. Tristan always comes to visit me in the hospital. That means he loves me at least a little bit, right?

Wait, Rowan. That's my memory.

. . . Samantha is walking in circles, talking to herself in the produce section of Star Market. Everyone is staring. I look at Juliet. Her face is bright red and she's fighting back humiliated tears. I go to get Mom, hoping that she doesn't start screaming this time. I can handle a lot, even the strung-out way she looks in public, but I can't handle it when my mom screams.

Rowan, cut it out.

. . . Tristan kissing me. I put my hands under his shirt and run them over his bare chest, feeling the smooth skin and firm muscles, down to his belly.

No.

. . . Tristan fumbling into his clothes in the dim bathroom. Miranda behind him. Is it shock or sadness or anger I feel? I can't believe how much this hurts.

No, Rowan.

. . . Scared faces above me. Everyone's staring at me, horrified.
My body twitching and clenching like I'm being struck by lightning.
I can hear my teeth clacking together and taste the blood in my
mouth. It pools in the back of my throat. I can't scream. I can't swallow. All I can do is wade through the panic and hope this seizure
ends soon.

Stop!

"—tern," Rowan finished.

Lily was thrown back into the noise and desperation of their
situation. So much had passed between her and Rowan, but almost
no time had passed at all. Thoughts really did move faster than words,
Lily supposed.

"I have it," she said. "I have your pattern."

Rowan nodded, as if he already knew as much, and steeled himself again. "Now"—he paused and swallowed hard—"usually, you'd
change the energy inside your own stone and then pour the power
into mine, so I don't even know if this is possible. But we did it with
your ankle, so we're going to give it a try. It's just more energy,
okay?"

"Okay!" Lily said, not really understanding but determined to
try if it killed her. "What do I do?"

"Come back in and fill me up."

Lily's question was interrupted by the crash of the door breaking
down. She saw a jumble of pincers, claws, armored shells, and long
thin legs, like the legs of spiders, only much, much bigger. Lily stared
at them, a scream choking in her throat. Each Woven looked like a
jumble of creatures, their parts pulled from a grab bag and stitched
together with bristling hair and teeth.

"There's no time!" Rowan shouted. He grabbed Lily's shoulders
and shook her until she looked at him, his words sliding into her head.

I'll try to guide you, but it's never been done like this before. Look into my stone. Take the heat of the fire. Change its energy into force inside my stone. Give it to me.

Lily forced herself to focus and looked into Rowan's stone. It was so beautiful.

The Woven charging toward them through the smashed door seemed to freeze. Lily didn't think. She just did what Rowan told her to do—she took the heat. Her skin inhaled the radiant energy of the fire and all the air in the room followed, as if she were a black hole. As the wind rushed in on her from all sides, it collided and got pushed up, blowing her hair and arms up with it. Rowan released her shoulders as a column of witch wind built, lifting her in the air until she hovered a few inches off the ground. The heat collected inside her, building into a bright ball like a mini sun gestating in her chest.

Change the energy into force.

The rational, logical part of Lily's mind, the part that knew about Einstein, understood that matter could be changed into energy. There was an elegant little equation that described it, too. But how was she supposed to change heat into force? Lily couldn't even begin to fathom that exchange, but she knew it had to be possible because Rowan had said it was. Directing the gathered heat in her chest into Rowan's willstone, she felt it start to change into force simply because she willed it to.

Lily's mind squinted at Rowan's stone to try to understand it. She *saw* the lattice of its crystalline structure ringing with vibrations as they altered the frequency of the tiniest shards of matter—which were themselves not actually *things*, but *vibrations*. Like a finger sliding up a violin string, the pitch changed, but the volume did not decrease. Nothing was lost. All of the energy she'd collected from the ambient heat in the air was turned directly into force.

The enormity of the power generated in this exchange staggered her, but her body took all that force back into itself as if it were the most natural thing it could do, like a lung pulling in a new breath after exhaling.

"Lily!" Rowan screamed.

She looked down at Rowan, bracing himself against the onrush of witch wind. The Woven were inches away from him. One of them extended a long, fanged snout from under its carapace. Its maw opened.

Give it to me. Give me the Gift.

She did. Rowan's chest swelled, and his head tipped back, an ecstatic look gracing his lovely face.

Light exploded inside Rowan's willstone. He leapt up from his knees, whirling in midair as he unsheathed his knife and faced the army of Woven that were charging into the cabin.

Lily could feel Rowan's body soaring, feel the rush of pure force pouring into his limbs. Knife in hand, he slashed through the armored back of a Woven and was on to his next victim before the killed creature could even scream. Caught in her column of witch wind, Lily kept absorbing more heat, changing it, and spilling it into Rowan as he used it. She was the hand of power inside Rowan, bearing him up so he could do impossible things.

His body leapt and spun. It crashed down with tons of force, smashing the Woven beneath him. His arms reached and whirled. He punched and grabbed, slicing through the ranks of invaders like they were no thicker than shadows. He pushed their enemies back, out of the confined space of the cabin and into the clearing so he could kill them more easily.

Even though she could no longer see the battle, Lily's senses still seeped into Rowan's. She was with him in his skin, feeling the thrill he felt with her power inside him. Every muscle was stronger than steel and every bone nearly unbreakable. She felt his lithe body all around her, moving and stretching. Her heart pounded with his, thrilling with the purest rush Lily had ever experienced. And right on the edge of his mind, she saw a flash of fear—fear that she would take him over entirely.

She realized that she could control his actions if she wanted. More. She could control his thoughts, his speech, even his dreams. And something in her pinched with lust at the thought of doing it, of taking all of him. Lily realized with a start that she desperately wanted something that she knew was despicable.

Don't give in, Lily. I know it feels good, but you have to let me keep myself. You don't know how to fight them.

Lily struggled with herself, resisting not only the desire she felt but the itch of curiosity. It was wrong, and she knew it, but still she wondered what it would feel like to own Rowan completely. Lily's conscience cringed.

I swear I won't, Rowan.

She schooled her thoughts and focused on the battle instead of her internal conflict. Out in the clearing, Rowan stood at the center of a pile of growing carcasses. The Woven had to climb up the dead to come at him. Several times one or two peeled off from the main group and tried to get past Rowan to the cabin. Rowan was vigilant and stopped all of them before they got close to Lily. Their numbers seemed to be endless.

As the fire behind Lily began to sputter and fail, the witch wind buffeted her unevenly, knocking her around like a doll. Lily gritted her teeth and waited for it to be over. Finally, the howls and squeals of the Woven ended.

They're all dead, Lily. Now we have to burn them.

I'm so tired.

We must. Or more are sure to come.

Still using the strength Lily was struggling to pour into him, Rowan pushed all the carcasses on top of the pile in the clearing and then set it alight. As the bonfire began to rise and Rowan's need for superhuman strength ended, Lily allowed herself to sever the loop of power she was channeling. The uneven witch wind stopped blowing, and Lily fell out of the air in a heap. A fatigue she'd never felt before hollowed her out from head to toe, leaving her motionless on the cabin floor.

She saw Rowan's boots coming toward her and thought about how she'd seen them up close like this before—when he had found her in the grate after chasing her through the streets of this other Salem. She wasn't in any better condition now than she'd been then, and the similarity made Lily chuckle.

"Shh, it's okay," Rowan said gently. "Don't cry."

Lily wanted to tell him that she wasn't crying, but her throat had closed off and her eyes were blurry with tears. He picked her up. His skin was wet and cool. He carried her to a cot and propped her against the wall, his fingers stopping to press several points on her body like he was reading something written in Braille under her skin. His hair was wet—all of him was wet, she realized. Lily ran her hand up his arm and over his bare shoulder, smoothing the beads of water away.

"Did you bathe because you were covered in blood?" she asked. Rowan nodded grimly and met her eyes. She had to look away, down at his chest where her hand had come to rest over his heart. "You're all scratched and bruised."

"I'll be fine. But you're exhausted and you need energy." Rowan stood and went to the pantry, returning with the jar of blueberry preserves. "Told you it was a good idea to save the jam," he said, a smile creeping onto his face.

"Jam," Lily repeated, the word flying out of her, halfway between a laugh and a sob.

Lily dreamed she was a man.

Her dreaming self didn't think it was strange at all to look down and see a flat, firm chest. Her hands were large, and she could feel the difference in their heft as she walked down the hallway of Salem High. She was tall, and her center of balance was higher to compensate for her thick shoulders and her narrower hips. She felt strong and healthy. She liked this body. It had smooth, caramel-colored skin that she wanted to explore.

Lily woke alone.

"Rowan?" she called out into the cold light of early morning. The smoky air smelled like burned hair and sizzling grease. She swallowed down a wave of nausea at the thought of all the burning bodies outside and got out of bed.

The cabin was too small to require a search. As soon as her eyes opened, she knew he wasn't there. At some point, he'd replaced the knocked-down door with a flap made of the same material as the rebel tents, but it didn't do much to keep the cold out. Lily stood in the middle of the frigid cabin, feeling raw and damaged. She really wanted her sister, but she didn't dare try to reach her with mindspeak. The last time she did that, she'd put Juliet in danger.

"Rowan?" she called again shakily.

She heard a noise outside and the flap raised. Rowan ducked under it quickly and placed a rock on top of the bottom edge to keep out the smoke as best as he could. He was wearing a piece of cloth tied around his nose and mouth and carried a large bucket of water. His jacket was dusted with ash. Watching his wide shoulders tip around the flap as he entered the room, Lily was taken by the sudden urge to run to him, but when he looked up at her, she couldn't meet his gaze. She felt strange and empty inside. Like she'd given him too much of herself the night before and didn't have enough self left over for her.

Rowan put the bucket near the fire and pulled his mask down until it rested under his chin. His dark eyes darted around. Lily realized that he was having as much trouble looking at her as she was having looking at him. He motioned to the water with one hand and rubbed the back of his neck absently with the other.

"So you can wash up. Are you hungry?" he asked. Lily shook her head. "We can't stay here. The smoke out there can be seen for miles around. And you used up a lot of salt last night."

Lily nodded, aware that she was craving salt like crazy. "Are we going back to Salem?"

"We have to."

"Do you think it'll be safe?"

"It's been a few days since the raid. And your hair is so different." He looked away. "I think I can sneak you in after dark."

"Okay."

Rowan turned to leave but stopped by the entrance. "Listen. I know you weren't ready for that. I wasn't either. I never meant to do that with you." He glanced at her, his eyes wide and uncertain. He shrugged, running out of words.

"Thanks for the water," she replied, shrugging back at him. She didn't know what to say, either. What had happened between them was done, and it couldn't be undone. He put his hand on the flap, but suddenly Lily didn't want him to leave. "Is it always like that?" she blurted out, stopping him. "Is it always so . . ." She couldn't find a way to describe it. Earth-shattering? Humiliating? Amazing? They hadn't even touched, but it had been the most intimate thing Lily had ever experienced.

"No. Non-magical people aren't as connected to their willstones as we are. They just feel a presence in their minds when they touch each other's stones. Sometimes they can share thoughts and memories if they are emotionally close, and physical sensation if they are attracted to each other," he said quietly. "But they don't feel anywhere near what we do. They aren't as vulnerable as we are."

"And what about between magical people? Is it always that intense?"

Rowan smiled and shook his head. "Mechanics can bond with each other, but that's different from being claimed by a witch. We call it stone kin—like Tristan, Caleb, and I. The bond is for life, but it's not nearly as overwhelming as a claiming with a witch. The rule of thumb is the stronger the witch and mechanic are magically, the stronger the shared experience." Rowan broke off suddenly, carefully considering his wording. "You and I are uncommon, Lily. The next time you claim someone, even if it is another mechanic, it won't feel like that. I don't want you to be afraid of it, okay?"

Lily nodded, frowning, and looked away. Her emotions had inexplicably flipped again, and she didn't want to talk anymore. She wanted to be alone. Rowan sensed that Lily had mentally checked out of the conversation and secured his mask over his nose. "I'll be right outside," he said reassuringly, and left.

She stripped down and stood in the bucket of icy water. It chilled her to the bone, but she didn't care. She washed herself from head to toe, marveling at how tender she was. How soft and small her body felt in comparison to Rowan's. She splashed water on her face repeatedly, trying to rinse away the memory of sharing his skin. She shouldn't want to wear Rowan like a pair of pants, or swallow him like a mouthful of chocolate. It just wasn't right.

She brushed off her wearhyde clothes and boots as best she could, giving them a good shake. Luckily, wearhyde seemed to be not only durable but also capable of staying fresh even after several days of hard use. Her linen shirt was limp and stained, but there wasn't much she could do about that. She finished dressing and tidied up the cabin while she let her hair dry. It still seemed strange to feel the ends of her hair touching the top of her neck and brushing against her jawbone, but she tried not to think too much about how it looked or lament its loss. Instead, she concentrated on folding and putting things away.

"Lily? Are you okay?" Rowan called from outside.

"Yeah," she replied. "You can come in."

He ducked under the flap and pulled his mask down, looking around. Lily had pretty much everything packed up and ready for them to go.

"Oh. You cleaned up," he said, surprised. Lily smiled at him, and looked away quickly. Everything he did seemed to make her blush. She felt ridiculous.

"I didn't know what to do with the empty jars of preserves and pickles so I washed them and left them to soak in the bucket of water you brought me."

Rowan pulled the jars out and left them on a windowsill to dry, then went to the chest, closed it, and sealed it with a shimmer from his willstone.

"I'll empty this and we can go." He picked up the bucket and gave Lily a puzzled look. "Thank you."

She nodded and shifted on her feet. "Well, I can't let you do everything for me. Even though it is tempting." He stared at her for a moment longer than usual. "What?" she asked when the moment dragged past the comfort point.

"Most witches expect their mechanics to do everything for them. They don't even think twice about it."

"I guess I'm not like most witches, then."

They stared at each other again with nothing to say. Lily edged past him and went outside.

The fire had burned itself out, but the mound of blackened bodies still smoked in the center of the clearing. Lily noticed that Rowan had dug a shallow ditch around it to contain any stray embers. She covered her mouth with her hand and stared at the jumble of mismatched body parts in the pile. She still had no idea how to classify the Woven in her head. Not one was exactly like another. Some were the size of a small dog, and others were twice the size of a man. Some stood upright, while others had no legs and had to slither. The majority of them resembled giant insects with claws and teeth, but there were some that seemed more mammalian or serpentine. It was the sheer wrongness of them that disturbed her the most.

"How many did we kill?'

"I don't know. Thirty or forty." Rowan threw the used water onto the smoldering remains, making them hiss. "Let's go."

He didn't want to remain there a second longer than he had to. Lily didn't blame him. She followed him to a water pump. He hung the bucket on the spout, adjusted his pack, and started into the woods without a backward glance.

They didn't speak for a while, but Lily could feel Rowan stealing glances at her whenever she wasn't doing the same to him. She kept imagining that there was a string connecting them—as if they'd been tethered together like two paper cups and something in each of them whispered to the other in the dark. The connection wasn't clear, but she could still feel something inside Rowan speaking to something inside of her. She didn't know how to initiate mindspeak yet, but she could tell there was something he needed to say.

"Go ahead," she said.

"What happened between you and Tristan?" His voice was tight and his hands wrung the strap of his pack.

"What do you mean?"

"It's just, I know him really well. Tristan and I have been stone kin since we were kids." Rowan watched Lily carefully, but she didn't look up at him. "We share mindspeak. So I know a lot of girls have forgiven him when he's—"

"Cheated," Lily finished for him. "Which means he isn't faithful in this universe either," she said, more to herself than him.

She expected to be disappointed about that, but she wasn't. Fair or not, she didn't feel the same way about Tristan. Things he did that used to seem unbearably charming to her now seemed staged—phony even. Lily knew she shouldn't judge the Tristan in this world by what her Tristan had done to her, but she couldn't help it.

She remembered Rowan's distrust of her when he first met her, and she wondered if he would always see Lillian when he looked at her. Something clenched inside of her at the thought. She wanted him to see *her*. She wanted—well, she didn't know what she wanted, but she couldn't bear the thought of going back to the time when he hated her. They'd shared too much.

"It's not that," Rowan said vehemently, bringing Lily out of herself and back to the conversation. "Tristan is the most faithful friend you could ever ask for."

"He was a faithful friend to me for years," Lily said, agreeing with Rowan.

Rowan was silent for a while. She could tell something was eating at him.

"What is it?" Lily asked.

"I was wondering if you'd forgiven your Tristan. That's all."

"No," she admitted. "The next morning we had a terrible fight, and then I let Lillian take me."

"Because of him?"

"Because of a lot of things." She glanced over and saw a muscle jump in Rowan's jaw. She was torn between being ashamed about what had happened to her and grateful that someone knew exactly how she'd felt. Rowan hadn't been just a spectator to Tristan's infidelity, and his anger wasn't just for Lily's sake. They'd shared more than memories the night before. What they'd experienced was a communion. For a few brief moments they'd literally become one. He'd felt just as hurt as she had in that moment.

But communion worked both ways. Lily had felt skin under her hand when they'd touched Lillian. And she'd felt their shared body swell when they'd climbed on top of her. Lily didn't know how to deal with that just yet.

"You showed me a gallows," she said quietly. "What happened?"

Rowan's face turned slightly away from hers. She hated not being able to see his expression, but she didn't push. Eventually, he changed the subject. "When you enter a mechanic, you don't have to give back, you know."

"What are you talking about?"

"You don't have to delve so deeply into him, or share anything of yourself if you don't want to. You're the witch. You're in charge. It doesn't have to be that intimate. You can keep your experiences to yourself."

"And what about the mechanic?"

"It depends on how strong he is and how strong the witch is. Sometimes, he can fight her off if she tries to view things he'd rather keep to himself."

Lily stopped walking and stared at Rowan. "*Fight* her off? That's awful, Rowan."

"None of this happens without the mechanic's consent. He has to let her in first." Rowan's lips twitched with the hint of a smile. "And a kind witch controls herself when she's in there."

"Like I didn't?" Her voice grated with guilt.

Rowan put his hand on her elbow, tilting his head down closer to hers. "You had no warning about how it would make you feel. It was your first time." He dropped his hand a little too quickly, and eased away from her. "I'm lucky you didn't eat me alive," he joked.

Lily's smile was forced. Did he *know* that she'd wanted to eat him alive? That she still wanted to? She cast around for something other than eating Rowan to talk about, and a thought occurred to her. "Wait. You've been calling me witch all morning."

"After what you did last night, you've definitely earned the title. Healing your ankle was medicinal magic. That's easy stuff—any crucible, even mechanics, can do it. But what we did last night was warrior magic. The highest level there is, save one. A simple crucible can't possess a body like that and fill it with the Gift." Rowan started walking again. "You're a witch. And you did it with no training and no willstone of your own."

Lily thought she heard him whisper the word "scary" to himself, and rushed to catch up with him.

"That's utterly ridiculous," sputtered Councilman Roberts.

Gideon shifted in his seat and swallowed the retort that caught in his throat. Councilman Roberts was a dried-out old fool as far as Gideon was concerned, but he had been serving on the Council for more years than anyone—even more than Gideon's father, Thomas Danforth. If Gideon and his father were going to get the rest of the Council to hear them, they'd need his support.

"I'm not quite sure we understand what you're saying," interjected Councilman Wake. He leaned into the round table and crossed his hands neatly in front of him. Wake was a younger man, barely thirty, but he had a reputation for being a shrewd tactician, which was why Gideon and his father had included Wake in this small and secret gathering. "Are you trying to say that the Salem Witch has created a copy of herself out of thin air?" Wake asked.

"Not created," Gideon interrupted, shaking his head. "We think she found another version of herself in another universe and brought that other self here."

A stupefied silence followed.

"What my son means is that there is the *possibility* that something impossible happened," Thomas Danforth said. He laughed nervously. "After all, you can't account for Lillian being in two places at once in any other way besides the impossible."

"Rumors," Roberts spat. "A bunch of drubs in the dungeons claimed they saw another Lillian gadding about the woods with Rowan Fall, when we could all attest that the Witch was in the Citadel. That doesn't make it true."

Thomas Danforth sat back in his chair, deflated. Gideon had always known that his father was not a strong man and that he often caved to the wishes of the other men on the Council. Danforth was well liked among them for exactly that reason. Knowing his father wasn't going to find the strength to convince the Councilmen, Gideon glanced up and looked into the corner of the room. Carrick stood with his back to the wall, huddled under a dark cloak, so that he nearly disappeared inside his own glowering shadow.

"Tell them what you told me about the shamans of your people," Gideon ordered.

"Now he's talking about shamans—the craziest of all the drubs," Roberts muttered incredulously to Wake, throwing up his hands. Roberts leaned imploringly across the table toward the final member of that evening's covert cabal, Councilman Bainbridge, who had until this point remained silent. "Don't tell me *you* believe any of this nonsense, Bainbridge?"

Bainbridge's face was stony. He wasn't nearly as old as Roberts, but he was just as respected. He had a lot of innovative ideas, and had been elected by the citizenry in his district by a huge majority. He also had more reason than most to hate the near-totalitarian rule of the Lady of Salem's Coven, as Lillian had squashed several of his pet projects for being "too scientific."

"I'm not saying I believe it or don't believe it," Bainbridge said equitably. "But I am wondering why Lillian's head mechanic would call this meeting to begin with."

Gideon knew what Bainbridge's problem was. Why would someone whose power hinged on the Witch want to meet with three men who had so long opposed the overreaching power of the Witch and her Coven? Gideon could sense Bainbridge's caution. Gideon could be working for Lillian, trying to root out those who opposed her. But these men of the Council could never understand Gideon's frustration. They had no magic. They had no idea what it was to be a mechanic who was claimed by a witch—no, *chained* to a witch— who wouldn't use him.

"Because I've worked with witches long enough to understand why the Council hates them." Gideon heard the edge of spite in his voice, and made no attempt to rein it in. "The Council is supposed to be equal in power to the Coven, and the two bodies of government are supposed to balance each other so no one group has too much power. But we know that's rubbish. If the Coven doesn't get what it wants all it has to do is put an embargo on electricity, medicine, meat, clean water—or any one of the dozens of things that witches supply the citizenry—until the people who elected *you* to stand up for *them* against the total control of the nonelected Coven demand that you give in to their wishes. How the hell is that democracy?"

"So all of this is for democracy's sake?" Bainbridge asked with one raised eyebrow. Yet despite his disdain, Gideon could tell he was intrigued.

"The witch system has to go," Gideon said finally, and watched the nervous glances dart around the table.

"Or rather, there needs to at least be an alternative to all the things the Covens supply the people, or the Council will never have any real power," Danforth interjected quickly.

Roberts was already shaking his head. "And where are we supposed to get these things? The people need energy and food and medicine—how are we supposed to supply that for them? Not even witches can pull something out of nothing."

"Really?" Gideon asked pleasantly. "Carrick. Would you please tell the distinguished gentleman of the Council about the shamans of your people?" he repeated pointedly.

Carrick's deep voice rose up out of the darkness around him, like a bit of shadow had been turned into sound. "The shamans say that there are an infinite number of worlds, all of them different, and that their spirits can travel to them and come back."

"And are these other worlds full of resources like energy and food and medicine?" Gideon asked.

"All that and more," Carrick promised quietly. "The shamans say that everything you could possibly imagine is real in some world somewhere."

"Nonsense," Roberts scoffed. "That spirit-walking stuff is a tall tale used to comfort poor Outlander children when they realize their lot in life."

"But what if it's true?" Danforth proposed quietly. "An infinite number of worlds with an infinite number of resources . . ." He trailed off dramatically, and for the first time, Gideon understood why his father was head of the Council. He had a knack for using greed to get everyone in line with his agenda.

"If Lillian has found a way to bring a person from one world into another, is it so hard to imagine that other things could be brought as well—the very things we lack, for instance?" Gideon added smoothly, after a suitable pause.

Bainbridge looked Gideon in the eye. "We'd need proof that other worlds exist before we make any move against Lillian."

"It's easy enough," Carrick suggested quietly. "Find Rowan Fall, and you'll find the other Lillian. Ask her where she came from."

Bainbridge grew quiet, internalizing all the ramifications. He shook his head suddenly. "No. Fall still has all of the Witch's favor and protection. She was always especially fond of him."

"And he profited by it," Roberts said lewdly. "I hear he owns the whole building he lives in. Great neighborhood, too. Could charge whatever he wants for rent in that area and make a fortune."

Gideon stifled another wave of frustration. The Council always was jealous of the Coven's wealth, and they begrudged how well the Coven paid anyone who worked for them—from the lowliest farmers who maintained the greentowers all the way up to the mechanics who were practically showered with riches.

"Does he still draw a salary from the Coven?" Wake asked, like the bean counter he was.

"No," Gideon answered sharply, hoping to end this line of conversation. "I'm Lillian's head mechanic now. What does it matter how well Lillian paid him?"

Roberts smirked at Gideon. "Proves how much the Witch cared for Fall, doesn't it? Their fondness for each other is practically anecdotal. The two of them may have had a tussle over that business with his father, but magical folk are queerly tied to each other with all of the claiming nonsense. Much more than regular flesh and blood and common sense would deem suitable, in my opinion. All of this hullaballoo could be that this 'other Lillian' is simply the Salem Witch visiting her favorite."

"In the Woven Woods?" Gideon interjected incredulously. "Not very likely."

"But far more likely than what you're suggesting," Bainbridge countered. "No, you can't openly challenge Rowan Fall without Lillian knowing. And even if he is no longer drawing a salary, she's made it clear that Rowan Fall is still to be afforded all the privileges of a head mechanic. Making a move against Fall is far too risky. You need to find your proof elsewhere."

"Yes," Wake agreed, his pensive tone matching Bainbridge's, "we'd need proof to convince the whole Council and a plan for how to access these other worlds, before we'd sanction you making any move against the Witch or Rowan Fall."

Even still, they were terrified of challenging Rowan. He was so legendary they wouldn't oppose him—even though Rowan no longer had the strength of the Salem Witch in him. *Gideon* was her head mechanic now, but they all seemed to overlook that fact. Either that or they knew that Lillian had never once given him the Gift. It galled Gideon. A disdainful breath escaped him, and Roberts was quick to chastise him for it.

"You're not the only one who'd swing if this cockamamie idea of yours turns out to be nothing but a middle-of-the-woods tryst between two reunited lovers," Roberts said hotly. "The Witch is awful fond of hanging people who oppose her these days, and you'll get no support unless you have enough evidence to get the *entire* Council on our side. I reckon not even she can hang half the government. In the meantime, I suggest you watch your thoughts carefully, young Danforth." Roberts gestured to Gideon's willstone, dangling at his throat. "If Lillian gets one whiff that you're disloyal, she'll root this meeting out of your memories in a heartbeat. And then, well— we'll all meet again at the gallows."

CHAPTER
8

LILY AND ROWAN REACHED THE EDGE OF TOWN AT DUSK. From a distance, Lily could see the towers of greenery soaring up into the air between the tall buildings, but as they approached, the colossal wall encircling Salem blotted out the city behind it. Lily tried to locate the end of the wall, but it stretched for miles in either direction.

"I'm going to have to smuggle you in. I hope the tunnel that leads to the Swallows is still up and running," Rowan mumbled, more to himself than to Lily.

"Tunnel?" Lily interjected nervously. She didn't like small, dark places, especially if they were underground. Lily didn't even like the thought of going down into her basement at home, let alone through a strange tunnel. She also didn't like the idea of going to any part of town named the Swallows, but that was the least of her worries. "My hair is so different, and it's getting dark," she argued. "Maybe no one will recognize me?"

Rowan shook his head. "You don't have a willstone, Lily."

"Yeah. And?" Lily asked desperately. She really didn't want to go underground.

"So you won't get in." Rowan let out a tense breath and dove in. "There's a string of numbers stored in everyone's willstone. It's your citizenship number. A related but much simpler kind of crystal— it's called a lattice—can locate and read this number and—" Rowan realized he was rambling and dragged a frustrated hand through his hair. "Basically, our willstones are our identification. Guards check everyone's willstone with a lattice for their citizenship number. You can't get through any of the Salem gates after dusk without one. On top of that, it's just *weird* to see someone over the age of seven without a willstone. You'd get stopped for that no matter who you look like."

"Okay," Lily said, backing off in the face of Rowan's obvious disquiet even if the thought of going underground still made her shaky. "Forget I said that. You lead, I'll follow."

"Oh, so you *can* be reasonable?" he quipped. "Every day, a new surprise."

"Quiet, you." Lily giggled as he took her hand and pulled her tight to his side. "Before I change my mind and throw a hissy fit."

The light mood didn't last long. Rowan's face darkened again as he brought Lily along the edge of the wall. Outside one of the huge gates was a shantytown of traders who had formed a rustic-looking fairground. The dark-haired, dark-eyed people in the caravan were packing in their wares for the night, pulling down the shutters of the armored carriages that doubled as merchant booths. Rowan led Lily into the maze of stalls, keeping her close.

"Don't look up at anyone," he whispered in her ear. Lily tilted her head down but she could still feel the Outlanders watching them. Rowan hurried her past the few who stopped to stare.

"Do they recognize me?" she asked anxiously.

"No. They're curious to see who's coming in from the Woven Woods alone, on foot, and uninjured," he answered. "It doesn't happen often."

Lily nodded her understanding and angled herself behind him, tucking as close as she could to the curve of Rowan's shoulder. She glanced up to the top of the city wall and could see guards moving around up there, the distance shrinking them to the size of mice.

"I don't understand," she said. "I thought Lillian was hunting the Outlanders."

"Just those pledged to Alaric. His tribe harbors scientists and fights for Outlander rights, but there are plenty of tribes that abide by Coven law." Rowan's mouth slid into a half smile. "Or so they say."

As they neared the center of the fairground, the muddy dirt paths turned to wooden walkways and the armored carriages grew larger and seemed more entrenched in their positions. Children ran around, playing chasing games. It was a neighborhood of sorts, protected by the carriages along the perimeter and by the guards on the wall a hundred feet above them. Lily could smell food cooking. She heard Rowan's stomach growl and thought for a moment that she could feel the twist of hunger inside of him.

"Can we buy food at one of the stalls?" she asked quietly in his ear. "You need to eat."

"I've got you," Rowan replied, pulling her more tightly to him. "Food can wait."

"Unbelievable. And you call me stubborn," she mumbled. She'd meant it as a joke, but as soon as the words were out of her mouth, she realized how true it was. She and Rowan were a lot alike. In fact, Lily didn't think she'd ever met anyone so much like her before.

"Fall," a man said, hailing them from the shadows. Rowan stopped, his hand sliding up to the knife at his belt.

Rowan said something to the man in a language Lily couldn't even begin to fathom. It sounded alternately guttural and nasal, and she thought maybe she'd heard it during the meeting of the elders, but she'd never guessed Rowan spoke it as well.

The man stepped into the light, revealing himself, and Rowan dropped his hand, tipping his chin up in a terse greeting. "We need to get into Salem," Rowan said quietly.

Without a word, the man turned and Rowan began following him.

What's the matter, Lily? You look startled.

What language was that?

It was a few words of Iroquois and a few of Sioux. I didn't know what tribe he was from, so I tried a couple.

So cool. I knew you weren't exactly white, but I didn't think you were part Native American.

Rowan looked at her strangely. *What the hell is a Native American?*

It's what we call . . . Forget it. Lily felt like an idiot.

The man brought them away from the main walkway and behind a row of larger, more ornate carriages that were nearly the size of houses. They turned a corner and entered a small, hidden alley. The man stopped, looked around anxiously, and then bent to lift a portion of the wooden walkway. Beneath the false boards was a tunnel and a rickety ladder leading down into the dark. Rowan briefly clasped the man's hand in thanks and began descending the ladder. Lily followed, never once looking up at the man, although she felt him trying to search her averted face.

As soon as the wooden slats were placed back over the hole, Rowan's willstone flared to life. It shed enough light so Lily could see the rungs beneath her hands but little else. Upon reflection, she decided that the fact that she couldn't see just how deep the drop went was a good thing. After a few seconds of descending, Lily got vertigo and stopped. She kept imagining a rung on the ladder breaking under her foot and then plummeting into the unseen depths below.

"It's okay, Lily," Rowan whispered. "These tunnels are only a few years old. The ladder is really strong."

Lily took a deep breath. "I hate the dark, Rowan. I've always hated the dark."

"I know. You're a witch." His voice was low and comforting, even though she didn't really understand what he was talking about. Lily felt his hand wrap around one of her ankles and him giving her a small stream of soothing heat and energy. "I won't let you fall."

Lily steeled herself and continued her descent. They went down one ladder, turned and went down another, and then started down a long tunnel. Beams buttressed the ceiling, but they offered Lily little comfort. They were down so deep, and the tunnel was so narrow that it seemed at any moment the walls could come caving in. The smell of earth and clay reminded Lily of her mother at her potter's wheel. Worry suddenly jangled through Lily like a sour note.

I'm okay, Mom, she thought fervently. *Please don't do anything stupid.*

After twenty minutes of walking through the tunnel, they reached another ladder and began to climb. Rowan went first. Lily could hear voices and the sound of footsteps above them. He turned and told Lily to stop when she was only halfway up the ladder.

"Stay here until I come get you," he whispered. Rowan reached the top, knocked at the hatch in code, and it swung open. He climbed out and quickly closed the hatch behind him.

In the dark, without even the faint blue glow from Rowan's willstone, Lily felt disoriented and vaguely dizzy. She held close to the ladder while she listened to Rowan talking to a few men and a woman above her. Lily inched up the ladder until she could make out what they were saying, her arms shaking with the effort to hold on.

"I haven't heard any word from Caleb or the sachem," the

woman was saying. "But Tristan's in town. I saw him at a bonfire last night."

"Is it true?" a man asked. "You captured Lillian?"

"No," Rowan said. "But I do have someone with me. And I need to keep it quiet."

"You've never hid anyone from us before," the woman said sharply. "Don't tell me she's *with* you." A pregnant pause followed. "Did you give yourself to a new witch?" she persisted, her voice shrill with jealousy.

"I need food, a selection of blank willstones, and your discretion," Rowan replied, clipping his words. "Now," he added quietly. Footsteps shuffled off in different directions.

A few minutes later, the footsteps returned. One of the men asked what the willstones were to be used for. Rowan didn't answer and instead requested that everyone leave the room. After another pause, Lily heard reluctant footsteps moving out of the space above her. The hatch opened and Rowan's head appeared. She sighed with relief and made her way up to him, her hands cramping from holding on to the rungs so tightly.

He pulled Lily up out of the hatch and kept her hand. Moving her quickly through the small safehouse and out into the bustling streets of the city, Rowan reminded her again to keep her eyes down and to stay behind him. She kept her head down as they moved through a place with brightly colored lights. An acid-purple flash caught her eye, and Lily had to look up to see what it was.

"What are *those*?" Lily gasped.

The streets were lined with rows of glowing trees on either side of the road. The trunks of the trees only gave off a little bit of light, but the leaves were bright enough to cast shadows. Oak trees canopied into purple brilliance overhead. Willow trees cascaded glinting pink branches. Lily glanced down a side street and saw hues of green and blue, while this street was predominantly pink and purple, almost as if the streets were color-coded.

"What are *what*?" Rowan growled. "Didn't I just tell you to keep your eyes down?"

"The trees, Rowan. The trees are freaking glowing."

"Yeah," he said, amused by Lily's obvious shock. "They share properties with deep-sea creatures that naturally create their own light. Witches married the aspects of the sea creatures that made them glow with the seeds of the trees to provide free light at night in the cities. They look normal during the day, though. They only glow in the dark."

"Bioluminescent trees instead of streetlamps," Lily mumbled, awed not just by the beauty, but also by the cleverness behind their creation.

"Oh, the richer neighborhoods still use streetlamps—just to prove they can afford it. Now will you *please* look down?" Rowan asked, smiling.

Lily obeyed. In the eerie, almost neon light, she couldn't see much more than the dirty concrete beneath her feet and the swing of pedestrians' arms and legs as they walked. But even with her eyes downcast, she noticed people stepping out of Rowan's way and then stopping to take a second look as he and Lily passed.

"Everyone's staring," she hissed.

"It's okay. They don't know who you are."

"Then why are they looking at us?"

"Because they know who I am." Rowan paused before continuing. "And they're not used to seeing me with a girl."

They wove through a brightly lit neighborhood that used electric lights as well as bioluminescent trees. They passed bars and restaurants that spilled strange, thumping music and even stranger-looking people onto the streets. Lily couldn't quite put her finger on the style of dress. Some of the women wore wearhyde breeches and boots with tunics or jackets over them, and some wore gowns and gloves. There was no distinct time period of dress, at least not any time period from Lily's world.

Walking quickly through what Lily assumed was the young and trendy part of town, they made their way to a quieter, more polished neighborhood. The buildings were a bit taller here, and instead of foot traffic, there seemed to be more of the silent automobiles that Rowan had called elepods.

"What do they run on?" Lily asked, watching a particularly sleek one glide by.

"Electricity," Rowan answered. He bounded up the outside steps of a six-story brownstone, his spirits visibly lifting.

Lily followed him up the steps. She gestured to a shining streetlamp. "What do you use as a power source? Oil, coal, natural gas?"

Rowan gave her a puzzled look. "Witches are our power source. I wasn't kidding when I made that comment about who runs this place. Witches literally run our world, Lily." He waved his hand in front of the door. His willstone glowed slightly and the door slid open. "And they never let us forget it," he added under his breath.

Rowan pulled Lily inside and practically ran up the steps to the top floor. He waved his hand in front of the penthouse door, and it opened, but before he let Lily inside, he paused and closed his eyes. His willstone glowed brightly and then faded. He opened his eyes and smiled at Lily.

"Come on in. It's safe," he said.

Lamps flared to life as Rowan passed them, revealing a large loft space with hardwood floors, soaring ceilings studded with skylights, huge windows along two sides, and graceful columns throughout the central area. Simple, elegant furniture created distinct living spaces like a sitting area, library, and dining room, without the use of walls. It was a beautiful, modern-looking space, vastly different from the tents and cabins that Lily had heretofore associated with Rowan. And yet both environments suited him. He was just as at home in this tasteful penthouse as he was roughing it in the woods. Lily followed Rowan through his apartment with an intrigued smile on her face, wondering if he was ever going to stop surprising her.

He headed straight for the kitchen, removing his backpack along the way. He shucked off his jacket, took the supplies he'd been given at the safehouse out of his pack, and placed them on the island in the kitchen before turning to wash his hands in the sink.

"Okay. So no meat for Lily," he mumbled, organizing the groceries on the counter. Lily sat on one of the stools on the dining room side of the island and watched while Rowan gathered pots and pans on the other. In a few minutes, he was whipping up an entire meal, stealing famished bites off an apple as he worked.

"You can really cook," she said, marveling at how he wielded his knife as he cut vegetables. "That's amazing."

His eyes flashed up at hers while he chopped, the relaxed look of them pinning her to her seat. "I love to cook. And not just in a cauldron." A pleased smile lingered on his lips as he put the veggies in a sauté pan and turned them with a deft flick of his wrist. His dexterity fascinated Lily, and she caught herself staring at him. "You can bathe if you want while I get this ready," he said, oblivious to her rapt attention. He lowered the heat under the sauté pan and wiped his hands on a dish towel. "I'll get you set up."

Rowan took her to a big bathroom and twisted the taps over a claw-footed tub. He tested the heat with his fingers and sprinkled some salts into the water. The scent that rose up with the steam was distinctly masculine. There was something intensely intimate about the thought of bathing in Rowan's scent, and Lily felt suddenly embarrassed.

"I can take it from here," she said, sitting next to him on the side of the tub. She tested the water with her hand and found that Rowan had chosen a perfectly cool temperature for her. *Of course*, she thought. *He knows more about my body than I do.* "You have a beautiful home. Thank you for letting me stay here with you."

His brow furrowed, as if what she'd said troubled him. "You're thoughtful. Considerate," he murmured. "You're still stubborn as hell, but you take other people's feelings into account. It's not all *your* way all the time. You have no idea how much that means to me." His eyes drifted down, and he lingered for a moment next to her, his fingers still stirring the water. "I'm sorry I was so horrible to you when we first met." Lily saw a glimmer of magelight under Rowan's shirt. In her mind, she saw an image of herself, crying and clutching at her twisted ankle in the dark forest. She experienced intense feelings of regret and shame—his regret and shame. "I'm especially sorry for that."

Lily couldn't get her voice to function so she just nodded. She knew that he'd opened himself up to her so she wouldn't just hear the word "sorry," but could feel how deeply he meant it. It was the most heartfelt apology she'd ever been given, and as soon as Lily grasped how generous it was of him to share such thorny emotions with her, she reached out to him in thanks. But he stood up and moved away before she could take his hand.

"Towel. Robe," he said, pointing to the items hanging from hooks on the back of the door as he named them, and then he left her alone.

Still shaken by Rowan's closeness and abrupt departure, Lily peeled off her clothes and lowered herself gingerly into the scented water. As she soaked away her aches and pains, she tried not to think too much about how she'd gotten them. She failed. The gruesome battle with the Woven and the memory of the fear-drenched hike through the forest made her restless even as she tried to relax. But it was the face of that old history teacher as he was being beaten to death that finally drove her from the incongruous comfort of the tub. She knew that experience would be with her for the rest of her life, and she hoped someday she would be able to make peace with it.

Lily dried herself off, wiped steam from the mirror, and took her first look at the new haircut. She didn't recognize herself. Wet, her hair looked black, and her eyes glowed bright green in contrast. Lily rumpled her curls with her hand, squeezing out the water. The back was clipped so short it felt nearly shaved at the nape. It didn't look bad, she admitted, just drastically different from what she was used to.

Still missing her long hair, Lily sighed and wrapped Rowan's robe around her. It was way too big on her, and the collar slouched down off her shoulders, but it was clean and comfortable. She left the bathroom and wandered down the hall toward the delicious smell coming from the kitchen.

Rowan was serving the finished meal onto plates when she joined him. He looked up at her and paused for a moment, his eyes resting on her bare neck. He turned and put the last pan in the sink and ran water over it. "Perfect timing," he said over his shoulder.

Lily waited for him to sit, rolling up the sleeves of his robe until she could actually find her fingers, and then they both descended on their food like vultures. He'd made her a lentil and pasta dish, steamed artichokes, and a baked red pepper stuffed with something like herbed polenta that she'd never encountered before. It was so delicious she made delighted noises while she ate, earning several satisfied grins from Rowan. When they were finished, they both leaned back in their chairs, too tired to do much more than stare at each other hazily.

"Thank you, Rowan. That was wonderful," Lily said. He nodded in acknowledgment. "You cooked; I'll clean." She stood and started grabbing plates.

"Leave them," he said, standing.

"I don't mind."

"Tomorrow." He came around the table and put his hands on Lily's wrists, guiding the plates back down to the table. His gaze was warm and his voice low. "I appreciate it, I really do. But it's bedtime."

Her eyes were level with Rowan's willstone, resting high on his breastbone under his clothes. She thought about touching it and about the sharp, almost painful awareness of him that had followed. The memory made her shake. Her eyes flicked up to his and she froze. His fingers fanned out across the insides of her wrists, smoothing over the soft, sensitive skin there before he suddenly pulled away from her.

"You need sleep," he said in a wavering voice.

He led her down the hallway, past the bathroom she had used, and into a large bedroom with a vaulted ceiling that was crowned with a faceted skylight. Stairs led up to a dais, where a wide bed dominated the otherwise uncluttered, almost empty room. Rowan led her up the steps, turned down the snowy-white comforter, and folded her between the crisp sheets.

"Sleep," he repeated, tucking her in, and then he turned and left the room.

The lights dimmed and went out as Rowan walked past them. Seeing his large silhouette pausing in the doorway for a last-second check on her filled Lily with a sense of well-being. Sleep seized her like a fever, wrestling her under within seconds.

Gideon let himself into Rowan's building and climbed the six flights of stairs. Rowan hadn't changed the outside wards, but Gideon was certain he'd changed the ones on his apartment. He'd had Carrick check them.

Gideon knew he wasn't supposed to do this. It had only been a few hours since the meeting with the Council members, and he still hadn't managed to swallow the bitter taste in his mouth. They were so frightened of Rowan. So scared of any miscalculation around the Witch that they would let the discovery of the century slip through their fingers.

The Council simply didn't have enough imagination to understand how important this other version of Lillian could be. She could change the balance of power in this world if Gideon could prove she existed.

Gideon knocked at Rowan's door and waited, ignoring the impulse to call to him with mindspeak. Not that it would work anyway. He and Rowan were no longer stone kin. Rowan had smashed his stone when he'd left Lillian and had been using a new stone for the past year, one that Gideon wasn't in tune with. Gideon touched the willstone at his throat, his skin crawling at the thought. He'd seen another mechanic suffering after his stone had been smashed, and Gideon could only imagine that it was like cutting off an arm or putting out an eye. After the guy had recovered, he'd bonded with another willstone, but it took weeks before he could do more than moan. Gideon had always known Rowan was strong, but to smash his own stone? That was something Gideon would never even consider.

He knocked again. He knew Rowan was home. He also knew that there was a girl with him. In all the years he'd known Rowan— and even during this past year when he hadn't had any contact with him at all—Rowan had never taken any girl but Lillian home with him. True, Gideon's spies had reported that Rowan was with a dark-haired Outland girl, but hair was easy enough to dye. Gideon knew she had to be this other Lillian that he needed. He felt it. And the Council would thank him for this later, even if he was going against their wishes.

The door opened. Rowan appeared to have just taken a bath. He wore only a pair of loose, drawstring linen pants, his hair wet, and there was a patch of stubble and shaving milk on his neck, still waiting for the razor. Gideon smiled, repressing the urge to hit the handsome bastard. He just kept getting better looking every damn year.

"Hi, Rowan," he said smoothly. "Bit late for a shave, isn't it?"

"Gideon," Rowan replied, his expression stony. "What are you doing here?"

"May I come in?"

"What are you doing here?" Rowan repeated. He angled his shoulders to block the door.

"I'm trying to help you." Gideon sighed heavily. "There's a rumor going around."

"A rumor," Rowan prompted blankly.

"Something that might get back to Lillian, make her ask questions." Gideon searched Rowan's eyes for a flicker of fear, or the uncertainty of a lie, but he saw nothing. It was strange to look at Rowan and have no way into his mind. He hadn't anticipated that, although he knew he should have. They'd never liked each other—in fact, Gideon knew that Rowan despised him—but being stone kin for so many years had forced them to be closer than brothers.

Up until a year ago, Lillian had not claimed either Gideon or Tristan, and they had been forced to work through Rowan's mind for years in order to remain in her inner circle. Gideon had never become stone kin with Tristan, but in order to even pretend he was a true mechanic, which many people doubted, Gideon and Rowan had, and they'd spent hours in each other's heads. Now all Gideon heard from Rowan was implacable silence. Gideon had never once considered that he wouldn't be able to read Rowan, and at the moment, all Gideon saw was a very large, very lithe Outlander with a razor in his hand. They were strangers now, and Gideon suddenly doubted the wisdom of coming here at all. "A lot of people saw you around town tonight with a girl."

"That was fast. You must have hired more spies." Rowan put his hands on his hips. They were hard hands—hands that were used to hitting things—unlike Gideon's. "Get to the point, Gideon."

"Is she here?" Gideon looked over Rowan's shoulder and saw two sets of dirty dishes on the table. "Apparently, she is. I'm surprised. It's not like you to leave a mess."

"We had better things to do than dishes."

Gideon raised an eyebrow at Rowan. If she wasn't the other Lillian, Rowan wouldn't work so hard to protect her from view. The fact that Rowan was fighting Gideon was a good sign. "May I meet her?" he asked casually.

Lily woke in Rowan's big bed. There was a palpable tension in the air. She got up and wandered toward the sound of voices. She couldn't make out distinct words just yet, but even so, Rowan's tone didn't sound right to her. She still wasn't sure exactly how to initiate mind-speak, but she reached out to him anxiously, and he sensed it.

Don't come out here, Lily. I don't want Gideon to see you.

Lily peeked around the corner and saw Rowan standing at the door, talking to a young man with blond hair and a doughy, pallid face. Gideon. He had just asked Rowan if he could meet her.

"She's sleeping, Gideon," Rowan replied. His voice slid down to an insinuating drawl. "And she's very tired."

"Really?" Gideon said doubtfully. "You know, I was convinced you'd never give yourself to another witch. She must be quite powerful to claim you."

"Hey, back up," Rowan said, laughing. "We just met. Nobody said anything about claiming anyone. I'm just having some fun."

"I don't believe that," Gideon said, shaking his head. "There isn't a witch in the Thirteen Cities who hasn't tried to claim you, and you've turned them all down. You'd never settle for less than Lillian. So whomever you've got in your bed is someone special. Someone powerful." His voice dropped conspiratorially. "Who is she?"

"I hate to break it to you, but she's not a witch. She's just some Outland girl I met." Rowan shrugged. "It's been a long time, okay? Would *you* go more than a year without a woman?"

Gideon smirked at Rowan. "Don't try to compare us. You're nothing like me, Rowan. You never have been," Gideon said, and realizing he'd get nothing out of Rowan, he turned and left.

Stay there, Lily. I have to strengthen the wards.

Rowan closed the door. His willstone sent a pulse of rippling magelight across the room. Every crevice in his apartment was touched by the undulating wave of oily light, and then it faded.

Following the strange string that connected her to him, Lily could sense a trace of Rowan's awareness lingering on everything that his magelight had touched. She took a moment to consider what he had done and understood that the windows and the walls were as sealed as the storage chest in the cabin had been, just on a much larger scale. Nothing they said or did could be seen or heard by anyone outside Rowan's ward of protection, and if anyone tried to disturb the barrier, he would know it as certainly as he would know if someone placed a hand on his shoulder.

"It's okay. You can come out now," he said out loud. Lily stepped away from the wall and stood facing Rowan. He was biting his lower lip, thinking, while he considered her with worried eyes.

"He was the kid I saw in your memory," she said. "One of Lillian's mechanics, along with you and Tristan."

"Yeah," he replied, his eyes far away. "He's her head mechanic now. He was the only one willing to do her dirty work when she came back so changed."

"He beat that old man to death," Lily said, shrugging his robe up over her shoulders.

"He's done worse to others," Rowan said quietly. "I've been inside his mind. Gideon doesn't feel things the way normal people do." Rowan shook his head like he couldn't believe it. "And now he's after you."

"Do you think he knows who I am?" Lily asked.

"He might. I don't know," Rowan replied.

"So why is he after me? Why does he care?"

"Why does he *care*?" Rowan repeated, frustrated. "You have no idea what you mean, do you?" His eyes searched hers.

Lily shrugged. She supposed her importance must have something to do with her being a copy of the Salem Witch. But Lily had no idea how to do anything even remotely witchy, at least not without Rowan telling her how to do it, so she didn't really see how that could benefit anyone except maybe Rowan. In Lily's estimation, she was just an odd glitch in the cosmological equation. She wasn't important. She was weird.

"Gideon's coming for you, Lily," Rowan continued in a hushed voice. "He's not going to stop just because I wouldn't let him into my apartment."

Rowan was scared of Gideon—as scared of him as he was of the Woven.

"Can you hide me from him?" she asked.

"Not forever. You need to be able to hide yourself. To defend yourself." Rowan's shoulders slumped and he seemed to give up. He suddenly moved to the kitchen. "I didn't want to do this. But I can't leave you helpless."

Lily followed him. He took a velvet jeweler's envelope out of his backpack, untied the strings and unfolded it, revealing a few dozen ovoid stones of varying sizes. They were such a dull gray color that at first Lily didn't recognize them for what they were.

"Willstones," she said, frowning. "But they look . . . I don't know. Dead."

"Because they're unkeyed. There's no mind inside them yet. Do you still want one?" Lily nodded, and Rowan regarded her seriously. "There's no going back after this. It will change you forever."

Lily was imagining herself back home, trying to explain her glowy necklace to Tristan, when she realized she hadn't thought about her own Tristan in days. Their failed attempt at a relationship seemed so far away after what she'd been through. She met Rowan's eyes. "I'm already changed forever," she said.

Rowan looked away, his mouth a grim line. "Okay."

He took a butter knife out of a drawer, picked up the velvet envelope, and led Lily down the hall to his bedroom. Straightening the mussed comforter, he directed Lily to climb onto the bed and get comfortable. Rowan sat opposite her and used the butter knife to separate the willstones on the velvet between them.

"Hold your hand about a foot over them, palm down," he directed. "Pass your hand over them slowly, one at a time. The stronger your talents are, the more this ritual affects you. This is going to be very hard, but whatever you do, don't pull your hand away."

Lily did as he said, and immediately felt a thrumming in her hand. "I feel something."

"Stay relaxed. Let it happen," Rowan replied. He leaned forward, watching her intently. "I'm right here, Lily. You're safe."

Lily looked up at him, his reassurance worrying her, and she wondered how strong the sensation was going to get. The stones began to shiver on the velvet, and the thrumming in Lily's hand became heat. She moved her hand over the array of stones slowly as Rowan had instructed. The heat grew to a burning itch under her skin. It spread up her arm, crawling under her skin like a disease.

"Is it almost over?" she asked through gritted teeth.

"I know it's hard. I'm right here." Rowan's voice was low and soothing. She felt the string between them tighten, as if he were pulling her closer to him without moving. "Breathe slowly, Lily. In and out."

Lily realized she was panting. Sweat broke out on her upper lip. She tried to slow her breath and relax as Rowan had instructed her, but the sensation was alarming. It was worse than pain. It felt as if she were being invaded. "I think something's wrong, Rowan," she gasped. "I don't think it's supposed to be like this."

"You're growing another limb made out of crystal. The rest of your body will try to stop it like it's an infection, but it isn't. Fight the instinct to pull your hand away."

The itch was intolerable. Her stomach churned with sick acid. Her heart pattered randomly like rain on a roof. "I'm scared."

"I'm here. Be brave, Lily. You can do this."

Her whole body felt like it was burning. Sweat trickled between her breasts, soaked her hair, and dripped off the end of her nose. The itch clawed at her until she wanted to dig her skin off. Lily forced herself to keep her hand over the willstones even though it felt like holding her hand over an open flame—like her flesh was crisping and melting off her bones.

"It hurts," she whimpered.

"I know, Lily. I know it hurts," Rowan said, his voice rough.

Three stones lit up and began to glow. A large one maintained a steady brightness, but two smaller ones twinkled and flared as if they were trying to muscle their way in and outshine the big one.

"You're nearly there. Keep going."

In desperation, a part of her reached out and grabbed on to the string connecting her to Rowan. She clung to it while the rest of her thrashed about in a sea of fire. Lily screamed in pain.

At the sound of her scream, all three of the glowing stones jumped off the velvet and smacked into the palm of her hand. Lily wrapped her fingers around them and crumpled onto her side.

The three stones pulsed in her hand, taking their first, tired breaths. Lily pulled her knotted fist up to her face and opened it carefully. Cradled in her palm were three new hearts she would wear outside her skin for the rest of her life. The littlest one had a shy golden glow to it. The medium-size one looked a bit pinkish and even though it was still exhausted from its birth, it somehow managed to flash at Lily like a cheeky little flirt. But it was the largest stone that commanded Lily's focus. It wriggled with platinum filaments of light that rose and sank in the smoky depths of the stone as if it were an endless well of light and dark. The large stone was strong and confident, and Lily knew it could outshine the sun if she asked it to.

"Three stones," Rowan whispered. His face grew fearful. "Unbelievable."

And then she passed out.

Gideon looked up at the window on the top floor. Rowan's wards were so strong that even though Gideon stretched his meager talent as a mechanic to its limits, he couldn't even sense that there were people up there.

A mechanic's first responsibility is to detect the physical needs of his crucible and to alleviate any block or discomfort while she is enspelled, sometimes to the point of keeping her heart beating and her lungs breathing for her while she is transmuting matter and energy. Mechanics were built to be sensitive to physical needs. Even the name "mechanic" came from the fact that first and foremost they were to tend to the machinery of a witch's body while every ounce of her being went into her willstone. And Gideon couldn't even sense a top floor of the building, let alone feel a heartbeat up there. Rowan's strength was terrifying. And infuriating.

When Gideon was young, he used to look at windows at night. Just behind the glass were perfect lives that glowed inside a perfect frame. They always seemed happy with what they had. Gideon didn't know if he envied those people or pitied them, but he couldn't deny that they fascinated him. He realized that he was staring at a window again, wishing he were on the other side of the glass. It had been so long since he'd done that.

"Are you sure she's up there?" Carrick asked.

"She's there," Gideon replied, failing to keep his tone in check. He never should have gone up there. Never should have shown his hand like that to Rowan. Carrick gave him a sideways glance, hearing Gideon's petulance.

"What are your orders?"

"Set up a permanent guard," Gideon snarled. "I want this building watched night and day."

"The Councilmen forbade this."

"The Councilmen are overcautious," Gideon said coolly, finally able to rein in his emotions. Carrick nodded in deference, and Gideon continued. "Only hire guards who haven't been claimed by Lillian. And no one with any ties to the Council or the Coven."

Carrick exhaled sharply. "You don't leave me many options." Carrick regarded Rowan's dark windows for a moment. "I'll need something in return."

Gideon gave him a calculating smile. "How much?"

"Not money," the Outlander replied. "At least, no more than it requires to find the special sort of help you need. No, if I'm going to run this right, I'll need more than money. I need the authority to do it. A title."

Gideon nodded once. "Done. You are now a—what do you think will fit? Captain of the city guard?"

It cost Gideon little to bestow that title. Carrick's salary would be paid by the city of Salem, not him. He could have his father arrange the appointment easily.

Carrick held out his hand, palm up, in the old way. Gideon laid his palm over Carrick's and slid his hand up until the two men were grasping each other's forearms firmly. Gideon briefly recalled that this was an ancient way of proving that you had no blades strapped to your arms and could therefore be trusted. He smiled. Sometimes the Outlander ways were so quaint.

"Done," Carrick replied.

Sunlight was streaming straight down through the skylight when Lily finally awoke. She sat up and looked around.

She felt completely rested for the first time since she'd come to this world. In fact, she'd never felt this good in her life. The sun was warm on her skin. Lily sensed that she could take that energy, change it, and use it for another purpose. She lay in bed, piecing together why she'd always hated the dark. It was because all kinds of heat and light fueled her, and being separated from the light weakened her. Lily opened her hand and looked at her three willstones. Rowan had been right. She was changed forever.

Lily sat up and saw a glass of water on the bedside table. A tiny card was propped up against it. It said, THIRSTY? in bold uppercase letters. Lily realized that she'd never seen Rowan's handwriting before. She stared at it, sipping her water, memorizing every swoop and curve.

She swung her legs out of bed and noticed that she'd somehow struggled out of his robe while she slept. Rowan had left a stack of clothes on the floor next to her, with its own accompanying card that read NAKED? Lily laughed quietly to herself and got dressed. The soft button-down shirt and pajama pants were way too big, but she figured it was better than the robe she'd drenched with sweat during the night.

Lily turned her willstones over in her hand, a stunned smile on her face as she dressed slowly, soaking in every detail. The shape and smell of Rowan's shirt filled her with so much tenderness that she didn't know if she wanted to laugh or cry. Lily realized with a start that she was changed in more ways than one.

She went down the hall, marveling at how aware she was of everything. The feel of the clothes on her body, the texture and springiness of the wooden floor under her feet, everything from the taste of the air to the muffled sound of her steps was clearer to her now. Sharper. Even something as mundane as walking down a hallway became a revelation. She was starting to discern all the different forces at play when she put one foot in front of the other. She could feel the air pressure changing as she moved through it and knew that with a subtle variation in energy—one tiny adjustment inside her willstones—she could will the air around her to be as motionless and silent as a vacuum.

She realized that this was how Rowan could move so quietly and sneak up on her. Thinking she'd give him a taste of his own medicine, Lily silenced her footsteps and moved toward the sound of voices coming from the dining area. She stopped at the same place she'd stood as she waited for Gideon to leave, wondering if Rowan would sense that she was there like he had the night before. She stifled a giggle, imagining jumping out and scaring him.

Rowan and Tristan sat at the table where she and Rowan had eaten dinner the night before. They were drinking tea and speaking in lowered voices. Rowan was dressed in all white—white linen pajama pants and a white T-shirt. She'd gotten so used to seeing him in all black that she was startled for a moment. His hair was tousled, and he looked younger and more vulnerable. He was beautiful. Lily had no idea how he'd become so precious to her so quickly, but he had. She lingered behind the corner, enjoying the rare opportunity of watching the person she adored without him knowing she was there.

"Whatever happened to keeping her out of your head?" Tristan asked, dismayed.

"I didn't have any other choice," Rowan said with a tired shrug. "Believe me. I'm regretting it."

Lily leaned back into the wall, the giddiness she'd felt suddenly chilling and turning to dread inside of her.

"What even gave you the idea?" Tristan asked.

"I thought about how she'd healed her ankle. It was a long shot, but I figured she'd already transmuted energy inside herself using my stone, and it was only one step farther to then pour it back into me."

"That's one hell of a step, though." Tristan paused, then his voice dropped. "Do you think she could invade a stone? Take it over without permission?"

"I don't know. But that is the next step after this one," Rowan said, allowing the thought to hang ominously in the air. He scrubbed his hands over his face a few times. "We're in a lot of trouble."

"Only if she goes bad," Tristan corrected.

Rowan looked at Tristan, and a tense moment passed between them. "She can work inside another person's willstone, she imprinted *three* of her own, and she's just as convinced that she's right about everything as Lillian ever was."

"So what are you saying?" Tristan asked in a low and serious tone. "That we can't trust her?"

Rowan's face looked pained for a moment before it grew unyielding. "No. I don't think we can."

Lily stopped breathing, too stunned to move.

"But she's still her own person, Ro, with a completely different background and upbringing. I don't think we should paint her with Lillian's brush just yet." Rowan didn't answer. "There are things about her that are different," Tristan continued. "She's funny. Did you notice that?"

"Lillian was funny," Rowan replied, a touch defensively.

"No, she wasn't," Tristan said, rolling his eyes. "Rose-colored glasses, my friend."

Rowan changed the subject. "Gideon came poking around. Looking for a witch strong enough to catch my attention."

"One of the prisoners he took from the raid must have talked. Gideon's been on the warpath looking for a new witch in Salem ever since."

A thought occurred to Rowan and he stiffened. "The Woven bodies at the cabin. I burned them, but it left one hell of an ash heap. If Gideon hears about them, he'll know that a witch was involved. A powerful one."

"We can have Caleb send a team up to get rid of them. How many did you kill, anyway?"

"Over forty. She's strong, Tristan. Just as strong as Lillian ever was."

Tristan cursed under his breath. Then he looked up at Rowan and gave him a knowing smile. "How was the claiming?"

Rowan looked down at his tea, frowning. "Too good. And too soon. I wish I could take it back."

They lapsed into silence. Lily wanted to crawl into bed and never get up again, but it would be Rowan's bed, and she didn't want to sleep there ever again. She decided it was no use trying to run away or hide. She took a step, making sure it was audible. Rowan's head snapped around in surprise.

"I didn't hear you come down the hallway," he said.

She shrugged at him coldly and his eyes widened. Lily hoped it was with hurt. She wanted to punish him. After everything they'd been through together, Rowan still believed she was evil. He'd been inside her head, shared some of her most intimate and painful memories, and yet he still thought she was going to become a tyrannical murderer like Lillian. She turned away from him, and toward Tristan.

"It's really good to see you," she said. She smiled warmly at him.

"And you. I like your haircut," Tristan said, smiling back. A blush reddened his cheeks. His eyes darted over to Rowan and his smile faded. "I have clothes for you." He picked up a bundle from beside his chair. "And a message from Juliet."

"Juliet?" Lily said excitedly. She crossed to Tristan. "Is she okay? What happened when she got back to the Citadel? Was she upset with me because I didn't try to mindspeak with her again?"

"Whoa!" Tristan said, holding up a hand. He passed the bundle to Lily, laughing under his breath. "I have no idea about any of those things. The letter's sealed."

Lily had to take the bundle awkwardly with one hand. "I need to put these in a necklace," she said, unclenching her fingers slightly around her willstones.

"May I see?" Tristan asked, leaning forward expectantly.

Lily suddenly felt shy. It was almost like he'd asked to see a mole or a tattoo she had on a sensitive part of her body. She reminded herself that everyone here wore their willstones around their necks and she shouldn't be so touchy about it. She opened her fingers and Tristan inhaled sharply.

"Beautiful," he whispered, his face entranced. His compliment pleased her enormously, although she wasn't quite sure why.

"Thank you," Lily said, grinning. "I'm quite attached to them."

Tristan laughed at her little joke, his breath brushing against her willstones. It sent a pleasant shiver up her back.

"One of each color. What do you think that means?" Tristan asked, and looked up at Rowan, who was watching the two of them with a guarded look.

"Do the different colored stones mean different things?" Lily asked.

"No," Rowan answered. "No one knows why most stones are smoke, some rose, and a very few are golden."

"That's not entirely true, Ro," Tristan countered. He looked at Lily. "Some people say the color of the stone can tell you about the personality of the wearer."

"So what does it mean that I have three stones? That I have multiple personalities?"

Rowan shrugged. "I've heard of powerful witches in the past imprinting more than one stone at a time because there wasn't an available stone large enough to harness her power, but your smoke stone is just about the biggest willstone I've ever seen. I think we're in uncharted territory here, and we need to wait and see." He stood and went to the kitchen. "Are you hungry?"

Rowan cooked for them while Lily changed into the new clothes Tristan had brought her, then took a moment to read Juliet's letter. It didn't say much, other than that Juliet was fine and that she hoped Lily stayed safe. Juliet placed extra importance on Lily staying far away from Gideon. She said he was lurking around, asking questions. Juliet begged her to stay out of sight for her own safety.

As Lily read the signature, "Ever Your Loving Sister, Juliet," it occurred to her that she had been missing from her world for six days. Her Juliet must have been frantic.

"Lily," Tristan asked when she joined them back in the kitchen, "was there bad news in the letter?"

"Not really," she said, smiling briskly. "I just miss my sister. Both versions of her."

For a moment, as Lily stared at her sister's name at the bottom of the letter, she felt as if she would cry. Tristan tactfully changed the subject. He started asking Lily questions about her trek through the woods, and they fell easily into conversation. It felt so normal to be sitting and chatting with him that she could almost ignore the fact that she was in a different world where she didn't belong, until she glanced over at Rowan and noticed him scowling at her. How had she overlooked his open animosity toward her when they were alone in the woods together?

"So, when can I start training?" Lily asked when breakfast was finished. Rowan and Tristan exchanged a look.

I know you two are sharing mindspeak, Rowan. Do me a favor and just say it out loud, okay? I'm not an idiot. Lily didn't even try to hide her annoyance. She wanted him to feel how upset she was, although she was careful to keep the root of that annoyance—how much he'd hurt her—to herself.

Rowan met her eyes, his mouth pursed in anger. "Tonight. If that's alright with you," he said with mock deference.

"The sooner the better," she replied, holding Rowan's angry gaze. *So I can get the hell out of here and away from you.*

Rowan looked away first, but Lily still didn't feel like she'd won.

CHAPTER

9

LILY SPENT THE REST OF THE DAY AT THE KITCHEN TABLE with Tristan, trying to make a necklace out of her willstones, while Rowan was out arranging a meeting with Caleb. During that time, Tristan gave her a crash course in willstones, their properties, and some of the complicated social conventions that had been established to accommodate them.

Even after just one day, Lily had already noticed some of the obvious benefits to having a willstone. She now had a photographic memory. Everything she learned from the moment she bonded with her willstones—every image that passed before her eyes—was recorded and dated and filed away neatly for her to reexamine at any time. All Lily had to do in order to recall an entire conversation, word for word, was think about it. She could read a page in a book and recall it without omitting one letter, although her willstone couldn't make her understand what she read any better. She'd already tested her comprehension by pulling *Meditations on First Philosophy* by René Descartes off Rowan's bookshelf and found it really hard to follow. For now, anyway. She was sure her reading comprehension would expand to keep pace with the library she intended to stuff into her head.

Tristan added to what she'd already discovered by teaching her how to open doors with her willstone by having it communicate with tiny shards of lattice—a willstone-like crystal, but much less complex—that were embedded in the doorframes. Lily thought it was *Star Trek* cool to open doors with her mind. For a good ten minutes, she walked through Rowan's apartment, watching the doors swish open and closed like, well, magic.

Once Tristan managed to get her to stop walking through doorways, he taught Lily how to seal up lattice-lined boxes so no one else could open them unless she willed it. There were so many different ways even a non-magical person could use their willstone that Lily thought it was like having a microcomputer with a ton of handy apps attached to her brain. Lily had always wondered why everyone in this world would choose to bond with a willstone if it made you vulnerable to a crucible or a witch's claiming, but now she understood. Even for the non-magical, willstones were as useful as a laptop, cell phone, keys, ID, and a strongbox combined. The way this world was set up, you simply couldn't get along without one.

But having a willstone *was* a vulnerability—especially for the magically inclined. Tristan stressed several times that while non-magical people couldn't really hurt each other by touching stones, Lily was different. She had to be careful. When she touched someone's stone, she could potentially claim that person if he or she allowed it. Even if the person didn't permit a claiming, Lily, as a witch, could still make that person feel things, both good and bad. A witch could make a person feel just about any sensation—whether taste, sight, sound, or touch—much more intensely just by touching that person's stone. And the stronger the witch, the stronger she could make that sensation. But intensified sensation went both ways.

"You must never, ever let anyone touch your stones. Not unless you really trust him or her," Tristan said. Again. "And only if it's with one of your claimed."

Lily kicked him under the table. "I heard you the first thousand times."

"I'm serious, Lily," he continued, even though he was grinning as though he'd never been serious in his entire life.

"Sure you are," Lily drawled, grinning back.

She suddenly wasn't sure if she was flirting with Tristan or not. It just was so easy to be around him. She wasn't walking on eggshells or constantly second-guessing every look or turn of phrase, as she did when she was with Rowan. She also wasn't hyperaware of Tristan as she was of Rowan. It was like Rowan's skin was always whispering to hers. Like there was another, more meaningful space inside the space between them. Everything felt bigger, brighter, and keener around him. Unfortunately, that included her insecurities as well. Lily's smile disappeared. So did Tristan's.

"Listen," he said, leaning back and regarding her with narrowed eyes. "Even if you're curious to try it with Rowan, just wait, okay? He's as sensitive as a mechanic gets, but he could still really hurt you if you two rush into it."

Lily remembered how Rowan had shivered with agony when she'd handled his willstone roughly. The stronger the magic, the stronger the bond with the willstones, and for witches having a willstone meant having a raw nerve laid bare on your throat. She looked at her three little hearts, beating at their own particular tempos in the palm of her hand, and knew that whatever pain Rowan had felt when she'd been careless with his stone would be ten times worse if he'd done the same to her.

And Rowan didn't trust her. In fact, there were times when Lily was convinced that he hated her.

"Okay," she replied quietly. "I get it, Tristan."

Since it was out of the question for Lily to allow anyone to touch her willstones, she had to make the necklace herself, and she wasn't exactly adept at arts and crafts. Lily finally managed to shake off the nagging sadness she felt over Rowan, but not because what she was doing was particularly soothing.

After three hours of struggling with a pair of pliers and what she was certain had to be the most uncooperative spool of silver wire in the world, Lily pushed through her brainfry and reached the goofy stage of overstimulation.

"It looks like I put them in an ugly cage," Lily said, turning her wreck of a necklace around in her hands. She started laughing. "What a piece of junk."

Tristan cracked up with her. "Three of the prettiest stones I've ever seen and you put them in jail."

Lily laughed even harder. They'd been at it for hours, and all she had to show for her painstaking work was a gnarly lump of metal with some rocks stuck in it. "I can't go out in public wearing this. People will think a fork threw up on my neck."

They heard the front door open, but the giggles had set in for both of them, and they were too wound up to stop.

"Are you two drunk?" Caleb asked from the doorway.

"Caleb," Tristan said, waving him over. "You gotta see this."

Lily held up her necklace. Caleb squinted at it.

"He doesn't even know what it's supposed to be," Tristan said, sending them both into another round of giggles. In the background, Lily saw Rowan come in with bags of groceries and start unpacking them silently. She wiped her streaming eyes and put on her ugly necklace.

"What do you think, Caleb?" she said, waggling her eyebrows at him. "You've got to admit, it takes a special talent to make something as hideous as this."

"It is pretty hideous," he said with a grin, but his smile faded fast. "Three stones," he whispered. "I've never seen that before."

The mood shifted from jovial to serious in seconds as Caleb regarded Lily cautiously. She could feel him fighting with himself, still not sure about whether or not he could trust her. Of course he still doubted her. He'd spent the afternoon with Rowan. As soon as Lily thought this, Rowan turned and came toward her.

"Here," he said, placing a velvet pouch in front of her. Lily opened the pouch and a gorgeous platinum chain spilled into her hand. "Lillian couldn't make her own setting either."

Rowan turned and went down the hallway to the spare bedroom, shutting the door firmly behind him. He'd made his point about how alike she and Lillian were, and the worst part was that he'd done it in a way that Lily couldn't dispute. Fuming, Lily resisted the urge to follow him down the hallway and yell at him. Instead, she untangled the chain and laid it out on the table so she could see it better.

The chain had an open platinum oval pendant that was shaped like a teardrop. Dangling from the teardrop were three smaller, detachable chains of staggered lengths. At the bottom of the three chains were three different-size settings, one for each of Lily's stones. The largest setting hung lowest, the medium above that, and at the top was a tiny, pea-size setting, waiting for her shy golden stone. Lily ran the small chains through her fingers, finding the clasps that detached them from the teardrop easy to work but stable. They wouldn't come off unless she meant to remove them.

"So I can take off two and hide them in my pocket. Make it look like I have the normal number of willstones," Lily said quietly, marveling at how Rowan seemed to consider everything. And marveling at the beauty of the necklace he'd brought her. "You think he could have told us he was going to do this so we didn't waste all day," she said, purposely turning her gratitude into frustration.

"Classic Rowan," Tristan said with a shrug.

Lily fitted her stones into the settings and tamped down the edges securely. She found that she didn't have to do much altering. Rowan had guessed the size and shape of her willstones almost perfectly.

"Where do willstones come from?" she asked, considering her necklace.

"They're grown," Tristan answered. "It's a long, frustrating process, but it'll be part of your training so there's no way out of it." Caleb looked at Tristan sharply. "We have to train her, Caleb," Tristan said out loud, even though Lily guessed that Caleb had just tried to initiate mindspeak. Lily appreciated that Tristan was including her.

"Tristan's right," Rowan said, returning and joining them at the table. He had changed into loose linen pants and a soft white shirt. "And we need to start now."

So you can get the hell away from me, right, Lily?

For a moment, Lily could feel Rowan's tangled emotions. He was furious with her—and with himself for some reason Lily couldn't quite understand. He pushed her mind out of his before she could figure it out.

"Okay," Caleb said, oblivious to the internal battle going on between Lily and Rowan. "But if you're going to train her, I want some kind of a promise out of her first."

"What are you talking about?" Tristan asked.

"I want to know she'll never fight for Lillian," Caleb said, like it was obvious. "She doesn't have to swear to fight for us, but we need to know you two aren't training another evil witch."

"No problem. I promise I'll never fight for Lillian," Lily said gladly. "Is that enough?"

"No, that's not enough," Rowan replied, his eyes narrowed mockingly.

"Well, apart from my word, what else can I give you?"

"Access," he answered. "You have to allow me to ask you questions about your loyalty—in mindspeak, where you can't lie—whenever I feel like it. If you don't answer me, or if you shut me out without allowing me to feel your deeper intentions, we'll kill you."

Lily felt like she'd been kicked in the stomach. Did he really hate her that much?

"Ro," Tristan said, interrupting the long silence. "That is totally out of line."

"No it isn't," Rowan said, turning his glare on Tristan. "If at any point in this process she shuts me out, I think it's fair to assume the worst."

"Because that's what Lillian did, right, Rowan? She shut you out," Tristan said, baiting him. But instead of anger Rowan responded with regret.

"And then she started hanging people," Rowan said quietly. He looked at Lily. "Do you agree to my conditions?"

"Do I have a choice?" she snapped. She sat back in her chair, her throat filling with frustrated tears. If she agreed, it would be like living in a glass room, without even the right to keep her thoughts to herself. But if she didn't, she'd never learn how to get back home. "You win, Rowan. I agree."

He nodded and stood. "Let's get started. Tristan? Do you want to change?"

"Yeah," he replied. He stood and went down the hallway. Apparently, he knew his way around Rowan's apartment because he didn't need to be shown the location of the closet.

"Was there a loose dress in that bundle from your sister?" Rowan asked Lily without looking her in the eye. She nodded. "Put it on. And don't wear anything binding under it."

Lily stood up and stormed down the hallway to the bathroom where she'd left the bundle of clothes. She didn't even consider arguing. This was Rowan's show, and she was just going to play her part until she'd learned enough to get home. Lily stripped naked, slid into what looked like a white silk slip, and joined Rowan back in the main room. He, Caleb, and Tristan were at the far end of the apartment, clearing a large space in front of the fireplace.

Tristan had changed into loose white pants like Rowan, and the two of them had taken off their shirts. Their willstones pulsed on their bare chests. Lily's willstones flared brightly in response, startling her. Rowan, Tristan, and Caleb saw the flash and looked at Lily briefly before returning to their tasks. Lily could feel static in the air. She glanced down and saw the hairs on her arms rising. The ritual was already beginning.

"Do you have enough wood stored?" Caleb asked Rowan.

"On the roof," Rowan replied while he moved a white sofa out of the way. "We're going to start small, anyway. Big magic is something she can do intuitively. It's small magic she has trouble with—it took her forever to figure out how to mindspeak. Just like Lillian."

Tristan rolled up the carpet, exposing the wood floor. "What were you thinking of starting with?" he asked.

"A water purification spell. We can send it as a gift to the sachem."

Rowan opened a door next to the fireplace and took out a large cast-iron cauldron, which he hung on a hook that swung into and out of the fireplace. Tristan shook out a black silk sheet and laid it on the floor in front of the fire.

"Sit," he instructed, leading Lily to the center of the silk sheet. He positioned her with her back to the fireplace.

"Is there anything I can do to help set up?" she asked. All three of the guys paused momentarily to exchange looks.

"I'll be right back with the wood," Caleb said.

"And the bucket of stale rainwater next to the pile, if you can?" Rowan called after him as Caleb left.

Lily waited, feeling a bit stupid just sitting there while Rowan and Tristan scurried around. Tristan laid out a collection of silver knives and a marble mortar and pestle in front of Lily.

Caleb returned with the wood and water. Rowan emptied the bucket of fetid, brownish water into the cauldron and started a fire. Lily could feel something in her switch on, like a factory coming to life.

Rowan knelt in front of Lily with a collection of herbs, flowers, and crumbly stones. He picked up one of the silver knives and after calling each herb by name, cut pieces of them and put them in the mortar. He picked up another knife, and after naming each element in what Lily now recognized as part of the ritual, he scraped different amounts of each into the mortar. He ground it all together, stopping every now and again to check the consistency. Then he held the concoction out to Lily.

"Let your thoughts be pure. Let your will remove all taint," he said, his voice low. "Breathe on it."

Lily leaned forward, feeling the touch of Rowan's mind guiding hers, and blew. Her willstones flared, the small golden one shining brightest, and for a moment, she saw the chemical compound that they had created. She also saw how the energy she had imparted on the mixture with her breath would strengthen it and make it multiply. Rowan's eyes closed briefly, and then he handed the mortar to Tristan.

Using a fresh silver knife, Tristan scraped the mixture into the cauldron and swung it over the fire. Lily could smell the change immediately. The rainwater went from spoiled to clean in moments.

She felt unbelievably tired.

Lily was aware of time passing, of Tristan and Caleb pulling the cauldron off the fire and testing drops of its water on rectangles of paper. She felt Rowan take her shoulders and lower her to her side. He kept his hand on her back, rubbing it gently while he and Caleb discussed where portions of the purifying water were most needed. A part of Lily was aware of the fact that she should be furious with Rowan for making her think that he cared about her when he was simply harnessing her power, but she was simply too comfortable to start another fight with him. The fire, his soothing hand on her back, and the spent contentedness in her muscles kept her from storming away from him. She was suddenly aware of Caleb's big white grin hovering over her eyes.

"Good work, witch," he said, smiling widely at her. She smiled back, but by the time she got around to it, he'd already turned away. There were footsteps, a door closing, and Lily felt herself being lifted off the ground. The change of position roused her from her torpor.

"How much dirty water can that one cauldron of potion clean?" she asked.

"Every batch is different, depending on the witch," Rowan said. She could feel his voice rumbling in his chest. He was carrying her down the hallway to his bedroom. "We think your ratio is about one to ten thousand." He sounded proud.

"Ten thousand of those huge cauldrons of water made clean by only one?" she mumbled as he tucked her into his bed. There was some reason she wasn't supposed to be sleeping in his bed, but she couldn't remember what it was. "That's not small magic, Rowan. Clean water is important. It can save lives."

He nodded at her, and his words slid into her head. *Lillian called it kitchen magic. It's taxing, and she resented how much energy it took from her when any novice crucible could be paid to do it—if only on a much smaller scale than she could.*

Lillian is an idiot.

Sleep.

Lily sat up in Rowan's bed, miffed. She felt like every time she used magic, she woke up twelve hours later wondering what bus had hit her. There had to be a way to do magic and remain conscious—and out of Rowan's arms.

She made his bed and thought about how he had treated her last night. Like he cared about her. It was misleading of him to rub her back, tuck her in, and still think she was evil. Or maybe he was only nice to her because he needed her to do magic. The thought made Lily go still for a moment. She set aside the small, chilled feeling that settled in her heart and got dressed. Whatever Rowan thought of her, she'd still done something good. Her magic had given people clean water.

She washed her face in the bathroom and thought about the water purification ritual. She knew what herbs they'd used—bay, rosemary, thyme, hyssop—and which elements—carbon, chalk, sand, and silver. Lily knew enough chemistry to know that none of these things would really treat dirty water and make it drinkable. She could *see* the change she'd made in the chemicals, though. She hadn't created any new elements. She'd only recombined them. It had to be some sort of science, she figured, just not one she had ever encountered before.

Lily went out to the main room to find Tristan, Caleb, and Rowan sitting around the kitchen table, the remains of a big breakfast spread out before them. Rowan's shirt was unbuttoned at the collar and his hair was pushed up funny in the back, as if he'd been rumpling it with his fingers. Lily looked away quickly when he noticed her watching him.

Caleb lifted his mug to salute. "There she is!" He grinned at her, and Lily found herself grinning back. Caleb looked big and scary when he just sat there, but when he smiled he looked like a giant teddy bear. If teddy bears had muscles like sacks of coconuts, that is. "The sachem thanks you for your donation to the rebel front and would like to encourage you to—wait, what did he say?" He looked at Tristan, who shrugged. "Something fancy about doing well."

"I take it Alaric's okay with me learning to be a witch?" she asked. Lily went into the kitchen and poured herself some tea.

"I made pancake batter for you. You hungry?" Rowan asked, standing. Lily nodded and took a seat on top of the island in the kitchen while Rowan crossed to the stove. She could tell he was trying to change the subject.

"The sachem is very happy you're learning to be a witch. Especially if you keep the water purifier coming," Caleb said. "Even better? We could really use some of those tabs that rid the body of infection. There's a fever going around."

"It's bad," Tristan added, looking at Rowan. Lily saw Rowan's brow pinch with worry before Caleb continued.

"And he wants you to know that he understands that you need to go home, and in exchange for your help, he's trying to locate the shaman for you. I'll let you know when we find him."

"Thanks. Why do I need the shaman?" Lily asked over the edge of her mug of tea. Rowan poured four dollops of batter into a skillet and sprinkled blueberries in them. "I love blueberries," she whispered. He smiled to himself—he already knew as much—and picked up a spatula.

"Rowan and I are Coven trained. And so is Caleb—well, a bit," Tristan said, waving a hand to include Caleb and Rowan. "None of us have any idea how to spirit walk. Maybe two people in the whole world do, actually. You have to see a shaman for that, and there's only one full shaman left."

"What is spirit walking?" Lily asked. "I've heard you all talking about it, but I don't think I understand it yet."

"It's where you separate your body and spirit and send your spirit elsewhere," Rowan replied. "Even other universes."

"Is it like astral projection?" Lily guessed. No one understood what she was asking. "No one knows how to spirit walk except for the shaman? Aren't there more than one?"

"No," Caleb said. "There's a kid out on a vision quest on the Ocean of Grass who's trying to become a shaman, but right now we only have the one. We need to find him before we can get you going."

Rowan flipped a pancake. "So you can find your home world, Lily," he said. "Right, Tristan? That's why we're doing this, isn't it? So she can go home?"

Everyone was quiet. Tristan and Caleb didn't move a muscle as they watched Rowan cook for Lily, and she got the sense that they were all sharing mindspeak. From what she could gather from their flashing eyes and tight mouths, the three of them seemed to be arguing intensely.

"Why does Lillian hunt scientists?" Lily asked. Her voice sounded uncomfortably bright in the quiet room.

"Because she believes they're going to destroy the world," Rowan replied, not looking up from his task. "She says science is corrupt."

"But that man. The one the soldiers killed in the woods," she said haltingly. "You said he was a teacher. Why lump him in with the scientists?"

"Because she's a power-hungry bitch who wants to rule the world with an iron fist?" Tristan offered. "A bitch we need to overthrow," he added, dart-like, at Rowan's back.

"That's an oversimplification, Tristan," Rowan countered calmly. He took the pancakes off the skillet and put them on a plate. "Lillian is killing teachers because most teachers teach their students critical thinking. And doctors, her other target, have to use the scientific method to diagnose and heal their patients. Both of these things promote free inquiry and, ultimately, science. Which she thinks is the devil. Do you want maple syrup?"

"Yeah, thanks," Lily said, taking her plate and the fork Rowan handed to her. There was so much going on in the room, so many hidden conversations that she could almost hear, but not quite, that she was getting dizzy. "But why does she think that? I've been noticing that magic is kind of like science. No—it *is* science. It's just a different way of manipulating the natural world. We use machines; you use magic."

"Magic is a science only people who are born with a particular talent can do," Rowan said. He poured maple syrup on Lily's pancakes. "Actual science can be done by anyone. Repeated by anyone. And there's no way for Lillian to control what people do with it or how far it spreads."

Caleb guffawed. "Like Tristan said. She's a power-hungry bitch who wants to rule the world with an iron fist."

Rowan rolled his eyes. "She's much more than that."

Lily wondered why Rowan would defend Lillian if he wouldn't defend her. Her throat stung. She didn't much feel like eating his pancakes and left them on the counter.

———

Juliet helped Lillian dress. The bodice hung loosely around her sister's wasted frame.

"We'll have to take this in. I've pulled the laces as tight as they'll go," Juliet said, with a hint of scolding in her tone.

"No. We'll have my tailor add padding," Lillian replied.

"Or you could eat more." Juliet waited, but her sister didn't comment. After a long pause, she continued. "I understand why you wouldn't want Gideon to touch you, but have you thought about what I suggested? About claiming another mechanic to help heal you? You've kept whatever this sickness is at bay for nearly a year now, but obviously you can't do it on your own anymore."

Lillian pulled away from Juliet's fussing and sat down at her makeup table. "I don't want another mechanic."

Juliet watched her sister dab blush on her bleached cheeks. She'd long suspected that the only reason Lillian allowed her and *only* her to touch her was because, as a latent crucible with almost no magic, Juliet was the only person close to Lillian who wouldn't be able to tell exactly how sick she was.

"People know you're sick now," Juliet said.

"I know they do."

"Then why not claim a mechanic—a good one—who can help heal you?"

As usual, Juliet got no answer. She tried for what must have been the thousandth time to reach out and share mindspeak with her sister. Again, she hit up against a wall around Lillian's mind.

Lillian sighed. "My sickness isn't the only thing I'm keeping to myself, Juliet. Please understand. I shut you out because I'm trying to protect you."

It was the same answer Lillian had been giving her since she came back from her mysterious disappearance, and Juliet knew she would get no more out of her. She glossed and smoothed her sister's curls in silence before helping her down to the main hall to hear the newest prisoner—a doctor.

There was a fever sweeping through the Outlanders. Citizens of the Thirteen Cities were entitled to free medicine from the Covens during a public health crisis such as this and they had nothing to fear from the fever, but the outbreak was killing Outlanders at an alarming rate. Children were the most vulnerable. Lillian had seized several Outlander doctors who had been feeding bread mold to the afflicted children. It was an open and shut case of child abuse as far as Juliet could see, but Lillian had insisted that the Coven and the Council hear the leader out before she sentenced them all.

Juliet still couldn't believe that anyone would be so inhumane as to feed mold to a sick child, but the Outlanders were brutish like that. Juliet had heard that they even *sewed* wounds together. Just the thought made her queasy. She had never condoned her sister's harsh punishments—she didn't agree with capital punishment for any reason—but she did agree that the Outlanders needed to accept magic as the one and only way. Sure, it was expensive to hire a healing crucible and her mechanic, but giving mold to children and calling it a cure? That was downright barbaric.

When they arrived in the main hall, Council Leader Thomas Danforth greeted Juliet and Lillian with an oily smile. Juliet returned it, not because she liked Gideon's rat-faced father, but because she knew her sister wouldn't, and the last thing they needed was to slight Danforth at the moment. Not when her sister's other self was running around stars know where, wreaking havoc everywhere she went. Juliet felt a surge of worry at the thought of Lily. She recalled Lily's frightened eyes and how they'd melted with relief at the first sight of Juliet at the top of the stairs. Her sister needed her, and . . . Juliet stopped herself. Lily *wasn't* her real sister, even though it felt like she was. Juliet shook her head to clear her confusion and focused on Lillian instead.

"Lady," Danforth said. The assembled hosts stood up from their seats behind one side of a long table that spanned the length of one end of the great hall. Danforth led the dignitaries in a respectful bow.

"You may be seated," Lillian said in a perfunctory way. She had never enjoyed the pomp and circumstance of being the Lady of Salem, and now that she was ill she barely tolerated it.

Juliet stayed close to Lillian, but she didn't help her into her grand chair at the center of the long table. She knew better than to make Lillian look like an invalid. Once Lillian was situated, Juliet took a seat on an unobtrusive velvet-cushioned stool that had been set up for her behind her sister's right elbow. Although seated in her imposing chair with the all-female Coven members on her right and the all-male Council members to her left, Lillian didn't need Juliet's cosseting to make her look like an invalid. Her giant chair seemed to swallow her frail body. It did not, however, swallow her voice or the authority it conveyed.

"Bring in the prisoner," Lillian commanded.

A tall, thin man was brought in. He didn't look overtly Outlander. He had brown hair and eyes, but he wasn't quite as dark as most of them were. Outlanders were a mix of many races. Some had even been citizens once and been expelled from one of the Thirteen Cities for one reason or another—usually for something criminal. It could be hard to tell where exactly someone came from. But Juliet saw streaks of red and black on the backs of the doctor's hands and on his cheek. He stood tall in front of the long table, facing the line of judges. Proud. He was definitely one of Alaric's painted savages.

"Michael Snowshower. You have been charged with practicing science," Danforth said, beginning the proceedings. "How do you plead?"

Snowshower spared Danforth one disdainful glace, and then looked at Lillian. "How do I plead?" he repeated quietly. "I plead for the lives of my people."

Juliet heard Nina, one of the senior witches of the Coven, make an exasperated sound and saw her roll her eyes. "After feeding them something that will only make the fever worse?" Nina asked sarcastically.

"The mold is an antibiotic. It saves some," Snowshower replied defensively. Juliet looked at him carefully and saw truth in his eyes. This was no charlatan. He truly believed the mold helped.

"But what you don't know is that the mold only kills most of the infection. Most. Not all," Lillian said. "What is left is the strongest strain, and it multiplies unchecked, getting deadlier and deadlier with every misuse of your *medicine*." Lillian said the word with such bitterness that Snowshower's eyes widened with surprise.

"Yes, but we've learned that if the mold is taken at a higher dosage for a full two weeks, it *does* kill all the infection," Snowshower argued back, if a bit uncertainly. "We've saved thousands——"

"And while you've been running your little scientific experiments about how long the mold should be taken and in what concentration, you've created a biological monster," Lillian said, silencing him. "Because of you——meddling in things you don't understand—— the fever has become so deadly that half the Outlander children probably won't survive the winter. Like all scientists, you promise a cure but you deliver greater hazards and more death. You are a murderer, Michael Snowshower."

Snowshower dropped his head, nodding to himself as if he were accepting responsibility for all that Lillian had said.

"But what other choice do we have?" he asked, raising blazing eyes to meet Lillian's. "The Covens will sell us spells, but few of us can afford them. Even if a whole family starved for it, most can't pay what a witch asks for one tab of your magic-made antibiotics. Should the Outlanders do nothing just because they're poor? Lay their sick down and let the weakest ones die?"

Lillian leaned forward in her chair, an angry red flush burning through the pink makeup on her cheeks.

"*Yes.*" Her eyes matched his for fire and her voice grated in her throat with passion. "Better a few die than to do what you have done. You have admitted your crime freely. No trial is necessary. Michael Snowshower, you will hang."

While the court clerks scribbled down the judgment and punishment in their little books, Juliet stared at her sister in disbelief. Snowshower was only trying to help as many of his people as he could. He was a good man, albeit misguided. She looked up and down the row of dignitaries, sitting in their plush chairs, nodding their heads in agreement with Lillian's decree. Not one of them tried to make a plea for the man.

Snowshower barely flinched. He'd known all along that he would die, and hearing it firsthand made little difference to him. Carefully, deliberately, Michael Snowshower got down on his knees in front of Lillian.

"Lady of Salem, I beg you to save the children of my people," he said, holding his painted hands out to her, palms up. "Please, Great Lady. Make a gift of your magic. Don't let them suffer and die."

Juliet's gaze flew to her sister's face. Surely, Lillian would do something to help. Juliet knew her sister was strict, harsh even, but Lillian would never allow thousands of innocent children to die. But instead of finding compassion in Lillian's expression as she expected, Juliet saw triumph.

"I want names, Michael. Three names in particular," Lillian said, a small smile on her dry lips.

Snowshower's outstretched arms dropped in defeat. "I don't have them," he said weakly. Even Juliet could tell he was lying.

"Then I don't have the spell." Lillian sat back in her giant chair, completely at ease. She looked down the row to her right at her Coven, her voice light. "Does anyone in my Coven have a spell to cure the Outlanders?"

They laughed. Juliet felt her heart shrivel at the sound. She looked at Michael Snowshower, still on his knees, as he realized that his fate was going to be worse than the death he'd already accepted.

"I'm sorry, My Lady," Nina answered with an obsequious smile. "It appears that the tithe for this particular spell is three names. The Coven can't work without a tithe."

"You have a choice, Michael Snowshower," Lillian said, her tone suddenly shifting from false gaiety to deadly serious. "It's not unlike the choice you made when you decided to use science. You see, when you chose to start meddling in things that you don't understand, you were choosing to save a few lives over the thousands who would suffer from the consequences of your actions. You are exactly where you put yourself, Michael Snowshower. Now you have the choice to protect three dangerous scientists who, like yourself, offer the world nothing but false promises and death, or save—what is it, Thomas? Twenty thousand?" Lillian asked Danforth, leaning to her left.

"If it's as bad a winter as we think it will be, estimates place the death toll at twenty-one thousand, Lady," Danforth replied with a sanctimonious frown.

"Twenty-one thousand dead," Lillian said slowly. She leaned forward, genuinely pleading with Snowshower. "You ask me to save the children, but it's in *your* power, Michael. I need three names. Three lives for twenty-one thousand. Please. Please save them."

CHAPTER
10

"NO. KEEP YOUR EYES CLOSED," ROWAN ORDERED. "USE
your stones to see inside the leaf, stage by stage. You have to
learn how to control this, Lily. Go easy. Don't just rush in."

Lily closed her eyes and tried to ignore her pounding head—
and the faint sense of *him* there in her mind with her, watching her as
she tried to complete the simple task of zooming in on a fern frond.
How was she supposed to calm down and focus if Rowan was es-
sentially breathing down her spinal cord? Especially since she enjoyed being close to him and feeling the touch of his presence in her
mind.

Today's lesson was about controlling her power, and Lily's continuing problem was an excess of strength. All Tristan and Rowan
wanted her to do was look at a fern and increase her ability to see into
it, as with a microscope, using slow, measured increments of magnification until she was down to the atomic level. To Lily, this was like
trying to hold a glass doll with a vice. Her problem wasn't ability. She
could look so closely that not only could she see into the atom, but
she could see down to the quarks and beyond to the squiggly, almost

alive-looking strings that jigged enchantingly through a dozen dimensions. She just had a slight problem doing it slowly.

"No," Rowan scolded when she skipped a magnification level. "I told you to stop before you could differentiate the cell walls. You're looking at a single cell's mitochondria. That's deeper than I asked." Lily groaned, but Rowan had no pity for her. "Stop there and observe it," he said. "Then draw for me, in all the exact stages, how the mitochondria turn sugar into energy by passing the spare electron around in a circle."

That would take forever. For a second, Lily thought she might start crying.

"Ro," Tristan objected. "She's exhausted. You can't expect her to observe a whole cycle."

"How else is she supposed to learn?" Rowan snapped.

"But I already *learned* this," Lily whined. "Mr. Carnello taught me this in eighth grade. It's the citric acid cycle discovered by Hans Krebs, like, seventy years ago."

"Try about two hundred and seventy years ago. Here anyway," Tristan said with a sympathetic smile. "And we've never heard of any Hans Krebs. The cellular energy cycle was first observed, understood, and manipulated by witches."

Lily threw up her hands in defeat. One of the things she was trying to absorb was that here, in this version of the world, *magic* had made all of what Lily knew of as *scientific* discoveries, and no wonder. With her willstones, Lily didn't need microscopes or chemicals or centrifuges to see and manipulate cells or—for example—unzip and recombine DNA. All she needed was a willstone and a deep understanding of the way DNA worked and she could do it.

Here, in this universe, what differentiated science from witchcraft was that scientists had fewer resources and couldn't magically manipulate the natural world by will alone. They had to fumble around until they found a chemical or developed a machine that achieved the same results. There weren't many people who called themselves scientists here, and not just because Lillian persecuted them. Witches were much more efficient at tackling the challenges of biology, chemistry, and physics, so why even try to be a scientist? That is, unless you were either in love with the profession or because you were desperate and had no access to a witch's cure-alls, as was the case with the Outlanders.

Witchcraft had done amazing thing in this world because manipulating the natural world was second nature to witches. It was, quite simply, what a crucible's body was meant to do. Because of that they'd achieved just about every scientific milestone a couple of hundred years before the scientists of Lily's world had. Witches had harnessed electricity, cloned animals, cured congenital diseases like cystic fibrosis and Down syndrome—and they'd being doing this for *centuries*. When witches needed a machine—like the trains, elepods, or lamps that lit the rich neighborhoods—they had their mechanics build them. Witches supplied the discoveries, and their mechanics made the gadgets they needed.

Scientists had always lagged behind. They had access to the knowledge that the witches supplied, but they had to come up with different methods for reaching the same goal. A scientist had to dream up a microscope and build it first, only to see something that a half-grown crucible could look at without even trying. Not a lot of glory in that job.

The one thing that the witches didn't have, but Lily's world did, was the driving curiosity that came built in to the culture of a well-respected scientific community. In Lily's world, scientists had the need to figure out for themselves how things worked, precisely because it did not come naturally. For some reason, Lily was strangely proud of the clumsy, sometimes downright destructive path of progress that her world had traveled as they fumbled toward the understanding that came maybe a little too easily to witches.

"Yeah? Well, you and your snooty, all-knowing witches have never been to the moon. My people have, because *it was there and it was a good thing to do*," Lily said in her best Boston accent. "So bite my scientist-loving *ass*."

Rowan and Tristan just stared at Lily for a while. The two young men looked nothing alike physically, but they'd spent so much of their lives together that they shared similar gestures and facial expressions. Right now the perplexed looks they gave her were practically identical.

"No John F. Kennedy in this world, I take it?" she guessed. "Culture shock really sucks."

"I think she needs a break," Tristan said.

"I think you're right," Rowan replied.

"What I need is fresh air," Lily said sullenly. "I want to go up to the roof." She looked at Rowan pleadingly.

He only allowed her to go up to the roof every few days, and always at random times. While his rooftop terrace was covered by one of his superstrong wards of protection, Rowan constantly worried that his ward would falter for a moment, and one of Gideon's goons, who were always watching his apartment, would get a glimpse of Lily and recognize her.

"Please. I just want to sit outside for half an hour," Lily begged.

"Fine," Rowan said, albeit reluctantly. "But wear a hat. And change out of that dress and into some wearhyde so you don't look so much like a witch."

Lily practically ran to her room, unlacing her dress on the way. Covering up wasn't exactly what she had in mind when she wanted so desperately to soak up what was left of the waning autumn light, but it was still better than nothing.

They had been training her for three weeks straight, and in that time she'd nearly perfected the water-purifying potion, a food-preserving charm, and a spray that cleaned soiled bodies, clothes, and hair with only one squirt of fine mist. "Kitchen magic" still drained Lily to exhaustion, and from what Rowan intimated, it probably always would. Small magic, while necessary, was definitely the grunt work of the magical realm, and it was the bulk of what Lily was learning.

She slept a lot, which served three purposes. Mostly, she needed the rest, but sleeping also killed a lot of time while Alaric tried to locate the shaman, whom Lily was desperate to finally meet. The sooner she started learning how to spirit walk, the sooner she stood a chance of figuring out a way to get home.

Lastly, sleeping a lot kept Lily from spending downtime with Rowan. She didn't want to watch him reading, or cooking, or sitting at the table talking with Tristan and Caleb. She didn't want to enjoy the way his voice sounded or how capably his hands managed to do the fiddliest little tasks. She didn't want to admire him or fool herself into thinking that there was something more between them than there was.

He seemed to be avoiding her as well. Despite the fact that he'd made such a big deal about being allowed access into her mind whenever he wanted, he hadn't once asked her questions about her loyalty. In fact, apart from when they needed to touch each other's minds during a ritual, they hadn't even shared mindspeak. Lily didn't want to miss sharing mindspeak with him, but she did. She remembered touching Rowan's stone for the first time. She'd never felt that close to anyone. And now that this closeness was gone, she'd never felt so alone.

The longer she and Rowan went without talking to each other, the more Lily wanted to be near him. She started to miss him, even though she saw him every day. The craving for any kind of intimacy with him drove her to sneak into the spare bedroom he'd been using one morning when he was out.

As soon as she walked in, she could tell the room had belonged to someone other than Rowan. It was a large room, but the bed was small and narrow, as if the owner had never adjusted to having so much space. The coverlet over the bed was a faded handmade ikat quilt of many colors. Lily trailed her hand over the dresser, lightly touching the trinkets neatly placed on top—a pair of glasses, a hand-carved comb, and a plain gold ring that Lily was certain was a wedding band. They were old items, scuffed, worn, and heavy with the memories of an entire life. A lost life.

There were no handy photographs announcing whose room this had been, but Lily didn't need them. She knew the room must have belonged to Rowan's father, but she didn't know how or why his father had died. Lily ached to ask Rowan about it, to exchange confidences with him again like they had in the cabin.

The longing for Rowan that was building in her and the energy it took to push it down was exhausting and made her intense workload harder to bear. When Lily wasn't sleeping, playing cards with Tristan, or making potions to supply Alaric's never-ending list of needs for the rebels, Rowan had also insisted that she learn camouflage magic. This type of magic would make her seemingly disappear in low light, as Rowan had when they'd been in the woods.

One of the camouflage spells she learned was how to cast a glamour, which worked on the same energy field principles as ordinary camouflage but didn't make her blend into the background. Instead, it shifted the way light hit her face, subtly altering the way she looked. Since Lily had learned how to cast a glamour, she'd been harassing Rowan and Tristan to let her leave the apartment and take a walk outside in the fresh air, which, considering they had her working double shifts and the fire was burning day and night, was getting harder to come by.

"You coming or not?" asked Tristan's voice outside the bedroom door.

"Yeah," Lily said, rushing to join him.

When they crossed through the living area, Rowan was sitting on one of the sofas, reading. Lily caught a glimpse of the book cover as she and Tristan passed on their way to the stairs.

"Was that a geometry book he was reading?" she asked when they got to the roof.

"Uh-huh," Tristan replied.

"Why? Rowan's way past geometry. I know he knows calculus."

"Yes and no," Tristan said, dodging an explanation. Lily stared at him with a cocked eyebrow until he continued. "You've noticed that your memory is crystal clear now that you have willstones, right?" Lily nodded. "That's because willstones are like extra memory space— not infinite, but really big. When Rowan smashed his first stone to get away from Lillian he lost a lot. It's not that he doesn't understand geometry anymore."

"But he doesn't have it memorized anymore," Lily finished for him. She thought about it for a bit, imagining what it would be like to make that kind of sacrifice, and desperately trying not to feel everything that touched Rowan as deeply as she did. Sometimes Lily thought that if someone were to pinch Rowan, she'd be the one to say ouch. "So that's why he's always reading."

"Trying to get back to where he was. He's been at it for months." Tristan shivered, then flipped a cushion on one of the two pieces of deck furniture before sitting.

This area wasn't really for recreation. Most of the roof was covered in potted plants, long dead now that the year was so deep into autumn. All of the roofs, terraces, and windowsills in this city functioned as growing space for edible plants. People grew what vegetables they could for themselves, and the best apartments—like Rowan's—had rooftop gardens. Few farms existed outside the walls of Salem, and those that did were surrounded by high walls and used mostly as pasture for horses and oxen or for luxury meat sources like cows, chickens, and pigs. They were called luxury meats because they came from entire animals that had lived and breathed, and not been grown one part at a time down in the Stacks.

Tristan had explained the Stacks to Lily, and since then they had occupied a particularly eerie place in her psyche. The Stacks were subterranean caves where the witches grew wearhyde on something they called skinlooms. If that wasn't creepy enough, it was also where they grew cuts of all kinds of meat, like chicken breast without the chicken, and pork loin without the pig, inside things called wombcombs. Wombcombs were shaped like giant honeycombs, but inside the hexagonal cells they grew either cuts of meat or the tame Woven who still protected the city.

Even the thought of the Stacks gave Lily the creeps, and if she hadn't been vegan before coming to this world, she was pretty sure she would have converted once she got here. Tristan and Rowan had both worked in the Stacks alongside Lillian, and Tristan's description of the place had not made the thought of eating meat appealing in any way. However, he had stressed how important the Stacks were for the survival of the city. Rowan had told her that the Coven barely broke even on the Stacks.

The Coven purposely tried to keep all of the basic needs services that they offered relatively inexpensive and accessible to all citizens. The Coven owned most of the greentowers and greenhouses in the city. They paid the farmers who worked them good wages, and they kept the price of food low, as they kept the price of wearhyde low. Hungry and cold people riot, which was something the Coven had learned to avoid at all costs inside a walled city that was surrounded by bloodthirsty monsters.

Most importantly of all, clean water and basic health care were completely free to all citizens. The last thing the Coven wanted was an outbreak of cholera or a crippling infectious disease inside such a closed space. Food, clothes, and health care: This was how the Coven had won the love of the people.

It was a system that kept the peace, refined over two centuries of confinement inside the thirteen walled cities, but of course there were still malcontents and rabble-rousers. This is where the Coven really showed their power. They had the right to banish anyone who disturbed the peace, and banishment meant a loss of citizenship from all thirteen cities. If you crossed any one of the thirteen Covens who ruled the Thirteen Cities, you found yourself outside the walls with the Woven.

Of the banished, only the useful, the honest, and the strong were invited to join Outlander tribes. Once solidly Native American, after two hundred years of assimilating all the different races banished from the cities, the Outlanders weren't any one particular race anymore, but a blend that was unknown in Lily's world. Only the lucky among the banished made it into a tribe, while the vast majority got mangled by the Woven on their first night outside the wall. Fear kept the people from rioting. Fear, affordable food, clothes, and health care seemed to be enough for the general populace to tolerate Lillian's hangings.

"Come here," Tristan said behind her, his voice rough. "I'm cold."

Lily turned to see him sitting again and noticed that his breath was a smoky cloud around him. Frost was settling into the dark corners where the falling sun failed to shine. She went to Tristan, sinking down next to him into the cushions of the patio furniture.

He picked up her hand and turned it over, exposing the underside of her wrist.

"May I?" he asked quietly.

After a moment, Lily nodded and Tristan laid the tips of his fingers against the pulse point on her wrist. He sighed deeply and leaned back, his eyes closed, and Lily felt her perpetual fever cool a little as he took some of her heat. She hadn't claimed him so they couldn't share mindspeak or memories, but there was something intimate about warming another person with your body. Feeding them with your heat.

"What does this feel like for you?" Lily asked. To her it felt like stepping into a cool pool on a hot day. It was refreshing, but there was something so rapturous about the look on Tristan's face that it made Lily think there was more sensation in receiving than in the giving. Lily couldn't help but remember how Rowan had looked when he'd taken some of her heat in the cabin. How his head had tipped forward and his eyes had closed with pleasure.

"Like drinking sunshine, I guess," Tristan answered. He turned and opened his sparkling eyes to look at her. "I can think of a few things that feel better. But not many."

Lily watched Tristan's face. His lips fell apart expectantly and his breath deepened. She'd seen this look on his face before, and she wished she felt something more.

Lily pulled away from Tristan, purposely ruining the mood, and looked out over the city. Her eyes skipped around, trying to take in everything that this huge walled city encompassed, all six miles long and three miles wide of it, and in some places, hundreds of stories high. Something strange caught her eye.

"Is that building over there empty?" Lily asked. She pointed to an elegant seven-story brownstone a few streets over that seemed to be shuttered. Real estate was the single biggest commodity inside the limited walls of Salem, and Lily couldn't recall ever seeing a tenant-less window, let alone a whole empty building before. Tristan stood from his seat and joined Lily at the balcony wall.

"Oh," Tristan said, following her line of sight. "That's the technical college Lillian started."

Lily looked at him, surprised. "She can afford to leave it empty?"

Tristan smirked. "Oh yeah. The Coven is the biggest landowner in Salem, and they don't have to pay taxes. Real estate is where they make their real fortune. They have lots of buildings that they can just sit on. Lillian took that one over when she outmuscled everyone else in the Coven and became the Salem Witch when Olga, the last Witch, died."

"How did she do that?" Lily interjected. "Wasn't she only sixteen?"

Tristan shrugged. "Didn't matter how old she was. The Coven chooses their leader in a simple way—the strongest rules until someone stronger comes along and knocks her off the throne. And no one has ever been stronger than Lillian. Especially not with Rowan as her head mechanic." A dark look crossed Tristan's face at the mention of Rowan.

"Go on," she urged. "Why did Lillian take over that building?"

"She was going to change the world, she said," Tristan continued quietly. "Lillian turned it into a school where promising non-magical youngsters—mostly Outlanders—were given full scholarship to study all of the Coven's writings on natural phenomena and apply those theories inside the newest and shiniest laboratories."

Lily let the words sink in. "She fully funded a college for *scientists?*"

"She did. Lillian started out as the most liberal Salem Witch in history. And then she changed." Tristan's face fell suddenly, and his blue eyes filled with sadness. "They were the first people she rounded up, you know. The people in *her own* college. The kids she sent to work camps. The older ones she hanged."

Lily stared at the dark windows, and imagined the horror of that last day of school. She could nearly hear the sound of marching boots and screams echoing through the now vacant rooms.

Tristan stood, ending the conversation. "Come on. He'll throw a fit if you stay out here any longer."

The fire was high, the cauldron bubbled and steamed, and the sun blazed through all of the windows and skylights in Rowan's apartment. The great room was already swelteringly hot when Lily joined Tristan and Rowan on the black square of silk in front of the hearth.

"It's a sauna in here," Lily complained. She flapped her hands, trying to wave a breeze into the robe Rowan had told her to wear to this afternoon's ritual instead of the silk slip. "What are we making today? Deep-fried witch?"

Rowan and Tristan smiled at her joke, but neither of them laughed. Their eyes were hazy and their breathing slow. Their willstones heaved with sluggish light, indicating that they were in a half trance. Lily had seen Rowan and Tristan in a trance-like state before. Every day at dawn, they did a series of exercises that Lily insisted was a form of yoga, even though they'd never heard the word. At the end of their exercises, they both sat cross-legged and meditated deeply. But this was different. They'd never put themselves in a trance for a ritual before.

Today, they were both wearing white shorts, and sweat slicked their nearly naked bodies. Lily wished she could focus on Tristan alone, but her eyes always seemed to wander back to Rowan. In front of his folded legs was a small wooden bowl, filled with a bright red paste, and next to it, a paintbrush. Tristan sat behind Rowan and to his right. In front of him was a long strip of gauze folded into a large pile.

"What are we making today?" Lily repeated, seriously this time.

"We're moving away from small magic and into the second level. Healing magic," Rowan replied, his hazy eyes focusing on Lily. "Sachem needs anti-infection tabs. There's been an outbreak of fever and lots of Outlander children are dying."

"Okay," Lily said with a firm nod. "What do I do?"

"Take off your robe and lie down in front of me," Rowan said.

Lily balked. She was only wearing panties under the robe. After a bit of hemming and hawing, she met Rowan's level gaze and sighed.

"Well, it *is* for the children," she said, and shimmied shyly out of her robe, covering as much of herself as she could with her hands. Rowan couldn't seem to help himself and cracked a smile, which helped to ease some of Lily's nerves. She lowered herself to the floor and stretched herself out in front of him, arms still draped over her breasts.

Even though it was unbearably hot in front of the fire, Lily's skin puckered with goose bumps. She could feel Rowan's breath falling on her from above. His gaze felt like touch, skimming over her like the downy edge of a bird's wing, over her belly, her breasts, and her thighs. Gently, he lifted one arm and then the other, and lay them by her sides, then picked up the wooden bowl and the paintbrush and positioned himself at her feet. Tristan stood and went to the fire, throwing a large cord of wood onto the flames. The fire roared. Lily's willstones echoed the power of the fire, and the rose stone flashed with a bright light. Lily felt herself fill with heat.

"Boil out the fever. Sweat out the sickness. Burn out the rot," Rowan chanted. He dipped his brush into the wooden bowl and began painting runes onto Lily's skin.

Lily's body flamed and roared like the fire. The cool touch of the brush made her shiver. The paint sizzled when it hit her feverish skin. Every stroke of Rowan's brush sent cooling waves through her, and her sweating body rose up to meet the touch of the bristles. She could feel the paint oozing into her system, mixing with her sweat and changing. Growing strong.

Tristan followed behind Rowan, winding Lily's painted flesh with the strip of gauze as if he were wrapping an injury. Sweat and paint and magic soaked into the wrappings, becoming medicine. Rowan painted all the way around one leg up to the thigh and stopped. Then he painted the other and stopped. The wrappings were removed and hung by the fire. Tristan lit a bundle of sage, flamed it out, and let the clarifying smoke waft up into the growing web of damp, red-blotted gauze. Rowan painted her arms in the same spiraling manner, with Tristan following in his wake with yard after yard of gauze. They stopped only to hang the saturated wrappings in front of the fire and to stoke the flames. Rowan eased Lily up to a sitting position and began painting her back. She could feel his breath on her drenched neck, could feel the paintbrush sliding and sizzling across her skin. More gauze was pressed into the design Rowan had drawn on her back, and then he laid her down again.

Rowan's hands shook when he started the spiral out from her navel. His brush traveled up, across her fluttering ribs, wrapping around her breasts. Lily could feel the tight coil of the spiral sinking into her, the heat settling low in her belly like a knot of want. The teasing touch of the brush became unbearable. She reached up and brought Rowan's lovely mouth down to her. His lips were so cool against her fire-bright skin that she sighed, drawing from them deeply as if she could drink him. Tristan's hands lifted her, wrapping her, brushing against her body while she kissed Rowan. Both of their eyes slid closed, and their willstones glittered on their chests.

Rowan broke away and paused, swallowing hard. Lily's hands were in his hair. He untangled them gently and moved determinedly to Lily's throat. Concentrating, he painted a small design around her willstones. The spell sank into her lungs, filling them with fluid and cutting off her breath. Gauze followed before she had a chance to panic, soaking in the sweat and paint, and lifting the heavy spell off of her. Her skin cooled. Her lungs cleared. She took a deep breath.

"It is done," Rowan said. His and Tristan's willstones darkened. Rowan stood and got Lily's robe, covering her immediately.

Lily sat up. The sun was down. The yards of gauze needed to dry before they could be cut into tiny tabs no larger than Lily's pinkie nail. Just one tab under the tongue could clear all infection out of a sick or injured person's body. Lily sighed, knowing that thousands could be healed by what they'd done in a few hours. The city sparkled in the darkness outside Rowan's huge windows. Instead of feeling tired, she was energized, her body humming with the adrenaline of two kinds of hunger.

"Let's go out," she said. "I want to go out. Actually, I think I *need* to go out."

Rowan and Tristan shared a look. "A crucible's craving is her mechanic's mandate," Tristan said. "You've already ignored that once tonight." There was a scolding note in Tristan's tone, like Rowan had done something they both knew was wrong. Rowan dropped his head.

"I know I did. But I still think it's too dangerous. Gideon has a man stationed right across the street, watching us," Rowan said.

"It's dark. I can use a camouflage spell, and he won't even see me," Lily said, standing.

"It doesn't matter if you get past that one guard," Rowan countered. "There are spies all over the city looking for the Outlander girl hanging out with me."

"So I'll bleach my hair blonde and go with Tristan," Lily replied, as if offering the simplest solution in the world.

You're not going to a bonfire without me!

Lily could sense that Rowan hadn't meant to initiate mindspeak. The thought had flown out of him in desperation, breaking three weeks of silence, but he closed himself off before she could sense anything more.

"So. Who wants to help me dye my hair?" Lily said through a grin. "I've always wanted to go platinum."

Tristan and Rowan were chemical geniuses. That, coupled with the fact that they also knew how to do magic, meant that two hours later Lily had white-blonde, pin-straight hair.

"I never thought anything could take the curl out," Lily said, fluffing her short, silky locks. "If you guys ever came to my world, you could make a fortune as hairdressers, you know."

"Here. Put this on," Rowan said, ignoring her frivolous comment and holding out a dress.

Lily pouted. "I like my wearhyde. It makes me look tough."

"Rebels and Outlanders wear wearhyde," he said, handing her the frothy pile of chiffon and ribbons. "Witches wear dresses."

There was no style in Lily's world to describe the dress, except maybe half-naked wood nymph meets couture, and she struggled with the complicated design for a good twenty minutes before she admitted defeat and called Tristan to help lace her up. The dress ended up being much skimpier than she'd thought. There was a lot of skin involved.

"I hope I don't catch a cold," she said jokingly.

"That's what the gloves are for," Tristan joked back, handing her a pair of opera-length gloves.

The dress, while complicated, kept her cool, and Lily had to admit it made a lot of sense. Crucibles and witches ran hot, and the dress managed to be sexy and structured but still airier than wearhyde.

"What are the gloves really for?" Lily asked Tristan as they went to join Rowan in the great room. Lily remembered from the walk through town the first night back from the woods that most of the women wearing dresses also wore gloves. It seemed to be more than a style or a trend.

"They're so you don't accidentally touch someone else's stone," he said, sliding a smile in her direction. "Bonfires can get a little wild."

Tristan's smile warmed, and Lily's eyes dropped to the willstone hanging at his throat. She was acutely aware of the fact that she hadn't touched it yet. It wasn't half as lovely to her as Rowan's stone, but she still wanted it. Lily realized she was staring and tore her gaze away.

Lily had spent the last few weeks trying to piece together the politics of the claiming ceremony. Apparently, a mechanic could assist with lower-level magic without being claimed by a witch, but in order to assist with warrior magic—the third-level magic she and Rowan had wielded against the Woven—he had to allow himself to be claimed. Lily had learned that even though Tristan had assisted Rowan with Lillian, he'd never been claimed by her. Lily didn't know why, but she did know it was up to Tristan to offer himself to the witch. Lily didn't want him to feel pressured to move any faster than he was comfortable. Until then, Tristan would be more of an assistant to Rowan than Lily's mechanic. He would assist in the preparation of the rituals and add his energy to Rowan's when they made a brew or wove a spell, but he wasn't pledged to Lily in the same way Rowan was. Tristan could still move on and offer himself to another witch for claiming if he chose.

Lily knew that if Tristan gave himself to her, it would be a life-long commitment. And with that much responsibility hanging over her, Lily didn't know if she really wanted to claim Tristan yet anyway. It was a big step, and Lily was wary of it. It certainly hadn't worked out too well for her and Rowan. And now they were stuck with each other—unless he wanted to go through the agony of smashing his stone. Lily swallowed down the lump of hurt that formed in her throat at the thought. If things continued to carry on as they had been between them, Lily didn't doubt that Rowan might consider smashing his stone an option.

When she and Tristan came back out into the main room, they saw Rowan sitting at the table, drinking a clear liquid from a short glass. He looked up at Lily and his mouth went rigid. "You're going to need to take two of the stones off your necklace," he reminded her, dropping his eyes.

"I think you should wear the rose stone," Tristan advised. "The smoke one is too big to go unnoticed, and the little golden one might get you teased."

Lily nodded and worked the clasps at her throat. She turned her back to the guys while she tucked the two stones into her bra, aware of the fact that they'd spent the day staring at her half-naked body and not caring that it made no sense to act modest now. Some standards had to be maintained or Lily might as well just walk around in her birthday suit all day long.

The guys put on their coats and turned. Their eyes darted all over, looking for her. She'd already cast the camouflage spell.

"Pretty good, right?" she asked. Tristan agreed enthusiastically, but Rowan only nodded and busied himself setting the wards on his apartment.

They had walked about seven blocks when Tristan finally spoke. "Ro. He's not following us," he said. "We can't get into the bonfire with her camouflaged. Their wards will show someone is with us."

"Alright," Rowan said shortly, his eyes scanning for witnesses. "Drop the spell, Lily."

Lily allowed herself to reappear, and slowed down to walk alongside Tristan.

"Don't forget your face glamour," he reminded her quietly.

Lily gave herself a slightly more triangular face, something pixieish to go with her new hair. That small change, along with all the makeup she was wearing, meant even Rowan had to admit that no one would recognize her. Tristan took Lily's hand and pulled her close.

"You look gorgeous," he whispered.

Lily smiled at him, wishing she felt more. This was the perfect opportunity to start over with Tristan. It was a gift, handed to her in what was otherwise a terrible situation, but now that she had his attention, she didn't want it. He'd broken the part of her heart that she'd given to him, and no matter how much Lily tried to convince herself that he was a *different* Tristan who deserved a fresh chance, she couldn't get the pieces to fit back together again in the same way.

She looked ahead at Rowan, walking in front of them. His shoulders were stiff and his back straight—every inch of him as unyielding as she was. They were so alike. How could she expect him to see past his distrust of Lillian and trust her when she couldn't do the same for this other version of Tristan?

Lily didn't feel like going out anymore, but she knew she couldn't change her mind now. They joined a group of people waiting outside a large warehouse-like building. Bass thumped through the walls. They didn't wait long. A female bouncer spotted Rowan and waved them over before they'd even joined the line.

"Rowan Fall," the woman purred. She held up her hand, making the air shimmer and bend as she dropped her ward to allow them to enter. "Do me a favor, precious. Try not to start too many catfights tonight."

Rowan paused and leaned close to her, letting his lips barely brush her cheek. It was so blatantly flirty that Lily felt more puzzled than jealous. It wasn't like him. The bouncer tried to wind her arms around his neck, but Rowan broke away with a cocky grin and led Tristan and Lily inside.

Bodies whirled around a huge, roaring fire that dominated the center of the room. Everywhere Lily looked, heads lolled and torsos writhed as people in varying states of undress spun in concentric circles around the bonfire. The music sounded almost tribal. It had a dark, driving rhythm juxtaposed against vaporous vocals that were mostly remixed whispers and sighs. In the background, Lily could hear chanting from people lurking in the dark. Many wore masks and little else. She looked up at the towering bonfire. There was no ceiling above it, just sparks floating up into the night sky.

Skirting around the edge of the circle of entranced revelers, they passed low tables surrounded by cushions and pillows. Lily peered through the veils draped over one such arrangement and saw a woman. She was sitting astride a young man, kissing him deeply. Her ungloved hand reached out to another man sitting next to them. She slid her hand up his bare chest and grasped his willstone. He threw back his head, his body shaking as he cried out.

"Oh my God," Lily gasped, clutching at Tristan's arm. "She's hurting him."

"Ah, a little," Tristan began tentatively. "But trust me, he's enjoying it. If she were really hurting him, you'd know."

"Is she *claiming* him right now?"

Tristan laughed uncomfortably. "Probably not. Witches and crucibles don't always claim a guy when they touch his stone. Remember—he has to *allow* her to claim him, and she has to want to take on all that responsibility. Claiming is a big deal. But touching stones can be just for fun between people who aren't looking for anything more. Or it can be awful." Tristan made an exasperated sound. "You have to understand *some* of this. You can't be that innocent."

Lily looked at the guy that the woman was straddling. He was definitely having fun. Then she looked at the guy who was separate from the couple. The woman barely touched his stone with her fingertips, and he was practically losing his mind.

"So, it's like sex?" Lily hazarded.

Tristan stared at her disbelievingly, like she was missing an important point. "Rowan really hasn't . . . ?" Tristan broke off before he finished that sentence, and pulled Lily along. "C'mon. I think we're getting a table."

Rowan was at the bar, talking to the slender bartender who had big blue eyes and bright pink hair. They clasped hands warmly over the bar, apparently good friends, and the bartender pointed to a booth off to the side that had a reserved sign on the table.

"Caleb's boyfriend, Elias," Tristan said, waving to the bartender and going directly to the booth.

"Love the pink hair. Should we go say hi?" Lily asked, curious to meet giant Caleb's itty-bitty boyfriend. She'd only heard mention of Caleb's partner, Elias, in passing and, sensing that Caleb was an intensely private person, hadn't wanted to pry. But she was curious—especially now that she saw how adorable Elias was.

"He'll come over when he's not too busy."

"He's really cute," Lily said with a devilish grin.

"No idea what he sees in a meathead like Caleb," Tristan said, grinning back.

Tristan and Lily sat down while Rowan accepted a bottle and three short glasses from Elias, then made his way to the booth. He hadn't taken two steps when a scantily clad girl wrapped her arms around Rowan's waist and pressed herself against him, nuzzling her face under his chin.

"And so it begins," Tristan said, sighing.

Lily watched as Rowan smiled sweetly at the girl, tucked the bottle under his arm to free up a hand, and pried her off of him. Lily turned to Tristan, an eyebrow cocked. "Seriously?" she asked.

"It gets worse," Tristan said, leaning back. "She was just a crucible. She's got no shot. Wait till a witch finds out he's here."

Lily tamped down a surge of jealousy while she watched Rowan run a gauntlet of girls who all reached out to touch him, trying to catch his attention or just feel him up for all Lily could tell. "But why? He's good-looking, but so are you."

"Because he's special. Gifted. He could take even an average witch and make her very powerful." Tristan smiled at her. "And thank you."

"My pleasure," Lily said, and flashed a smile back at him.

Rowan finally made it to the booth and sat down. "Moonshine?" he asked, looking between Lily and Tristan. He didn't wait for a response before starting to pour.

A bare leg and a whirl of gauzy material flashed over Rowan as a woman took a seat astride him. She was in her mid-twenties, beautiful, and she had long, light brown hair. Lily hated her instantly. Rowan didn't seem too surprised to have a witch in his lap, and Lily supposed sitting on a guy was the way witches shook hands at a bonfire.

"Hello, dearest. Come to let me claim you?" the woman asked.

"Hello, Nina," Rowan replied pleasantly.

Without any more chat, Nina leaned forward and kissed him. Lily felt Tristan take her hand under the table, stopping her, and realized that she'd leaned forward to stand up. She wanted to launch herself across the table at both of them, but then she noticed that Rowan wasn't returning the kiss. He was simply tolerating the witch, like he didn't have a choice. Nina tightened her thighs on his hips and ran her right hand up his chest, searching for his willstone. She wasn't wearing a glove on that hand. Rowan grabbed her wrists hard, and she pulled away.

"Don't touch," he said. Rowan's smile was polite, but his eyes had knives in them. He released her wrists and sat back, looking at her lazily.

"Romantic Rowan. You have to be more realistic," she cooed condescendingly. "I know Lillian set you up handsomely, but eventually you're going to need another witch to look after you. And you know I'm not only talking about money." She smiled and ran her fingers over his face. Lily wanted to slap her, and not just because she was jealous. She wanted to slap her for treating Rowan like a piece of meat. "Everyone knows that after Lillian, I'm the strongest witch in all the thirteen Covens. And with you as my head mechanic, I could be just as strong as she ever was."

Rowan jerked his head away, dodging her touch. "Nina? You're delusional."

"Am I?" she asked acidly. "Come on, Rowan. You must miss it. You must be *dying* for it. Unless Gideon's right and some new, unknown, and unbelievably powerful witch has claimed you?" She meant it as a joke, but when she saw Rowan's willstone flash, her smile quickly faded. Her eyes darted down to Rowan's stone, and her face hardened. "Who is she? What Coven is she from?"

Rowan stood up, taking Nina with him. He unwrapped her legs from around his waist and placed her back down on her feet—hard. "I belong to myself, Nina. And I intend to keep it that way."

Rowan sat down and turned away from her, leaving Nina to fume at his back. Belatedly, she noticed Tristan and Lily, sitting on the other side of the booth. Tristan still had his arm around Lily's shoulder, and she felt it tighten when Nina began to scrutinize her. Nina's eyes dropped to Lily's willstone. Confusion clouded her eyes.

"Rose?" she mumbled to herself. She looked at Tristan's affectionate posture, down at his stone, and then dismissed all three of them with a flick of her long hair as she turned and stormed away.

Rowan's chest swelled with incensed breaths. He finished pouring out three shots of moonshine and passed them around. He didn't wait to toast before drinking his and pouring himself another. His cheeks were flushed with anger and embarrassment. Lily felt bad for him.

"'I'll get you, my pretty, and your little dog, too!'" she said, and gave her best Wicked Witch of the West cackle. She got blank looks all around. "That means something where I'm from. Trust me—it's *really* funny."

Rowan smiled at her, his eyes softening at her attempt to cheer him up.

I'm sorry about that, Lily.

Lily didn't have a reply for him. She couldn't tell him in mindspeak that it didn't bother her, because it did.

"Our funny Lily," Tristan said. He squeezed her and kissed the top of her head. Rowan looked away.

"Little witch, if you're not going to drink that, pass it over," Caleb said as he slid into the booth next to Rowan. Lily gladly passed her untouched shot of moonshine across the table to Caleb. He looked tired, and his right eye looked swollen. Lily glanced down at his knuckles and saw that they were all bloody.

"Were you in a fight?" Lily asked, her voice louder than she intended.

"No," Caleb replied casually. He did his shot and looked over his shoulder. "Where the hell is my boyfriend?"

"What happened?" Rowan asked.

"The city guards have been going crazy for weeks now. There's a new captain. An Outlander," he replied, disgusted by the betrayal.

"It's not a big deal. They're just roughing up anyone who comes in and out of the city a lot." Caleb looked anxiously over his shoulder again for Elias and then turned back.

Lily watched an understanding pass between him, Rowan, and Tristan and knew they were sharing mindspeak.

Tell me what's going on, Rowan.

It's the supplies we're sending the rebels. The quality and volume are too high. Lillian's been seeking three Outlander scientists and clamped down hard. She's given Gideon and his new captain a whole squadron of inquisitors to harass Outlanders, and our gifts to the sachem got noticed.

But we can't stop yet. They need the antibiotic we made tonight.

It's too risky. Gideon may be hunting those scientists for Lillian, but he is also hunting you, and now he has more power to do it. He's following the supply chain back to the source, and he's linked our product to Caleb and Elias. Coming here was a mistake.

But the fever, Rowan. The antibiotics—

It's over, Lily.

Lily was just about to open her mouth to argue with Rowan properly when Caleb burst up from his seat, nearly knocking over the table, and ran toward the back of the building. Tristan and Rowan jumped up as well, chasing after him. Lily followed in their wake, alerted by the fear she felt ringing through Rowan, and knew that something bad was happening.

Lily burst through the back exit and found herself in an alley. To her left was a dead end. To her right, dozens of soldiers blocked the outlet onto the main street. Unconscious on the ground, in the middle of the alley, lay a slender young man with pink hair. Elias. Behind his slack figure, Caleb struggled with four soldiers as he screamed. The soldiers were beating him with cudgels, trying to bring him down. Rowan and Tristan ran to help Caleb.

Lily saw a bright flash before she heard the crack of gunshots.

"No," she gasped quietly.

She raised her hand and felt the raw energy exploding out of the soldiers' guns. It was a compressed heat, hotter for a split second than an open flame, and it contained enough energy to fuel her mechanic for hours if she asked it to. A witch wind gusted down the alley as she absorbed all the heat and momentum from the bullets, and they fell to the ground, pinging off the pavement like a bagful of dropped marbles. Energy flooded Lily's stone in a hot rush.

So that's why they also carry crossbows here, and not just guns. Explosions feel wonderful.

To a witch and her mechanic, they do. Give it to me, Lily. Give me the Gift.

Lily didn't have to struggle to recall Rowan's pattern. It was right at the forefront of her mind. Already changing the energy she'd harvested from the firearms, Lily unlocked Rowan's stone with his pattern and started channeling force into him. She shared Rowan's thrill as their bodies filled with power. His back arched, his will-stone beamed with light, and he launched himself at the soldiers surrounding Caleb.

"Witch!" someone screamed in terror.

I've missed you.

Lily didn't know if the thought was his or hers. All she knew was that she was fighting with herself not to take Rowan over completely. She had to remind herself over and over that she didn't own Rowan. You can't own a person, no matter how close to him you feel, she kept chanting inwardly.

Don't give in, Lily. Please let me keep myself.

Rowan wove his way through the four soldiers surrounding Caleb, catching their attempts to hit him with their cudgels. His return blows came so quickly that the soldiers seemed to fall down on their own as he moved past them. Then he turned to face the rest of the soldiers still blocking the end of the alley.

The soldiers ran. Only one man among them rode forward on his horse, a dark-eyed Outlander who appeared to have been in command of the now-scattered soldiers even though he didn't wear a uniform. Light from a streetlamp struck his face and Lily thought for a moment that he looked familiar. Rowan stopped, his arms falling with uncertainty to his sides.

Lily suddenly saw from Rowan's perspective. This time she was more prepared, and immediately went along with Rowan as he relived one of his early memories . . .

. . . A boy, maybe sixteen. He's skinny and he's got bruises everywhere. I'd feel bad for him if he didn't pick on us little kids. Dad says I'm to stay away from him, even though we had the same momma before she died when I was just a baby still. Dad says Carrick's father did things to him—things that turned him bad. Dad says there's no help for him now. I don't know my half brother at all, except for his name and gossip about the things he's done, but I know he's always hated me. It won't matter. Dad says I'll go to the Citadel soon and never see him again.

And I haven't until now, Lily.

The man who had once been that bruised sixteen-year-old boy looked Lily in the eye and smiled. Now that Lily knew who he was, she noticed how much he looked like Rowan.

Rowan. He knows who I am. He recognizes me.

Lily felt fear thrill through them. Rowan stepped in between Lily and the man, trying to shield her from his view.

"I don't want to hurt you, Carrick," Rowan said.

"Then you'll lose," Carrick replied. Rowan took a threatening step forward, his willstone still blazing with power. Carrick wheeled his horse around, his face twisting with scorn, then he rode away.

"Rowan!" Tristan barked. "We have to get out of here!"

Lily ran over to Tristan, who was still trying to help Caleb stand.

Rowan went to Elias and began picking him up, but then stopped. He looked up at Caleb, his eyes wide with compassion.

"I'm so sorry, Caleb," Rowan said. He lowered Elias's body back down to the ground.

Caleb's bloody face seemed to crumble. He made a small sound and took a step toward Elias. People from the bonfire started spilling into the alley.

Rowan rushed forward to intercept Caleb, catching him in a bear hug and pushing him back. "He's gone, Caleb," Rowan said, holding his friend tight. "We have to leave him. You know we have to leave him."

Tristan and Rowan forced Caleb to turn around and started hurrying him down the alley. Lily went after them and nearly tripped over one of the soldiers' dead bodies. She stared down at the corpse, frozen. He was young, and his cheeks were still pink with life. She'd killed four men, using Rowan as her weapon.

Lily!

She shook herself and started running.

Gideon arrived in the alley before they took the bodies away.

"Four men dead, sir," a soldier reported. "Five, including the rebel."

Gideon waved him off. He didn't need to be told what he could see for himself. "Did anyone go *after* them?" he asked, the edges of his teeth scraping together with frustration. The soldier's eyes widened.

"No, sir," the soldier replied, trying to hide his shock. "Fall has been claimed by a new witch." He paused and shrugged helplessly. "He would have killed us all if we'd followed them."

Gideon rubbed his eyes tiredly. If they'd caught the girl then, in the middle of committing the crime of attacking the city Guard,

Gideon could have dragged her before the Council and hanged Rowan Fall. If the guard had managed to survive apprehending him, that is. From the back of his horse, Gideon looked around at the dead bodies lying on the pavement. They had died from having their necks snapped, chests caved in, and skulls crushed. Rowan hadn't even used a weapon—he'd killed them all with his bare hands.

"You may go," he said, dismissing the shaken soldier, who gladly scurried off.

"I saw her," Carrick said as he rode forward and pulled alongside Gideon. "Different hair, but it was her."

"Did any of the other soldiers recognize her?"

Carrick sighed. "Not well enough to swear by it before the Council, I don't think. The alley was dark."

"So we still need proof or the Council will never back us." Gideon waved at the carnage. "Especially not now that they have even more reason to fear Rowan Fall and his 'new' witch. How bad was it?"

"He tore through men like they were made of paper," Carrick replied in his shadowy voice. "I wouldn't doubt that he could have taken twenty mounted men, or I would have chased him myself."

Gideon studied his new captain. Carrick's voice was surprisingly level, but somewhere in his eye was genuine hatred. And maybe even respect.

"Proud of your fellow Outlander?" Gideon guessed.

Carrick looked away and changed the subject. "If you close off the city, there are only so many places Fall can take her," he said. "There are several Outlander safe houses used for smuggling rebels into Salem."

"Start with the safe houses, but go easy," Gideon said approvingly. "I don't want him to feel hunted. Wherever he takes her, I want them to relax and settle in while we think of a plan and look for the Council's proof. Will you need bribe money?"

"I may." Carrick furrowed his brow. "Let me see where they land first. There are plenty of Outlanders who hate the Salem Witch and wouldn't feel too badly about turning in her double. If for no other reason than to avoid having to deal with two of them."

Gideon nodded his approval. As Carrick wheeled his horse and galloped off, Gideon wondered if the drub wasn't getting a bit *too* smart for his own good.

CHAPTER
11

THEY RACED THROUGH THE CITY STREETS, CUTTING through alleys, jumping fences, and skirting around the roaring guardians chained to the bottoms of the greentowers.

The neighborhood changed and became more residential, but it wasn't a nice part of town. Lily thought she recognized this place. They were in the Swallows. Few people were out on the streets. They slowed their pace, still not speaking. Caleb's head was down, his massive shoulders hunched. He wasn't even looking where he was going, and Rowan had to lead him. They reached a small building. Tristan entered first, opening the door with a wave of his hand and a flash of magelight.

As Lily entered, she realized it was the safe house with the tunnel beneath it. A plain-faced woman in her mid-twenties met them in the hallway, the question in her eyes turning to alarm when she saw Caleb.

"What happened?" she asked, rushing forward to help.

Lily recognized the woman's voice from her other trip through the safe house. Mostly, she remembered how possessive the woman had sounded when she'd asked if Rowan had given himself to a new witch. The woman had brown hair and brown eyes, but she wasn't quite as dark as most of the Outlanders. Lily looked at her willstone and found it uninteresting. Low strength, Lily realized. This woman was not a witch. Lily recalled Nina's confusion when she'd looked at the rose-colored stone at her neck, and finally understood it. Nina had seen power in Lily that didn't fit inside the flirty rose-colored stone she wore. Lily snapped herself back into the present moment and tried to smile in a friendly way at the woman who tended the safe house. The smile wasn't returned.

"City soldiers tried to take Elias into custody," Tristan replied.

Caleb broke away at the mention of Elias's name, storming down the hallway. Rowan went after him.

"Elias is dead, and so are four soldiers," Tristan continued when Caleb was out of earshot. "We need to leave Salem now, Esmeralda."

"The tunnel's blocked. There was a cave-in almost a week ago," Esmeralda replied. "We haven't been able to clear it because Gideon had his guards put seismic wards all along the perimeter. One little jiggle underground, and the tunnel, the safe house, everything is lost. They're clamping down, Tristan. Hard." Esmeralda's gaze leapt over to Lily. She narrowed her eyes. "Who are you?" she asked in a less-than-friendly way.

"I'm Rowan's witch," Lily said bluntly, taking a challenging step toward her.

Esmeralda took a step back, her face blanching. "Lillian," she whispered fearfully. Too late, Lily remembered that glamours didn't hold in direct light. She hadn't meant to scare the woman.

"Not exactly," Lily replied in a less combative tone. "It's complicated."

Lily. Please come.

"Rowan needs me," Lily said, excusing herself with a polite nod. She left Tristan to explain to Esmeralda as much or as little as he thought prudent, and went after Rowan and Caleb.

She found them in the kitchen. Rowan had Caleb backed into a corner. He was holding out his arms to keep Caleb from running. Caleb's face was bruised, bleeding, and his eyes wild with grief.

"Lily," Caleb said. "Claim me."

"Would you just *wait*?" Rowan pleaded. Caleb tried to get past him, but Rowan was still coursing with the power Lily had poured into him, and he easily detained the larger man. "You're not yourself, Caleb."

"Of course I'm not myself!" Caleb screamed. "And I'll never be myself again, Ro. Not really. Not without him. You, of all people, should know that."

Rowan sighed and dropped his arms. "Yes. I know it."

"I wasn't strong enough. Now I've got nothing." He broke off, and his chest fluttered with the tears that he managed to choke down. "It's my decision. I'm ready to be a witch's fist." Caleb's swollen eyes locked with Lily's. "Claim me."

Lily looked down at Caleb's willstone. It didn't call to her the way Rowan's had, but it was still beautiful and she wanted it badly. Caleb had power—not as much as Tristan, and nowhere near as much as Rowan, but he was still strong. Lily wondered why he wasn't some other witch's mechanic.

Lily. Don't. He doesn't know what he's saying.

Just because you hate that you gave yourself to me doesn't mean he will.

What are you talking about?

Lily opened her memory to Rowan. She showed him himself, telling Tristan that he regretted giving himself to her.

Is that why you were so cruel to me, Lily?

You think I was the one who was cruel?

She let him feel how much he'd hurt her. How much she'd learned to care about him and how all of that was ruined when she found out he didn't feel the same.

He looked stunned.

"That's not what I meant," he said quietly.

"I notice you didn't say that in mindspeak," Lily replied, disappointed. "Why? Are you hiding something?" She hadn't expected him to blurt out that he didn't think she was like Lillian at all anymore, but she'd secretly hoped he would. Rowan tried to continue, but Lily strode forward and cut him off. "This is between Caleb and me. You shouldn't be interfering."

Rowan's face hardened and he stood back. "You're right. I have no right to tell a witch what she can and can't do. I hope you're paying attention, Caleb. This is your life from now on if you become a witch's fist."

Lily ignored his comment, or tried to. She busied herself by re-attaching her willstones to her necklace, wondering why she felt so guilty. Rowan was acting like she was laying down the law, but she wasn't. She wasn't in charge here; she was just doing what Caleb wanted. Wasn't she?

Lily shook off her doubt and stood across from Caleb. He was in so much pain that she could feel it spilling out and around him like a halo. She took his hand in hers.

"Are you going to fight the Citadel?" Caleb asked.

Lily paused. Over the past few weeks she hadn't thought twice about supplying the rebels with whatever Alaric asked of her. But her motivation for learning magic was not to stay in this world and fight. It was to go home. She looked into Caleb's desperate face, knowing that she had to make a choice. Did she want to stand up against Lillian? Or more importantly, could she live with herself if she didn't?

"For as long as I'm here, I'll fight Lillian," she replied, hushed by the weight of her decision.

"I need your word."

Lily thought of that old history teacher in the woods again. She wanted to know his name but wondered if it would be easier or harder to forget him if she did. "I give you my word that if they attack us, I'll fight her with everything I've got."

"Then you've got me."

Lily's hand darted out hungrily of its own accord. She noticed that it was moving too fast and managed to snatch it back at the last second. She heard Rowan suck in a sharp breath.

"Sorry! I'm sorry. I've only done this once before," she said, grinning sheepishly at Caleb.

"Well, I've never done this with a girl," he said shakily. "Let alone a witch, and I hear that's something else entirely."

"No grabbing," Lily promised, and crossed her heart.

He took a second, and then nodded at Lily. She raised her hand and ever so slowly took his willstone between the tips of her fingers. Caleb's eyes closed and he shivered from head to toe. Lily had Caleb's pattern. She played it back to his stone and saw one of Caleb's memories. From Caleb's perspective she saw . . .

. . . A beautiful blond boy, maybe twelve, sitting on a brick wall. My dad makes me go back. He's seen that Elias had his head on my shoulder when he picked me up after lessons, and he tells me I have to go back and punch the sissy in the nose. I don't want my dad to know I'm like Elias. I walk back. My throat feels tight, but I hit him.

You don't have to show me anything you don't want to, Caleb.

. . . The sachem walks across the room quickly. The meeting is over. The sachem stops and holds his hand out to me. He says I've grown. The way he says it makes me laugh. I'm as big as two of him, and I'm not even fifteen. Elias sees the sachem notice me. I'm so proud. Someday Elias will notice me again, too. He'll forgive me for what I did. Forgive me, Elias.

I wasn't there for him, Lily.

. . . Elias lies in the alley. He's not moving. They tried to take him to get to me, to make me submit. Help me, Rowan. There are too many of them.

I'm so sorry, Caleb.

It's happened to both of us, you know.

. . . Rowan is bucking and screaming. I try to hold him back, try to pull him away through the crowd. Curses fling out of him, every one of them for Lillian, standing stock-still on the scaffolding next to the hanged body of his father. River Fall is dead. Rowan's voice shreds through the silence of the crowd as he screams how much he hates her. None of it will bring his father back, but his vows to kill Lillian with his bare hands might just get him the noose, too. Tristan comes. Together, we drag Rowan away. I'm scared he's going to hurt himself, so I don't leave him all night, even though he struggles to get away. But no matter how hard I hold him down as he sobs, I know it won't hold together everything that's broken in him.

Lily dropped Caleb's stone as if it had burned her. She looked over at Rowan.

"Hey!" Rowan exclaimed, stepping forward to catch Caleb as he fainted. Lily put up her hands just in time, and together, she and Rowan guided Caleb's slack body to the floor. "You can't just tear yourself away from that kind of deep contact with someone, Lily."

"I didn't know," she said, avoiding his eyes. She couldn't look at him. "I didn't know," she repeated, seeing a black-haired man dangling lifeless from the end of a rope.

Lily and Caleb sat next to each other on the floor of the kitchen. Caleb didn't want to be healed, he just wanted to sit in the dark with his back up against the refrigerator for a while. There was a lamp on in the next room, sending cutouts of light and shadow through the legs of the kitchen table and chairs toward them. Neither felt like getting up and joining the others.

"They need us to love other people," Caleb said, breaking the long silence.

"Who are they?" Lily asked quietly.

"The Citadel—the Council, the Covens, Lillian and her army. And I almost allowed myself to be a part of it." Caleb shook his head bitterly. "You know I was accepted as a mechanic when I was seven and given citizenship? When I was eleven, I dropped out. I didn't want to be claimed and become a puppet. A witch's fist. That's what we Outlanders call mechanics." Caleb glanced at Lily, smiling sadly. "The Citadel needs another way to control people like me. Lillian needs our permission in order to take over our willstones and rummage through our minds until she get names out of us. So she finds out who we love the most and hurts them until we submit. At least, Elias didn't have to go through that."

"No, he didn't," Lily said, squeezing Caleb's hand. "Is that what happened with Rowan and his father?"

"That was different." Caleb looked at Lily. "Did you know he was a doctor?" Lily nodded and Caleb continued. "River Fall was in my father's tribe. That's how Rowan and I know each other. We've always been friends, even after I left the Citadel and returned to my people. Everyone respected River Fall. Loved him, even. Lillian didn't have to kill him. He wasn't a rebel. All he wanted to do was help sick people who couldn't afford a witch's magic. But when she outlawed being a doctor, she went after River first."

"Why?" Lily asked. She remembered the elders' bowed heads at even the mention of River Fall. "Why him first when so many loved him?"

"To make her point," Caleb said. "She did it so everyone in the Thirteen Cities would know that no one, not even the father of the person she loved most in the world, would be spared. And for the most part, it worked," he said with a sad shrug that rolled his gigantic shoulders. "When people heard that she'd hanged River Fall, everyone in the Thirteen Cities fell in line. The other Covens, the Council, everyone."

"In line?"

"With her doctrine. No science. No research. No inquiry. Witchcraft is the one true way." Caleb laughed bitterly. "In a way, killing River Fall was the dumbest thing Lillian ever did. It left a lot of people with no choice but to join Alaric. All the Outlander tribes, city-bred teachers and doctors, and a lot of people who were just plain angry or scared, came from all over to pledge their lives to Alaric's cause. Including Rowan, Tristan, and me."

"Is that when the three of you touched stones?" Lily guessed.

"Right after Rowan had bonded with his second stone," he said, nodding. "We became stone kin that night."

Lily's mind was still entangled with Caleb's from their claiming ceremony, and she caught glimpses of Tristan and Rowan from over the past year. Tristan and Caleb had worked hard to keep Rowan from falling to pieces after losing his father and Lillian, and they were there for him when he smashed his first stone. Lily saw a skinny body sweating under a sheet as Rowan wasted away for weeks in agony. She saw Tristan helping Caleb as the two of them brought Rowan back to health slowly, lovingly. Like true brothers.

That time together had brought the three of them together quickly. Lily had always known the bond between the three men was strong, but now she understood just how strong. They would die for each other. And they had grown that close because of what Lillian had done to Rowan.

"How can Rowan think I'm anything like Lillian?" Lily asked. "She's evil."

Caleb's eyes narrowed in thought. "You have her strength of mind, Lily. When you believe in something, you follow through, whatever it takes. He loves that about you. And it scares him to pieces."

Lily rubbed Caleb's meaty hand in hers and let her head tilt back and rest against the refrigerator, thinking about why Lillian had chosen *her* out of the infinite number of versions of *them* available. She decided that there was one thing Lillian must not have considered— that strength of mind works both ways. If Lillian would do anything to follow through with her beliefs, so would Lily. And what Lily believed now was that Lillian had to be stopped.

"She's dying, Caleb. I'm sorry it wasn't in time to save Elias." Lily's throat caught as one of Caleb's memories of Elias, laughing on a summer day by a lake, flashed through her mind. Elias. He shone like the sun. Losing him cut into Lily as if she'd loved him her whole life. As Caleb had. "But trust me. It'll be over soon."

Even if I have to kill her myself.

"Slow down, Lillian," Juliet said anxiously. She tried to take a hold of her sister's arm as they flew down the dungeon stairs, but Lillian yanked it away.

"Don't fuss, Juliet. I feel better than I've felt in ages," Lillian said, her eyes gleaming.

The robe she'd thrown on over her nightgown was untied, and Juliet could easily see a red flush sweeping up her sister's pale chest and the dewy sheen of a fever sweat forming on her cheeks. Lillian was too excited to realize that she shouldn't be out of bed, but Juliet knew there was no stopping her now. Citadel soldiers had just brought in the three scientists Michael Snowshower had named, and they were waiting in the dungeon below the keep.

"This could be the end of it," Lillian whispered hopefully.

Juliet had no idea what her sister was talking about, but she didn't bother asking. She was too worried that the flickering torch-light would make one or both of them miss a step and go tumbling down the spiraling granite staircase to spare a thought for her sister's obsession. And *obsession* was the only word for it.

Since the three scientists—Hakan, Keme, and Chenoa—had been named, Lillian had hunted them with every resource at her disposal. She'd claimed Michael Snowshower and dug through his mind for any information about the unlucky three. She'd sent out spies, restricted access in and out of the city, and raided every known Outlander caravan from Salem to Richmond. She was so consumed in the hunt she'd even seemed to have forgotten about Lily, although Juliet hadn't. She thought about Lily all the time.

"Lady," chorused the soldiers. They stood at attention when she swept into the guardroom at the center of the star-shaped passage-ways that radiated out to the prisoner's cells.

"Captain. Where are they?" Lillian asked, barely containing her eagerness.

The captain led them to a nearby cell. Lillian waved her hand at the wall sconces and they burst into flame, revealing two men and one woman behind the bars. She smiled with relief. She'd seen their faces in Snowshower's mind and knew that her soldiers had found the right scientists.

"Hakan, the builder," Lillian said, her eyes trained on a dark man in his early thirties. "Keme, the problem solver," she said, turning her gaze on a frightened young man. Despite the fact that he had an old Outlander name, he was fair-haired and light-eyed like a citizen. Juliet guessed that he couldn't be much older than her twenty years. Lillian repositioned herself and made one of the sconces flare more brightly for a moment, illuminating the woman. "And Chenoa, the dreamer."

Lillian stared at Chenoa the longest. She was the most important. She was older, and looked close to fifty. Her cinnamon-colored skin was creased with thick lines around her eyes and mouth, and her black hair was shot through with white. She was a little thing, but her presence seemed to fill up the whole cell. She looked back at Lillian, her eyes narrowing as she assessed the Salem Witch.

"Have them separated, Captain," Lillian ordered, suddenly turning away. "Put them all on different levels of the dungeon and make sure their cells are on opposite ends of the passageways—as far away from each other as possible." Lillian looked back at Chenoa. "She goes on the lowest level."

Juliet hurried after Lillian, feeling relieved. "So you'll have your Coven make the medicine for the Outlanders now?" she asked. Lillian remained silent. "Would you like me to get word to Nina to start work on that, or do you feel strong enough to do it yourself? I know yours would be better than hers, but maybe you need to rest?"

"Juliet," Lillian said, stopping on the stairs and turning to look down at her. "You know I can't do that."

"What are you talking about?" Juliet said, her voice dropping. A knot was forming in her chest. "You promised."

Lillian's face was as smooth as glass. "You think that medicine will go to heal children—and some of it will—but you must know that some of it will also go to warriors. Alaric's savages are going to try to get Chenoa, Hakan, and Keme back. The more of them that die of fever, the fewer of them will be left to kill my soldiers."

"But, you said—"

"Stop it, Juliet. You can't possibly be that naive," she said impatiently. "What I'm doing will save the lives of the men and women who defend this city."

"At the cost of how many innocent Outlander lives?" Juliet fired back. She stared at her sister, as if seeing her for the first time. "You're a liar."

"I'm much worse than that." Lillian looked away for a moment, and Juliet saw that flicker inside of her again—that inner turmoil that Juliet could nearly hear even without mindspeak.

"Do these three scientists mean so much to you that you'd allow tens of thousands to die? They're *children*," Juliet said, choking on the word.

Lillian didn't respond.

"Who are you?" Juliet swept past Lillian, leaving her to struggle up the treacherous staircase alone.

They had to spend the next few days hiding out at the safe house. Since the fight in the alley, Rowan's apartment had been crawling with Citadel soldiers, and they'd had to abandon it and move in with Esmeralda. She brought them supplies and even gave Lily a few of her own dresses to wear. Lily tried to reach out to her, feeling badly about how she had treated her on their first meeting, but Esmeralda was slow to thaw and never really warmed up to her.

Every day, they went down into the tunnel to rebuild the collapsed passage as carefully as they could. They brought candles and Lily sat close to their lambent light, channeling energy into Caleb and Rowan. With Lily's assistance, they could pick up huge boulders with one hand and carry them out silently, one by one. It was slow work, not because the earth was difficult to move with so much strength flowing into them, but because they didn't dare do anything that would disturb the seismic wards above. They couldn't even talk aloud or tread heavily while they were underground.

For Lily, it was like living in a grave. There were many times she felt panic steal her breath and she'd have to rush out—back up through the hatch and into the sunlight. Fear of the dark, confined space wasn't the only thing Lily had to contend with. She was more exhausted every day. The guys got their energy from her, and even though she was the one sitting while they worked, Lily was the one who ended up feeling drained by it.

The enforced silence of the hideout left Tristan outside Lily's reach for many hours a day. He could mindspeak with Caleb and Rowan, and they could relay his thoughts to her, but it wasn't the same. Not only was Tristan unable to work without tiring the way Rowan and Caleb could with Lily fueling them, but he was also cut off from her in a way they weren't, and when the workday was done, she was usually too tired to spend any time with him. Tristan was getting left out, and tension had begun to build between him and Rowan. By the end of the third day, Tristan had had enough.

"I want everyone to hear this," Tristan said, breaking out of mindspeak with Rowan. "I want Lily to claim me. It doesn't make sense for me to be blundering around down there without her strength."

"We'll be through it in another day. Don't, Tristan." Rowan wasn't pleading, he was ordering.

"Why not?" Lily asked. "We should have done this weeks ago, when you two first started teaching me. Why are you so against me claiming him?"

Rowan didn't answer.

"Because he thinks we need someone outside your influence, just in case," Tristan said.

"In case of *what?*" Lily asked. Fatigue finally made her lose her temper. "In case I suddenly turn psycho and start hanging everyone else's fathers?" Rowan looked at Lily, his mouth parted in shock. "Rowan," Lily began, knowing she had gone too far. He turned and left the room before she could continue.

She stood very still for a moment, hoping that if she didn't move she could somehow figure out a way to take back what she'd said, then darted after him, following him upstairs. He'd shut the door to the room he, Tristan, and Caleb had been using as theirs. Lily knocked, but he didn't answer.

Rowan. Let me in.

Get out of my head, Lily.

No. We need to talk.

There's nothing I want to say to you.

"Open the damn door before I kick it in," Lily said, her voice louder than it should be.

The door flew open. Rowan grabbed her, pulled her into his room, and slammed the door behind her. He was so angry he was shaking.

"I'm sorry," Lily said, meaning it with her whole heart.

She opened her feelings up to him, the way he had when he'd apologized to her. She showed him a fragment of Caleb's memory, one of Rowan crying, and she let him feel how ashamed she was for being so careless about something that meant so much. He looked surprised for a moment, and then all his anger left him in a rush.

"When did it happen?" she asked.

"Seven months ago," he replied, his voice low. "I begged her." Lily felt a flash of desperation and disbelief—his feelings when he pleaded for his father's life. "But she'd made up her mind."

Rowan opened up a memory for Lily to share.

. . . A courtroom. This farce of a trial is over and it devolves into a circus of people screaming and shouting around me. At the center of the chaos is Lillian. She just stands there—silent. She won't let me in her head, won't answer me, won't acknowledge if she can feel my hurt. I send it all to her. I hope the hurt goes away soon and turns into hate. I let her know that, too. How I can't wait to hate her . . .

The betrayal Rowan had felt—and how staggeringly empty it had left him when he'd lost both his father and Lillian in one devastating moment—knocked the wind out of Lily. It was nothing like what had happened between Tristan and her. There was no comparing their betrayals. "How can you even stand to look at me?" she asked breathlessly.

"That's the problem. I should look at you and see her, but I don't anymore. Not since we spent that night in the tree." He shook his head, smiling at the memory. "You'd been in shock for days. I woke up the next morning, and you told a joke. You did that for me. To put me at ease so I'd worry less about you. You're still the most stubborn person I've ever met, but you also admit when you're wrong. You're thoughtful and kind, Lily."

"You say that like it's a bad thing," she said.

He lifted his hand and touched her face, his fingers cupping the curve of her jaw. "Because I want to trust you. I want you to be everything I loved about her and nothing I hated. I want it so badly that I know I shouldn't trust myself enough to trust you. But I guess I'm doing it anyway, even though I know you're not staying."

"What do you mean?" she asked, her voice shaking.

"You want to go home. And when you've figured out how, you're going to leave us, aren't you?" Rowan ran his hand down her throat. His fingers slid lightly over her neck and collarbone, just barely touching the platinum edges of her willstones. Every place he touched tingled and tightened. She didn't have an answer. Rowan suddenly released her and went to his bedroom door. "You need salt," he said. "And I'm a bad mechanic for ignoring it."

Rowan took her hand and led her downstairs. She followed him clumsily, her knees still wobbly, not sure what had just happened between them. Caleb and Tristan were in the kitchen, about to sit down to dinner.

"Oh good," Caleb said. "No one's bleeding."

"We worked it out." Rowan smiled and pulled a chair out for Lily, then sat down next to her. Tristan looked between them, his face stony. He stood up suddenly, his food untouched. "Tristan?" Rowan said. "Do you still want Lily to claim you?"

Tristan turned back. "Oh, so now you're okay with it?" he said sarcastically.

"Would you just stop?" Lily said through a laugh. "Rowan's had a hard time trusting me. I get why now, and we're figuring it out. But even though this is hard for him, it really is your decision, Tristan, and no one else's. So, you let me know when you're ready."

"I'm ready," Tristan said, like he was on his last nerve. "I'm sick of being left out."

"Okay. But later?" Lily asked plaintively. "I'm starving."

After dinner, Lily claimed Tristan. She was much gentler than she'd been with either Rowan or Caleb, even though the urge to take him over completely was strong. She didn't grab him or break off contact too soon. She tried to allow Tristan his privacy as she had tried with Caleb, but some kind of memory exchange seemed to be part of the process. Lily saw several of Tristan's formative memories, some of the many women he'd been intimate with, including something currently with Esmeralda. But mostly she saw Lillian and Rowan. She wondered if Rowan knew how much Tristan both admired and resented him.

He knows.

Then why did you let me claim you, Tristan? Why not find another witch so you don't feel like you're always second to him?

Because you need me, Lily, and so do Rowan and Caleb. I can be a selfish person sometimes, but in the end I'd rather help my friends than help myself.

I know. That's probably why I've always cared about you. No matter what universe we're in.

Gideon kicked off his shoes and dropped down into his chair. The meeting with Roberts, Bainbridge, and Wake had not gone as he'd hoped. Gideon had told them where the other Lillian was hiding. One raid, and they would have the physical proof they needed that there were other universes and that Lillian had learned how to access them, but they'd balked. Roberts had sputtered like a fool, saying that they would need Coven approval for a raid, and if they were wrong, they'd hang. Gideon wondered how long that petulant old man would be alive and debated whether or not it would be useful to try to help him along with dying.

"You'd think they'd want to at least *try* to capture the other Lillian," Gideon said, disgusted.

"Not necessarily." Carrick stood by the window, looking out. "Being able to access other worlds may mean that the people no longer need witches to get them what they need. But if they no longer need witches, they may decide they don't need Councilmen either. They're afraid."

Gideon cocked his head at Carrick, studying him. Whatever the Outlander lacked in formal education, he made up for with keen intuition. He certainly had an uncanny understanding of what people feared.

"Whoever holds the most power is the one in control," Gideon countered. "And there is no greater power than this."

"But you still need a witch in order to do it," Carrick reminded him. "And the problem with witches is that they tend to do the controlling."

A very good point, but Gideon hadn't given up yet—wouldn't give up until he solved this problem. Too much was at stake. If he could find a way to control just *one* witch, he might not need the Council or the Covens. With the ability to access other worlds, the possibilities were endless.

"The Council will never back us," Gideon said. "We need to move without them. Get in touch with the traitor."

"Are you sure?"

"Yes. Let's do it tonight."

Caleb didn't want to wait until morning to start work on the tunnel. With three witch-powered mechanics hauling rubble and shoring up the braces, Rowan figured they could have the rest of the tunnel dug out before dawn. It was decided that arriving in the Outlander caravan outside the walls would be safer at night, and the sooner they got out of Salem the better. Esmeralda had already needed to call in a few favors to hide the extra supplies they required, and no one wanted to tempt fate another day.

Reluctantly, Lily climbed down into the hatch with her candles in a knapsack, already exhausted from a full day's work. The stuffy air choked her and made her light-headed. The dark smothered her, making her feel weak. Luckily, they didn't have to go far before Rowan put down a square of black silk for her to sit on and began setting up the candles in a circle around the square. He lit the wicks, and their warm glow instantly filled her with energy, soothing her fears.

"It'll be over soon," Rowan whispered in her ear. He brushed his lips across her cheek, startling her. Before Lily could even gasp, he'd disappeared down the dark tunnel after Tristan and Caleb.

Lily sat down in her circle of light, desperately hoping that Rowan's brief show of affection hadn't been an accident. She closed her eyes and touched her mechanics' minds to let them know she was ready to start channeling energy into them.

Finally! I've been waiting for this my whole life.

The thought had come from Tristan, and Lily could feel his elation when she unlocked the particular pattern that had grown between his mind and his stone and filled him with power. It wasn't as overwhelming as when she'd poured all that power from the fire into Rowan's stone when they'd fought the Woven. She still felt a thrill, but it was manageable, and she easily resisted the temptation to posses him. As Rowan and Caleb echoed Tristan's exhilaration, she reached out to Rowan for an explanation.

Rowan? Why doesn't this feel the same as it did in the cabin, or when we were fighting in the alley where Elias died?

It isn't the Gift. It isn't warrior magic. The scale is smaller, and the bond between us isn't as intense.

But it still feels good?

Of course, Lily. It's amazing.

Rowan? Are witches addictive?

I don't know. Is being close to someone addictive?

No. It's necessary. Everyone needs to feel close to someone else.

Then witches are necessary.

Lily knew there had to be a flaw in his thinking—people got on just fine in her world without witches—but she was too taken with the idea to pursue it. In her world, she'd been loved—by her sister, her mother, and even her Tristan—but Lily had never been necessary.

As the night wore on, Lily felt the tons of rubble moving under the hands of her mechanics because she fueled them, felt the circle of minds wrapped around hers because she was the touchstone, and she knew that Rowan had been right. In this world she was able to contribute things that really mattered to people, like clean water and antibiotics. She was important. Just as Lillian had said she would be.

Lily? We're through to the other side. I'm coming back for you.

Lily stirred. She realized that she was lying on her side in the dark, and she couldn't breathe.

Hurry, Rowan. The candles have burned out.

Why didn't you tell me sooner?

I think I passed out. There's no air in here.

Esmeralda was supposed to leave the hatch open for you.

It's shut. Please hurry. I'm cold, Rowan.

Cold?

Lily could feel a thrill of urgency race through Rowan. It pierced past the haze of fatigue that pressed down on her. Lily sensed Tristan and Caleb responding to Rowan's alarm. They chased after him as he ran down the tunnel. Lily didn't have the energy to give them any extra speed.

Lily heard a distant boom and the ground above her shook. Earth fell from the ceiling in a sheet. She felt rocks hitting her, cutting her. Then everything went silent.

Lily felt someone grab her. She screamed.

Rowan!

Lily, we're cut off. There was an explosion aboveground that triggered a cave-in. We've been betrayed. I'm digging.

A strange man hovered over Lily in the dark. She could feel rough hands on her bare arms and legs. She was so weak she couldn't even draw magelight from her stones.

"Lillian," oozed a voice. It wasn't totally foreign to her. She recognized it from Rowan's memories.

"Carrick," she whispered.

Rowan, help! Carrick—

Lily felt a web of ice wrap around her heart. Her body went rigid, her limbs wriggling with agony as Carrick ripped her willstones off her neck.

CHAPTER
12

Gideon took the steps in his father's keep two at a time. The Danforth Keep, much like the Citadel, had been built hundreds of years ago when the first witches rose from their pyres after the Salem Witch Trials and took over the continent. If only the witches had been hanged and not burned, they would have been wiped out, but apparently the constables of Salem hadn't known that a rare breed of witches known as firewalkers had recently emerged. Since Carrick had explained to him how parallel universes worked, Gideon often wondered what his world would have been like if that one choice, burning over hanging, had been made differently.

Gideon had been rushing since he got the message. The Danforth Keep was on the opposite end of Salem, as far away from the Citadel as one could get without breaching the city walls. And he'd had to traverse the city at first light, when every greentower was undergoing preparation to capture the scant hours of sunlight left during the autumn months. The traffic was murder, but unfortunately, there was no way to bring Danforth closer to the Citadel.

His father's keep had been originally built to protect the Danforth family from the witches, and then later when witches and mechanics were found in the Danforth line, it became a satellite to the Citadel on the other side of town. It was widely known that Gideon's ancestor, the original Thomas Danforth, was the judge who sent half of Salem to the pyre. Gideon supposed that his father, the current Thomas Danforth, was not so different in temperament from his predecessor. Since the trials, hanging had become the customary way to execute all enemies of the Witch State, and many in Salem had dangled because of Thomas's dedication to rooting out the scientist heretics for the Lady of Salem.

Gideon had gotten word from Carrick that his father wanted him to come directly to the dungeons, and Gideon shivered as he descended the many steps. He hated how medieval it was down there, but he knew that the cold and dark were necessary to deplete a witch. Even the solid stone construction served a purpose, no matter how ghastly it looked in the pale glow of magelight. The naturally occurring stone of the area, good old granite, had a hefty dose of quartz crystal in it. The single, clock-like vibration of quartz acted as a buffer from the varied and mutable vibrations created in willstones. If the walls of granite were thick enough, they could keep a witch protected from the magic of another—or keep her cut off from the outside. A witch could still do magic inside a granite keep, but it was nearly impossible for her spells to penetrate its walls.

At least, usually it was. Gideon knew that a witch as powerful as Lillian could do just about anything she wanted, which was why he was rushing when normally he would have waited for the green-tower farmers to get where they were going before trying to brave the gridlock. His father wasn't a mechanic. Thomas was a politician. He had no idea how powerful this Lily could potentially be.

Gideon arrived at the lowest level of the keep. He looked down and saw a slip of a witch with short, platinum-blonde hair lying on the damp floor in front of his father. Her whisper-thin dress barely kept her decent. She shivered and shook on the ground. Tears streamed from between her shut eyes. She was mostly unconscious, but still crying in agony. Gideon had to look closely to recognize her face, but the angular features, alabaster skin, and those heart-shaped lips that were so like Juliet's were exactly the same. She was Lillian, but not Lillian. Carrick stood over her with something gleaming in the palm of his hand. Gideon froze when he realized what he was holding.

"You'll kill her." Gideon strode forward and offered his handkerchief. "At least put them in silk."

"She's managed this long," Thomas said indifferently.

"Carrick, put them down." Gideon allowed a hint of malice to enter his voice as he said the Outlander's name. Really, it was beyond the pale that a drub was allowed to fondle a witch's willstones, let alone a drub who had gone behind his back and played up to his father. He'd given Carrick too much power by making him a captain. But he'd deal with Carrick later. "Father, a witch's bond with her stone is much deeper than the average person's. This could injure her to the point where she's of no use to you."

His father nodded quickly, not wanting their prize too damaged. Carrick balked. After a moment, he reluctantly slid all three stones into the silk handkerchief Gideon had proffered. He obviously didn't want to give up the feeling of strength coursing through him at the touch of a great witch's stones. Gideon knew the feeling. Even through the silk, he could feel the thrum of power reaching into him. It was intoxicating.

The girl curled up into a ball. She tucked her knees under her chin, her ribs still shuddering with sobs. The crying stopped, but she began to whimper. Gideon opened his hand and saw the three stones.

"We'll have to move her. Get her out of the city. Lillian can never know about this," his father was saying fearfully, but Gideon was only half listening. "She can't stay here. I won't risk getting caught imprisoning a witch."

"But where? There aren't many prisons that can hold her," Carrick said.

"I know where we can take her," Gideon replied testily. Lillian had just reminded him of the perfect place not six months ago, asking if it was still of use. She hadn't explained why she needed it, but when he had checked it out for her, he'd found that it was sound. "It's old and very strong."

"Is she going to die?" Thomas asked.

"No," Gideon replied. He forced himself to hold only the edges of the silk so the stones swung free of his touch. He felt the lack of her essence immediately and understood something about Rowan that he hadn't before. "We need to discuss this, Father."

"I should think so," Danforth said with a satisfied smile. "The Council will have to believe us now."

"No," Gideon interrupted. "Don't tell them yet. Why should they benefit when they were too spineless to back us in the first place?"

"We're going to need support, son," Danforth said.

"Yes." Gideon stared at the girl, his mind turning over rapidly. "But *after* we figure out how to control her for ourselves." He looked at Carrick. "Do you know how to spirit walk at all?"

The Outlander looked away and shook his head. "But I know of one who does. The shaman."

"Find him," Gideon ordered. "In the meantime, I'll work with her."

"And how do you intend to do that?" Thomas asked. "With her stones she could crush us, and without her stones she's like this," he said, gesturing to the girl's prone body.

Gideon looked down at the stones in his hand again. Golden, rose, and smoke. Something clicked in his head. He had no idea what it meant that Lily had every color of willstone possible, but he knew one thing. The fact that there was more than one made him the luckiest man in the world.

"Yes, but there are three of them, father. Three willstones," Gideon said excitedly. The idea was still solidifying in his thoughts. He removed the huge smoke stone from his palm and held it in his other hand. He looked at his father and found understanding and approval. "Divide and conquer."

Lily dreamed of the Woven. They were chasing her through the forest. Their bodies were a jumble of fur and barely stitched-together skin. Raw bones showed through their sores, and their eyes and tongues were rotting in their heads. One of them looked like it was half human, half boar—caught in the middle of a painful transformation. The wereboar had yellowed tusks growing out of a human mouth and called Lily by name as it chased her.

Rowan told her to climb, and Lily tried to dig her fingers into the walls of the stone cabin, but she kept slipping. She broke her fingernails down to the quick as she tried to scrabble up the impossibly high wall.

The Woven pulled her down by her ankles. They didn't wait to kill her before they started eating her. Somewhere, Rowan was screaming her name, but he was too far away, and she was in too much pain to reach him.

Juliet hurried through the market. She was sure now that the young man with the dark hair and light eyes was following her. He had the muscular, lean frame of a fighter, and the enormous willstone at the base of his throat was crawling with the bright filaments of power.

He was definitely a witch's mechanic—a powerful mechanic to a powerful witch.

She turned down a quiet alley and glanced around the corner anxiously, waiting for him to pass her by, but when she looked again, she couldn't find him anywhere.

"Juliet," said a deep voice behind her. A familiar voice, she realized, even as she jumped. Juliet spun around, and her pursuer dropped his face glamour. Juliet relaxed when she saw that it was Rowan. "I need your help," he said desperately.

He looked awful. His eyes were sunken in shadow, his clothes were rumpled, and he hadn't shaved or combed his hair.

"What happened?" Juliet breathed.

"They've taken Lily. Please. I can't hear her." He was nearly frantic. "I think they've taken her willstones away."

Juliet's skin crawled at the thought. "What can I do?"

"She could hear you even without willstones. You're sisters," Rowan said. He took Juliet's hands in his, begging her. "I know your loyalty is still with Lillian . . ."

"I'll help," Juliet said, cutting him off. It hurt her to even think of it, but she didn't know who she was loyal to anymore. "What do you need me to do?"

Rowan's eyes closed briefly with relief. "Thank you, Juliet," he whispered. "Come with me."

Juliet followed Rowan, knowing full well that every step she took with him brought her farther away from Lillian.

Lily? Where are you?

Lily heard Juliet's voice in her head, waking her. She opened her eyes. It was so dark she may as well have kept them closed. Her head pounded and she felt dizzy. She tried to reach out to Rowan, Tristan, and Caleb but all she felt was an intense, stabbing pain when she tried to mindspeak with them. A seasick feeling gripped her, as if she were pitching around in the bottom of a ship. The pain had lessened somewhat, but it was still all she could do to keep from throwing up.

"Are you awake, girl?" a man's voice asked.

"Where are you taking me?" Lily rasped. Her stomach heaved but nothing came out. She was completely empty inside.

"We're not going anywhere, girl. Nowheres at all, at least not on this earth," the man said. His voice rumbled with a mix of sympathy and amusement. "It's the vertigo of being separated from your willstones that makes you feel like you're being tossed about on the ocean."

Lily put her hand under her and felt straw, and under that, rough stone. "Well, since there's never been a boat made out of rocks, I'll believe you," she said, even though she could feel herself rising and falling on giant swells.

"Careful, girl. Logical thought like that could get you hanged," the old man said, chuckling.

Lily sat up and tried to steady herself with her hands. If she could just fix her eyes on something, it might help. "Is there any light?"

"The only light they allow down here is magelight so as not to give you energy. This is a witch's prison. An old, forgotten one."

"And are you a witch?" Lily asked, swallowing down the bile burning her throat.

The old man laughed. "Not a lot of male witches running around, and most of them that are witches don't rightly know it," he replied, amused by something that Lily didn't understand. She'd never even heard of a male witch before. "No, girl, I'm something they got no prison for, even if she did stick me in here."

Lily lay back down, her eyes closing. She fought her mounting confusion and asked the most relevant question. "And what are you?"

"I'm a shaman, Lily," he said. All traces of humor left his voice. He sounded serious and steady. "I'm going to teach you how to spirit walk."

"So this is where you've been," Lily mumbled as sickness overwhelmed her. "I've been waiting for you."

"Sorry I'm late," he said with genuine regret. "I was detained."

She knew she should care that she'd finally found the shaman, but all Lily could feel was spinning blackness pulling her down and all she could think of was her sister. If she listened very hard, she could almost hear Juliet's voice in her head.

Lily? Where are you? I'm trying to feel where you are, but there's too much granite blocking the way.

Help me, Juliet. I'm in the dark.

Lily came to and saw a glimmer of magelight. She lifted her head—her neck complaining of a vicious kink—and quickly glanced around.

She was in a small room, no more than two paces in any direction. Three walls were solid stone and the fourth, all bars. There was a raised pallet with a thin mattress for her to sleep on behind her, but Lily awoke to find herself on the floor. She recalled being placed on the bed, but she must have rolled out of it when the vertigo became too much to bear. In one corner was a bucket; in the other a bottle of water. Lily memorized the placement of everything in her cell because she knew she would be given little chance to see it again.

Beyond the bars was an alcove, and then a hallway. Lily saw other cells surrounding the alcove, but they were empty. The shaman's cell must be directly next to hers, out of her line of sight.

The magelight came from the hallway. At the foot of the hallway was a small desk. Lily crawled closer to the bars of her cell and peered at the source of light. A figure was bent over the desk. The middle drawer was open, and the man was looking inside it with a rapt expression. She couldn't see what was in the drawer, but she could feel his eyes on its contents.

A shiver of fear went through her. It was Carrick, staring at her willstones.

"Please don't," Lily begged softly. "Please don't touch them, Carrick."

He startled and straightened, as if he'd been caught doing something he shouldn't. Then he relaxed, as if he remembered that he was the one in charge. He brightened his magelight until he could see Lily clearly, and she could see him. His hawkish face held traces of Rowan, but the resemblance wasn't a comfort. The chill in his dark, vaguely familiar eyes only made her more terrified of him.

"But you let my half brother touch them. Am I so different from him?" he asked.

"Rowan's never touched my willstones. He wouldn't hurt me like that."

Carrick sneered at her. "But I would?"

Lily wanted to answer him. She wanted to say "obviously" but she didn't dare. The drawer was still open and she was still his prisoner. She shut her mouth.

"What did my half brother show you about me?"

"One memory—a fragment of a memory, really. You were skinny and bruised."

"Did he pity me?"

"He felt bad for you."

Carrick's eyes flashed. "Then why didn't he help me?" he said through clenched teeth.

"Because he was just a little boy." Lily shrugged, like her answer was obvious.

"*Later*," Carrick barked. Lily jumped, sensing his anger unhinging him. His eyes had a wild look to them. "I mean later, when he was set up at the Citadel and his life was nice and plush. Did he ever think to find me or help me?"

"I don't know. Maybe," she pleaded. "He only had one memory of you. Carrick, he didn't know you."

"But he knew what I was going through. What was happening to me." He broke off for a moment to calm himself. "Everyone knew."

"He was too little. He didn't understand." Lily threw her hands up, losing patience. "*I* don't understand."

"But you defend him." Carrick stared down at her willstones. "You defend him because you love him. And you love him because he's special. Because he got taken to the Citadel when he was seven while I got taken to hell."

His hand hovered over Lily's stones. She pulled herself up the bars, tears already streaming down her face at the thought of him touching her three little hearts.

"Have you ever heard the saying, 'Whatever doesn't kill you makes you stronger'?" Carrick asked. Lily nodded desperately, hoping for any way to relate to him, to reach out to his humanity. "It's a lie," he said quietly. "There are things that a person can live through that make him weaker. Things that can leave you less than you were before. Maybe you're about to experience one of them."

Suffering descended on Lily like a claw from the sky.

Lily? Where are you?

I don't know, Juliet. They haven't said. This is all I have.

Lily replayed the brief images she'd seen—the cell, the alcove, and the desk.

Darn it. There are oubliettes like that everywhere. Can you be more specific?

Gideon and Carrick. That's all I've got, Juliet. Find them and you'll find me.

Easier said than done, Lily. They've disappeared. No one's seen them in the city for days. Are you okay?

I'm in pain.

"Hey, girl. Lily girl. Are you dead?"

Lily uncurled herself from the ball she'd rolled into. Her nerves were still twitching with pain, but at least the worst was over. After she'd stopped screaming, Carrick had put her willstones back in the drawer and left. As a parting shot, he'd asked her whether or not she felt stronger, but she'd been in too much agony to engage in his repartee. She wanted to kill him. She counted that as a good thing. It meant she was still alive and kicking.

"Not yet," she croaked in answer, unclenching her cramped fists.

"Good to hear. Let's get started," the shaman said enthusiastically.

Lily crawled through the dark toward the bottle of water. "Are you serious?"

"Best time to learn how to spirit walk. Right after a near-death experience or a great shock, like a fever or a seizure."

"Huh. Go figure." She thought about the seizure she'd had at Scot's party, and how she'd seen herself from afar, like she was floating over her own body. "That actually explains a lot," Lily said, and raised the bottle of water to her lips.

"Put down that water, girl," he admonished. "You're starved, which is fantastic, but dehydration is the real key."

"Fantastic?" Lily asked, not too sure she agreed with his word choice. Her mouth was so dry it felt sore. "Can't I have one sip?"

"Absolutely not," the old man replied. "Usually I'd take you to a sweat lodge after your fast. You'd be allowed water there because you'd be sweating it out faster 'en you could drink it. But there's no hope for a sweat lodge in this freezing cold, now is there?"

"Not really," she said, putting the water down. It was mostly ice, and she'd have only gotten a few drops out of it anyway. "Wait. How did you see me pick up the bottle? It's pitch black in here."

"Darker than the inside of a cat, isn't it?" The shaman cracked himself up.

"Ah, sure?" Lily said hesitantly. She didn't have much experience being inside cats.

"Darkness is good for our purpose," he said, without answering her question. "Now. You need to lie down and relax."

"That's the best thing you could have possibly said to me right about now." She felt her way across the straw-covered floor until she found her bunk, then gratefully pulled herself onto it.

"Now, here's the hard part, girl," the shaman said seriously. "I need you to empty your mind."

"Piece of cake," Lily mumbled.

"No. Don't fall asleep." The shaman's voice was urgent. "Your spirit is a weak force. Like gravity. It works over vast distances, but the much stronger forces of the body and mind overwhelm the spirit in the short run. You must make the choice to put the spirit first. Let your will direct your spirit, and you can travel vast distances."

Lily let the shaman's words hang above her like thought bubbles in a comic book. Each idea was something she could see, suspended above her in black and white, but she didn't try to think about them too hard. She just accepted them. Her spirit was whisper thin, easily overwhelmed by the howling demands of her body and the hard machinery of her logical thoughts. But as thin as it was, her spirit reached out past the stars and into other worlds.

"Okay. I see it," she whispered.

"Good," the shaman breathed. "Now, what do you hear?"

Lily. Are you in pain? We're trying to find you.

"My sister. She's looking for me."

"You must go past that." The shaman sounded sad. "I know you love her, and the other versions of the people who you love will guide you like bright lights into the other worlds. But Juliet's mind-speak keeps you tethered to this world. In order to spirit walk you must go up, Lily. Jump up."

She jumped. For a moment, Lily felt suspended. She looked down and saw her body lying on a dirty mattress. Her torn dress hung off her in ragged threads. Her face was streaked with filth, and her elbows, hands, and knees were rubbed raw and bleeding. She wasn't looking with eyes—there was no light to see anything in the dank, cramped prison her body was trapped in—but Lily could see perfectly. She flew out into the alcove and looked around.

The shaman glowed like a pillar of fire in the next cell. The light of a thousand strange suns illuminated his body. Each sun showed him as a slightly different man. Lily saw him as old, young, beautiful, and dying at once. His spirit held every stage of his life inside him and refracted them back to Lily's new farseeing eyes as if through a prism. He was everyman.

"There you are, girl," he whispered, looking up at her. "Welcome home."

Lily! Where did you go? Your mind went silent. Don't leave me!

The screams of her sister brought Lily slamming back into her body.

I'm here, Juliet. I'm back. I'm sorry.

Lily pulled in a shuddering breath. The demands of her body assaulted her immediately, and she regretted coming back to such a dismal state of being. Everything ached. Without her willstones, she was cut off from the world again. Sick. She heard the shaman sigh.

"I couldn't ignore her," Lily mumbled, realizing she'd done exactly what he'd told her not to do. "She thought I'd died."

"Well. I guess it would be worse if you didn't love anyone that much," he said. His voice sounded old and tired. "Get some sleep. We'll try again tomorrow."

Gideon was excited to start work. He didn't know for sure if this divide-and-conquer strategy was going to succeed. He almost couldn't believe that no other mechanic had tried it, except for the fact that it was really rare for a witch to have more than one stone. Maybe witches avoided bonding with more than one stone for this very reason, although if witches did it on purpose, they didn't tell mechanics that. This other Lillian probably hadn't known to limit herself to one stone.

It was small things like that which made Gideon suspect that this other Lillian didn't have much experience with magic. He was even beginning to believe that she came from a world where there were no witches or magic at all. Gideon looked forward to going there one day. He imagined he would seem like a god among the non-magical people, which would be a welcome change.

Gideon saw how people looked at him, like he had no talent. He'd only gotten his position because of who his father was. It was true that he'd been presented to Lillian when they were children because his father was on the Council, but that was common enough. Lillian had claimed dozens of Councilmen's sons, but Gideon was placed in her inner circle. He was supposed to have been special. Then she'd favored Rowan and Tristan over him and ignored Gideon. His one consolation was that Lillian had never claimed Tristan either. Gideon didn't know why. Lillian had claimed hundreds, but in her inner circle, those who she saw and worked with every day, she'd only claimed Rowan and Juliet. A year ago, she'd been forced to claim Gideon and make him her head mechanic—but he was that in name only. And *everyone* knew it.

This was Lillian's fault. She'd pushed him to this. She'd claimed him, but then refused to utilize him, leaving him with no other option. If he couldn't find true power in the witch system, then that system had to be overthrown.

Gideon had big plans. He was already talking to mechanics who specialized in growing willstones. They'd told him it might be possible to tailor them and make it so witches routinely bonded with more than one stone. His father was already drafting the legislature that would make it the law for all witches to bond with multiple stones so that they too could be controlled by their mechanics. Once that was pushed through the Council, the world was going to change. Witches would be ruled by their mechanics. They would still be a power source, of course. But Gideon saw a day when they wouldn't be the *only* power, as they were now. In fact, after he surveyed all that the other worlds had to offer, the witches might just find themselves obsolete. And begging *him* for a job.

Carrick was already in the oubliette when Gideon climbed down the rope and joined him. The girl was crouched in the far corner of her cell with her arms over her head. Her willstones were out on top of the desk, and Carrick was staring at them. That was unfortunate.

"Let's get something straight, Carrick," Gideon said, sighing regretfully. "You're not to try to touch her willstones, or even look at them again unless I tell you to. Are we clear?"

Carrick looked up at Gideon with a confused expression on his face. For a moment, Gideon thought he saw something foreign in Carrick's eyes. Carrick shook his head as if to clear it, and his usual coolness returned. Gideon angled himself in between Carrick and the stones. He couldn't take them from the oubliette. That kind of distance between a witch and her willstones would make her too ill to do anything.

He was going to have to find some kind of safe to keep the stones in so Carrick wouldn't be tempted. It might take a few days to get something like that out here, but Gideon knew he'd have to make arrangements. Gideon had been avoiding Salem, lying low. He'd have to go all the way to Providence to buy a safe, but he didn't have a choice about that now. Carrick was becoming attached to her willstones— and maybe to her.

"Are we clear, Carrick?" Gideon repeated.

"We're clear."

"Good. She should be weak enough now that it'll be safe to run a little test." Gideon picked up the edges of the handkerchief and went to her cell. The girl hugged her stomach, biting her lower lip to stop the nausea. It must be so disorienting to feel your willstones picked up by another and moved around while you sit still, Gideon mused. He didn't know. He'd never had the displeasure.

"We can give her the littlest stone, and see if she can transmute a *tiny* bit of energy with it, while I hold the other two for safekeeping." Gideon met her eyes, pleased to see a wealth of anger there. She really was just like Lillian. This was going to be so much fun for him. "I'm always going to keep at least one of your stones with me. Wouldn't want you to get any ideas above yourself. Now would I, Lily?"

The girl's glare dissolved into pleading. *Now* she was starting to get it. With two of her stones held hostage, Gideon was the one in control of her magic. Unless she wanted to suffer, she'd better do every thing he said exactly as he said it.

"This is a power storage cell," he continued, putting a heavy but small black box in front of the bars of Lily's cage. He handed her the smallest willstone. "I am going to give you a tiny bit of heat and I want you to turn that heat into electricity and put it into the storage cell. Do you understand?"

Lily nodded blankly. "You want me to charge that battery."

"We'll start there and work our way up. If you're good, we can move on to something more fun. Remember, there's a gauge on this battery, as you called it, so don't try keeping any power for yourself. I'll be watching." He squeezed her other two willstones, still cupped in the palm of his hand to give her a taste of the punishment she'd get if she tried to trick him. Lily gripped her head, stifling a scream in the back of her throat. "If you're good, we'll keep working our way up to higher and higher levels of energy. Who knows how far we'll go? Maybe all the way into another world."

Rowan has a way to find you, no matter how deep they bury you. Please don't lose hope, Lily. We're coming for you.

I haven't lost hope, Juliet. What's the plan?

Um. Well. I can't tell you. You're a prisoner, and they can make you talk. The less you know, the better.

I understand.

Really?

Yeah.

You're just going to trust us?

Of course I am. You're my sister.

That's. Wow. That's great.

Juliet? How is it I can hear you when I can't hear Rowan, Tristan, or Caleb?

Because we're family. Hold fast. We're coming.

Lily woke up amused. She didn't know if she was dreaming of her sister to comfort herself or sharing actual mindspeak with Juliet while on the verge of sleep.

It didn't really matter. Lily wasn't going to wait to be rescued, no matter what Juliet and the guys planned. The next time Gideon gave her a stone, even if it was just her golden stone, she was going to take it and whatever energy he gave her in his attempt to "train" her, and use it to stop his heart. She would be punished. Carrick might even smash her other stones, trying to kill her, but Lily would survive. Like a wolf chewing off her own leg to get out of a trap, Lily knew she would survive. And then Carrick would have to come into her cell to get her, or leave her to open the lock on her door with her golden willstone and whatever energy she had left in her body.

It had been a long time since she'd eaten. She had to try to get away now, or she had no chance of opening the lock. Lily was actually hoping that Carrick would dare to come into her cell. Then she could lay hands on him, drain all of his body heat, suck the electricity out of his nerves, and leave him a corpse at her feet. As she should have done when he'd taken her captive in the tunnel. Even though she was dazed and weak, she could have taken power from him. It would have killed him, but as long as Lily was conscious and had even one of her willstones, she could always take the life-force of another to fuel herself. She'd had to come to the point where she was ready to kill in order to even consider that an option. She was ready now.

In fact, she had dreamed about killing Carrick, but she didn't count on it happening. She couldn't count on anything anymore. The only thing she knew for certain was that once she got out of her cell, she had to get the shaman out, too. She didn't know what kind of shape he was in—neither of them had been fed since she'd been brought here—but if the brilliant aura she'd seen on her spirit walks was any clue, he had oceans of energy that she could borrow to break him out. Then they would get away together.

Out into the light.

"Lily girl? Are you dead yet?" the shaman asked. The sound of his voice warmed her and gave her strength. She might be in the dark, but at least she wasn't alone.

"Not yet," Lily answered, smiling.

"Then let's get back to work. You've got a lot to learn."

Lily lay back and made herself comfortable. She was dehydrated and literally starving to death, but as soon as she stepped out of her body, she would no longer notice it. She took a deep breath, looking forward to a spirit walk. When she was just on the verge of jumping up, she heard the shaman's voice.

"The universes branch out, sort of like a great tree. Every choice we make—every fork in the road where we have to decide to go left or right—is actually two new universes bubbling up and being born. In one universe, we go left; in the other universe, we go right," he said in his soothing voice. "And so it is with every choice we make."

"That's a lot of universes," Lily mumbled.

The shaman laughed. "So many, it gets awful confusing. It's powerful easy to get lost in the worldfoam."

"Worldfoam. I like that. It sounds fluffy."

Lily thought about a universe where Tristan hadn't left her to find Miranda at that party. He'd never cheated on her. She'd never had a seizure. They'd never fought and she'd never allowed herself to be taken by Lillian. Somewhere in the worldfoam this had happened. And *that* Lily had never learned she was a crucible. She'd never felt the touch of another person's mind in hers or the raw rush of power when she transmuted energy. There was a Lily who wasn't kept prisoner in the dark—a Lily who had never met Rowan. She wondered if that Lily was happier than she was.

"Why are you teaching me all this?" Lily asked. She wasn't entirely sure she'd spoken aloud until she got an answer.

"Because I made a terrible mistake," the shaman said sadly. "I violated a sacred law, and now you're paying the price for it."

"Is that why you're here in the oubliette? Because you broke a law?"

She heard the shaman chuckle to himself. "I don't believe the Great Spirit punishes, but I do believe I'm here with you for a reason. And that reason is to restore the balance by teaching you how to get out of this prison and go home."

"Home," Lily mumbled.

"Yes, home. You must go home as soon as you are able, Lily," the shaman said stridently.

"Why?"

"You don't belong here. And I'm to blame for what you're going through right now."

"You taught Lillian how to spirit walk, didn't you?"

The shaman didn't answer right away, and when he did, his voice sounded heavy and sad. "Witch magic and shaman magic should've never come together. I taught Lillian how to spirit walk because we thought we could cure this world of the Woven. But we were wrong, Lily. And now Lillian's just about tore this world apart because of my arrogance."

Lily took a breath to argue with him. The shaman was a lot of things, but he certainly wasn't arrogant. The shaman spoke over her. "Do you hear me, girl? You can't stay in this world for anyone or anything."

Something about this bothered Lily, and it took her a moment to untangle what that was. Leaving this world meant she would never see Rowan again. But she knew that was a foolish argument. If she stayed in this world, she was going to die in this oubliette. Still, leaving meant leaving him.

Grasping at straws, Lily came up with the only rational argument that presented itself to her. "Not even you? What if I could get you out of here?"

"Especially not for me. I'm a used-up old fool." Lily could hear him smiling as he said the words. "This is an opportunity for me to set things right, and I feel blessed to be able to have it."

"I guess I'm blessed, too. I don't think I'd have made it if you weren't here with me." Genuine gratitude warmed Lily through and through. She knew that she would have given up days ago if she hadn't had a friend down there with her in the dark. "Thank you."

A few moments passed before she heard the shaman speak again. "Alright, enough now," he said gruffly. "Settle down and get to work."

"Aye, aye, captain," Lily said, and then she turned her attention to her breathing. She focused on relaxing until she could feel her soul about to leave her body.

"Okay, you're ready," the shaman said. "But this time, don't just jump up. Jump up and *out*. You'll know you've done it if you feel like you're a drum and the whole world is a-beatin' on you. But be careful. If you see a wall of ash, fall back into yourself, and try again a moment later," he said.

"A wall of ash?" Lily whispered, confused.

The shaman paused. "There are more versions of the world that have failed than have succeeded," he said carefully. "Many worlds have died in mass sickness, and many more than that in great holocausts. There is no point in sending your spirit into either of these kinds of worlds."

"How many more?"

"There is an infinite number of universes," the shaman said, brushing past her question. "Just focus on finding a *living* one. Leave the cinder worlds to the dead who burned 'em."

"But—"

"Please, Lily," he said. His voice was impatient, but behind his impatience was fear. "If you see ash or sickness, fall back into yourself. Immediately. It won't do you any good to dwell on the cinder worlds."

"Okay," Lily said, struggling to accept what the shaman said.

Then she jumped.

A pounding vibration tingled through her. It was so complex and varied even her skin shivered independently over her muscles. For a moment, it felt like the vibration would shake her to pieces, but then it stopped. A moment later, another one started—just as complex and overwhelming as the first. Lily tried to make sense of it, tried to piece it apart, but she couldn't keep up with all the changes and variations. She could sense that it was different from the first vibration, but she wasn't fully aware of how it was different. She was too awed by its enormity to get her head around it. Then the second vibration stopped.

Lily found herself spirit walking a few feet above a forest floor. There was a dusting of snow on everything. She drifted up, disembodied, exulting in the brightness and beauty of the world around her. She was free of the darkness of her cell, and even though she couldn't feel the world with a body, having her spirit partake of it was a joy. It was late afternoon. Lily saw huge lichen-covered boulders hunkering in the thin, brilliant light refracting off the winter snow. She realized that it had to be late December. The boulders around her formed a slight cliff above her that spilled down in a V formation.

She kept drifting up. She thought she recognized the place, but she couldn't be sure. It looked like a Massachusetts forest with lots of tall trees and trails, except there were more rock formations than usual. Something from her memory kept telling her she knew this place. She floated up and up, then saw a parking lot and a freeway. There were no freeways in Lillian's world.

"Lily. You must come back now," the shaman called.

She fell back into her body—and was about to tell the shaman that she'd done it, she'd made it into another world—when she saw magelight illuminating the alcove. She took a breath but kept her eyes closed.

"She's not dead," Carrick said. "I can see her breathing."

"Well, she wasn't breathing a second ago," snapped a woman defensively.

It was Esmeralda. Lily hadn't had much of a chance to figure out how Carrick and Gideon had taken her, but now it all made sense. Esmeralda had only to do one little thing—shut the hatch—and even with her three nearly invincible mechanics, Lily was nothing but an unconscious armload.

"How long has it been since you fed her?" Esmeralda continued, badgering him. "Gideon made it clear that she was to be kept weak, but you're killing her."

Carrick was silent for a moment. "You can go now," he said.

"No, actually I can't." Esmeralda sounded annoyed. "Gideon had me come out here while he's gone for the next two days, because he doesn't want you left alone with her."

"And where is he?" Carrick asked.

"Halfway to Providence, I expect."

Lily heard a fast movement, followed by a cry of alarm from Esmeralda. The sound of her scream was abruptly cut off. Lily wanted to open her eyes, but fought the urge. She heard stumbling steps, grunts of exertion as Carrick and Esmeralda fought hand to hand, and then the sound of a body hitting the floor hard.

"Gideon will kill you for this," Esmeralda said in a strained and whispery voice. Lily could hear fluid gurgling in her lungs.

"For what?" Carrick asked pleasantly. "You never arrived. I'm afraid the Woven must have gotten you on your way here."

"People know I'm here. The soldiers in the camp up there," Esmeralda said.

"Oh. You mean the same soldiers who know you were brought up in the Coven, then changed sides to become a rebel, and now because you've been ignored by a man, you've changed sides a third time?" Lily could nearly hear the smile in his voice. "Soldiers hate turncoats. I won't even have to pay them off to keep this from Gideon."

"It wasn't like that. It wasn't just about Rowan," Esmeralda pleaded. "It's *her*. She's exactly like Lillian, but none of you can see it."

Lily heard crying.

"Was he worth it?" Carrick asked, like he didn't understand. "Was Rowan really worth all this?"

"I had to get rid of her," Esmeralda said, sniffling back tears. "After everything she did to him, he still fell in love with her again. Tristan, too. Everyone loves Lily," she said bitterly. "They're too stupid to see she's going to betray them all over again."

A few moments passed. Lily heard gasps, choking coughs, and finally, Esmeralda's death rattle.

Carrick approached the bars of Lily's cell. From behind her eyelids, she saw his magelight brighten. She kept her eyes clamped shut, feigning unconsciousness, as he looked her over carefully. He seemed to stare at her forever, but after several harrowing seconds his magelight dimmed and he turned back to Esmeralda's corpse.

Lily listened as he struggled with her body. The only way in or out of the oubliette was by rope, and although she knew he was strong, Carrick would have no easy task getting her dead weight up it. She wondered why he didn't call for the help of the soldiers above if they were as keen on getting rid of Esmeralda as Carrick had said. He must have been lying.

Either that or he wanted some time with Lily without the soldiers knowing he was down there alone with her, which was probably the whole point of killing Esmeralda in the first place. Carrick wanted complete control over Lily and her willstones. She shook at the thought, fighting back tears, until she managed to calm herself again.

Several times, Lily heard the damp, smacking sound of Esmeralda's body hitting the floor and her stomach twisted. Esmeralda had orchestrated Lily's capture in the tunnel—she'd weakened Lily, timed it perfectly, and probably set the charges aboveground that brought the ceiling down—but Lily couldn't hate her now. She didn't have the energy.

After a lot of grunting and swearing, Carrick made it up the rope with Esmeralda's body. He'd managed that faster than she thought. That probably meant he'd be back soon. The tears started again. Lily wiped them away and sat up. The blackness around her buzzed, her head felt hot, and she felt something against her cheek. Was she still sitting up? The darkness was so complete it confused her sometimes. Up and down hadn't mattered in days, but she was pretty sure what she felt on her cheek was her mattress. She'd fallen back down onto the bed. Her body was much weaker than she'd thought. She tried to remember when she'd last tried to stand. It must have been days.

Magelight glowed at the end of the hallway. Lily heard the creak of the rope as he descended. So soon. She hadn't figured out anything yet, and she was having trouble putting together the motions required to sit up and face him with some spunk. She was going to die lying down. The thought galled her.

"Lily?" called a voice—a deep, lovely voice.

"Rowan?" Lily managed to turn her head on the mattress. She saw him, his gorgeous willstone throwing his particular brand of shimmering light around him. He ran to her cell. His face went blank and his hands clutched the bars as he stared at her. He was breathing hard. Her upper lip tore when she smiled at him and she tasted blood.

"Where are your willstones?" he whispered.

"The drawer."

Rowan turned and rushed back to the desk, opened the drawer, and lifted his hand to take them. A whimper escaped Lily in anticipation of the agony to follow. Rowan's head turned, and he looked at her, his eyes narrowed.

"He didn't touch—" Rowan saw the terrified look on Lily's face. "He did." Rowan took a steadying breath. "I won't hurt you."

He reached into the drawer and picked up Lily's stones. She braced herself, but instead of pain and nausea she felt warmth and comfort. Lily sighed with the odd pleasure that was simply the absence of pain and realized that she'd been hurting for what felt like forever.

"You're going to have to come the rest of the way to me. I can't reach you." Lily opened her eyes and saw Rowan, his arm stretched toward her, straining against the bars. His face was desperate. "Please. You have to try."

Lily rolled onto her side. She had no hope of standing. Her legs wouldn't hold her. She flopped out of bed onto the floor. A wave of sickness overtook her, and she retched but nothing came out.

"Just a few inches. Come on. You can make it."

Lily's head wobbled on her neck as she raised it. Rowan was on his knees on the other side of the bars, every inch of him trying to push closer to her. Her arms shook as she crawled toward him. She reached out her hand and Rowan grabbed it, touching her willstones to her palm. She melted with relief and heard a thought racing across Rowan's mind.

Could still die. Please, no.

Rowan dragged her the rest of the way to him and held her through the bars. He was warm and solid in her arms.

"Tilt your head back and drink this." Rowan held the back of her head in one hand and a canteen in the other. "Just a little sip."

Lily felt warm, sweet liquid wet the inside of her mouth. It had an herbal flavor that she couldn't quite place, but it immediately made her feel a bit more alert. She took the canteen from Rowan and felt him uncurling her fingers. She let him. His hands shook a little as he carefully reattached her willstones to her necklace. Every time his fingers brushed across her stones she felt it inside her body. It didn't hurt, not exactly.

"Keep drinking that," Rowan said. He propped her against the bars and dug into the pack slung across his back. He took out candles and lit them quickly.

"How did you find me?" she asked in between small sips of her brew.

Rowan's face darkened. "My half brother," he said bitterly. "He doesn't know enough about the craft to guard himself from me, and he's never told Gideon who he really is. Whenever Carrick went outside the granite grotto that we're in, I could sense where he was. He didn't leave often, which is why it took me so long to find you."

His voice slid into her head. *It's freezing, Lily. Lean over the flames if you can.*

Lily reached her hands over the candles. Her body throbbed with pleasure as her stones gorged on the power of the flames.

"I know this is going to be hard for you," Rowan said. "But I need your help to get you out of here."

Lily nodded and brought a candle close to her chest, absorbing as much warmth as she could. A witch wind whistled down the rope hole and blew across Lily's face.

"Move back," Rowan said, his willstone flaring with power. He grabbed the door of the cell and pulled it off its hinges. He tossed the metal aside, reached down and scooped her up, leaving the candles behind.

"We have to get the shaman," Lily said, clutching Rowan's shoulder.

"The shaman?" he asked, confused.

"He's right there," Lily said, pointing into the cell next to hers.

"There's no one there."

"Shaman?" she called. She struggled in Rowan's arms until he put her down. Her legs gave out, and she stumbled and fell against the bars of his cell. "Wake up, lazy! We're rescued," she called into the cell, impatiently. "Rowan, rip the door off."

"Lily. Don't," Rowan said, simultaneously trying to hold her up and pull her away from the bars.

Lily brightened her magelight until she could see inside the cell. A heap of rags lay on top of the mattress. She squinted. Among the rags was something that looked like shriveled leather. It was shaped like a hand.

"It's not possible," Lily said, backing away, knees buckling. "He taught me how to spirit walk, Rowan. I couldn't have imagined that."

"Lily, he's dead," Rowan said. He picked her up. "We can try to come back to give him a proper burial later, but right now we have to leave."

She stared at the cell in disbelief as he carried her down the hallway. "I'll come back for you," she whispered to the dark, cold hole where the shaman's bones and spirit waited to be put to rest.

Rowan slung Lily over his shoulder and climbed up the rope. It was far, several stories at least. As they neared the top, Lily heard Caleb and Tristan in her head.

He's got her!

We need to move. There are more soldiers coming.

Lily felt hands sliding under her arms. Caleb took her while

Rowan swung up and out of the hole. They were in a rock shelter built over the oubliette, much like the stone cabin in the woods where Lily and Rowan fought the Woven. Four dead bodies were scattered around the room. Lily looked out the window of the cabin as Caleb carried her past it. It was dark out, but she thought she saw two more bodies lying in the snow. Something slithered over one of them. Feeding. Lily shuddered and looked away when she saw the Woven rise up to pull off the dead man's arm.

Caleb laid her down in front of the small fire burning in the simple hearth. "We don't have much time here," he said. "The sentries will be changing soon."

"Give her some more of the brew," Tristan said.

"She finished it already," Rowan said. They stood over her anxiously while Lily tried to absorb as much of the heat of the fire as she could. A faint witch wind whipped around the room, but Lily still didn't feel stronger. She felt heat, but not power.

"She's not transmuting energy properly," Tristan said. He looked at Rowan sharply, and Lily could nearly hear what they were saying to each other in mindspeak even though they were shutting her out. That she might be past the point of saving.

Caleb went to the window and looked out. "We're going to have to move her," he said.

"She's too weak," Rowan argued.

Lily struggled up onto her forearms, her head spinning. "No, Caleb's right, Rowan. I won't let you three get caught." Lily thought of the Woven outside and immediately squelched the wave of fear that followed. "We need to go."

Rowan nodded reluctantly. He lifted Lily while Tristan and Caleb gathered up their packs, supplies, and weapons. They breezed through the room efficiently, picking over the bodies for what they needed and leaving behind what they didn't without a backward glance. Rowan shook out a blanket, wrapped Lily in it, and carried her outside.

Still strengthened by the tiny bit of energy Lily had given him, Rowan leapt from boulder to boulder, carrying her out of the rocky ravine. At the bottom, Caleb and Tristan were already waiting for them with horses.

"Hurry, Ro!" Tristan hissed.

"Woven coming in from the south and east!" Caleb said urgently.

Rowan jumped onto the horse Tristan was leading and held Lily in front of him as he rode away. Everything was bouncing around and her head hurt, but as they passed a narrow crack between two gigantic slabs of granite, Lily finally remembered where they were. She recognized this place from her world.

"That's Fat Man's Misery," Lily said, pointing with a sweaty arm. "We're in Purgatory Chasm, way out in Sutton."

She felt Rowan squeeze her tighter with worry. "We call this place Witch's End."

"I came here with Tristan and his parents when we were kids, before I started getting sick all the time. It was far," she mumbled incoherently. Her head fell against Rowan's chest. "Rowan? Is Carrick dead?"

"No," he replied in a low voice. "Not yet."

The dark forest blurred by as Rowan reached more level ground and urged his horse to pick up speed.

CHAPTER
13

THE JARRING MOTION OF THE GALLOPING HORSE SEEMED to go on forever, and Rowan kept wrapping her more tightly in the blanket even though she was pouring sweat.

Lily twisted in his arms, trying to stretch her aching back and free herself of the insufferable constriction. She wished she could just fall asleep, but every time she closed her eyes, her senses sharpened unbearably until every fiber in the blanket stuck into her skin like pins and the gamey smell of the horse and the leather saddle made her stomach turn. Hours passed, each one worse than the hour before it.

"Here!" she heard Tristan yell. "The river is up this way."

Rowan turned the horse and headed for Tristan's voice. They rode faster, and the rocking motion as the horse hit a canter nearly had Lily screaming.

"Get a fire going, Tristan," Rowan said, pulling the horse up sharply. Lily closed her eyes, trying not to throw up, and felt herself being passed down into Caleb's thick arms.

"She's as hot as a lit match," Caleb said.

"Don't touch her bare skin, it'll burn you," Rowan warned, dismounting. He took off his jacket and shirt.

"Are you sure about this brew?" Tristan asked uncertainly. "Birch bark could give her the grippe."

"Just do it," Rowan snapped, ending the argument. He pulled off his boots and stripped off his pants, shivering violently with the cold, and turned back to Caleb. "Give her to me."

"I'll scout up the riverbank for Woven." Caleb handed Lily over, and then put out an arm to stop Rowan. "What if you freeze to death in there?"

Rowan paused to grasp Caleb's shoulder. "She won't let me die, brother. Not from the cold," he said, smiling.

Caleb helped Rowan get down the riverbank and to the iced-in edge of the river.

"Is this the Charles River?" Lily asked blurrily. "'Cause the Charles is totally polluted."

Rowan laughed through a shiver. "It is the Charles, actually. I can't believe we call it the same thing. And don't worry. It's not polluted at all here."

"Oh. That's nice. But nothing's polluted here, is it? It's just my world that's a big mess. All the glaciers are melting and the polar bears are starving."

Rowan was too preoccupied to answer, or even try to figure out why Lily was mumbling about bears. He broke the ice edge with his heel and stepped into the frigid water. "Hold your breath, Lily."

She felt cold water slosh over her. Rowan held on to her underwater and kicked them both back up to the surface. He shouted when they crested, his whole body convulsing with shock. Lily wrapped her arms and legs around his torso, letting the blanket drift away on the current.

Steam rose off Lily's skin and the water around them bubbled and hissed like they'd poured hot fat into it. She pressed her chest against Rowan's, trying to keep his heart warm, as he paddled with his arms and legs to keep them afloat. Lily tipped her head back into the icy current, trying to cool her head. It didn't help. She felt so hot she thought she might explode from it. She wondered if this was what a dying star must feel like—never hotter than just before it goes supernova.

Rowan? Am I dying?

"No," he said roughly, working against the current. They were being swept downstream. "You're not going to die."

You didn't answer me in mindspeak.

Don't ask me to answer, Lily. I can't—

"Ro! Reach for this!" Upstream, Caleb hung over the edge of the ice, holding a stick out to Rowan. Rowan managed to grab on to it as they passed, stopping them.

The water around them roiled. Rowan's face was a grimace. Lily released him and floated away a bit so she could look back at him. Even in the pale moonlight, she could see an angry red burn where she'd been holding him. Lily kicked away from him and into the current, but he grabbed her wrist before she got away.

"Let me go," she cried. "I'm hurting you."

"Like that's anything new," he said, managing to smile at her through chattering teeth. The hand that held her wrist shook with effort. Rowan was fighting every instinct to hold on to her even though her skin was burning him. The water around Lily was boiling. Her head was so hot.

"I can't stop it, Rowan," Lily said, trying to tug her wrist out of his grip. "It's just getting worse."

"I know." Rowan's face suddenly fell. "Cold water isn't going to be enough to put out the fire. We have to suffocate it."

He pulled Lily to him with a scared look on his face. "I'm sorry," he said. His eyes pleaded with hers for a brief second, and then he pushed her head underwater.

Lily looked up at him through the shifting surface, too stunned to do anything else. The moonlight and the bubbles distorted his face, making his sharp features elongate until they seemed hawkish. The unseeing gleam in his black eyes was familiar to Lily.

Carrick.

Even though she'd run from him, he'd found her somehow and now he was trying to drown her. Lily struggled under his hand, thrashing violently. He grabbed a hank of her hair and pushed her down even farther. Water burned as it rushed into her nose and mouth. Lily grabbed his wrist, trying to twist herself free. More water rushed into her lungs. She grew cold and sluggish, staring at Carrick's face above hers. She wanted to fight him, but she felt so heavy.

Lily heard a familiar voice slide into her head. Her own voice. This time, Lily knew that it was Lillian and not herself she was talking to.

No. Don't you dare die, Lily.

I don't want to live. There's no one here in the dark with me.

I'm here, Lily. And so is Rowan. You have to fight, Lily. He can't handle losing us both.

You don't want me to live for Rowan. You want me to live for you. You brought me to this world for a reason, and you can't let me die because you want to use me somehow.

Everyone wants to use you. But don't think for a second that I don't care about what Rowan feels. Loving Rowan is what made me who I am now.

How dare you blame your evil on him? You killed his father.

No one can lie in mindspeak, Lily. Everything I did, I did for Rowan. Everything I am doing to you now is to save Rowan by saving the world he lives in. You will stay here and finish what I started—for him. You may as well accept it, Lily. You're stuck here. There's no one left to teach you how to worldjump.

How can you know that? You killed the shaman, didn't you?

I left him to die.

You failed, Lillian. You killed his body but not his spirit. He taught me how to spirit walk. Sooner or later I'm going to figure out how to worldjump, and I'll leave this place. Your battles are yours to fight. I don't belong here.

And what happens when Gideon or Alaric comes to your magicless, mindblind world to pillage it for resources? Will you still sit on the fence then?

Alaric? He wants to help me. He would never come to my world to pillage—

What did I tell you? Everyone wants to use you. You think Alaric would allow you to claim three of his braves out of the kindness of his heart? Or did he plan on you claiming them, loving them, so you would join him? I was seduced by that dream once, too. I started down this path looking for a way to rid my world of the Woven so no more Outlander children would have to grow up in fear as Rowan did. Have you experienced his night terrors yet? Have you woken up next to him when he's sweating and crying out?

No. But I can feel the shadow and sadness inside him when he looks up at the trees in the woods. I hate it like I've never hated anything.

I know. I hate it, too. The Woven are Rowan's sad shadow. That's why I begged the shaman to teach me how to worldjump. There are an infinite number of universes. Somewhere out there is a world that figured out how to eradicate the Woven. I was going to go there and learn how to free all of the Outlanders. I was going to save the man I loved from the monsters that hunted him in his nightmares. And look at me now. I was a fool, but I was a powerful fool. And so are you. Ask Alaric what he really wants from you. Open your eyes. Get angry. Your fight has only just begun.

Someone was hitting Lily hard on the chest. *Thump, thump, thump.* It was almost like a heartbeat, except it came from the outside. Her eyes focused. Carrick was pounding on her chest like he was trying to crack her in two. Hot liquid surged up the back of her throat and spurted out of her mouth and nose. Carrick grabbed her by the neck, twisting her head to the side. As the water poured out of her, she found the strength to fight him. She pushed at his hands and kicked her legs, her hoarse voice pleading for him to stop.

Oh God. He's really going to kill me this time.

"Enough! You're scaring her!" Tristan yelled. He pushed Carrick aside.

"Tristan," Lily gasped. She reached out her arms to him, her best friend. A big man came and helped Tristan pull Carrick off her.

"He comes down every day," she continued through hiccups, scrambling hysterically to get away from her tormentor. "He's been hurting me. He's been—" Lily couldn't find the right words to describe what Carrick did to her. She thought it instead and saw Tristan recoil for a moment before he pulled her close to him.

"Caleb, she thinks he's Carrick. Get him out of here," Tristan ordered.

Carrick looked sad. He went sort of limp, and Caleb didn't have any trouble dragging him away through the snow. The last thought Lily had was that Carrick was wet and nearly naked. He might freeze to death if she was lucky.

Lily felt Tristan's arm, heavy and smooth, draped over her shoulder. They were lying on their sides and he was tucked against her back.

She'd woken up with Tristan holding her like this before, but now instead of sheets, pillows, and white curtains dancing on the breeze, Lily saw only dry leaves and dirt.

Her arm reached out to hold the hand of another boy. Caleb lay across from her, his giant hand swallowing her wrist and his boulder-like shoulder rising and falling with his gusty breaths. The ground under them was seared and brown. The air radiated up from their little circle, wavering with heat like a mirage. Lily's heat.

She edged out from under Tristan's encircling arm and sat up. The ring of heat Lily had created was edged with ice and snow. She looked up and saw snow hissing into steam above her as if it were hitting an invisible dome that vaporized it.

Lily tried to move her leg. Her ankle was being held. She looked down and saw Rowan sitting up, guarding them while they slept.

"I'm not Carrick," he whispered.

A flood of images from the night before rolled over Lily from Rowan's perspective. How she'd screamed and scratched him. How she'd shied away from his hands and cried. How he'd burned and froze, burned and froze, over and over to keep her alive.

Lily reached for him and pulled him into the circle of heat. Tristan and Caleb rolled over and complained wordlessly through the gooey glue of sleep. Rowan's hand was cold. She held it close to her chest and tried to forget everything that they and their doppelgängers had done to each other. A nagging thought pestered her mind as it trudged back toward unconsciousness.

Something troubling about Alaric.

It was still snowing at dawn when Lily awoke. The guys were up and clustered around the cauldron, talking quietly. She wanted to get up and join them, but she couldn't. Lily could barely lift her head.

"She's awake," Rowan said, ending their conversation. He looked over at her.

Who am I?

You're Rowan.

He smiled at her. *Don't forget it again.*

Tristan brought her a small bowl of broth while Caleb and Rowan saw to the horses. The broth didn't go down easily. After just a few swallows, Lily felt uncomfortably full and oddly shaky. She almost threw it up. The guys exchanged worried glances as they packed. They were probably all arguing inside their heads about what to do about her, but Lily knew that they only had one choice. If they didn't push on, they'd be found by Gideon's men, or eaten by Woven. They had to make it the rest of the way to the sachem's camp outside of Salem, or they didn't stand a chance.

"How much farther do we have to go?" Lily asked Tristan.

"Just a few hours' ride. Can you make it?"

She smiled weakly at Tristan as he helped her sit up. "Every morning—at least I think it was in the morning—the shaman would ask me if I was dead yet."

"The shaman?" he asked. Tristan gave her a worried look, like he thought her fever was making her lose her senses again. She patted his shoulder, a lump forming in her throat. She hadn't had a chance to mourn her lost friend. He'd been there for her when she needed him, but she'd been too late to help him. Much too late.

"I'm not dead yet, Tristan," she said roughly through her tight throat. "I'll make it."

Caleb helped put her on the horse in front of Tristan. It wasn't until she was mounted that she realized she was wearing a different dress. She wondered if it was another one of Esmeralda's, taken from her pack hurriedly as they rushed out of Purgatory Chasm. She tried not to think too much of the sound Esmeralda's body had made when Carrick kept dropping her as he tried to make his way up the rope. She saw Rowan mount his horse carefully.

Why aren't I riding with you, Rowan?

You're still blazing hot.

Lily noticed that his right hand was bandaged, and she could see the outline of more bandages under his shirt. Her chest shrank with guilt. She let Rowan feel how terrible she felt.

Are you very badly burned?

I'll be fine.

That's not what I asked.

He looked over at her, and his eyes softened when he smiled at her, but he avoided answering her in mindspeak where he couldn't lie to ease her guilt.

The snow hissed when it hit Lily's skin. As they rode, she leaned her head back, resting it on Tristan's shoulder so she could catch as many flakes on her face as possible. She could sense how tense they were. Rowan's eyes constantly scanned the trees above them. Tristan stiffened at every noise from the forest. Lily tried to use mindspeak to ask what was wrong, but her head hurt too much.

"What is it?" Lily croaked. "Are there soldiers out there?"

"No. Woven nest," Tristan whispered. His breath was tight in his chest. *"Shh."*

They managed to slip by the nest, and at some point as they made their way as quietly as they could through the forest, Lily fell asleep. When she woke again, she was riding with Caleb.

"We're nearly there," he whispered in her ear. He wiped sweat from his forehead. "Which is good because I think my horse has heatstroke."

"Poor horse," Lily muttered. She wanted to joke with Caleb, wanted to make him laugh and ease his fear, but she didn't have the energy.

When they entered the sachem's camp, Lily's head was nodding, and her eyes opening and closing on their own. She heard voices and saw row after row of the Outlanders' armored caravan carts and faces—lots of faces looking up at her anxiously as she and Caleb rode past. Something didn't feel right. There was something she was supposed to remember about Alaric and his tribe, but she couldn't.

"It's okay, Lily," Rowan said soothingly. "You're safe here. I swear it."

Lily felt her arms being restrained. She felt her legs being held down as she was lowered onto a cool bed. She saw Rowan's eyes over hers and tasted something bitter in her mouth. She tried to spit it out but found that she couldn't. She decided that it would take less energy to swallow Rowan's nasty brew than reject it, so she did. She tried to tell him in mindspeak that she didn't like the taste, but her head hurt.

Lily opened her eyes, but it was so dark she might as well have kept them shut. She was back in the oubliette. Maybe she'd never left. Fear stiffened her spine, and she sat up, clutching at her neck.

"Lily, what is it?" Rowan said into the dark. She grabbed at her necklace, feeling all three of her willstones but not fully believing they were there. She felt Rowan's hands on her shoulders.

"Did he catch you, too?" she asked thickly. "How did he catch you?"

Rowan's willstone glowed with magelight, revealing his worried face. Lily looked around and saw that they were in a tent. Tristan and Caleb were with them, and just starting to stir.

"No one caught us. You're safe, Lily," he said, easing her back down onto her sleeping bag.

"Safe," she whispered, and wondered if she would ever really feel safe again. "It didn't kill me. But I'm definitely not stronger."

"You will be," Rowan promised. "You'll heal if you let us help you."

I'm not talking about my body, Rowan.

Neither am I, Lily.

Juliet tugged at the collar of her dress. She'd never minded the elaborate gowns or the intricate piles of braids and curls on top of her head before, but lately everything about her position as Lillian's sister seemed to squeeze her too tightly or weigh too heavily on her head. She swirled her ribs over her hips to loosen her lower back and folded her hands neatly in her lap, waiting patiently as she'd always done.

"Let the prisoners come forth," cried the bailiff.

The courtroom was packed with Coven, Council, citizens, and Outlanders, and all turned as one to see the doors of the dungeon open. Sibilant hisses and low murmurs rose up from the mixed crowd. Hakan, Keme, and Chenoa emerged, blinking at the bright light of noon after days spent underground.

Thomas Danforth rose from his seat at Lillian's left and waited for the accused to take their places in front of the jury. From her front row seat in the audience, Juliet noticed that the jury was made up entirely of citizens. Outlanders were held accountable to the laws of the Thirteen Cities—they could be tried and hanged like anyone else—but as noncitizens they had no say in shaping the laws that took their lives. They didn't even have representation to speak on their behalf during a trial. Instead, they were forced to make do with defending themselves, even if they were unfamiliar with the laws of the cities. This had always seemed perfectly natural to Juliet before, and for that she was now ashamed.

"Hakan, Keme, and Chenoa. You are charged with practicing science," Danforth said in a sonorous voice. "How do you plead?"

"Is there any point in pleading with you?" Hakan retorted. "You've already made up your minds to hang us."

A surge of murmurs came from the courtroom. Lillian raised a hand and all fell silent again. "If you denounce science as evil and give us the names of other scientists, we may show leniency," she said.

"Evil?" Chenoa said, shaking her head. "Science is a tool, like witchcraft. It's people that are evil. But you know that better than any of us, don't you?"

The court erupted with noise, mostly hisses and boos, but the few Outlanders that dared to watch from the back cheered Chenoa. Lillian leapt to her feet and strode toward the scientist, her body rigid with rage. The room went silent with shock. The Lady of Salem had presided over many trials like this, but never once had she shown her anger in public before. Not even when she'd hanged River Fall and many had shouted every dirty name in the book at her. Chenoa was different somehow. Juliet knew that Chenoa was the linchpin for all of her sister's fears; she just didn't know why.

"Evil is as evil does, and your brand of science is the *most* evil because it causes the most harm," Lillian said, finally controlling herself.

"Is it evil to try to bring cheap, bountiful energy to your people?" Chenoa countered calmly. "We Outlanders don't have witches to light our lamps for us. We must find another way."

"An evil, impure way," Lillian corrected. "Isn't it true that elemental energy creates a dirty byproduct that is dangerous to all living things for thousands of years?"

Chenoa nodded her head stiffly. "It does."

"And that it is very unstable? That even in your small experiments it often runs out of control and creates major damage?" Lillian pressed, her eyes gleaming.

"Yes. But we're working on making it safer."

"Safer. But not safe. Not entirely," Lillian said leadingly. Chenoa didn't answer. Lillian relaxed, leaning back and looking down on her adversary with triumph. "And, isn't it true that elemental energy could be used in warfare to make an explosion so great that all of Salem could be obliterated in a fraction of a second?"

Nervous whispering rose up from the crowd. Chenoa narrowed

her eyes at Lillian. "How could you know that? I've never told anyone that. Not even them," Chenoa said, gesturing to Hakan and Keme, both of whom looked genuinely shocked.

"It doesn't matter how I know it," Lillian said sadly. "All that matters is that I know it's inevitable if we start down this path. You know it, too, don't you?"

Chenoa's shoulders stiffened. "Not all of us are out to destroy the world, Lady."

"All it takes is one," Lillian said. Her sad expression suddenly changed to pleading. "Which is why it's so important you tell me who else knows about your work with elemental energy. Please, Chenoa. Turn away from this madness. Give me a name."

Chenoa looked at Hakan. He gave her a brave smile of solidarity. Then she looked at Keme. He was scared. He looked so young and fragile, but even still he shook his head at Chenoa, telling her no. They were all ready to die.

"Juliet Proctor!"

Juliet stood on shaky legs and met her little sister's stunned eyes. She was aware that people were shouting and trying to get her to sit down and shut up, but she shook them off. She'd been silent long enough.

"You want a name? I just gave you one," Juliet said, coming forward and taking a stand in between Lillian and the three condemned scientists. "*Juliet Proctor*. If you're going to hang them, you'll have to hang me first, Lillian."

Lily woke up—really woke up for the first time since coming to this world.

She spent a long time staring at the tent over her, piecing together what Lillian had said when she was dying on the edge of the Charles River. She wanted to believe that Lillian had found a way to lie in mindspeak, but no matter how Lily turned the story over in her mind, it all added up to the same thing.

Lily was as stiff and sore as if she'd been kicked down a flight of steps. And for once, she was actually chilly. She staggered up off her sleeping bag on unsteady feet and managed to make her way to the basin in the corner. She sat down on the only piece of real furniture in the tent and peered into the mirror at her gaunt face. The angry red of the fever was gone. She looked pale. And sad.

The guys had left their shaving stuff scattered around the basin and Lily had to shuffle through their razors and soaps until she found a toothbrush. After washing her face and brushing her teeth she felt better. She still looked like death warmed over, but at least she was refreshed. Lily ran her hand through her hair and noticed that she was growing some pretty impressive red roots. They looked almost pink in contrast with the bleached white tips, and Lily thought it looked sort of cool. She wondered in an offhand way if Juliet would like it, and suddenly missed her sister desperately. Juliet, it appeared, was the only person in this world who *wasn't* trying to use her.

Juliet?

There you are!

Are you okay?

Not really, Lily. I've gotten myself into a bit of trouble with Lillian.

What happened?

She's going to hang three people on New Year's Day. I tried to save them. I'm just glad you're alive.

Lily felt Juliet leave her mind. An emptiness took her sister's place. Knowing she couldn't put this off any longer, Lily stood up and rifled through the different piles of boys' clothes stacked around the tent until she found a dress. She slid it over the slip she was wearing and struggled to do up the laces herself. It was a gorgeous dress—beautifully tailored and embroidered with gold thread. She wondered who it had belonged to and where it came from. She wasn't naive enough to think that Alaric's tribe had bought it for her in a store, she just hoped no one had been killed for it. She dug in the clothes pile some more and found a cape that looked like it would fit a girl. She threw it over her shoulders and went out into the snow barefoot.

She could feel where her mechanics were. Lily made her way through the camp, turning heads wherever she went. Everyone who looked at her immediately glanced down at the three stones lying on her bared breastbone and hurried to get out of her way.

The camp was much larger than she'd thought. Lily had to walk a fair distance to make her way out of what she assumed was its center, where her tent was hitched, to find Rowan and the others, all the while heading toward the looming walls of Salem. As she felt her way through the grounds, Lily passed row after row of booths, tents, stalls, and stables. There were thousands, possibly even tens of thousands, of people camped here—and most of them were heavily armed.

There was urgency in the air. Lily looked up at the walls beyond the camp, and saw flashes of light. The great wall surrounding Salem bristled with soldiers. A chill ran down her spine. Lily had zero battle experience, but even she knew that the two sides were facing off with each other. A war was brewing.

Lily hadn't seen much of the city while she was there, but she did know that it was modern, rich, and filled with resources. It also had a witch who could fuel her claimed with superhuman strength. As she passed through the camp, it seemed centuries behind. The carts and clothes were handmade. The children worked alongside the adults at the forges and the bakeries rather than attending school. Lily thought of the two sides of Rowan she'd seen—the Rowan who fit so perfectly in his sleek city apartment, and the Rowan who knew how to make do in a simple survival cabin in the woods. She remembered how happy he was when he was serving a huge meal to his friends at his stylish table, and how one jar of jam had been so important to him that he'd have rather starved than take it from another Outlander.

This camp was filled with Rowan's people. They were a people who had never had any resources apart from the kind they found inside themselves, and as noble as that was, Lily knew they didn't stand a chance if it came down to a fight. The Citadel was too strong.

Lily arrived at a huge armored cart surrounded by fierce-looking Outlander warriors. They had streaks of red and black paint on their faces, eagle feathers in their hair, and their dark wearhyde clothes were so similar they could have been uniforms. When she tried to pass, they stepped in front of her. They barely glanced at her or her stones. These were not the kind of men or women who were impressed by willstones and witches.

"I need to speak to Alaric," Lily said loudly.

Half a second later Rowan appeared at the door. He looked her up and down with a funny expression. Her heart pinched at the sight of him, and then hardened. Why was it that every time she gave her heart to a guy, he almost instantly broke it?

Lily! You're awake.

And I plan on staying that way. I've been asleep for too long.

Lily could feel confusion swirling around inside of Rowan as he picked up on her anger.

Is something wrong?

Lily didn't respond. Rowan's confusion turned to frustration.

I'm glad you're awake, but don't go through the camp alone again. Call to me first and I'll come to you.

Why?

The Woven like to pick off loners and strays.

324

Lily's stride hitched and her skin crawled.

But this camp is huge. They can still get inside?

Outside the walls of the cities, no one is safe.

"Let her pass," Caleb ordered.

Tristan joined Rowan and Caleb at the doorway, smiling brightly. Lily could sense Caleb's and Tristan's happiness at seeing her up and about, but she took no comfort in it.

The Outlander warriors stepped out of Lily's way. She took a few steps toward the carriage, but didn't enter it.

Lily? What's the matter with you?

Lily ignored Rowan. "Alaric!" she called. Confused thoughts from Caleb and Tristan ate away at the edges of her anger. It was hard to stay mad at them when their thoughts were laced with so much concern.

Alaric limped out of the war carriage, his face inscrutable. "My Lady of Salem," he said smoothly.

"Lily," she replied sharply. "My name is Lily. I'm not the 'Lady' of anything."

"What can I do for you, Lily?" Alaric said politely.

"You can tell me what you want from me." She glared at Rowan. "And *he* can tell me whether or not you're lying in mindspeak."

"I want you to help my people," Alaric said immediately.

Lily looked at Rowan.

He's telling the truth.

"And how do you want me to do that?" Lily asked Alaric.

"By going to other worlds to get me the technology my people need to survive if necessary," he responded. "But I'll take whatever I can get from you. Clean water, antibiotics, whatever you've got."

Lily didn't need Rowan to confirm what Alaric just said, but he did anyway.

He's telling the truth.

And what about you, Rowan? Were you ever going to tell me the truth?

"I've never lied to you," Rowan yelled out loud.

"But you didn't tell me the whole truth, either. Did you?" Lily yelled back. "You weren't looking for the shaman so I could find my home. You were looking for him so I could learn how to steal things for you."

"Don't you *dare* tell me what my motives were," Rowan said warningly.

Like a slap across the face, Lily got a memory from Rowan.

. . . the meeting with the Outlander elders, right before the camp got raided by Gideon's men. The elder from Huron says there could be an answer to all the Outlanders' problems on other worlds and that the girl could get those answers. The elder from Choctaw is so hopeful. He says that the fighting and dying and running from the Woven could end tomorrow if the girl can get the power source they need from the farworlds. The elder from Cherokee, the wiry woman with the mane of gray hair, cuts them all off. She says that first they have to find the shaman and then they have to find a way to get the girl on their side. She looks at me, and I know what she wants me to do. She wants me to seduce Lily. The elder wants me to tell Lily I love her so she'll follow me anywhere. How I want to. But this girl is an innocent. I can't. I won't. I'm scared she'll break my heart—again.

Rowan's mind skipped ahead.

. . . Gideon has just left. Lily is standing there, swamped in my robe, trusting me to protect her. How can I protect her if she can't give me the strength to do it? Gideon is coming for her. I can either lose her or train her. Everyone wants a piece of her, and I can't stop them unless I make her a powerful witch—the witch everyone wants me to make of her so they can use her. I don't know what's right or wrong anymore, but I know I can't lose her. How the hell did that happen so fast?

The memory changed again.

. . . making blueberry pancakes for Lily. She's sitting on the island behind me, so fresh and lovely it hurts. She has no idea Tristan, Caleb, and I are fighting in mindspeak. Neither understands what my problem is. The way Caleb sees it, Lily would have to learn from the shaman to get back to her home, so what's the problem with us training her? Tristan adds that if she wants to help us rebels, she will. If not, it's not like anyone could make her do it so what was the harm? I ask them sarcastically if they also think I should do as the elders want and sleep with Lily to seal the deal. Tristan offers to do it for me, whether it seals the deal or not. I nearly hit him. I take a breath and flip the pancakes. I tell them again that I won't have any part of it. If the shaman shows up, I'll stop training Lily. I won't trick her into fighting this war for us.

The memories ended, and Lily stood, looking into Rowan's offended eyes.

"But you're the only person I told about the shaman in the oubliette. That he taught me how to spirit walk," she said, feeling chastised. "Why did you tell Alaric about that if you didn't want him to use me?"

Rowan smiled at her, shaking his head. "You told *everyone* about the shaman when you were delirious."

"I did?" Lily looked at Tristan and Caleb.

"You wouldn't shut up about him," Tristan said.

"You kept trying to make us go back for his bones because you hadn't learned how to worldjump yet and you needed to bury him," Caleb added, his nose wrinkled with distaste.

Lily turned to Alaric. "I don't know how to worldjump. Not completely. I can send my spirit to other worlds, but I have no idea how to get my body there. So I doubt I'll be of any use to you," she said bitterly, happy to ruin his plans to manipulate her.

"We'll find someone else to train you," Alaric replied with a shrug.

"I can't believe you!" Lily said, shocked by his audacity. "You're just going to bald-face admit that you want to use me to raid other worlds?"

"If it comes to that, yes," Alaric replied heatedly. He spread his hands wide to include the camp. "I want you to help my people, and I don't care if you feel like I'm using you. I'm doing it so *they*—" Alaric jabbed his finger angrily in the direction of the camp, "—don't *die*. Which is far more important to me than your feelings."

As hurt as she was at being misled, she honestly couldn't fault Alaric for his intentions. Even on her brief walk through the camp she'd seen how much these people needed help. "You still should have told me. If you want me on your side, you can't keep things from me."

"I need your help, Lily," the sachem said pleadingly. "*We* need your help. Ask me whatever you want, and I'll try to give you an honest answer."

Lily felt the skirt of her plundered dress between her fingers. No matter how much she sympathized with the Outlanders, was she really ready to raid other worlds for Alaric? She looked at her guys and could feel how much they wanted her to at least listen to the sachem. She sighed. "I'll listen. But I'm not promising anything."

"Fair enough." The sachem gestured for Lily to join him inside the carriage.

Thank you, Lily.

I'm trying, Rowan, for your sake. But I don't trust Alaric yet.

Lily couldn't help but think about Lillian, and what she was willing to do for Rowan's sake. She felt him put his hand on the small of her back as she climbed the steps and knew it wasn't just to help her up. They were still tightly connected after sharing his

328

memories and he wanted to touch her. She wanted to be physically near him, too, and she pressed herself against his hand.

It was her first time inside one of the Outlander carriages. Lily looked around at the scaled-down furniture and how everything seemed to either fold up or have multiple functions. Beds served as couches, and tables could easily be stowed into the walls. There were papers all over the place—maps and designs and lists of names. Lily saw a glass box on a ledge by the window. The inside of the box crawled with crickets. She looked at Rowan, her lips pressed together with mirth.

Dinner.

With a little salt, they're not as bad as you'd think. Crunchy.

I'll stick to pickles.

I don't blame you.

Rowan? Did you grow up in a place like this?

Yes. Except ours was much smaller, and we shared it in shifts with another family. They worked nights and we worked days.

But it's so small. Lily widened her eyes at him, and he smiled and shrugged.

We were poor, Lily.

Lily sat close to Rowan, pressing her leg against his. Whether Rowan had intended to win her over for the Outlanders or not, she couldn't help but think the elders had won. A part of her knew she'd do anything for Rowan, and she wondered how deep *anything* went.

"Now then," Alaric said briskly when they were all seated. "What would you like to know, Lily?"

"I guess my first question is, why are you parked on Lillian's doorstep and not hiding in the woods somewhere?" Lily asked.

"No point in hiding anymore," he replied, throwing up his hands. "Not when Lillian is about to hang three of my best scientists."

"Okay. What's this really about? Lots of people have been hanged. Why are these three scientists so important?" Lily asked, leaning forward and looking the sachem in the eye. "You have God knows how many Outlanders ready to go to battle against a force that can crush them. For what?"

Alaric looked at Lily with respect. "Power, of course, but not political power. The kind of power that can fuel cities, fight the Woven, and make it so the Outlanders can finally get out from under the thumb of the Covens. Real power."

"Elemental power, Lily," Tristan said reluctantly.

"You mean nuclear power?" Lily asked.

Tristan nodded. "They're going to hang three scientists," he said. "Lillian destroyed all their notes, killed all their students, and these three are the last who know how to turn elements into energy—without a witch."

Lily looked around at Rowan, Tristan, and Caleb, her eyes wide. "Nuclear power is really tricky," she said fearfully.

"Tristan already told me that you're against it," Alaric said, his expression unreadable.

"I'm sorry, Lily," Tristan said contritely. "I didn't mean it as a betrayal."

"No, Tristan. It's fine. My position isn't a secret." Lily ran a frustrated hand through her hair. "Sachem, you can't really understand the scope of this, but there have been huge disasters in my world because of this kind of power. A lot of people have died."

"But how many people are there in your world, Lily?" Rowan asked. "How many millions?"

"Billions. There are *billions* of people in my world, Rowan," she said. A stunned silence followed.

"And you use this form of energy widely?" Alaric asked.

"Yes," Lily said.

"And it's helped you grow in numbers, all across your world?" he persisted.

"It has," Lily admitted. "It had been used safely in many countries for many years. But it's also done a lot of damage along the way. In my world, it was originally developed as a weapon. A bomb. That bomb was used to end one of our great wars, and it wiped two cities off the map. The shock of that kind of power stunned my whole world. Even today when it's used for peaceful reasons, sometimes it gets out of control and poisons the land and the water for miles."

"Then maybe in another world you could find some other type of energy we could use? Something safe, that will both free us from the Covens and help us fight the Woven?" Alaric asked.

"I could look for you—" Lily began optimistically, and then broke off.

She thought of what both the shaman and Lillian had told her. Lily didn't have Lillian's entire story yet, but she knew that Lillian hadn't lied to her. She had been trying to save the Outlanders. She wanted to eradicate the Woven and save Rowan's people, but instead she must have seen something or learned something on one of her worldjumps that made her come back determined to eradicate science instead.

Lily felt Rowan's mind pressing up against hers—a gentle nudge, wanting to know what she was thinking. How could she ever tell him any of this? How could she tell Rowan that, behind it all, Lillian had done this for *him*?

"The shaman warned me against this," Lily continued nervously, careful to leave Lillian out of it. "Stealing technology from other worlds—even if it seems like the right thing to do at the time— has disastrous consequences. And I agree."

"You realize, you don't leave me with many options." Alaric's intense eyes captured Lily's. "You say elemental energy is too dangerous to use, but finding another option is too dangerous as well?"

"I know." Lily met his eyes. "I don't have a solution yet, but I'll try to think of something."

"Unfortunately, we don't have the time for that." Alaric's gaze drifted down in serious thought. There was a knock at the door. "I will let the elders know your position. Now if you'll excuse us."

Dismissed, Lily and her mechanics stood and headed toward the door. She could feel Rowan's disappointment, Tristan's frustration, and Caleb's sadness. At odds with herself, Lily stopped.

"Alaric," she said, turning. "I don't agree with using this type of energy. But I also don't agree with murdering people just because you're scared of what they think. I'm not Lillian."

The sachem narrowed his piercing eyes at her. "Whether you agree or don't agree, three people have been tried, found guilty, and they will be hanged at dawn tomorrow. And everything they know will die with them unless we go to war and try to stop it."

"You can't win," Lily whispered.

"It not about winning. It's about having nothing else to lose." The sachem smiled at her, a brief flash of pain crossing his face. Lily wondered what it was that Alaric had lost. "You must leave now, Lily Proctor."

Lily stepped outside the carriage. A group of men and women filed past her to join the sachem. Lily recognized a few of the faces. She nodded at the wiry elder from Cherokee with the salt-and-pepper mane, who smiled back, looking pointedly at Lily and Rowan and how close they stood to each other. Lily's natural instinct was to move away from Rowan so as not to give her the satisfaction, but instead she decided to lean closer to him, her willstones pulsing possessively. Just to make her point, she sent a surge of power through all of her mechanics' willstones, making them glitter prettily across their faces.

"Lady Witch," the elder said, tipping her head respectfully.

"Elder," Lily replied, staring her down.

Not very friendly, Caleb whispered in her head. *She's known Rowan and me our whole lives, you know.*

Well, then, it's about time she backed off, Lily thought, earning a devilish smile from Caleb.

She waited until the door to the war carriage was closed before turning to her men.

"Why does Lillian give the scientists a trial if she's just going to hang them anyway?" Lily asked.

"She doesn't just want to kill them," Rowan answered. "What good would that do anyway? Eventually someone else will make the same discoveries as they did."

"Lillian always has trials for high-profile scientists," Tristan explained. "It's not about proving they're guilty, but proving to everyone that what scientists do is evil. She puts science on trial."

"And it's working," Caleb said. "People are actually starting to believe that science is evil and that doctors do nothing but harm."

"She traps the people on trial," Tristan said. "She gets people to admit that science makes chemicals that pollute the world and that doctors make drugs that get people addicted, while witchcraft does everything that the people need without all the side effects."

"Except for the small side effect of tyranny," Rowan said quietly.

"There's only one thing for us to do. We have to get those three scientists." Her mechanics looked at her, surprised.

"Are you sure?" Rowan asked.

"You don't think I'd actually let a *war* start because I'm not a fan of nuclear energy, do you?"

"Uh. No?" Caleb said innocently.

"I wouldn't," Lily said, punching Caleb in the shoulder. "But I can't speak for you guys. It'll probably be really dangerous."

"Probably," Tristan said dryly. "I say we do it." He looked at Rowan, who was frowning and deep in thought. "Rowan?" Tristan asked.

"Yes," Rowan answered. "Caleb?"

"I'm in, too," he replied.

"Okay. We need a plan," Lily said, nervously rubbing her hands together. The enormity of what they were going to do was starting to sink in for her. She dropped her shaking hands and steadied herself. "You three are the jailbreak masters. What do you suggest?"

Tristan and Caleb shared a look, conferring in mindspeak. When they'd finished, Caleb looked at Lily.

"Even with you fueling us, it's going to be a close fight," he said.

"We can't just barge in there, blind. We need someone on the inside," Tristan added.

Rowan nodded, picking up on their thoughts. "You have to ask Juliet for help, Lily. Or we don't have a chance."

CHAPTER
14

H EY, JULIET?

Lily. This is sort of a bad time.

It can't wait. I need a favor.

What is it?

You know those three scientists you tried to save? You wouldn't happen to know exactly where they are, would you? Like, what cell they're in and stuff?

Actually, I do.

Juliet sent Lily images of where the scientists were. She walked Lily through how to get from one cell to another, as if she had been down in those dungeons many times. Lily saw that each scientist was being kept on a different level of the dungeon, as far from each other as they could possibly be.

You're the best. One last thing. Are they going to be in their cells all night?

I think so. Should I ask what's going on, or should I just keep out of it?

You'd better keep out of it. I'm sorry, Juliet.

It's okay, Lily. Just don't do anything stupid.

How are you? You seem strange.

Um . . . you just worry about yourself, Lily. I'll be alright.

Lily felt Juliet break the connection and frowned.

"What is it?" Rowan asked.

"It's my sister," Lily said. "She's acting all cagey and weird. I don't like it."

"Did she tell you where the prisoners are?" Tristan asked.

"Yeah," Lily said, distracted. The guys shared a look.

"Do you think we can trust her information?" Caleb asked. Lily glared at him. "I'm just asking, Lily," he said, backing off. "It seems to me like she's hiding something."

"Shh," Tristan hissed.

There's someone behind you.

Lily and Caleb shut their mouths, and they all turned to stare conspicuously at the man and woman loitering behind them until they moved off. The sachem had ordered that the rescue attempt be kept top secret. There were spies on both sides of the walls and you never knew who had been turned or when. Esmeralda had proved that.

What did Juliet tell you? Rowan asked.

Lily showed them all the images of the dungeons that Juliet had shown her, and in a few seconds, they were discussing strategy in mindspeak. There were still a few more hours until dark, and the team used that time to gather the supplies they'd need, then eat. Rowan spent half of supper arguing with them in their heads.

I still think Lily should stay here. She can charge us with enough energy to get over the wall and back, Rowan thought.

Tristan looked at Rowan angrily and answered him. *If something goes wrong in the dungeon—if we have to fight our way out and we use up what she gave us—Lily won't be able to give us any more energy with all that granite in the way. We'll be trapped, Ro. And we'll all hang, the scientists included.*

I'm going, and that's final, Lily thought as gently as she could. Rowan's eyes flashed, but Lily shook her head, stopping him. *I mean it, Rowan. I'm going or this isn't happening.*

Rowan pursed his lips in an expression that Lily was getting to know quite well.

Let's go over how to detonate a pocket bomb again, he thought.

Lily saw Caleb roll his eyes and laughed, but went through the sequence of pin, lever, clip for the hundredth time anyway for Rowan's sake.

The camp settled down for the evening. There was a heightened tension in the air. As Lily walked back to her tent to change out of her dress and into darker wearhyde clothes, she could hear music being played around the campfires. Some songs were rousing, martial songs, others sad, like the singers were already lamenting the people who would be lost in the pending battle.

As Lily neared her tent, she paused to listen to one woman with a haunting voice. She sang with her eyes closed, her back arched slightly and her head tipped back, as if the music were trying to leap right out of her heart and into the sky.

"I love this song," Rowan whispered in Lily's ear.

"It's beautiful," Lily agreed. She felt Rowan take her hand.

Thank you, Lily.

For what?

For proving me wrong.

Rowan gave Lily another memory.

. . . I'm exhausted after days in the woods, and after last night— the confrontation with Gideon, and then Lily bonding with her willstones. I didn't meet Lillian until after she bonded with hers. Last night was an experience between Lily and me alone. Tristan is sitting across the table, angry with me for giving myself to Lily. I can tell he wants me to share the memory of my claiming with him, but I don't want to. I don't want to share her. I'm telling Tristan we can't trust her, but that's not it. She didn't ask for any of this. It's not her I don't trust, it's me. I don't trust myself around Lily.

So you do trust me, Rowan?

Yes. Except for one thing.

"What?" Lily asked aloud, hurt.

Rowan smiled at her, and led her away from the fire. He brought her inside his tent and pulled her close to him. She leaned against him, her limbs suddenly light and her insides lifting like she'd jumped off a cliff. Rowan was breathing fast as he lifted her hand to his willstone. Lily hesitated for just a second, wondering if he really meant it, and then gently laid her fingertips on it. She took a deep breath, resisting the urge to grab it and crush it in her hand, and managed to hold it gently even though she wanted it. Rowan shivered and sighed, his willstone glittering.

A world of tenderness wrapped around Lily and filled her up, as if the air had turned into Rowan and she was standing in him and breathing him in. Lily saw images of herself—a pile of rags and pale skin in the oubliette, a human cinder that muttered and twisted with fever, a pleading white mask under dark and icy water.

This is why I don't trust you, Lily.

He looked her in the eye. "I don't trust you not to go and die on me," he said aloud. "You're stubborn and brave and you don't listen to me."

Lily smiled up at him nervously, her throat tight. "I've never been good at doing what I'm told. I'm sorry, Rowan. I know you want me to say that I won't go tonight for your sake, but I can't."

"I know," Rowan said. "You wouldn't be you if you could."

He kissed her, softly at first, but then more deeply, until Lily felt herself falling open under him. Rowan dropped his head to the side and kissed her neck.

"See?" he whispered against her jawbone. His fingers were inching her skirt up her thighs, his knee sliding between her legs. "I can't trust myself around you."

Rowan opened himself up to her completely. He let her feel what he was feeling in his body, all his excitement and anticipation. He showed her the ways he wanted to kiss her and touch her and how urgently he wanted it. Lily's body lit up with sensation, but her mind fumbled somewhere between eagerness and fright. She wanted to open herself to him, but she had nothing to share back. And inside her was a nagging thought. She'd never intended to stay in this world, and although she still had no idea how to get home, that was still what she wanted to do.

At least that's what she thought she still wanted.

She was falling in love with Rowan, and yet she still intended to leave him—didn't she? Lily froze. Rowan pulled away and held Lily at arm's length, abruptly shutting off the stream of feelings.

You've never been with a man, have you?

No.

Rowan's face darkened and he took a step back.

"But you and your Tristan. You showed me the two of you together," he said carefully.

Lily shook her head, suddenly feeling very small and exposed. She crossed her arms. "You didn't see all of it. I would have, but he didn't want to."

"Idiot," Rowan whispered.

"No," Lily said fairly. "I'm lucky he stopped."

"I meant me." Rowan smiled and came to Lily. He unwound her arms and stepped into them. "I knew you were shy with your body."

Lily narrowed her eyes. "Actually, you called me a Puritan," she chided gently.

"Well, to us you sort of are. Seventeen and never been with a man?" Rowan teased. "You've got so much catching up to do I might have to draw you a chart."

Lily tried to break out of his arms, but he only held her tighter. He took energy from her to do it, too.

"You're cheating!" she said with disbelief.

"I'm your mechanic." He pressed his hand into the small of her back, sealing her against him. "My strength flows from you. I can't cheat you."

"Is that all you are?" Lily asked uncertainly. She felt embarrassed heat pouring out of her, and she knew that Rowan could feel it, too. "Are you just my mechanic?"

He shook his head slowly, never taking his eyes off of hers. His willstone glittered high on his chest, just under his throat. She watched the light inside his stone writhe and fall with mesmerizing grace.

"You have the prettiest willstone," she murmured. "I've never seen anything that even comes close. And I don't think I've ever wanted anything more."

He was still and silent for too long. Lily looked back up into his eyes. They looked hungry. "Did I say something wrong?"

"Slowly, Lily." His breath caught in his chest. "We're going to go very slowly, for both our sakes."

He tucked his face into her neck and just held her. She could feel the pull of want in him, like a tight thread inside. She felt it, too, but he wouldn't let her turn her mouth to his and kiss him.

"Hey! Sorry," Tristan said from the entrance of the tent. "Didn't mean to interrupt." His eyes slid away from them, and Lily could sense that he didn't want to look at them holding each other. She wondered if she should be worried about that or if it would go away on its own. "It's almost time," he said.

"Alright, both of you out," Lily said, easing away from Rowan's embrace. "I need to change."

Rowan and Tristan shared a look with each other and then turned to Lily, smirking like they thought she was crazy.

"I know, I know. You've both seen me naked a jillion times, and I've noticed that nudity is no big deal in this world, but I don't care," Lily said, shoving Rowan toward the exit. "I'm actually conscious this time, and it's not like we're doing a spell to save a bunch of dying children. So get the hell out."

They obliged, laughing with each other as they left the tent. Once Lily had finished changing, she joined Tristan and Rowan outside the tent and went with them to an open field near the sachem's council carriage on the edge of the camp. A huge fire was already going, and as they arrived Caleb threw another log onto it, sending sparks crackling up out of the white-hot center. The sachem was there, along with four of his elite guards with the painted faces.

"Watch the trees," Alaric said to his guards. "There were reports of simian Woven out there."

The warriors swept past them and set up a perimeter between them, the rest of the camp, and the dark canopy of trees.

Got your pocket bomb? Rowan asked anxiously.

Lily smiled at him and patted the small bulge in her skirts. *Of course.*

The sachem stepped forward and went with Lily to the edge of the fire. Rowan and Tristan set wards in a circle around them to hide the night's witchcraft from both the camp and the soldiers on the wall. Caleb trailed behind them, watching and following their instruction. He hadn't finished his training as a mechanic as they had, and each new situation was a chance for him to learn. Arcs of light sprang out of their willstones and wove together until a hazy screen formed into a large dome over the group. Lily and the sachem stood with their backs to the fire, waiting for her mechanics to finish.

"You're taking quite a risk," said the sachem.

"I'm not doing it for you," she replied. "I'm doing it for them." Lily made a gesture toward the camp.

"Good." The sachem smiled slowly at Lily, and she found herself smiling back at him. She didn't know how she felt about Alaric just yet. She wasn't ready to trust him, but she did respect him.

The sachem looked up and watched as the spell trails of the wards dimmed. "Beautiful," he whispered. Lily's mechanics joined her, kneeling in front of her so that the darkness was at their backs and the fire behind her lit up their eyes. Alaric turned to Lily and tipped his head.

"Good luck, Lily Proctor," he said, before limping off into the night surrounded by his ghostly guard.

Ready? Lily asked her three charges.

Ready, they answered as one.

Lily took a breath with her whole body, breathing in air through her lungs and heat through her skin. A witch wind kicked up immediately, knocking all three of her mechanics forward with its ferocity. Lily's skill and strength had grown with training. She wasn't overwhelmed by warrior magic anymore, as she had been in the cabin the night she'd claimed Rowan. In fact, she craved it. The column of air collided with Lily and lifted her up off her feet, her arms and face reaching toward the dark sky. Lily felt her three stones rise up off her breastbone, begging for power.

The harvested heat grew inside her chest like a seed sun. Her smoke stone floated in front of her, wanting it the most. Heat piled on heat inside Lily's body. As the witch wind shrieked around her and flew her high into the air, Lily knew that this was the most power she'd ever taken into herself. She looked down on her three mechanics, waiting on their knees, and saw how small they looked several stories' distance beneath her. She was afraid for them. How could she give this much power to them without crushing them?

Help me, Rowan. I don't want to hurt you.

It's okay, Lily. Give me the most, Tristan the second most, and go easy on Caleb. He's not as experienced as Tristan and I are.

I'm afraid for Caleb. Show me how much is too much for him.

Spill it all into me, and I'll Gift Tristan and Caleb. Don't worry about hurting me. I can take it.

All of it, Rowan?

At this level, I can take whatever you can gather, Lily.

There's another level?

Firewalking. Don't think of it now, just Gift me.

Her smoke stone opened like a book of light. She poured all her power through it and into Rowan and gave him the Gift. Giving the Gift was different from the dribs and drabs of power she'd been channeling into her mechanics to dig tunnels and climb ropes. This was on a different level entirely. It turned her mechanics into gods who could do the impossible. It filled them up and set them free so that only the limits of their imagination limited their physical abilities.

She was getting better at transmuting energy. Every calorie of heat from the fire changed easily into raw force inside her willstone. This much power also tempted Lily to take them over, to steal their will. She wanted to own each of them so badly she ached, but she wanted Rowan most of all. He was the strongest by far, even though both Caleb and Tristan were physically bigger than he was. Rowan's mind was like a diamond—strong, clear, and so tightly bound onto itself that he could handle enormous amounts of pressure.

Let me keep myself, Lily.

Yes. I will. I'm sorry.

It's okay. It's time to start over the wall. Let go of the heat. I'll catch you.

The witch wind ended abruptly and she fell from the sky. Rowan rose up to meet her and caught her in midair. Lily saw that Tristan and Caleb were with him, and all together they sped to the great wall around Salem. The landscape swept past her so quickly, and they climbed over the hundred-foot wall so fast that she thought they might be flying. They crested the wall and slipped past the sentries, hidden by the darkness and their incredible speed. In moments, they were over the wall, and through the strip of no-man's-land on the other side. When they reached a busy city street they slowed.

Rowan held Lily high against his side with his left arm. He swung her down to the ground and she released her tight hold on his neck.

Face glamour, Lily. And tuck your stones under your shirt.

They continued down the street, melting into the crowd like they belonged there.

Rowan? Why aren't we running?

The streets are too well lit, and there are too many people to try and maneuver through.

Lily glanced over at Tristan and Caleb. She could easily see the excitement they felt. They were enjoying this. Caleb looked border-line giddy, and because all four had been linked through mindspeak for most of the night, the sensation spread through all of them.

Tristan led the way, although it was easy to see where they were headed—the Citadel. The giant granite structure was across the city, at the edge of the ocean, but the ramparts were still visible through all the other soaring structures of Salem. They wove through the streets swiftly, and as they neared the giant gate that Lily had entered on her first day in this world, their excitement turned into focus.

Tristan and Caleb peeled off to the left and right and disappeared in the dark. Lily knew that their camouflage magic wouldn't work once they got inside the Citadel and clashed with Lillian's wards, but camouflage still worked along its perimeter. Rowan lifted Lily and sent the signal.

Over.

Rowan brought Lily over the Citadel wall in one leap. When they landed inside the inner courtyard, she could hear muffled thumps and gasps as Tristan and Caleb took out the guards. They were exposed, but Rowan moved across the courtyard quickly enough so that no one would be able to see them in the dark. He stopped at the portcullis that led down to the dungeons. By the time Caleb and Tristan were done hiding the guards' bodies behind the scaffolding of the gallows, Rowan had bent the bars of the portcullis and made an opening.

The small raiding party swept down the steps together. They only had minutes to find the scientists and get them out of there before they were discovered. Rowan reached out to all of them.

When we split up down there, the granite will block our willstones from each other, and we won't be able to mindspeak. Once you release your prisoner, take him, and run as fast as you can through the city. If you get held up in a fight, Lily and I will be right behind you to help. We'll rendezvous back at camp. Good luck.

They raced silently down the torch-lit steps. Lily felt the chill and smelled the stone all around her. It was the smell that got to her. She hadn't anticipated this. Her heart began to pound and panic fizzed in her blood.

I don't know if I can go back into the dark, Rowan.

It'll be okay. This isn't a prison for witches, Lily. It's made to hold regular people, so there will be light and heat all the way down. Stay calm.

I'm trying.

Caleb stopped his descent and went down the passageway off the main staircase to retrieve the scientist on the topmost level. The rest of the party went down two more flights, while Tristan broke off to retrieve the scientist on that level. Lily and Rowan descended all the way down to the lowest level. At the bottom of the steps were four small passageways that radiated out in different directions. The largest passageway led straight ahead to an alcove. It was filled with guards.

Rowan put Lily down at the base of the steps and stepped in front of her. All the guards turned to look at him.

A mad scramble began as the guards lunged to grab whatever weapon was closest. They came at Rowan with swords, daggers, maces, and spears. He strode down the passageway toward them, his chin down, his fists at his sides as he covered the distance, and then he burst into a flurry of motion.

Rowan grabbed weapons by their blades and yanked them out of the guards' hands. He turned with the swords and spears that they would have used on him and ran them through with their own weapons. Fountains of blood followed Rowan's path through the cluster of doomed men. His willstone flashed with pulses of light, and Lily threw back her head, exulting in the feeling of power she shared with Rowan.

"Witch!" a guard screamed, pointing past Rowan and zeroing in on Lily.

Get down!

Hails of arrows were loosed. Rowan snatched dozens out of the air as Lily hit the floor.

Roll to your left!

Lily did as Rowan instructed, rolling down one of the side corridors off the stairway. More arrows streaked past the opening of Lily's passageway.

I need more strength, Lily.

Lily scrambled back up onto her feet and grabbed the nearest torch off of its sconce on the wall. She took in the torch's heat, and a witch wind whistled toward her from all directions. Lily changed the gathered heat into force and fed it to Rowan. The sounds of the fight in the corridor picked up again.

Go get the scientist, Rowan. We're almost out of time.

I'll lose contact with you if I go for Chenoa. She's all the way down a corridor at a right angle from yours. It'll put fathoms of granite between us.

It's okay if we're out of contact for a bit. You draw off the guards, and I'll start up the steps while you get her. I'll meet you aboveground.

I don't like it.

I'll be fine. Just do it, okay?

Okay. Go quickly.

"Lily?" Juliet said, her voice ragged.

Lily's head snapped around, and she saw that she was standing in front of a dark cell. Juliet was in there.

"What are you doing down here?" Lily said disbelievingly. She put the torch back in its sconce and grabbed on to the bars of Juliet's cell. Her sister came to her and hugged her through the bars.

"I told you I got into a little trouble with Lillian," Juliet replied.

"How could she do this to you?" Lily said, her teeth grinding together. She called out to Rowan in mindspeak, but she got no reply.

"I told Lillian if she wanted to hang them, she'd have to hang me first. The scientists, I mean," Juliet admitted sheepishly. "I couldn't stand back and let one more person die. And apparently killing them means more to her than I do."

The sisters broke apart and Lily looked at Juliet. "I need a vessel. I can't rip this door off, but if you let me claim you, I can give you strength and you'll be able to."

Juliet shook her head, her eyes filling with tears. "Lillian claimed me when we were kids."

Lily knew that two witches couldn't claim the same person. Juliet was stuck with Lillian unless she smashed her willstone and got a new one. Lily looked down the long corridor. There were more cells. Lily saw faces pressed against the bars, and even a few mirrors sticking out, as the inmates tried to see what was happening down the passageway.

"Who wants their freedom?" Lily screamed.

"Me! I'm not a scientist, I'm a tanner. I was only looking for a better dye for my skins," one woman said loudly. She came forward and clutched the bars of her cell. She was an Outlander. Her face was covered in bruises, and her thick wrists were rubbed raw as if she'd been kept in iron shackles.

"I was accused because my neighbor wanted the reward money! I've never even dabbled in the scientific arts!" yelled the man across from her. He was waving his arms through the bars. His nails were long and grubby, and his sleeves threadbare rags. "Help me, witch! Help me, please."

More voices joined theirs—all of them protesting their innocence. A great clamor erupted down the passageway. Arms waved and people banged on their cell doors.

"Everybody settle down," Lily yelled, holding up her arms for silence. The noise stopped. Lily could still hear the clash of swords far off down one of the passageways and desperately hoped that Rowan was okay.

"Who here *has* been claimed by a witch?" Lily asked as she walked down the passageway and looked into each cell.

"None of us," the tanner replied. "If we had, we could've proved our innocence in mindspeak. But witches don't care who's innocent or who's guilty. They just want more names."

Lily's brow furrowed. It was so easy for a witch to find out the truth. All Lillian had to do was share mindspeak with a suspect, ask a few questions, and she'd know if that person was a scientist or not.

"Did you refuse to let Lillian claim you?" Lily asked.

"No," the tanner replied, offended. "She refused us."

"She needs us down here," another woman said. Her voice was weak. When Lily looked in on her, she saw that she was an old woman. "We're the example so all those that the Citadel can't reach are too scared to even try to learn science."

Lily nodded and stepped forward. She positioned herself halfway down the corridor so as many inmates as possible could see her. "Who wants to be claimed by me?" she asked. Silence. She didn't have time for this. "Let's try that again. Who wants to be claimed by me so you can free yourself and fight the Citadel?"

The clamor erupted again. Arms reached toward her. Lily went to the nearest, the tanner, and took her stone between her fingertips.

. . . A baby. My sweet little man. He needs me.

Lily gathered the pattern and released that stone, moving on to the next.

. . . A pretty little yard. I just want to go back home and see my garden.

Lily moved on to the next stone.

. . . A stack of books. I have so much reading to do. And I'll never get it done before testing time, especially not if I'm stuck in this stupid hole. I don't want to die here.

Lily sped up as she went. By the time she arrived at the last few cells she was swimming in other people's loves and losses. She didn't have time to process any of it. She just gathered the patterns and the most basic sense of each individual. The clock ticking, she ran to the nearest wall sconces and pulled down a torch.

A witch wind rushed toward her, moaning as it raced down

the passageways. She changed the heat into energy and poured it into her newly claimed willstones. She didn't turn the heat directly into force. She didn't know what the Gift would do to people who weren't trained mechanics. Her instinct proved right. Most of the prisoners could only handle a tiny bit of power, barely enough to pull the bars of their cells apart, but still they gasped with awe at their first taste of a witch's strength.

Lily grabbed the Outlander tanner by her shoulder as she raced by. She was physically the strongest of all the prisoners, but more importantly, Lily had noticed that she could handle a huge amount of power in her willstone. Briefly, Lily wondered why she hadn't been trained as a crucible because she certainly had the talent.

"Free my sister," Lily said, pointing to Juliet's cell. The woman looked into the cell, recognized Juliet, and then peered into Lily's face. She began backing away fearfully.

"You're *her*," the tanner whispered.

"No. I'm not," Lily pleaded, reaching out again. The woman easily threw off Lily's arm and began to run away.

The rest of the freed prisoners had already fled. Lily couldn't let her go. No matter what she had to do, Lily knew she would do it to get her sister out of that cell. She hesitated a moment, but knew she had no other option. Lily played back the woman's pattern to her willstone, unlocking it, and did what she'd promised Rowan she would never do. She took over the woman's will. As Lily filled the woman like a hand in a glove, she resisted reveling in the delicious feeling of being in total control. She found the woman's name in her mind and called to her.

Stop, Dana. Turn around. Come back.

Dana had no choice but to do as Lily commanded. Lily smothered a triumphant laugh, reminding herself that this was wrong.

Pull the bars apart.

Dana obeyed. Juliet slipped out from between the bent bars and hugged Lily. Then she looked at Dana.

"Did you—" Juliet asked, unable to finish her thought aloud. Lily nodded and grabbed Juliet's hand.

"Let's go," Lily said, pulling Juliet along. "Good-bye, Dana. I'm sorry I did that to you, but I had to. She's my sister."

Lily gave Dana back her will, even though she had to force herself to do so.

Go be with your son. Good luck.

Wait, Lily! I'll never make it over the wall without you.

"I'm out of strength. Give me some more power so I can fight my way out," Dana called aloud. Lily stopped and turned. "You owe me," Dana said in a low voice.

The torches flickered with witch wind, and Dana's willstone flared with power. Dana smiled and rolled her meaty shoulders as a huge measure of strength filled her.

"Now *I* owe *you*. Get behind me, you two," Dana said, rushing down the corridor. "If anyone comes up from the rear, you holler and duck."

And if you ever try to possess me again, I'll find a way to kill you, Lily. Understood.

Dana paused at the end of the passageway to look up and down the abutting main hallway. She waved Lily and Juliet forward, and then darted down the main hallway to grab a sword from a fallen guard.

"Oh my," Juliet breathed when she saw all the bodies.

Lily had helped create this slaughter. It was inhuman to have enjoyed it as much as she had, and she wondered what had happened to her to make her so bloodthirsty. Was it the thrill of power, or was there something sinister growing inside her? She thought twice about possessing Dana, and still she did it. That worried her.

"Come on!" Dana said, charging toward the stairs. "Don't get squeamish on me now."

Lily and Juliet raced after Dana, taking the steps as quickly as they could. They encountered a pair of soldiers on the stairs, and Dana ran them both through before they could even call out. Their bodies slid past Lily and Juliet. Juliet shied away from the corpses, her hand at her mouth, and Lily had to pull on her arm to get her to move again. As they got closer to the surface, Lily tried to touch the minds of her mechanics.

Rowan? Tristan? Caleb?

She heard nothing in reply and kept climbing. Both she and Juliet were drained, and they were flagging. As they reached the surface, Lily heard the shouts and clangs of a huge fight. The three women passed through the broken bars of the portcullis and came out into the courtyard.

"Rowan!" Lily screamed.

He was fighting in the center of at least three dozen soldiers, his legs planted around the crouching figure of a woman. He was bleeding.

Lily! Help me.

"Get back!" Lily yelled at Juliet and Dana. She yanked the pocket bomb out of her skirts, pulled the pin, squeezed the lever, and slid the clip over the lever to keep it in place. Dana recognized what was in Lily's hand and tackled Juliet, who was staring at her sister, slack-jawed.

Lily threw the pocket bomb at her feet just as it exploded. The white-bright fire expanded, slowed, and then retreated back on itself as Lily devoured its energy. Instead of the deafening clap of a bomb there was silence, followed by the shrieks and howls of a fierce witch wind as it rushed over the ramparts. The wind hit Lily like fists on all sides and pushed her high into the air, arms straight up, head thrown back, and lips parted like she were trying to jump up and swallow the moon.

She sent the Gift to Rowan and felt him exalt in it.

The shrieking wind was nearly overshadowed by the screams of the soldiers as Rowan renewed his attack. He quickly blazed a path through the circle surrounding him and pulled the scientist out with him. He managed to stop himself from turning and facing the rest of the guards in the circle. He didn't want to kill them all.

We need to run, Lily, before Lillian comes.

Wait, Rowan. My sister is down there. I have to Gift Dana to get them out of here.

Lily took the last of the heat from the smoldering wreck of the bomb, turned it directly into force, and channeled it into Dana's stone. She felt Dana's elation at this new and much more intense level of power and had to fight to stay focused.

Get my sister out of here, Dana. Don't wait for me.

Alright. Good luck, Lily.

With its energy source almost completely spent, the witch wind grew weak and began buffeting Lily unevenly. Lily looked down as she was being tossed about violently and saw Dana pick up Juliet, throw her over her shoulder, and climb up the wall in a few fluid movements. She heard Rowan in her head.

I'm coming.

Rowan jumped and snatched Lily out of the air. He landed once, rebounded, and leapt over the Citadel wall, holding Lily on one side and the exhausted scientist on the other.

As they sped through the city, knocking stunned and frightened people out of the way, Lily heard Lillian's voice in her mind.

Give them back! They must be hanged, Lily.

No, Lillian. I won't let you do this.

You don't know what they're capable of. You don't know because you haven't worldjumped on your own. You haven't seen the cinder worlds yet. Do you have any idea how many of them there are? I won't let this world burn, too. Think of it, Lily—a few lives to save an entire world, a beautiful world. I know you agree with me. I know what you believe, and I know you're strong enough to do what has to be done, no matter how hard it is. Deep in your heart, you ARE me.

No, Lillian. You're wrong.

Am I? I didn't want to do this, but I don't have a choice anymore. I'm going to show you a version of your world I found on a spirit walk a month before I found you.

Lily tried to block it, but Lillian shoved the memory into her head so forcefully, Lily went board-stiff in Rowan's arms.

. . . My spirit arrives to empty streets and abandoned cars. It's a cinder world—yet another Earth that has been devoured in a holocaust of ambition and stupidity. Houses are burning down at the end of the block, and if the wind off the water picks up, the rest of the neighborhood will go up in flames as well. I can feel a version of myself down below, beneath the ground, even though she hates it down there. She's with Juliet. I tell myself to get out of here. This is just one of millions of wasted worlds, but the pull to see what's happening to them is strong, even though I'm sure I will see nothing but heartbreak.

I send my spirit through the poisoned air and down underground to find them hiding in the cellar. They are skinny and covered in sores. They won't live much longer. If they're lucky, the fire will suffocate them in a few hours. Better that than—

Lily finally managed to shove Lillian out of her mind.

"Lily!" Rowan squeezed Lily, trying to snap her out of it. "What happened? You're shaking."

Tears blurred Lily's vision. She buried her face in Rowan's neck to try to blot out the horrid image of herself and her sister suffering. "Lillian's going to come for the scientists," she whispered to Rowan.

"I know," he replied, and launched them over the outer wall and into the dark forest.

CHAPTER
15

GIDEON FOLLOWED LILLIAN THROUGH THE CARNAGE IN the courtyard. The wounded had been taken inside to be healed, but the dead still lay where they'd fallen, waiting to be dealt with. Lillian stood among the bodies, her pale face unmoving. The hem of her long gown was dark with blood.

"You'll lead the army out," Lillian commanded in a flat tone.

Gideon smirked at her. "You're joking. I'm not a soldier."

"I know that, Gideon," she said tiredly. "You're also not a jailor, but you didn't have much of a problem playing that part when it suited you."

Gideon froze. He knew that Lillian had heard about Witch's End. There was no way to conceal so many dead bodies, not from the Witch, but Lillian had seemed satisfied to apprehend Carrick, throw him in the dungeon, and leave Gideon out of it. He realized that he'd been wrong, and he sifted through his mind quickly to try to find a way to amend his miscalculation.

"You know, you're only hurting yourself if you have me lead out the army," he said equitably. "I'm not a natural fighter, Lillian, not even with a witch's strength in me, and I know you're not foolish enough to shoot yourself in the foot just to punish me."

"I'm not punishing you," she said. Lillian turned away from Gideon and called out to one of the guards on top of the wall, "Captain Leto! Have a pyre built on Walltop!"

"My Lady!" Captain Leto replied eagerly.

"And if there are any soldiers who have not been claimed by me but wish to be before the battle, have them arrange themselves in the courtyard," Lillian ordered.

"No one will wish to go into battle without your strength, Lady," Leto answered proudly.

The soldiers were looking forward to receiving the Gift, as was Gideon. But someone of his breeding belonged at the back of the fray, enjoying the feeling of the Gift and the spectacle of the fight. He wasn't supposed to actually fight.

Lillian turned back to Gideon. "You'll go out first, but you won't be in charge. I have a well-trained army and plenty of generals for that."

Gideon's hands went slick with sweat. He wiped them on the sides of his thighs as casually as possible and blinked his eyes so they didn't stare at Lillian with walleyed fearfulness.

"So why send me out at all?" he asked as jauntily as he could manage. "I'm not a soldier, I'm not a general."

"No, you're a politician, Gideon. Or at least, you're trying to be," Lillian said, her eyes narrowing. "That legislation you and your father are working on—that pathetic attempt to make it a law that witches must bond with multiple stones so their mechanics can control them? That will go away tonight."

"My dying won't make it go away." Gideon smiled at her sadly, as though she wouldn't understand on her own—like it was a good thing that he was there to walk her through it. He even moved closer to her, as if to take her into his confidence. "If you want this multiple willstone nonsense to go away, the best thing would be to work with me. Give me a little something. A bit more freedom, a bit more power in exchange for what I'm willing to give up. We can work together on this."

Gideon felt himself go rigid against his own accord. His body marched back, away from Lillian, and got down on its knees in the mud and blood in front of her.

"You are going to go out there tonight like a brave man," she said in a low voice. "Your father is going to watch you do it. Many Council members will recall that *they* have sons that I've claimed, and now that we are officially at war with the Outlanders, they'll remember that at any moment their sons, like Thomas's, could be called into battle by me. They'll also recall that if their sons smash their willstones during wartime, I have the right to declare them traitors, and they'll hang."

Lillian gave Gideon his will back and he staggered to his feet. She'd never taken him over like that before, although she'd done it to Rowan a few times by accident when they were young and clumsy with their powers. Gideon knew about the feeling of helplessness through him, but he'd never experienced it directly before. Now that he'd angered her, he wished he had more than that slim warning. That way he would have known what he was up against. He'd never really understood how trapped he was until now.

"Lillian. I'm your oldest friend," he pleaded. He felt his breath catch in his throat and let it happen, in case crying might convince her. "I stayed with you when Rowan and Tristan left."

"Only to plot against me," she said with mock consolation for his gathering tears.

"Only because you shut me out," he countered accusingly. "I would have been your ally, but what else was I supposed to do when you wouldn't even pretend I was wanted?"

"Gideon? I know you're not really hurt, nor are you my ally, so let's skip the act. You can either go out there, receive the Gift, and revel in the battle with the rest of my army, or I can possess you and work you like a puppet."

Gideon opened his mouth to protest, and Lillian shut it for him with a painful snap. He tasted blood in his mouth. She'd made him bite off the tip of his tongue. Lillian strode toward him, her nearly black smoke-colored willstone now pulsing with an eerie blue light and her green eyes narrowing to slits as her anger rose up inside of her like a steep wave.

"And I promise you, if you defy me, you won't even be able to lift your arms to defend yourself when they come to cut you down. This is the only choice you've ever had. I'm not going to work *with* you, Gideon. You work when I *tell* you to. Now," she said, the wave of anger ebbing out of her. She eased away from him, and her livid face drained, leaving it white and smooth again. Gideon bent forward, spitting out a mouthful of blood and the tip of his own tongue. "I think it would be wise for you to arm yourself with your shiniest weapons and your flashiest uniform because you, my oldest friend, are about to die a glorious death."

Juliet let go of Dana's neck as soon as they reached the Outlander camp. With barely a backward glance, Dana ran off to find her son. Having no place to go, Juliet spun around and looked up at the walls of Salem. She knew this wasn't over. Lillian would send out her army. Juliet glanced around at the Outlander camp. There were tens of thousands of people here. There was no way they'd be able to break camp and get away from Lillian's army in time.

Beyond the borders of the camp, Juliet saw branches moving violently and heard the synchronized shouts of the perimeter guards as they repelled a Woven attack. Even if they tried to get some of the women and children out before the battle, trying to run through the woods at night would be suicide. The Outlanders had to stand and fight—all of them—or they'd die.

"Lady Juliet," a deep voice called. Juliet snapped herself out of her morbid thoughts and peered into the half dark. She saw a man, flanked by warriors, coming toward her. He wasn't exceptionally tall or large, but there was something about the set of his shoulders that marked him as the leader. As he got close, she noticed that he had a limp.

"Alaric," Juliet said, and then corrected herself. "Sachem," she said, tilting her head down in a respectful nod. Her knees were shaking. Juliet had spent most of her teen years terrified of Alaric Windrider and his tribe of painted savages.

"I heard what you did for my people in the courtroom," he said. "I thank you and welcome you to my camp."

Juliet hadn't expected him to be so polite. She looked up at him, wondering how old he was. His hair was salted with gray at the temples, but up close he didn't look much older than thirty. He was handsome. None of the stories about him had mentioned *that*, although they seemed to mention everything else, including what had happened to him to make him the most feared leader of the Outlander tribes.

The story, legend now, said that ten years ago his wife and infant girl died during a brutal snowstorm. The young family had been right outside the Salem gate, but because they were Outlanders, the guards wouldn't let them in after dark. With the Woven in the woods behind them, and implacable guards on the wall above, he had to watch as his wife and child froze to death in his arms. The story went that he got his limp that night trying to kick down the Salem gate in a blind rage.

Juliet didn't know if any of this were true, but she did know that after that night, Alaric went wild. He built an army to topple the Thirteen Cities, and five years ago when Lillian had grown strong enough to replace Olga, the old, dying Salem Witch, he vowed to destroy Lillian's Coven himself. He killed guards, raided the underground train lines that linked the cities, and started demanding that Outlanders had the right to own property and govern themselves. Many felt as he did, and thousands of warriors from dozens of different tribes pledged themselves to him. When Lillian outlawed science, he'd grown even more powerful, as citizens and Outlanders alike flocked to him for protection.

Alaric hadn't been born a sachem. He became one by strength of will alone. And all to avenge his lost wife and child. Juliet had often wondered what drove a man like that—what fueled so much fire. She used to think it had to be hatred, but she wasn't so sure anymore. The look on his face as he stared down at her was almost gentle.

Juliet shook herself, realizing that she and Alaric had been standing there staring at each other for ages. Even the disciplined warriors in his personal entourage were starting to look uncomfortable. Juliet blushed and quickly dropped her eyes.

"I-I just did the only right thing left for me to do," she stammered, mortified. "Not that it did any good. This isn't over, Sachem. Lillian will go to the pyre for this."

"How do you know? Can you hear her thoughts?" Alaric asked. His eyes narrowed. "Can she hear yours?"

"No. Lillian shut me out a year ago," Juliet replied, shaking her head emphatically. "There's something in her mind she doesn't want me to see, and she's willing to never share thoughts with me again to keep it from me." Juliet smiled at Alaric ruefully. "And I know when she's trying to spy on me by sneaking into my thoughts, so don't be afraid of her stealing any of your plans through me. Remember, she was my nosy little sister long before she was the Salem Witch. Which is why I know she'll attack."

"I don't doubt you," he said, almost like he was surprised he was saying it. Alaric suddenly lifted his hand and rubbed the back of his neck in agitation. "But you can still hear Lily?"

"Yes."

"Good. We have to get her and the scientists to safety."

Lily and Rowan hurried through the camp, feeling their way toward Caleb and Tristan. Cheers followed them wherever they went. Lily felt the success of their mission buoying the Outlanders as they prepared for battle. A few Outlanders even came up to Rowan to shake his hand.

"Now that they've got to come out from behind the walls, we can win this!" one man shouted enthusiastically as he thumped Rowan on the back. The crowd took up a rallying cry, all of them eager to fight.

Lily glanced over at Rowan as he broke off and led her away. His smile faded fast and a grim look descended on his face.

What is it, Rowan?

They're deluding themselves. We can't win, Lily.

Why not?

Lillian will be fueling everyone who takes the field for her. None of these people have ever faced a witch's army, or even seen what someone can do with a witch's strength inside of him. It'll be a slaughter.

"No, it won't be," Lily said, disliking Rowan's defeatism. "If Lillian is going to fuel her army, I'll fuel everyone who fights for the sachem."

Rowan stopped dead and grabbed Lily by the shoulders, his face flushing with anger. "No, you won't! You are not ready for the pyre. You'll die."

"The pyre?" Lily asked uncertainly. Rowan let go of her and stepped back.

"Firewalking," he said. "You don't stand in front of the flames, you go into them." His voice dropped. "In order to get enough energy to fuel an army, we have to burn you, Lily."

She stared at Rowan, her thoughts turning over rapidly. "Lillian can do it? She can firewalk and live?"

"She started with little things, like holding her hand over a flame for five minutes." Rowan paced in a circle, dragging his fingers through his hair. "And at first, she hurt herself. A lot. I had to heal her over and over again. It took years for her to be ready for the pyre."

"But she was young, right? She hadn't come into her power yet, had she?"

Rowan stopped pacing and looked at Lily, his eyes sad. "Just once in your life, please listen to me. You're not ready to firewalk, Lily."

Lily looked around at the camp. Men and women were focused and united as they prepared themselves for war. They had their scientists back and the promise of an independent future if only they fought for it. She could feel their optimism, their hope for a better life for their children, and she knew Rowan was right. They had no idea what they would be facing. Lillian's bewitched army would mow them down.

"If I don't go to the pyre, are you still going to fight?" she asked. He looked away.

Answer me. Are you going to fight, even without my strength?

Yes.

Even if that means you'll die?

363

Yes.

"Then what difference does it make if I die on the pyre or not?" she said, taking his hand. He looked baffled for a moment, and then his face changed suddenly to pleading.

"Don't do this for me," he said.

"I know. And it's okay, Rowan," she replied. She thought about Lillian, and how she was so willing to hurl herself across the universe and into the unknown for this man. She smiled at him. "I get it now."

"There you are!" Juliet called out, relieved. She ran over to Lily and grabbed her arm, pulling her away from Rowan before he could protest any further. "We have to get you out of here. Lillian's having a pyre built on the wall. The sachem told me he wants you and the scientists to hide in the woods."

Lily paused. She looked over Juliet's shoulder at all the people who would die tonight without her.

"Where is the sachem?" Lily asked. "I want to see him."

"I'll take you."

Juliet led Lily and Rowan a short way through the camp. When they joined up with the sachem, they found all three of the scientists were with him, along with Caleb and Tristan. Lily also recognized a few of the faces from outside the sachem's council carriage. She nodded at the elders in greeting.

"Lily. We all want to thank you and your mechanics for returning our scientists," one of the elders said. When she came forward through the crowd, Lily saw that it was Dana.

"Just a simple tanner, huh?" Lily replied, shaking her head.

"I was once," Dana said through a grin.

"I'm just glad we all made it out," Lily said. She grimaced suddenly at the irony of the situation. "For what it's worth."

Dana nodded, her eyes glinting with understanding. "It was

worth a lot. Outlanders are used to dying, but if we die tonight, at least this time it will be for something we believe in."

Lily frowned in thought. "I've always been big on fighting for what I believe in." She laughed at herself. "Which, in my world, means I wore a lot of T-shirts and donated my allowance to groups I wished I could join. I was always too sick and too weak to actually fight." She looked over at Rowan. "Until now."

"Lily," he whispered, his face pleading with hers. "Don't."

"I have to, Rowan." She reached out and took his hand again. "You know I do."

"What's going on?" Tristan asked.

"Lily wants to go to the pyre," Rowan said, never taking his eyes off hers.

"That's insane," Tristan said with a laugh. A silence followed his outburst. "This is ridiculous," he continued, his tone serious now. "Ro, she can't handle it yet. You know she can't."

"It's not my decision," Rowan replied. "It's hers."

"Lily," Juliet said calmly. "You're no good to the rebels dead."

Lily nodded, dropping her head. "If I don't do this, there'll be no rebels left to help, Juliet," she said. She looked up at Rowan. "I'll need to claim everyone who's willing. We'd better start now."

You're not going to listen to me, are you, Lily?

Please, Rowan. I couldn't live with myself if I didn't try to do this.

Brave and stubborn and determined to break my heart.

"Yeah, we'd better," Rowan said blankly, pulling his hand out of Lily's. He looked around at the sachem and all the elders. "Have everyone who wants to live through the night come before Lily to be claimed."

The sachem nodded and called over his shoulder to his painted warriors. "Do it," he ordered, and half of them raced off into the dark.

Rowan turned to Tristan and Caleb. "Come on. We have to build Lily's pyre." He brushed past Lily, heading toward the back of camp. Tristan followed him, barely looking at Lily as he passed.

"I hope you're a fast learner, little witch," Caleb said, looking down at her with a worried frown. He put one of his huge hands on her shoulder and squeezed.

"Me, too," she replied, smiling up at him weakly. "Caleb? Do you think I'm doing the right thing?"

"Yes, I do. I just don't want you to die."

"Me neither."

Caleb gave her a fierce hug. He released her quickly and left her with the sachem. She stood next to him solemnly, trying not to shake too much.

"Will you take care of my sister if I don't make it?" Lily asked the sachem.

"Lily," Juliet began, but the sachem cut her off with a gently raised hand before she could continue.

"I swear to you I will," he said.

"Thank you, Alaric."

Outlander braves began to gather in front of Lily, waiting to be claimed. They were anxious. Their eyes darted over to the sachem, as if to ask if it were okay with him that they were giving themselves to a witch. Alaric had to wave people forward, encouraging them to step up, although Lily noticed that he didn't offer himself to her. She didn't ask, either. Lily assumed there was a reason he'd never had his knee healed by Rowan or Tristan, or any of the other competent mechanics that were sworn to him, and she assumed it was because he didn't trust witchcraft, even if he could see its usefulness.

Alaric wasn't alone in that sentiment. Most of the Outlanders had spent their lives hating and fearing the Covens, and more than a few had lost loved ones in Lillian's witch hunt for scientists. Offering themselves to her was a big leap, and Lily didn't take their trust lightly. Every time she went to take a stone between her fingertips, she remembered what it was like to have a hateful person touch her little hearts like that, and she focused on being as gentle and as quick as possible.

Thousands of lives flashed inside her mind. She saw good people, bad people, weak and strong. Lily saw love and trauma tangled together inside almost everyone that came before her. Some people were damaged and still hopeful, while others had fallen down under the weight of their misfortunes. Lily learned the rhythm of them all. The patterns she gathered from their willstones stacked up inside her mind, like she was listening to thousands of songs, catching the main tune in each one and filing it away. Somehow she knew that if she ever heard that particular person's song again, she would recall the refrain, and her willstones would be able to play it back. In under an hour, Lily had the keys to thousands of minds.

Lily. It's time.

There are more waiting to be claimed, Rowan.

It's too late. Lillian is opening the Salem gates. Her army marches out now.

"Sachem, I have to go," Lily said, stumbling back. Alaric nodded at Lily in understanding and she turned to go. The warriors still waiting clamored to be claimed. "I'm sorry," Lily cried. "But it's time."

"Lily!" Juliet said, clutching at her sister's arm. "Be strong. And come back."

"I will." Lily hugged Juliet quickly and sped off.

She ran through the last of the waiting braves, brushing her fingertips across their bared willstones. She heard their patterns in her head, but didn't have time to process any of them as she ran through the crowd, past the outstretched necks and pleading eyes. She had no idea if it was enough, or if she'd missed these soldiers and they'd have to fight without her strength.

The shouts of the sergeants marshalling the foot soldiers rose up behind her as she ran to Rowan. She heard the troops being rallied into ranks and marching out as she ran to the back of the army, where her pyre awaited.

Lily could see the heap of wood towering high above the heads of the scrambling men and women like a huge hill of sticks. At the very top, a single stake stuck up from the pyre. Even from a distance, Lily could see iron shackles dangling from its top. Her stomach twisted with fear.

Rowan, Tristan, and Caleb met her at the bottom of the pyre. A rough staircase had been built into the side of the giant stack of wood, leading up to the stake. They waited for her at its entrance.

"Take everything off," Rowan said, gesturing to Lily's wearhyde gear. He held a white slip of silk in his hands.

Lily untied her boots and stripped off her clothes, her fingers fumbling and her knees shaking. As soon as she was undressed, Rowan dropped the white slip over her naked body. She shivered as the slippery cold silk whispered across her skin and flared out around her thighs.

"Good luck, Lily," Tristan whispered, kissing her softly on the cheek.

"Don't die," Caleb said, trying to smile bravely. Lily nodded and swallowed hard but couldn't smile back.

Rowan took her wrist and led her up the precarious steps to the stake. Her bare feet padded up the rough-hewn edges of the recently harvested logs. The turpentine smell of sap and abraded wood surrounded her. Clumsy with fear, she stumbled along behind Rowan up the steep and wobbly way. Her tender feet filled with splinters and began to bleed. On top of the pyre was a single plank that led to the stake. Rowan guided Lily across the plank and pushed her back against the stake.

"Are you doing this for me?" he asked, pressing against her. His face was pale and his eyes were wide and vulnerable.

"No. I'm doing this for all of us," Lily replied, happy he hadn't asked her that question in mindspeak. "What are the shackles for?"

"When you start to burn, no matter what your mind wants, your body will try to leap off the pyre. It's a reflex."

Rowan took her wrists in his hands, looking down at them. Slowly, he raised her left arm over her head, and clasped it in one shackle. Lily started shaking all over.

"What do I do?"

"Gift as many as you can as fast as you can. If you feel yourself burning and you can't get rid of the energy quickly enough, send it to me. No matter how much it is." He raised her right arm over her head and locked it in the second shackle. "I can take it."

"Oh God, Rowan. I'm scared." Her eyes filled with tears and her chest swelled in and out with panicked breaths.

I'll be with you. Rowan kissed her quickly, crushing her against him. *Always.*

He tore himself away and ran down the rough steps. "Light it!" he yelled to Tristan and Caleb.

Lily could hear her breath rasping in and out, and the iron chains jingling over her head. She looked across the battlefield and saw a bright fire at the top of the wall. Lillian's pyre was already aflame.

She smelled the smoke first. It billowed up from underneath, choking her. Lily coughed so hard she doubled over until the chains stopped her, and saw the flames flickering below. Then she felt the heat.

Her feet were suddenly burning. An animal need to get away from the flames possessed her, and Lily tugged violently on the chains. The flames rose quickly. There was no way to escape them, no matter how she twisted or turned, and she began to burn. Screams tore out of her, horrible shrieking sounds that she'd never made before.

Lily. Take the heat. Change it into force. Give it to me, or you'll die.

Writhing in agony, Lily took the heat in and found that as she did so, the flames felt cooler. She pulled in more and more heat until she thought she would burst with it, then turned the gathered heat into force. The roar of the flames silenced for one brief moment. Lily looked up and saw a bright column of light beaming straight up from where she stood, hundreds of feet into the sky. A witch wind howled high up in the atmosphere, spinning the clouds above like a hurricane. It made an eerie sound, like the sky were moaning. Across the battlefield, Lillian's hurricane spun above the Citadel, a twin to Lily's.

Give it to us, Lily.

Lily recalled the patterns of every willstone she'd ever claimed. Thousands of different rhythms flashed across her mind, forming a complicated series of vibrations that she experienced like a song of buzzes and hums in her body. There were so many, but the pain helped her focus on each and every one. Lily unlocked all the stones in her army and filled them with power.

Thousands of bodies arched with euphoria and thousands of minds reached for Lily, sharing the experience with her. At the front of all the minds, strong and clear, was Rowan's. Near to him in strength and familiarity were Tristan and Caleb, and close behind, Dana. Lily poured the lion's share of power into their stones and connected each of them with the minds of the soldiers she sensed around them. Lily's newly appointed generals led her army out onto the battlefield at a run.

Her body hanging limply from her chains, Lily's mind thundered with them toward the oncoming army in her mind. She felt her fighters clashing with Lillian's, felt the front lines charge through each other and pass in a blur of bodies and steel. She was there with Rowan when he cut off Gideon's head in the first second of battle.

Lily shared in the experience of battle with her soldiers. She thrilled with them at the feeling of invincibility that so many of them had never experienced before. She also felt it when they died. A one-of-a-kind rhythm would suddenly stop, and that unique part of the symphony would be lost forever. Every time it was a shock to her. Every time, she gasped at the loss. But feeling the loss drove her even harder. The flames bent toward Lily as she greedily pulled their heat into her core and changed it into force in an ever-increasing loop. When she felt one of her soldiers' strength fail, she would flood his or her stone with power.

The two bewitched armies were evenly matched, and the fighting went on and on. The pyre began to collapse as the wood was consumed. A firestorm whirled around Lily in a tornado of sparks and ashes. She had to fight to breathe among the oxygen-hungry flames. The stake she was chained to crumbled, and Lily easily pulled her shackles free of it. She was so tired. Her skin began to burn as she fell to her knees, struggling to stay conscious. She heard Lillian's voice in her head.

You can't win. And I don't want you to die. I'll pull my army back if you get off the pyre, Lily.

Why, Lillian? I would think you'd want me dead at this point.

Not at all. You are everything I hoped you would be. I need you. That's why I brought you here to begin with.

There are an infinite number of us, Lillian. Why not get another one?

No. You're perfect. And I'd never get Rowan to train a third.

Lily knew Lillian couldn't lie in mindspeak and wondered if

she'd meant to say this, or if she was struggling over there on her own pyre and, in pain, she'd let it slip.

You led me to him that first day, didn't you, Lillian? You guided me through the city right to him. You needed me to meet him.

Rowan is loyal to a fault. Even to cafes. I knew he would be there, and I knew that even if I found a replacement who had every ounce of my potential, without Rowan, she'd never match it. I needed Rowan to train you as much as I needed you.

You used us. You betrayed us.

I betrayed myself, Lily. And because of that, I know I'll never get this chance again. You're the only replacement who will be capable of truly being me. I'm pulling my army back. You must get off the pyre. Now, Lily!

Spent logs gave way under her, and Lily fell into the white belly of the inferno. She thrummed with a giant vibration. She felt herself lifting up and out of her tortured body and sighed with relief. Spirit walking, she looked back down on herself, her blackened skin bubbling and crisping. She was dying. She had to get her body out of the pyre—a universe away if need be. She thought of the shaman. Instead of just jumping up, she jumped up and out into the worldfoam.

Lily heard a new vibration. It was huge. Even though she'd managed to wrangle thousands of individual vibrations and keep them all under control during the battle, what she was experiencing now was so far beyond that she didn't know how to begin to decipher it. But she'd felt it twice before: once when she'd dived through the worldfoam, and once before that, when Lillian had first brought her here. Lily finally understood what it was. The vibration was so mind-bogglingly complicated that it could only be the key to a whole universe—the key *into* another universe. It was so huge, Lily knew instinctively she couldn't store it in her willstones. If she even tried it, her stones would crack.

Lily hovered somewhere in between life and death while she fed this new vibration into her willstones, following a feeling more than precise memory. Her stones pulsed with different lights, each of them trying to process the rhythm of a whole universe and play it back in sequence. Lily didn't even know what universe she held the key to, where she would end up, or if she would ever be able to find her way back, but it was too late for that now. Ears ringing, Lily's awareness skipped in and out of her dying body.

She saw burnt logs falling and heard shouts all around her. Fresh air rushed in, feeding the fire in a giant plume of heat. Someone was trying to dig her out of the pyre.

Rowan.

He was burned and bloody. He beat savagely at the glowing wood around her with an ax and pulled her out of the fire with his bare hands. Lily fell back into her body, inhaling a lungful of air.

"Rowan," she whispered. "You have to let me go."

"Never."

"But—I'm leaving."

The last sequence of the vibration played in her willstones.

Not without me.

The pyre collapsed, and a stream of pressurized heat rushed toward Lily and Rowan. She had no choice but to change the heat into energy or they'd be incinerated. Her willstones took the massive kick of energy, catapulting them both out of one universe and into another.

The people who love you will guide you like bright lights into the other worlds.

The shaman had told her that. Lily desperately searched for a light.

She saw nothing. Felt nothing. Not her own pain, nor Rowan in her arms. She couldn't even feel the weight of her skin on her bones. The complete absence of light and sensation was terrifying.

Don't be scared. I know it's confusing, but focus on finding me. It's time to come back.

Mom? I'm coming. I'm coming home.

ACKNOWLEDGMENTS

Great notes—the kind that make you smack your forehead and say, "*that's* what I meant"—are a godsend to a writer, so thank you, Jean Feiwel and Holly West at Feiwel and Friends for my sore, but grateful, forehead. Special thanks to Mollie Glick and Tara Kole, my brilliant agent and savvy attorney, for supporting me through a rough and tumble year. Thank you Rachel Petty in the UK for having my back. Thank you Ippolita Doulas Scotti Di Vigoleno at Giunti in Italy, and Astrid Muschkowski at Dressler in Germany for taking such great care of both of my series overseas. A big hug to the Wearboar Sisters—they know where the bodies are buried and would never tell. And finally, all my love to my husband, Albert.

Deleted Scenes from

TRIAL BY FIRE

BY JOSEPHINE ANGELINI

"The Lillian Letters"

I'm going to write this story in my willstone. I need to leave a record of my thoughts before this sickness robs me of my clarity. Like a message in a bottle. Someday, I may contact you directly, but it's still too soon. You wouldn't understand. You probably hate me right now. But if I die before you're ready to hear me out, I need to leave some way for you to access my thoughts. To understand why I have done what I have done. I owe you that much, at least.

The first thing I want you to know is that you and I are the same person, Lily. We are not sisters, or twins. We are the same. Had you been born in my universe and I born in yours, we would have made all the same choices and lived identical lives. The only difference between us is the experiences we've had up to now.

Our nature is one, even if our nurturing has been different.

* * * * * * * * *

I see you with your shirt slogans, calling out to save the whales, the polar bears, and the children. I think you even have a shirt that actually reads "Save the World." You are just like me, and I know that given the same choices, you would do what I did. What I'm still trying to do. I wouldn't have you any other way. This is why I chose you.

But I don't want you to save the world. I want you to save mine.

I've sent you to someone who will show you everything you can do. He will guide you, and defend you, and most importantly, he'll love you. It may feel like I'm punishing you right now. Like I've stolen you from your life. But what I've given you is the greatest gift anyone could ever give another.

A purpose.

Creating Woven is a time suck for the crucibles of my Coven, but the natural way is unthinkable. No Woven created by the Covens can ever be made to be fertile again. We made that mistake once before and we've been suffering the consequences ever since.

It was the Woven, and my arrogant hope to eradicate them, that started me down the hellish path I've been on for the past year. No— that's not entirely true. Originally, I was trying to help my mother. But I could never blame her for my terrible choices.

My mother's affliction was getting worse. I've watched you struggle with your version of Samantha, so I know you know what I mean. One day, my guard summoned me to the top of the city Wall. Samantha was in her nightgown, and her hair was wild. She was balancing on the very edge of the Wall, threatening to throw herself off if anyone came near her. She was saying that in another world, the Wall was not there and that if she squinted her eyes, she could convince herself that she was walking on air. She begged me to believe her, to believe that she saw all of these other worlds and that she couldn't block them out. Then she begged me to help her make the visions stop. I didn't know what to do. Rowan was with me. He helped me talk her back from the edge. No one was ever more patient with my mother than Rowan was.

Later, after I had cried myself out on his shoulder, Rowan told me that Samantha's rants reminded him of the Shamans of his people. He said that there was a special kind of Shaman who spoke of other worlds that were similar to ours, but different. He called these Shamans spirit walkers. Then he laughed and said that everyone in his tribe thought spirit walkers were crazy, but I asked him to find one for me anyway. I was desperate.

I didn't realize then that I was doing something that had never been done before. To me, having a Shaman come to the Citadel to help my mother was a simple choice, even if it went against centuries of prejudice on both sides. Shamans hate witchcraft. They think it's an insult to change what the Great Spirit made by transmuting matter and energy. They refuse to wear willstones. And witches have always maligned anything that came from the Outlanders. They'd laugh in your face if you even tried to suggest that Shamanism was more than a hallucination. But I didn't see a painted savage when I looked at an Outlander; I saw one of Rowan's people. I'm not blaming Rowan for my choices any more than I'm blaming my mother, but it was my love for Rowan that brought two different kinds of power—spirit walking and transmutation—together for the first time.

We kept it the darkest of secrets, of course. If my Coven or the Council found out that I had a Shaman at the Citadel, there would have been a huge scandal. Rowan and Juliet were the only two who knew.

At our first meeting, the Shaman told me that Samantha was a rare thing—a female Shaman—and after just days of training with him, my mother was already better. Whether I wanted to believe in spirit walking or not, I couldn't deny that his teaching was helping her. Then the Shaman told me that I had the gift, too, and that the older I got, the stronger it would become. Without training, it would take over my mind, as it had Samantha's.

I was terrified. I didn't tell anyone, not even Rowan. I was afraid that if anyone knew, I would lose my position as the Salem Witch, and at sixteen, I was one of the youngest Salem Witches in history. I knew that my Coven would turn on me in a second if they found out, and I was afraid. Pride and fear, Lily. I let them make my choices for me and I started training with the Shaman in secret.

I know what you're thinking. Why didn't I tell Rowan?

You already know it wasn't because I didn't trust him. I didn't tell Rowan because I was ashamed. I can't tell you how much it hurts to admit it now that she's gone, but it's true—I was ashamed of my mother. I was ashamed of the crazy woman with the dirty nightgown and the frizzy hair, and I was ashamed of others thinking that I might become like her. Especially Rowan.

* * * * * * * * *

I run through my system, looking for the tainted cells. I can kill them with a thought—they're actually quite fragile—but strength isn't what makes them lethal. What makes them lethal is the same thing that makes the Woven lethal. They reproduce more quickly than you can kill them, and if you leave even one alive, in a few weeks, you are overrun again. My body is lousy with useless cells that do nothing but reproduce. Even when I sift every last one out my tissue, blood, and bones, my system has been so damaged that a previously healthy cell will turn, and the plague crops up anew. This is the price I must pay for the mistakes I have made.

I told you already that this whole mess started because I was trying to save my world. I'm still trying to save my world, but my understanding of what that truly means has changed. Initially, I was just trying to save it from the wild Woven.

After I asked the Shaman if he thought it were possible for me to use my willstone in order to affect other universes, he guided my spirit to a world that was still very like ours, except that the Woven had been exterminated.

It was glorious.

Outlander children didn't have to grow up in fear like Rowan did. They could go to school, learn to read, and just be young. I know you claimed Rowan last night. You and I are connected, and I felt it, as I would feel it if you died. It woke me from my sleep. The air around me seemed to swell up and down like a giant wave, and all I could see was Rowan. I assume you also shared his bed last night. Does he still have night terrors? He used to shake in his sleep and cry out for help, or mercy . . . or his father. When I would drop into his nightmares to try and guide him to a safe place inside his mind, his dream-self was always a little boy, running from monsters. It used to break my heart. Now that you've felt his heart beating in your chest, you can understand why I wanted to end that, can't you? No matter what I had to do, I wanted to end that nightmare for Rowan.

The Shaman told me that he had been watching the Woven-free world for over a year, and he still hadn't learned what it was that had killed the wild Woven off. He didn't even know if it was some kind of poison, a device, or a virus, but he did know that it had been because of the efforts of the Salem Witch. Me. Actually we, Lily. Another version of us had saved that world, and she'd died doing it. In fact, everyone that the alternate version of me had ever loved—Rowan, Juliet, my mother— had died. But so had the Woven.

*   *   *   *   *   *   *   *   *

My sister has been missing all day.

I climb to the top of the outer Wall and stand a step away from where my mother nearly jumped so long ago. I send my mind out and into my claimed. I join them together, like so many drops of water uniting to form a wave, and gently steer that swelling wave in the direction I want. My claimed feel my presence in them like a tenderly whispered word against their cheek.

I ask . . . **Juliet?**

The tide goes out with my question and a sea of information rides back in to hit me. The city of Salem spreads out beneath me in a patchwork *of different perspectives. Not for the first time, I think that this must be how a fly sees the world with its compound vision. Every pair of eyes belonging to my claimed feeds back into my mind. But I don't just see the Now as a fly would. I see every time a woman who looked like Juliet walked past any of my claimed during the whole day. It's not just space that is fractured around my mind's compound eye—it's time. It is dawn. It is mid-afternoon. It is ten minutes ago. The sun blinks around the sky like a strobe light as I shuffle through the memories of my claimed like a deck of cards. The frenetic light hurts my inner eye.*

My head aches. Time flits around me. The horizon is Juliet, and space and time undulate around her. I am made seasick on four dimensions instead of just three.

I sway where I stand.

"Lady," a guard says—his voice wavering, his hand at my waist, trembling, as he steadies me. I notice his hunger.

*I've entered the minds of my claimed so rarely this past year. They are all eager for my presence. I can feel their loneliness pressing against me like a penitent pet. I take a moment to send them comfort. I stand next to each inside his or her mind and whisper . . . **"I am here."***

A bright web spins out, connecting us all.

The brief communion of minds is met with relief, but I can't sustain it long. Individually, none of them has the power to pull thoughts out of my head the way a trained mechanic or my sister might, but together, they pose a threat. If I try to maintain this bond, I will bleed my own thoughts back into them and I will show them what must stay hidden. It's why I can't share mindspeak with Juliet anymore. It's why I pushed Rowan away as soon as I came back from the cinder world. I cannot connect when I have so much to hide.

I break the web of minds and wrangle each of the many thousand mind-threads under strict, emotionless control. I press my claimed until their heads hurt, too. I don't like to hurt them, but if I must, I must.

Again, I ask . . . **Juliet?**

There she is. Was. One of my claimed offers up an image. His mind has filtered out all the noise of the "possible Juliets" and, at my urging, zeros in on something he saw out of the corner of his eye. It was a brief moment. His eyes only grazed across her shape for half a second, but I recognize my sister in the image—slurry like a flash of crimson on a desert dune. And the shape next to her is one as dear to me as the shape of the sun in the sky.

Rowan.

His face is glamoured. His willstone is foreign to me. It hurts that I don't recognize the whirl and flux of his gorgeous mind inside that new stone—it hurts like chewing on your own cheek hurts. A self-inflicted wound. You tell yourself to stop, but you keep tearing at the swollen skin with your teeth anyway.

But try as he might, Rowan can't hide from me. I may not know his new willstone, but I know the shape of his back, and I recognize the way his hands move.

He takes Juliet down an alley. This memory ends, but before it does, I see another of my claimed not too far away from where Rowan and Juliet hide. I mark her—my claimed—and the place of the sun in the sky and slide into her mind. Using the position of the sun as my timepiece, I send her mind back to that moment. She was talking with someone else and has no conscious memory of two people having ducked down the alley just behind her, but in the background, I can hear the faint rumble of Rowan's voice.

The mind is in incredible thing. Even if your attention is elsewhere, there is a part of your brain that stores background information for a short while. I hold the memory supplied by my claimed in my thoughts and filter out everything but Rowan's voice.

They've taken Lily. Please. I can't hear her.

My claimed happened to move at that moment. She went too far away for me to get any more of the conversation. I shuffle through a thousand minds and get a brief glimpse of Rowan, his face still glamoured, and leading my sister into a house on the bad side of town.

I have collected as much information as I can, and release the minds of my claimed. The entire exchange took seconds.

I stand on the Wall, looking out at the Woven Woods. To my right, the trees shake violently. I know you're not out there. I can sense you. You're sleeping now—or unconscious—it's difficult to tell the difference sometimes. I feel an urge to send my army out to find you.

But I can't.

Rowan must be the one to find you. Juliet will help. She'll be able to hear your mindspeak no matter where you are, and the two of them will save you. You can't be far because Gideon will need to keep you close—and yes, I have no doubt that Gideon is behind your abduction.

I'm sorry I underestimated Gideon, and even more sorry that you're suffering for my mistake.

You are suffering, but I can't come get you. Someone else needs to save you. Danger has a way of bringing people closer together, and I need you to feel close to the people in this world. But I'll know if you're near death, and believe me, I won't let you die.

I'm sure you're scared, but you shouldn't be. There are two things I know all the way down to the ground. One—that Rowan will come for you. And two—that Gideon will pay for this with his life.

GOFISH

JOSEPHINE ANGELINI

Marc Cartwright

What was your inspiration for The Worldwalker Trilogy? How did you come up with the idea?
I'm a bad sleeper and a remarkably stubborn person. I go through regular bouts of insomnia and refuse to take any kind of sleep medication. So, I spend a lot of time staring at the ceiling at night. Weird things pop into your head at 3:00 in the morning. One notion that kept plaguing me a few years back was the thought that if I ever met another version of myself from a parallel universe, we'd probably be enemies. I have no idea how that idea got in there, but once it was there, I had to build a world around it so it would leave me alone.

Which character do you most identify with in *Trial by Fire* and why?
Right now, after finishing the second book, *Firewalker*, it's Lillian. Funny thing about writing a series instead of stand-alone books is that your sympathies often wander from one character to another.

What made you decide to make Lily and Lillian Witches?

I'm from Massachusetts and I grew up with the lore of the Salem Witch Trials all around me. My parents' house is right across the street from the town forest, and in the center of that forest is a cliff with caves in it. Those caves sheltered people accused of witchcraft in Salem who were fleeing persecution. My sisters told me many died—froze to death—in those caves. Try sleeping with that right across the street from your bedroom window. Maybe that's where my insomnia comes from, come to think of it. I've been thinking about witchcraft my whole life, and I knew that someday I would write about it.

New Salem (as a setting) is modern and fantastic. How do you picture it in your mind's eye?

Basically, I take the skyline of New York, enlarge it by another half mile, cover it with greenery, and wrap a colossal wall around it. The people of New Salem can't leave the city because of the Woven. There is no such thing as farmland. They grow all of their food inside the city on soaring hydroponic scaffolds called greentowers. Every roof and wall that catches light is a garden.

The Woven are so creepy. What was your inspiration for them?

I harvested the concept of the Woven from another world that I built called Nineland. The world of Nineland is crystal clear to me, as are the characters, but I couldn't get the story right. Luckily, the Woven fit perfectly with the magical system that I created for The Worldwalker Trilogy, so I transplanted them. It's funny how ideas get recycled and repurposed. I still want to write Nineland someday, but that is probably the most complicated idea I've ever had for a series and I need to mature as a writer before I try to tackle it again.

It was important to you to work out the science behind the magic in this series. Why?
Because it's *fun*. This is where I get my kicks at 3:00 in the morning. Creating something that rings true despite the fact that it's pure fantasy is exciting. I want people to read my stories and think that the systems and the worlds I create could possibly be real.

How long did it take you to write *Trial by Fire*, from your first thoughts to the last page of the final draft?
The trouble with me is that I come up with ideas and can't get them out of my head even when I'm supposed to be working on something else. I started thinking about *Trial by Fire* years ago, but only started seriously outlining it a year before I finished it. It generally takes me a year to get a world mapped out and a first book written. Second and third books take about eight or nine months. I'm a slow writer.

Where did you write *Trial by Fire*?
I have the most boring writing space imaginable, and this is on purpose. Every now and again I'll trek out to a coffee shop to work, or if I'm traveling, I have no problem working on planes, trains, hotel lobbies, or wherever. But day-to-day, I work on a tiny bare desk that faces a blank wall. I have two choices—write or go crazy. Usually, I write. Usually.

How much of *Trial by Fire* did you share with your family and friends before you submitted it to your agent?
No one sees what I'm working on until it is done. For a series, I pitch the basic idea to my husband first and then to my

agent just to see if the idea has any traction, and so far, they've responded to my pitches. For second and third books, I've had to submit brief summaries along with the manuscript to my publishers, but that's it. No one ever sees my outlines or reads the first few chapters while I'm working. I don't take notes as I go, or bounce ideas off of anyone. Please understand, this is a *bananas* way to work and I am excruciatingly aware of the fact that I could write an entire book and it might come out horribly. Most authors don't work this way, but I need to get the idea down in its entirety before I'm ready to show it. That's just my creative process.

What are your favorite memories of reading as you grew up?

As a child, I remember reading *Where the Sidewalk Ends* by Shel Silverstein outside in the sunshine. As a tween, I devoured *Are You There, God? It's Me, Margaret* and The Dragonriders of Pern series by Anne McCaffrey—both of which were read in marathon-like stretches where I didn't eat or sleep.

When I was a teen, I remember reading *The Mists of Avalon* by Marion Zimmer Bradley, and my sister Martha and I reading everything by Jane Austen aloud to each other while it snowed outside.

And now? Oh, boy. This is tough because most of my fans aren't familiar with the books I've read, probably because I've been an adult for much longer than most of them have. Apart from Shakespeare and the Greeks, college was all about *One Hundred Years of Solitude* by Gabriel Garcia Marquez, *All the Pretty Horses* by Cormac MacCarthy, and *Possession* by A.S. Byatt. Later, it was the entire Earthsea cycle by Ursula K. Le Guin and everything by China Miéville, especially *The Scar*. Now, I read whatever my friends are working on and books that I'm being asked to blurb. I just read *Blackbird* by Anna Carey and *Eternal Night* by Carina Adly MacKenzie, both of which were fantastic and will be out soon.

Where do you believe your love for storytelling came from?

Late nights, obsessive thinking, a free-floating sense of optimism, and sheer pigheadedness. When I ask myself "what if," I don't censor myself just because the answer I come up with is outside the boundaries of normal. I choose to believe that I can create a type of reality from complete fantasy, and I am just stubborn enough to keep going until I do it.

If you had the chance to bond to a willstone, would you?

Heck, yes! Being able to do any kind of magic would be amazing, even if bonding with a willstone leaves you vulnerable in the system I created.

Would you let a Witch claim you?

No. I'd be the Witch, of course.

Why write a young adult novel?

I think my natural voice as a writer fits this genre. It's more like YA chose me. Plus, I adore the YA audience. YA readers have such open minds, and when they love something, it's with fervor that an adult can seldom match. I remember what it was like to love a book when I was a teen. To know that something I wrote is loved in that way is humbling and deeply gratifying.

SQUARE FISH

DISCUSSION GUIDE

TRIAL BY FIRE
by Josephine Angelini

1) In our world, Lily's greatest weakness is that she's allergic to everything, but in the alternate Salem, that is exactly what makes her so powerful and important. Can you imagine a scenario in which your greatest weakness becomes a source of power?

2) While Lily struggles to be seen as different from Lillian, they both share an unyielding stance in the rightness of their beliefs, even when it makes things difficult for them. Is this a strength or a weakness?

3) Although Lily knows intellectually that the Tristan in this world is different from the Tristan she grew up with, she can't forgive him for the other Tristan's betrayal. What would you have done in that situation? Have you ever been mad at someone for something that wasn't their fault?

4) Everyone in New Salem has a willstone, and Lily is quick to insist that Rowan give her one as well, so she can progress in her magic, but they also have drawbacks. Would you choose to have a willstone if you had the chance?

5) The Shaman says that the decisions people make are what causes the worlds to split. Thinking about the choices you've made in your life, can you imagine a universe where you chose differently?

6) In this new Salem, women Crucibles are powerful and rule the land, while their male mechanics support and care for them. Does this feel strange to you? How is it different from the typical gender roles in our world?

7) Witches find it very hard not to completely take over someone they have claimed. Lily wants to take over Rowan completely, but fights with herself to leave him with his free will. Have you ever seen this kind of potentially controlling dynamic in relationships in real life?

8) Tristan spent years refusing to let Lillian claim him, yet he insists that Lily claim him, even knowing that she is also in love with Rowan. Why do you think he made these choices? What would you have done?

9) Lillian believes that nuclear power will destroy her world, and Lily enters new Salem wearing a No Nukes T-shirt. Yet, Rowan and Alaric are intrigued by nuclear power and the idea that this kind of energy could support their people and help them fight against the Woven. Do you think that nuclear power can be helpful if handled responsibly, or is it too destructive to mess with?

10) Lillian says, "I know what I must do, even if it makes me the villain of my own story." And through the course of the novel, she does some terrible things. However, she does them because she firmly believes that these actions are in the best interests of her entire world. Do you believe that she's a savior or a villain?

I'M A WITCH. AND WITCHES BURN.

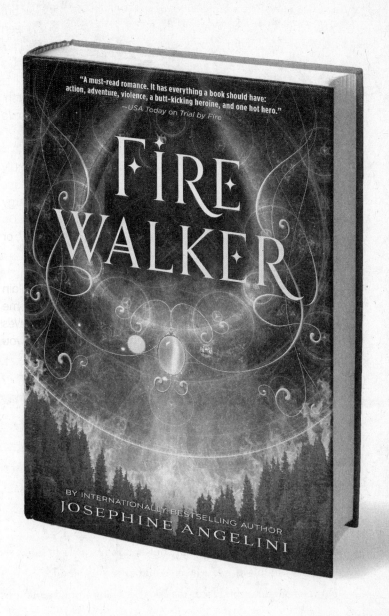

KEEP READING FOR A SNEAK PEEK!

CHAPTER

1

LILY LAY FLOATING ON A RAFT OF PAIN. TERROR KEPT her clinging to it. If she slipped off the side, she knew she'd drown in the smothering darkness that swelled like an ocean under the sparking surface of life. She wanted to let go, but fear wouldn't let her. When the pain became too much to bear, she hoped that at least the fear would end so she could allow herself to slip weightlessly into the hushed waters of death.

But the fear didn't end. And Lily knew she couldn't let go. She was a witch. Witches don't die quietly in the cold, muffled silence of water. Witches die screaming in the roaring mouths of fire.

"Open your eyes," Rowan pleaded desperately. Wading her way back to the sound of his voice, Lily forced herself to do as he said. She saw his soot-smeared face, smiling down on hers. "There you are," he whispered.

She tried to smile back at him, but her skin was tight and raw and her face wouldn't move. All she could taste was blood.

"Do you recognize this place?" he asked, looking around anxiously.

"I've never seen anything like it." He tilted her up in his arms so she could glance around.

It was nighttime. Lily felt pavement under her hand and realized they were lying in the middle of the road. She heard a jingling sound when she moved. The shackles and chains from the pyre were still bound to her wrists, the weight of them dragging down her arms. She focused her eyes and looked up the street. It was snowing. The streetlamps were few and far between. Woods surrounded them, but not the impossibly dense, old woods of Rowan's world. These were young woods. Her woods.

The winding road and rolling hills were familiar. Lily knew this place. They were two towns away from Salem in Wenham, Massachusetts. She hadn't realized her pyre had been that far from the walls of Salem. The battlefield in the other Salem must have been enormous, and she had filled it with blood.

"I think we're on Topsfield Road," Lily croaked. "There's a farm up ahead."

"A farm?" Rowan said, squinting his eyes as he tried to peer through the trees. There was a flash of light and Rowan's head snapped around.

"Headlights," Lily rasped, her voice failing. "We have to get out of the road."

"You're badly burned," Rowan began hesitantly.

"Have to. We'll get hit."

Rowan reluctantly started gathering her up in his arms, but Lily screamed before he could pick her up. It felt like he was tearing off her skin.

The raft of pain rose up again, lifting Lily up and out of herself. The headlights grew closer, blinding her. Tires squealed. Car doors slammed. As she drifted away from it all on her raft, she heard a familiar voice.

"Go help him, Juliet," the voice commanded. "Careful! She's burnt to a cinder."

"Mom?" Lily whispered, and then gave herself to the wet darkness.

Juliet stared at the charred girl lying in the middle of the road, momentarily unable to accept that she was looking at her little sister. The skinny girl was burned and bloody all over, but her raspy voice was unmistakable. It was Lily.

A frantic young man clutched her to his chest. Juliet had never seen anyone quite like him before. His hands and forearms were burned as well, but the rest of his leather-clad body was drenched in blood. Juliet got the sickening feeling that the blood was not his own. He was carrying two gore-tipped short swords strapped across his back and his sooty hands looked as if they knew how to use them. At his waist was what seemed to be a whole kit of silver knives arrayed from his belt and strapped down the side of his right thigh. He looked like an utter savage.

"Go, Juliet!" Samantha ordered. Her mother's voice, strangely calm and in control for the first time in ages, was what snapped Juliet out of her shock. She strode forward and knelt down next to the stranger and saw a flash of silver around her sister's wrists.

"Why is Lily wearing chains?" she asked accusingly, her voice pitched low to keep it from shaking. When she lifted her eyes to meet the strangers', her gaze was caught by something at his throat. It was a large jewel that seemed to throb with dark light—if there was such a thing as dark light, Juliet thought. She blinked her eyes and looked away, both disturbed and drawn to the odd jewel at the same time.

"Samantha, do you know me?" the savage asked. Juliet stiffened in fear. Who was this guy?

"How do you know my mother's name?" she asked, certain that it hadn't been said in his presence.

"Yes, I know you, Rowan," Samantha answered, waving an impatient hand in Juliet's direction to keep her quiet. "What do we need to do?"

"We need to get her by a fire so I can start to heal her," Rowan said. He started to lift Lily, and she moaned in pain.

"What? We need to call 911 and get an ambulance," Juliet yelled. She reached out a hand to restrain Rowan from moving her. "You're hurting her!"

"I know that," he shouted back, his expression desperate. "But we have to move her. I can't heal her here."

"Mom!" Juliet screamed. "For all we know, he *did* this to her."

"No, he didn't. Listen to him, Juliet. He's the only one who can help her now," Samantha said sternly.

Juliet searched for any sign in her mother's eyes that she had lost it, but all she saw was cold, hard sanity—something Juliet hadn't seen in her mother in a long time.

Samantha knew exactly what was going on, even if Juliet didn't, and it was Samantha who had said she knew where to find Lily and she'd forced Juliet to take her to this stretch of road in the middle of the night. Juliet had no idea how her mother could know where to find Lily after three months of her being missing, but right now there were more pressing matters, like saving Lily's life. And at the moment that seemed doubtful. Juliet had candy-striped in hospitals and trained as an EMT. She was going to med school at Boston University and she'd seen enough to know when someone was dying. Although Juliet said under her breath that they should be taking Lily to an emergency room, she knew it would make no difference at this point. Her little sister was going to die whether they got her to an ICU or not.

Rowan kept Lily on his lap in the backseat of the car while Juliet drove as quickly as she dared through the falling snow. She gripped the wheel as if she were trying to wring it dry in order to keep her hands from shaking. Her sister, missing and thought to be dead, was back. And she was dying in the backseat of Juliet's car.